NEWMAN'S JOURNEY

MERIOL TREVOR graduated (in Litterae Humaniores) from Oxford in 1942. She worked in a London day nursery during the War and later as a steerer on the Grand Union Canal. In 1946 she was sent to Italy with a volunteer group of relief workers under UNRRA, based in the Abruzzi on the Adriatic coast. Back in England, after a spell in a family farming venture in North Devon, she became a Catholic (in 1952).

Meriol Trevor's first publications were books for children and historical novels. She then embarked on the two-volume biography of Newman which won the James Tait Black Memorial Prize in 1962. She was elected a Fellow of the Royal Society of Literature in 1967. Altogether she has written six biographical works, eighteen historical novels and thirteen books for children. Her biography of James II, *The Shadow of a Crown*, was published in 1988. She has lived in Bath since 1962.

Biographical works by Meriol Trevor

Newman: The Pillar of the Cloud
Newman: Light in Winter (Macmillan, 1962)

Apostle of Rome: A Life of Philip Neri, 1515–1595
(Macmillan, 1966)

Pope John (Macmillan, 1967)

Prophets and Guardians: Renewal and Tradition in the Church
(Hollis and Carter, 1969)

The Arnolds: Thomas Arnold and his family
(The Bodley Head, 1973)

The Shadow of a Crown: the Lifestory of James II
of England and VII of Scotland (Constable, 1988)

FOUNT CLASSICS · BIOGRAPHY

NEWMAN'S JOURNEY

Meriol Trevor

Fount
An Imprint of HarperCollins*Publishers*

Fount Paperbacks is an Imprint of
HarperCollins*Religious*
Part of HarperCollins*Publishers*
77–85 Fulham Palace Road, London W6 8JB

Newman Pillar of the Cloud and *Newman Light in Winter* first published by
Macmillan & Co. Ltd in 1962 © Meriol Trevor 1962
Newman's Journey, an abridgement of these volumes, first issued in Fontana Library
of Theology and Philosophy in 1974 © Meriol Trevor 1974

This edition first published in Great Britain
in 1996 by Fount Paperbacks

1   3   5   7   9   10   8   6   4   2

Copyright © 1996 Meriol Trevor

Meriol Trevor asserts the moral right to be
identified as the author of this work

A catalogue record for this book is
available from the British Library

ISBN 0 00 628009 9

Printed and bound in Great Britain by
Caledonian International Book Manufacturing Ltd, Glasgow, G64

To the Fathers of the Birmingham Oratory
Past, Present, and to come

CONTENTS

Biographical Summary

1801 *21 February*: born in London

1808–16 at Ealing School

1817–20 at Trinity College, Oxford

1822 *12 April*: elected Fellow of Oriel College

1824 *Trinity Sunday*: ordained deacon in Church of England; curate of St Clement's. *September*: death of father

1825 Vice-Principal of St Alban's Hall, under Whately. *Whit Sunday*: ordained priest in Church of England

1826 College tutor: gave up St Alban's Hall

1828 Vicar of St Mary the Virgin, university church

1830 Resigns tutorship after difference with Provost

1833 Mediterranean tour: fever in Sicily (May). First *Tracts for the Times* (September)

1836 *28 February*: death of Hurrell Froude. Hampden row. *May*: death of mother, marriage of sisters

1841 *27 February*: *Tract 90*. Tract series ended

1843 *September*: resignation of St Mary's; farewell sermon at Littlemore

1845 *October*: resignation of Oriel Fellowship; received into Catholic Church by Fr Dominic Barberi CP. (*9th*) *Essay on the Development of Christian Doctrine*

1846 *22 February*: left Littlemore for Maryvale; *September*: left England for Rome

1847 *Trinity Sunday*: ordained priest in Rome; with companions joined Oratory of St Philip Neri; in England by Christmas

1848 *2 February*: English Oratory founded at Maryvale

1849   *2 February*: Oratory opened at Alcester Street,
        Birmingham; *May*: Oratory at King William Street,
        London

1850   *May*: *Lectures on Anglican Difficulties* at London Oratory.
        Papal Aggression agitation

1851   Lectures on *The Present Position of Catholics* at the
        Birmingham Corn Exchange; libel case brought by
        Achilli

1852   Birmingham Oratory removes to present site,
        Edgbaston. Lectures on *The Scope and Nature of
        University Education* given in Dublin; *June*: Newman
        loses libel case

1853   *31 January*: condemned by Judge J. T. Coleridge and
        fined

1854–7 Rector of Catholic University in Ireland

1855–6 Difference with London Oratory resulting in separation

1859   *2 May*: opening of the Oratory School. The *Rambler*
        episode; delation of Newman to Rome

1861–2 School reorganized after resignation of staff

1864   *Apologia Pro Vita Sua* issued in weekly parts

1866   *January*: *Letter to Dr Pusey* on doctrine of Mary

1867   Bishops forbid Catholics to attend English universities

1870   *March*: *An Essay in Aid of a Grammar of Assent*.
        Newman's attack on Ultramontane clique leaked to
        press during Vatican Council I

1875   *January*: *Letter to the Duke of Norfolk*, on infallibility and
        conscience, in answer to Gladstone

1877   Elected first honorary fellow of Trinity College, Oxford

1879   Created Cardinal Deacon of San Giorgio in Velabro by
        Pope Leo XIII

1890   *11 August*: died at 8.45 p.m. Buried at Rednal

INTRODUCTION:
NEWMAN THEN AND NOW

What is there to interest people living at the end of the twentieth century in the life story of a man who was born in 1801 and died in his ninetieth year in 1890? Half his adult life was lived as an Anglican in Oxford and the later half as a Catholic priest in Birmingham, but all of it as a dedicated Christian. Surely Newman cannot have any understanding of our time, when so many people doubt the existence of the personal Creator-God of the Bible, believing that the new scientific discoveries – particularly in the fields of astrophysics and biology – draw a very different picture of the observable universe, and of humanity, accidentally evolving from primeval forces.

This view was mine, too, in my twenties (the 1940s). I was a conscientious humanist but not a materialist, exploring Jung's psychological theories of dreams and the self, psychic and mystical experiences, until the reality of this supra-natural, supra-temporal sphere led me to believe in Christ's resurrection appearances to his disciples. It then seemed right to join the ancient Church, there from the beginning and always teaching the same faith. But as I was then living in a remote part of the country I could not do that at once, and I happened to pick up a copy of Newman's essay, *The Development of Christian Doctrine*, written in 1845, just before he was received into the Catholic Church at Littlemore.

At the beginning is a marvellous description of the way *ideas* develop through the give and take of many minds over many years, and then he applies this to the way the basic beliefs of the first Christians were gradually developed over centuries, subject to the collective authority of bishops in Council, with the successor of St

Peter at their head. Newman perceived the Church as a fact of history, not an ideal; a collective organism rather than an organization, growing in time as a person grows but still the same embodied being; and with Christ at the centre, his presence in the eucharistic sacrifice the energizing spiritual food for every believer.

This historical developing view was so new at the time that many Catholic theologians were suspicious of it, but it has proved to be central to the way many twentieth-century people can believe in the Church. Newman's influence was recognized in some of the decrees of the Second Vatican Council (1962–1966), as it is now in the new Catechism, based on the Council, as the old Tridentine Catechism was based on the Reforming Council of Trent in the mid-sixteenth century. Newman's influence is also strong in the ecumenical field where, as he wrote in a letter, we must work for a 'union of hearts' first; his motto as a Cardinal was *Cor ad cor loquitur*, heart speaks to heart. He has also been declared Venerable, the first formal step in the process of canonization as a saint, in recognition of his practice of Christian virtues 'to an heroic degree'; patience, I feel, being the foremost, especially with difficult colleagues and suspicious superiors.

All this has happened since I first became interested in Newman and is as much due to his teaching on Conscience as on Development. As far as I can discover, Newman was the first to bypass the God v. Science controversy (still in public discussion) by showing that Conscience is, so to speak, the direct line to God. Conscience is part of human rational self-consciousness; it is the discernment of good and evil with the obligation to choose the good and the true. Truth, justice and goodness are real, but non-material; the knowledge of them is universal among human beings, primitive and modern, and on our planet to no other animals, who act by instinct (collective subconscious inherited habits). Conscience, of course, may be misapplied in circumstances, but the fact of its existence as the faculty of moral judgment is undeniable.

Newman once wrote in a prayer: 'I see Thee not in the material world except dimly, but I recognize Thy voice in my own intimate

consciousness.' Conscience – commanding truth, justice and goodness – is the direct communication of the creating Spirit to the
human creature. This explains why the Bible writes in human terms
of God, and why the story of Israel is uniquely important; starting
like all tribal peoples, they were gradually led to recognize God as
the supreme Righteous One, the One who revealed to Abraham that
(unlike the pagan gods) he did not want human sacrifice but right
living, who revealed to Moses the Ten Commandments for man-in-
society, and who inspired the Prophets to recall the people to obedience. When Jesus came, he confirmed the moral way of the
Commandments, summing them up in two positive commands:
Love God, and love your neighbour; he told the story of the good
Samaritan to show that your neighbour is anyone – even an enemy –
in need. In his parable of the judgment, moreover, this love of the
neighbour was the criterion for salvation.

These two insights of Newman's – Development in the Church
and Conscience as the way to God – were aspects of his lifelong
pondering on Reason and Faith, which he finally put into form in
The Grammar of Assent philosophically, but with the last hundred
pages written, as he told Miss Holmes, 'especially for such ladies as
are bullied by infidels and do not know how to answer them.' He
always wrote for the ordinary intelligent reader.

These words cheered me when in the late 1950s I began the task of
writing Newman's life, suggested by Fr Charles Stephen Dessain,
who was then beginning on his great work of editing the *Letters and
Diaries*, and told me there were 20,000 letters which had never been
published in full, and many more from the correspondents, and that
Newman himself thought letters the best basis for biography. I knew
that Newman, when he started on what became his *Apologia*, in
answer to Charles Kingsley's fierce attacks on him and through him
on the Roman priesthood as liars and manipulators, decided not to
counter-attack but to write a 'History of my Religious Opinions', not
blaming others or criticizing their opinions but telling his personal
story. In so doing, he won the attention of the English public and,
indeed, their continuing sympathy and respect. So I thought that if

I wrote a *personal* life of Newman, not a critical assessment of his ideas (which I was not competent to do, and has been done by many others), it might serve to introduce him to general readers, especially those like myself once doubtful about God. I hoped that the learned would not react like the priest to whom I was introduced by Fr Dessain at an international Newman conference in Luxembourg in (I think) 1960, who exclaimed: 'A *woman* write the life of *Newman?*' But some did!

Those thousands of letters, then unpublished and all in folders, I read in Newman's own handwriting. They are so natural, directly expressing his feelings and thought, that it was fascinating to follow him through his energetic life; for he was *not* the scholarly sensitive recluse he has so often been imagined to be – an impression perhaps gained from the *Apologia*, which concentrated on his 'religious opinions' and left out everything else. Nor did he allow anything to appear about his difficulties in the Catholic Church, within the Oratory he founded in England, or with the clerical leaders in London and Rome, especially at the time of the First Vatican Council. All this could not be brought out in one volume, and so it was published in 1962 as two volumes, carefully *not* divided at 1845, since he was definitely the same person all through: *Newman: The Pillar of the Cloud* and *Newman: Light in Winter*.

Ten years later, because by then about a dozen volumes of the *Letters and Diaries* edited by Fr Dessain had appeared, I was able to make a shortened version for paperback which I called *Newman's Journey*, published by Collins in 1974. Now I have been asked to write a new introduction for this third edition, for a new generation of Newman readers. I thought, therefore, that I had better give an historical account of its origins before I leave this mortal scene. As I have now lived through three-quarters of this violent and quarrelsome twentieth century, I wonder more and more at Newman's prophetic inspiration and creative imagination, in the tradition of his beloved ancient Greek Fathers of the Church.

Meriol Trevor
February 1996

1

BEGINNINGS

In the autumn of 1805 a child of four lay in his cot and stared at the candles stuck in the windows of his home, flames against the dark, to celebrate the victory of Trafalgar. It was one of the first events John Henry Newman remembered by its date in history, at once definite and mysterious. Light within and darkness outside, victory far off at sea: the image remained in his mind.

The house and the world in which he lay belonged to the eighteenth century; in England the old order reigned, though the nation was profoundly disturbed by the repercussions of the French Revolution and the birth pangs of industrialism. John Henry Newman was born with the nineteenth century and died at the beginning of its last decade; he was to see the whole face of his country change, and he was one of the few who foresaw something of the century to come. Not that he was a prophet of events, but his profound insight into the conflict of ideas behind the transformation enabled him to forecast the trend things were likely to take. His was the century of evolutionary theories which shattered men's idea of a static world, just as the astronomical theories of the sixteenth had shattered the image of a static earth, set between external poles of good and evil. Newman often compared these two revolutions of thought, which have radically altered the human perspective and seemed at first destructive of all traditional beliefs and values. But from his study of early Christian history Newman thought out a theory of the development of ideas which antedated the theory of the biological development of mankind: his mind had already made the transition from the static to the dynamic view of the world which his contemporaries found it so hard to make.

To an extraordinary degree Newman's thought and his life were one; his own story is one of development, in ideas, in action and in personality. His course can be traced in detail because of his exceptional self-awareness and the fact that the Victorians were great keepers of letters; and Newman's letters are marvellously direct and alive, nearly all written in haste, except in controversy, when drafts were made and corrected. The *Apologia Pro Vita Sua*, through which many people first approach Newman, is in a sense deceptive because, as he was telling the story not of his life but of his religious opinions, he inadvertently gives the impression of an intellectual recluse, a dreamer of dreams from earliest childhood.

'I used to wish the Arabian Tales were true:' Newman wrote in the *Apologia*; 'my imagination ran on unknown influences, on magical powers, and talismans. I thought life might be a dream, or I an Angel, and all this world a deception, my fellow-angels by a playful device concealing themselves from me, and deceiving me with the semblance of a material world.'

Yet this child was so observant of the external world that he could remember the plan of a house he had left before he was five, and the border of the dining-room wallpaper which he admired before the birth of his sister, when he was not quite three. He remembered coming downstairs saying, 'This is June' and seeing the breakfast things shining on the table; he remembered the loft at his grandmother's, with apples on the floor and a mangle. It was the same child who recited ' The Cat and the Cream Bowl' to the assembled company on his fourth birthday and who sent his mother a broom flower when his second sister, Jemima, was born in 1807 and he was six. And who made a servant laugh by the heavy sigh with which he forecast for himself the inevitable future of school, business and marriage. None of this got into the *Apologia*; it is gathered from scraps and memories in letters.

The house where the candles were stuck in the windows to celebrate Trafalgar may have been 17 Southampton Street (now Place) near Bloomsbury Square, or Grey Court House at Ham, not far from Richmond, which was the family's country retreat. Both were

Georgian, the house at Ham big and square, three storeys high and standing in its own garden next to the Royal Oak Inn where the carriage horses were stabled. There were several other big houses near, and not far off Ham House itself, and the river Thames. Newman loved this house so much that he said he could have passed an examination in it. 'It has ever been in my dreams.' It was given up before he was seven and soon afterwards he was sent to school; the double break isolated for him the Golden Age, the time before time that lies at the beginning of all lives. Years later he wrote that when he dreamed of heaven, as a boy, it was always Ham. Happy the man to whom heaven is home.

His home, his childhood, were indeed exceptionally happy. John Henry was the eldest of six children, born in London on 21 February 1801 and baptized in the church of St Benet Fink. Church and house have long disappeared under the London Stock Exchange. Next to John came Charles, then Harriett, Francis, Jemima, and lastly Mary, who was nearly nine years younger than John.

Their father, John Newman, was a banker, the son of a man from Swaffham in Cambridgeshire, who had come to London and done well enough in the grocery trade to give his son a better education than his own. The Newman forebears were small farmers and village tailors in the seventeenth century; there were Newmans in East Anglia back to the late middle ages, none in the least distinguished. Grandfather John Newman died just before his son married but Grandmother Elizabeth (born Good) and her daughter, Aunt Betsy, were well known to the children, who often stayed with them. The mother of the six was Jemima Fourdrinier, the only girl in a family of brothers, the daughter of a paper manufacturer of French Huguenot stock. She brought her husband a dowry of five thousand pounds, which she kept intact through many vicissitudes, leaving one thousand to each of her surviving children. The Fourdriniers were perhaps of slightly higher social standing than the Newmans, but both families were good bourgeois, rising with every generation to more importance in the English scene.

In England, manners and education have always helped to raise people in the social scale and the young Newman couple were both musical, fond of plays, dancing and 'routs'. John Newman belonged to the Beefsteak Club. He was thirty-three when he married; his bride was twenty-eight; they were well matched and both delighted in their children. Mr Newman was easy-going, his quick temper as quickly subsiding; he was conventional, conservative in habit but liberal in opinion, and belonged to the established Church. The Newmans have often been described as Evangelicals; they certainly were not.

In a Fourdrinier family picture Mrs Newman, as a young girl, stands by her father, gay and graceful, with dark ringlets; she was affectionate and happy in her domestic world, but not a dominating type. There was no forcing, moral or intellectual, in that household and the memories of childhood were happy for all of them.

John, the eldest, was often the leader, writing burlesques for his brothers and sisters to act, but neither of his brothers would yield an inch of independence and even Harriett would answer back, so there was no danger of his becoming the despot of the family. And they were all too close in age for him to live an isolated life. Moments of fancying himself an angel might occur, but so did the excitement of making a kite with glass eyes, so did a neighbour's cockatoo, and the romance of all adventure was embodied in Eel Pie Island on the Thames.

John was lucky in that the school where he was sent at the age of seven did not break the trusting and loving disposition that had thrived in the psychological security of his home. It was a private boarding school at Ealing, run by a Dr Nicholas, quite fashionable in its day; Marryat and Thackeray at different periods were there and a contemporary and friend of Newman's was Westmacott, the designer of the Hyde Park arcades. Discipline was mild and Dr Nicholas a kind man and a friend of Mr Newman's. In the memories Fr Neville took down from Newman in his old age it is recorded, 'Once Dr Nicholas said, "Why, John, it's your birthday – won't they be drinking your health at home today? I must go to London today

– suppose you get up behind the carriage and then you can say I shall be glad of a dinner too.'"

John was always fond of music and when he was ten his father gave him a violin. Dr Nicholas gave musical evenings and once discovered him listening at the door. 'What, do you like it? Come in and sit down.' Ealing was undoubtedly a civilized school; the maximum penalty was six strokes of the birch, and Newman, though once ordered it for impudence to an undermaster, was let off by the head – which did not endear him to the usher.

John Henry was a prize pupil; Dr Nicholas used to say that no other boy had passed so rapidly up the school – he was at the top when he was fifteen and reciting in Greek on prize days, and playing in Latin comedies, once before the Duke of Kent. He was later to introduce these to the boys of his own school, who never forgot the vigour of his rehearsals, when he was over sixty.

He did not care much for games, then casual affairs of marbles and unorganized cricket, but his schoolboy diary is full of entries of bathing, in the river. He learned to ride, then almost a necessity; he was a tough walker, at Oxford ready to go seventeen miles before breakfast to visit friends. He went boating on the Thames and there is a casual reference to an attempt, when he was about fifteen, to row round the Isle of Wight, despite a sea fog. When he was only nine he and Charles climbed up a cliff at St Leonards and got stuck there.

Nor was he a solitary at school, but the ringleader of a secret club and the editor of newspapers modelled on the *Spectator* – his were the *Spy* and *Beholder*. A cartoon of the Spy Club survives, done by 'our enemy' in which Newman, nose already prominent, appears in command of the meeting. Bored for lack of opposition he invented his own, writing the *Anti-Spy* as well. The *Portfolio* was political and contained a contribution from the American Minister, John Quincy Adams (later President) whose son was at the school.

This happy and successful life received a sudden shock when, in March 1816, Mr Newman's bank failed. The end of the long wars brought ruin to many private banks and businesses; the Newman family always blamed their father's partner and insisted that all the depositors were paid. The house in Southampton Street was let and by the autumn Mr Newman had settled his family at Alton in Hampshire and was trying to manage a brewery there. But he was nearly fifty and was never to recover confidence, moving slowly but inexorably towards bankruptcy.

John was fetched home to hear the news but then sent back to Ealing where he stayed at school through all the summer holidays. He was ill while he was there and the sick room at school became a symbol of horror and desolation, immediately returning to his mind during his serious illness in Sicily in 1833. The fever of 1816 and the experiences 'before and after, awful and known only to God' as he later expressed it, were the occasion of his first conversion, an experience so crucial that it always seemed to him to have made him a different person.

He was fifteen and at a critical point of his development. He had of course been brought up a Christian and was early conscious of his religion. 'What am I? What am I doing here?' he remembered asking himself, before he was five. But at school he began reading sceptical literature. At fourteen he read Tom Paine's tracts against the old Testament and some of Hume's essays: 'So at least I gave my father to understand; but perhaps it was a brag,' he wrote modestly in the *Apologia*. He copied some French verses denying the immortality of the soul and thought, 'How dreadful, but how plausible!' And he decided that he would like to be virtuous but not religious – the classic ideal.

In 1859, when Newman, nearing sixty, was in the throes of another crisis, his mind returned to this crucial event of 1816 and he wrote in his private journal, addressing his Creator: 'Thy wonderful grace turned me right round when I was more like a devil than a wicked boy ...' And in a meditation he wrote, 'Was any boyhood so impious as some years of mine? Did I not in fact dare Thee to do Thy worst?' He saw in himself the sin of intellectual pride, the evil spirit of self-sufficiency.

But God 'mercifully touched his heart' and his whole being was changed, an event to him more certain than that he had hands or feet. Yet because he did not go through the usual sudden and emotional experience of conversion, many Evangelicals afterwards assured him that he had not been converted at all. To them it had to be an apocalyptic event, but Newman gave it a duration of five months, from August to December 1816. He called it 'a great change of thought' in the *Apologia* and treated its intellectual aspects, recording the influence of some books lent him by Walter Mayers, a young Evangelical clergyman who taught at the school.

The two most important were *The Force of Truth* by Thomas Scott and Milner's *Church History*. Scott (grandfather of the Victorian architect George Gilbert Scott) was the son of a Lincolnshire grazier who, starting as a Unitarian, had become convinced of the truth of the Trinitarian doctrine of the nature of God. He not only implanted in Newman's mind an enduring love of this mystery, but presented religious truth as a quest and the understanding of it as a personal development. 'Growth the only evidence of life' became an axiom to the young Newman.

Milner's *History* had an equally profound effect for here Newman first discovered the Fathers of the Church, the great Greek and Roman thinkers of the fourth and fifth centuries. He was immediately attracted by this 'paradise of delight' as he significantly called it, and compared their thought to music, his favourite art. Greek clarity of reasoning met the concrete symbolism of the Hebrews in a fusion of intellect and imagination which appealed instantly to a mind in which these forces were held in unusual balance.

At the time of his first conversion Newman became convinced that God willed him to lead a single life. He called it 'a deep imagination' – an exact phrase, indicating that it was neither a mere fancy nor a rational decision, but something rising from the depth of the self beyond conscious awareness. He knew very well, when he mentioned it in the *Apologia*, what would be the reaction of his contemporaries: one review ran the heading 'The Boy Celibate' and concluded that he was 'lacking in elementary vitality'. Probably the reaction today is similar, if expressed differently. But to Newman it was an element in what he felt to be a total dedication to God's service, a following of Christ in becoming 'a eunuch for the kingdom of heaven's sake'. It is needless to add that this element in his conversion was anathema to the Protestant Evangelicals of the day.

So Tom Paine and the modern sceptics were put aside and the fifteen-year-old boy began to pray earnestly and to strive to live according to the moral standard of Christ. Life was beginning, school was already over, and in December 1816 he was matriculated as a commoner at Trinity College, Oxford.

'Trinity? A most gentlemanlike college.' With these words Dr Nicholas reassured John, who had never heard of it before. His university entrance was altogether a haphazard affair. With the post-chaise at the door, Mr Newman had not decided whether to make for Oxford or Cambridge. It was the curate of St James's Piccadilly who settled it, going with them to Oxford, and though he failed to enter John at Exeter, his own college, succeeded in getting him into Trinity.

He was not able to go into residence till the following June and then arrived just as everyone was going down. However, he met his tutor, Mr Short, and a youth whose birthday was on the same day as his own, though he was three years older – John William Bowden, who was to be a lifelong friend. He was a handsome creature with a Byronic mop of hair and an amiable smile; his father was a director of the Bank of England and they had West Indian connections. In spite of all this, it was Newman who took the lead from the start.

It was lucky for Newman that he made this friend at once, for his first year was a difficult one. He was two years younger than most men of his year and came from a very different background. Trinity was certainly gentlemanlike – nobody did much work and everybody drank a lot of wine. Mr Short, kind man, was continually surprised at the boy's knowledge and did little to guide his reading. Newman 'fagged' to keep up with Bowden, a year ahead in studies; his long hours overtasked a growing physique and he suffered from sudden bouts of faintness or fell asleep over his books. But he did not spend all his time working; he went boating and walking with Bowden and visited the cold plunging bath in Holywell very frequently. He went to concerts in the Holywell Music Room and later joined a small orchestra.

Playing the violin was not then considered altogether gentlemanly, and in his first term Newman was asked to bring it to a wine party by some young men who thought it would be amusing to make a fool of him. When he arrived he heard a smothered laugh as he was announced: 'Mr Newman and his fiddle.' Put on his guard, he refused to oblige with a tune, and when they pressed him to drink, took only three glasses and left in good order. Baulked of their sport the gang burst in on him some ten days later, and locking the door began to press him to come to another wine party, and when he refused they mocked him. The ringleader was six foot three, but the sixteen-year-old refused to be rattled and the giant came back next day to apologize, telling Newman he had 'seldom or never seen anyone act more firmly'. After this, he seems to have been left alone.

Newman's first year ended gloriously with his winning a college scholarship which had just been opened to all comers. When he went back to Alton that summer his proud father greeted him, beaming: 'What a happy meeting this!' The scholarship was worth £60 a year for nine years – no mean sum in those days; it was more than Newman was to receive as Vicar of St Mary's.

So he was able to attend his first Gaudy in all the glory of his new scholar's gown, only to discover that the sole object of the feast was to get drunk. Since the Gaudy preceded the annual college communion, Newman was disgusted and walked out. It took some courage to do this and the next year, men whose support he had gained in the interval crumpled up and gave in. But he did not. In telling this incident, in a memoir he wrote (in the third person) in 1874, Newman, while treating it lightly, remarked in passing, 'in spite of his gentleness of manner, there were in him at all times *ignes suppositi cineri doloso*, which as the sequel of his life shows, had not always so much to justify them ...' Fires under the deceptive ash – many people were to discover that, with surprise.

With his scholarship behind him Newman launched confidently into his second year, going to lectures on geology and mineralogy;

like Shelley, about eight years his senior, he tried some experiments in chemistry. Shelley, in 1811, had been sent down for writing *The Necessity of Atheism*, but Newman had already got past his youthful scepticism and was filling notebooks with prayers (mostly destroyed later) and learning passages of the Bible by heart.

However, he had not lost his literary bent, and in 1819 collaborated with Bowden to produce a periodical, *The Undergraduate*, which, starting pompously, became more comic with every issue; but when it got about that 'Newman of Trinity was editor' the bashful journalist handed it over to the printers and it soon died. Another collaboration the same year was *St Bartholomew's Eve*, a narrative poem, described by Newman in his old age as a romance. 'The subject was the issue of the unfortunate union of a Protestant gentleman with a Catholic lady, ending in the tragical death of both, through the machinations of a cruel fanatic priest, whose inappropriate name was Clement ... There were no love scenes, nor could there be, for, as it turned out to the monk's surprise, the parties had been, some time before the action, husband and wife by a clandestine marriage, known, however, to the father of the lady.' Newman said Bowden was responsible for the historical and picturesque parts, he for the theological. But he marked the passages and the truth emerges: Bowden wrote the dull descriptions and Newman the dramatic episodes – for instance, the last meeting of the ill-fated pair:

> *The faint wild shriek with which she sounds his name*
> *'Julian!' – 'My wife, my dearest, then again*
> *I see thee, love! I have not pray'd in vain!*

In this year, when Newman was eighteen and beginning to feel his powers, he wavered as to his future career. His father had always intended him for the Law, in those days the entrance to the political life of the nation for those not born to power. The Union was not yet founded; Newman was one who suggested there should be a university debating society and had it existed he would certainly have been a member. Bowden, too, who took his schools this year, was to read law in London. But in the summer of 1820 Newman gave up these secular ambitions, returning to his old intention of taking orders, and fagged so hard for his finals that he broke down in the examinations. He was called a day sooner than he expected, lost his head and left before the end. Even so he could hardly believe it when he saw the list: 'his name did not appear at all on the Mathematical side of the paper, and in Classics it was found in the lower division of the second class honours, which at that time went by the contemptuous title of "Under-the-line", there being as yet no third and fourth class.'

'It is all over and I have not succeeded,' he wrote to his father, overwhelmed by the disappointment he was causing them. Father and mother wrote anxiously and he pulled himself together to answer them: 'Very much I *have* suffered, but the clouds have passed away.' Indeed, the situation was not irreparable. He was only nineteen, still had his scholarship, which would enable him to stay at the university till he was old enough to take Holy Orders; he could earn money by coaching pupils and later try for a fellowship. His failure was due to nerves, not to laziness or stupidity. But it was a typical beginning; so many, less gifted, passed easily into a chosen career – Newman slaved for all he won, and suffered humiliating defeats before every prize.

Morally his defeat did more for him than success. The boyish precocity, the alternating moods of hilarity and solemnity, settled into a more mature balance, preparing him for the responsibilities which early came to him as the eldest son in a family where the unfortunate father was declining into bankruptcy and premature death.

Mr Newman was declared bankrupt in 1821, and all the family possessions were sold – Newman lost his music, which happened to be bought, in his old age, by someone who knew him and made inquiries, so that, as he told his sister, Jemima, he was 'obliged to shuffle' to shield their father's name. He always tried to keep his father's failures secret, 'for his sake who laboured and spent himself for us', as he wrote in a note on Alton.

And this in spite of the fact that in his adolescence he often clashed with his father, who thought he was getting too religious for his own good. As recorded in John's journal, one can almost hear his voice. 'It is very proper to quote Scripture but you poured out texts in such quantities. Have a guard. You are encouraging a nervous and morbid sensibility, and irritability, which may be very serious. I know what it is myself, perfectly well. I know it is a disease of the mind. Religion, when carried too far, induces softness of mind … Depend upon it, no one's principles can be established at twenty … I know you write for the *Christian Observer*. My opinion of the *Christian Observer* is this, that it is humbug.' That newspaper was the organ of the Evangelicals and Newman was to come into conflict with it later when his opinions, as his father had surmised, *had* changed.

At the time, of course, John thought they never would. His younger brother Francis had now come under the influence of Mr Mayers and was a more intransigent Evangelical than John; a painful scene with father occurred when Francis refused to copy a letter on Sunday and John backed him up. John confided these family quarrels to his journal but always with strong criticism of himself, couched in the religious jargon of the day; he noted that he was vain of his attainments and too conscious of social differences – much more difficult sins to admit to in youth than bad temper and bad thoughts, which also figured in the list.

The bad temper was chiefly aroused by Francis, whom he took back to Oxford with him and coached for university entrance. Frank was a clever boy but obstinate (like all the Newmans), and on his own admission almost humourless. In December 1822 Newman copied into his journal what he had said or written to his mother: 'I have felt while with Francis at Oxford, a spirit of desperate ill temper and sullen anger rush on me, so that I was ready to reply and act in the most cruel manner to intentions of the greatest kindness and affection. So violent has this sometimes proved, that I have quite trembled from head to foot and thought I should fall down under excess of agitation.'

Yet most of this feeling was suppressed for in 1845, when he was about to become a Catholic, Newman wrote to his brother to ask forgiveness for his bad temper and cruelty in their youth, and Francis, who was not given to making allowances for him, replied that he could not remember any. Even in his *Recollections*, written as a jealous old man out to smash the image of the saintly Cardinal after his death, Frank spoke of John as a generous and kind brother. What annoyed him in John had nothing to do with cruelty.

Newman was naturally troubled by other passions besides anger; sexual temptations seem to have been recorded chiefly as 'bad thoughts' which came most often during the difficult vacations at home. Any details must have been pruned out later, but he does not seem, as the *Apologia* reviewer surmised, to have been 'lacking in elementary vitality'. Newman was well aware that the high standard of chastity he preached laid him open to what he called 'slurs'. In a sermon of 1849 he wrote of the saint: 'He grows up, and he has just the same temptations as others, perhaps more violent ones. Men of this world, carnal men, unbelieving men, do not believe that the temptations which they themselves experience, and to which they yield, can be overcome.' Worldly men, he said, thought a resolute Christian, 'a hypocrite, who practises in private the sins which he denounces in public; or ... they consider that he never felt the temptation, and they regard him as a cold and simple person, who has never outgrown his childhood, who has a contracted mind, who does not know the world and life, who is despicable while he is without influence and dangerous and detestable from his very ignorance when he is in power.'

But although he overcame his temptations, Newman never developed an obsession with sexual sin, as some religious people do; his journals show that even when he was young he considered his pride and vanity more insidious dangers to Christian living, and in later life he was to keep the same sensible balance in dealing with others. There survive some Latin prayers written twenty years later to help an adolescent boy he was teaching at Littlemore. The prayers are directed at specific youthful difficulties, but with brevity and simplicity, and God is invoked as *caritatis amator* – the lover of true love.

Newman's struggles with bad temper and bad thoughts went on through years of great strain, when he was slaving to earn money to help his family, to start Frank on his career, and allowing himself sometimes only four hours' sleep at night. He thanked God once for his 'strong frame' and it must have been strong to stand the pace. He was reckoned by his contemporaries to be fairly tall in his prime, and must have reached his full height about now; he was thin but wiry and had great resilience, recovering quickly from physical or mental prostration brought on by overwork. He walked fast, he worked fast; his letters were rapid talk. But he thought things out slowly, even if he often began with a flash of intuition. By this time he was probably wearing spectacles; he had become slightly short-sighted. They were small, with metal frames. His eyes were grey-blue, his hair light brown, soft and silky. He had a strong prominent nose, determined chin, and the wide full mouth that seems to have come from his mother's family. At this time he was particularly devoted to his sisters; his affections were bound up in the family circle. At Oxford he was lonely, going for solitary walks; Bowden and his Trinity friends had gone down.

In February 1822 he was twenty-one and in April he stood for an Oriel fellowship.

2

ORIEL

Newman nearly repeated the collapse of his Schools with the Oriel election, and it only made him the more anxious that he had a feeling he would succeed. On his twenty-first birthday he wrote in his journal: 'Thou seest how fondly, and I fear idolatrously, my affections are set on succeeding at Oriel. Take all hope away, stop not an instant, O my God, if so doing will gain me Thy Spirit.' He seemed to be taken at his word and during the first day of the examination felt so ill that he had to break off and walk up and down Oriel Hall.

He was saved by kind Mr Short, his tutor, who was having an early dinner in his room and made Newman sit down and eat lamb cutlets and fried parsley, telling him he was doing very well. Sitting once more in the hall he saw up in the stained glass of a window the motto *Pie Repone Te* – 'rest in your dutifulness' perhaps expresses the meaning, or 'in devotion compose yourself'. He went to bed calm.

The next day, Friday, 12 April 1822 – 'of all days most memorable' – he was playing his fiddle in his lodgings when the Provost's butler arrived, and using a time-honoured formula of which Newman was ignorant, said he feared he had 'disagreeable news to impart' – he was elected and required to present himself at Oriel immediately. Newman, thinking the man impertinent, took it coolly, but the minute he had gone 'he flung down his instrument and dashed downstairs with all speed to Oriel College.'

In the Common Room he was overwhelmed with shyness at meeting his new colleagues; though mostly youngish men they were a brilliant set, and one of the cleverest was also the quietest: John Keble, barely thirty. 'When Keble advanced to take my hand,'

15

Newman wrote to Bowden, 'I quite shrank, and could nearly have sunk into the floor'.

Back to Trinity went Newman, to find his college in an uproar, and bells set ringing in three towers ('I had to pay for them,' he noted). The day ended with his taking his seat in Oriel Chapel and dining in Hall, where he sat next to Keble and tried to get used to the familiarity of calling his colleagues by their surnames. 'Thank God, thank God,' he wrote in his journal and remembered the date with gratitude all his life.

Now he had a home, an income, and a career before him, but because he felt himself responsible for his family he did not cease to work; in lodgings still, he had a 'little wretch' of a pupil all through the summer vacation: 'How I longed for it to be over!' he wrote in pencil in 1856, reading over his journal. This was his probationary year; he was fully admitted in 1823, but still lived in lodgings with Francis, who went to Worcester College in May, his expenses paid by his brother. For a young man it was a hard slog, on a few hours of sleep at night and worried for every penny. 'I find it very irksome to be so tied down as I am,' he admitted to his journal. 'I am too very solitary ... Pound me, Lord, into small bits; grind me down, anything for a meek and quiet spirit.'

But he began to make new friends. The first was Edward Bouverie Pusey, six months his senior but elected the following year to Oriel; a Christ Church man, he had from the first been in intellectual circles at Oxford. His family were wealthy landowners; his father was despotic and old, having refused to marry till his own mother died, by which time he was in his fifties. Edward was the second of three sons and was brought up by a straight-backed Lady Lucy Pusey in the old High Church tradition. When scarcely more than a boy he had fallen in love with Maria Barker, a girl his father disapproved simply for her family's politics. Newman, in his memoir of 1874, vividly described the young Pusey: 'His light curly head of hair was damp with the cold water which his headaches made necessary for comfort; he walked fast, with a young manner of carrying himself, and stood rather bowed, looking up from under his eyebrows, his shoulders rounded and his bachelor's gown not buttoned at the elbow but hanging loose over his wrists. His countenance was very sweet and he spoke little.' He spoke a lot, however, on their walks together. Newman, while admiring his goodness and humility, had some evangelical doubts as to whether Pusey was 'regenerate'.

Newman could talk away to Pusey but in the Oriel Common Room he was struck so dumb that the Fellows began to think they had made a mistake in electing him. So Richard Whately undertook to see what he was made of; he liked to lick cubs into shape, if, like the dogs of King Charles's breed, they could be held up by one leg without yelling – as Newman recorded of him. Whately was recently married and had a living at Halesworth, but Suffolk did not agree with his wife, so Whately gladly put in a curate and returned to Oxford, where he was known as the White Bear – bear for manners, and white for the rough coat he wore.

Although now a huge man with a huge appetite and an aggressive manner, Richard Whately had been the puny runt of a large family and timid at school; he had cured himself of shyness by becoming insensitive to the feelings of others. A great intellectual, small-talk bored him; he was a formidable logician and a Whig. Newman slyly remarked that Whately 'was a great talker, who endured very readily the silence of his company'. But having held young Newman (metaphorically) upside down in mid-air, Whately pronounced him to have the clearest mind he knew and put him to work assisting him to hammer out articles on Logic for the Encyclopaedia Metropolitana, which he afterwards made into a successful book. Newman cut his teeth as an academic writer on this Encyclopaedia, earning money with articles on Cicero, Miracles, and (later) Apollonius of Tyana.

It was said that the Oriel Common Room 'stank of logic', and men passing the college would shout, 'Porter, does the kettle boil?' Tea, not wine, was imagined to be its staple beverage. Newman ought to have felt at home there, but he was uncertain of himself among the group of older men, mostly liberals, except for Keble, who spent much of his time in the country, assisting his old father as unpaid curate. Sometimes known as the Noetics, these Oriel men were philosophers and politicians; to them the Church represented the moral order of society and Whately objected to Parliamentary interference from liberal rather than religious principles.

A contrast was Lloyd of Christ Church, afterwards briefly Bishop of Oxford, whose theological lectures Newman and Pusey attended. He was Regius Professor of Divinity, of the High and Dry school, and though he found Newman promising, was irritated by his Evangelical opinions. Fat and snuff-taking, as he walked up and down he would sometimes stop and 'make a feint to box his ears or kick his shins' – naturally making him feel 'constrained and awkward'.

These theological lectures were part of the preparation for ordination and it was on Trinity Sunday, 13 June 1824, that Newman was ordained deacon in the Church of England. 'It is over,' he wrote in his journal. 'I am thine, O Lord; I seem quite dizzy and cannot altogether believe and understand it. At first, after the hands were laid on me, my heart shuddered within me; the words "for ever" are so terrible. It was hardly a godly feeling which made me feel melancholy at the thought of giving up all for God. At times indeed my heart burnt within me, particularly during the singing of the Veni Creator. Yet, Lord, I ask not for comfort in comparison of sanctification. I feel as a man thrown suddenly in deep water.'

He was thrown at once into the deep water of pastoral ministry, for he had accepted the curacy of St Clement's, a poor parish just over Magdalen Bridge, which carried a stipend of £45 a year and surplice fees. The Rector, Mr Gutch, was eighty and often bedridden; the church small and old and a subscription had to be raised to rebuild it; the population had doubled in the last year owing to the increased trade brought by canal traffic. 'When I think of the arduousness, I quite shudder,' Newman wrote in his journal. 'O that I could draw back, but I am Christ's soldier.'

He started visiting, especially the sick, and keeping notes. Often he was taken in by pious talk and afterwards discovered that the person was a drunkard or had deserted his wife and children. From the dying he tried to elicit penitence and induce them to take the Sacrament which, as he was only a deacon, he could not administer himself. The case of a sick girl was very painful – 'it is like a sword going through my heart.' And there was a young married woman with consumption. 'Her eyes looked at me with such meaning I felt a thrill I cannot describe – it was like the gate of heaven.' She died half an hour after he left, much comforted by his reading from St John, though very ignorant of religion, as most of these poor people were.

Meanwhile, from the rich he collected over five thousand pounds for the new church – though he was not responsible for its design. Pusey paid for a gallery to seat the ninety-five children Newman had collected into a catechism class; he prepared them for confirmation and they never forgot him – two later turned up in Birmingham and became Catholics. Miss Gutch the Rector's daughter helped him and the parishioners immediately fixed up a match between them and were quite surprised that it did not come off. When Newman returned to Oxford as a Cardinal, over fifty years later, he went to visit old Miss Gutch.

Newman started his whole congregation singing, probably the psalms in metrical version – and the official singers walked out, in his first parochial row. He preached regularly, but his first sermon was delivered at the tiny church at Over Worton, seventeen miles away, where Mr Mayers was now curate. Newman's text was: 'Man goeth forth to his work and to his labour until the evening.' It was to be a long day's work for him.

In September 1824 Mr Newman died, after only a short illness. John reached London in time to see him. 'He knew me, tried to put out his hand and said, "God bless you."' He died peacefully two days later, his family praying round him. Newman wrote in his journal: 'On Thursday he looked beautiful, such calmness, sweetness, composure and majesty were in his countenance. Can a man be a materialist who sees a dead body? I had never seen one before.'

They buried him the next week and John recorded his thoughts: 'When I die shall I be followed to the grave by my children? My mother said the other day she hoped to live to see me married, but

I think I shall either die within a College walls, or a Missionary in a foreign land – no matter where, so that I die in Christ.' Immediately after his ordination to the diaconate in June he had gone to make inquiries at the Church Missionary Society in London, where they told him that short sight and a weak voice would not prevent his acceptance. But when Mr Newman died, not yet sixty, leaving John the only earning member of the family, the prospect of dying a missionary in a foreign land became extremely unlikely.

After her husband's death Mrs Newman joined his mother and sister at their little school at Strand-on-the-Green, at Kew; the grandmother died in the spring of 1825, the wish of her heart satisfied – to see John in the ministry. Charles left the family, saying they were too religious to live with; Bowden got him a clerkship at the Bank of England which he kept for the next five years – longer than he was to keep any job afterwards. In him the high-strung Newman temperament reached the point of unbalance; he became an argumentative unpredictable oddity. Francis was only nineteen and still had to be seen through Oxford. Then there were the girls: Harriett was twenty-one, Jemima seventeen and Mary fifteen. John supplemented their education by post and loved them all affectionately, but perhaps especially Mary, who wrote him laughing, teasing letters. Mrs Newman had already come to rely entirely on her eldest son. 'I have no fear, John will manage,' she said to her husband, after the bankruptcy.

John managed. He accepted Whately's offer to make him his Vice Principal at St Alban's Hall – later to be absorbed by Oriel. Although it had only a dozen students, so idle and dissipated as to earn it the nickname of Botany Bay, it was worth Whately's acceptance since he became thereby Head of a House with a seat on the Hebdomadal Board and a voice in the affairs of the university. He was made a Doctor of Divinity and was now on the way to a Deanery or Bishopric; in the event he became Archbishop of Dublin. But Newman, who did most of the administrative work, though he needed the extra salary, had no ambitions beyond the university.

About this time he got to know Edward Hawkins, then Vicar of the university church of St Mary the Virgin, since both of them stayed up during the Long Vacations of 1824 and 1825. Hawkins criticized Newman's sermons. 'Men are not saints *or* sinners,' he said sensibly. Newman was already discovering at St Clement's that people could not be divided into sheep and goats in this world and that progressive sanctification, rather than sudden conversion, was to be aimed at. Hawkins also made Newman understand the importance of Tradition in the life of the Church: Christian faith was handed on down the generations as a recognizable body of teaching. Hawkins, an establishment man if ever there was one, did not realize what he had done in getting Newman's mind off the Evangelical track and into history.

Newman was ordained priest in the Church of England on Whit Sunday, 29 May 1825. It was a calmer occasion than the diaconate which for him had represented his break with the secular world. At the beginning of August he celebrated the Holy Communion service for the first time, and for the first time Jemima and Mary took the Sacrament, and from his hands.

'O how I love them,' Newman wrote in his journal. 'So much I love them, that I cannot help thinking Thou wilt either take them hence, or take me from them, because I am too set on them.' Scarcely more than two years were to pass before Mary's sudden death.

In January 1826 Newman was made a college tutor with an income of £600 a year. Since he had always felt his vocation lay in teaching, he gave up St Clement's at Easter, and St Alban's Hall too, though Whately offered to make his salary equal to a tutor's, so eager was he to keep him.

Now Newman had rooms in college, the famous rooms on the first floor in the corner of the front quadrangle, next to the chapel and oriel window. Mary wrote to him: 'Dear John, how extremely kind you are. Oh, I wish I could write as fast as I think ... I hope the "brown room" is not quite so grave as the name would lead one to suppose ... I did not imagine, John, that with all your tutoric gravity and your brown room you could be so absurd as your letter (I beg your pardon) seems to betray ... ' John had written cheerfully about

the cake they had sent and mentioned a project which might take 't!
e!! n!!! ... years??? – to trace the sources from which the corruptions
of the church, principally the Romish, have been derived.'

In the vacations Newman took duty for an ex-Oriel Fellow,
Samuel Rickards, at Ulcombe, a tiny place on a ridge overlooking
mile upon mile of the Weald of Kent. Harriett went as housekeeper
and the two families became great friends. Going back to known
difficulties at Oriel, Newman wrote to Rickards: 'My spirits, most
happily, rise at the prospect of danger, trial, or any call upon me for
unusual exertion; and as I came outside the Southampton coach to
Oxford, I felt as if I could have rooted up St Mary's spire and kicked
down the Radcliffe.'

He needed all this giant strength to deal with the young men who
now came under his charge – himself only twenty-five. 'The College
is filled principally with men of family, in many cases of fortune,' he
wrote in his journal. 'I fear there exists very considerable profligacy
among them.' Tom Mozley, the son of a Derby printer and
publisher, and by no means a prig, who came up in the spring of
1826, wrote home that the undergraduates of Oriel were getting
dreadfully dissipated, as bad as any in the university.

What particularly disgusted Newman were the drunken orgies
before and after the corporate college communion. When he spoke
of it to Tyler, the Dean, he said, 'I don't believe it, and, if it is true, I
don't want to know it.' When Newman asked the Provost if there
was an obligation for all the men to communicate, Copleston said
briskly, 'That question, I believe, has never entered their heads, and
I beg you will not put it into them.'

Newman, however, like Socrates, was soon to be notorious for the
questions he put into young heads, and instead of letting the young
gentlemen go on as they pleased, he issued warnings and reprimands,
thereby making himself very unpopular. Long afterwards, in 1885,
when Newman was eighty-four and a Cardinal, one of these ex-
undergraduates gave his reminiscences about Newman as a tutor,
making him out to have been the feeble butt of youthful pranks,
unable to defend himself. Frederic Rogers, by then Lord Blachford,

a later pupil who became a friend, defended him in the newspapers, pointing out that most of Lord Malmesbury's anecdotes were told of other college characters and saying that Newman had been 'very kind and retiring, but perfectly determined ... master of a formidable and speaking silence calculated to quell any ordinary impertinence.'

Blachford had criticized the old Cardinal's drafts of a reply as showing too much feeling; Newman had talked of 'high and mighty youths' who had attempted indignities and insults against him. 'I am sorry you dislike "high and mighty",' Newman said to Blachford. 'I could find nothing else to intimate that from the first they thought me "only a tutor" and that of *course* their conduct cowed me.' But he acutely observed of Malmesbury's story of his nearly being turned from High Table by Copleston's shouting at him for mutilating a haunch of venison, that it was probably 'a mythical representation of what was the fact – viz, that I was not supported in my reforms by the high authorities of the College.'

Snubbed by the Provost, evaded by the Dean, and despised as socially inept by riotous young noblemen, Newman held his course and was eventually to win respect. A gentleman commoner was once seen coming out of his room, considerably subdued. '"What did he say to you?" – "I don't know, but he looked at me."'

Meanwhile there were his mother and sisters to settle. John prospected at Brighton. 'I prefer it to Bath,' he wrote home, '– it is magnifiquo – and the waves are breaking so soft, bluey green and white.' They moved into 11 Marine Square in the autumn of 1827, John managing everything, wallpaper and upholstery included. His letters overflowed with fun. 'Love to all, saucy H, sly J, silly M,' he scribbled in one, and in the next, 'by way of making amends – Love to sensible H, sober J, and sprightly M.' And at the end of another, 'I am laughing so much I cannot write.' Lloyd, made Bishop of Oxford, had appeared unrecognizable in his wig – 'People say he had it on hind part before.'

One of the new Fellows was a Spaniard, an ex-priest called Blanco White, with whom Newman began to play Beethoven's quartets. He had a passion for Beethoven, who died this year. Newman once said he was 'like a great bird singing'. Blanco White liked this clever young Englishman, who was to travel in the opposite direction from himself. 'Farewell, my Oxford Plato,' he wrote later.

This year Newman had congenial pupils at last – Tom Mozley, who was to marry his sister Harriett, and Henry, youngest son of William Wilberforce, who came up at Michaelmas 1826. His elder brother Robert was elected a Fellow that year. Henry was 'small and timid, shrinking from notice, with a bright face and intelligent eyes,' Newman wrote after his death in 1873, in a short memoir undertaken at the request of his widow. Henry was only temporarily timid, partly because he had never been to school. By nature cheerful and sociable he found Oxford dreadfully devoid of young ladies and soon was flirting with Newman's sisters, when he stayed with them in the holidays. 'I am just wishing to be able to write as fast as H. Wilberforce speaks,' wrote Mary. Newman met the famous old father just before he died, and was touched by the affection of his four sons for him.

In the autumn of 1827 Newman was appointed a University Examiner; he felt his own failure in the Schools redeemed and worked hard to prepare for it. Suddenly there came shattering news from Strand-on-the-Green: Aunt's school had failed and she was £700 in debt. Although in the event Francis was able to help with this, at the time it seemed likely to fall entirely on John, who had already had to pay more than he expected for the house in Brighton. On top of this came the news that Copleston had got his bishopric at last and so there must be an election for a new Provost of Oriel. This excitement precipitated a kind of nervous crisis – Newman's mind went blank and he had to leave the Schools in the middle of the day. Trying to describe it in his journal afterwards he said, 'It was not pain, but a twisting of the brain or eyes. I felt my head inside was made up of parts. I could write verses pretty well but I could not *count*. I once or twice tried to count my pulse, but found it quite impossible; before I had got to 30, my eyes turned round and inside out, all of a sudden.' For this alarming condition the doctor bled him with leeches on his temples and then Robert Wilberforce took him home to the family medical adviser, Mr Babington, whom Newman consulted from now until his death in 1856.

However, he seemed quite recovered when he went home for Christmas, and began writing to his friends about the college election. It was between Hawkins and Keble, and Newman influenced his friends in favour of Hawkins, thinking Keble too gentle to control the wild set. If they were electing an angel, it ought to be Keble, he said, making one of the Fellows laugh, but they were only electing a Provost. Thus it was largely through Newman's offices that Hawkins was elected, who was to oppose him so strongly in years to come; and for Keble it meant a lifetime in country parishes. The election took place on 31 January 1828 and was celebrated on the annual Gaudy day, 2 February, feast of the Purification of the Blessed Virgin Mary, under whose patronage Oriel had been founded. With Hawkins's promotion to the provostship, Newman became Vicar of St Mary's, the University Church.

But by then he was writing in his journal: 'O my dearest sister Mary, O my sister, my sister, I do feel from the bottom of my heart that it is all right – I see, I know it to be, in God's good Providence, the best thing for all of us; I do not, I have not, in the least repined – I would not have it otherwise – but I feel sick, I must cease writing ...'

Mary had died suddenly, at Brighton, on the eve of the Epiphany, 5 January 1828. She was only just nineteen.

A new friend, Maria Rosina Giberne, was with them on the fatal evening; fifty years later she wrote to Newman, 'Dear Mary sat next to you, and I was on the other side; and while eating a bit of turkey she turned her face towards me, her hand on her heart, so pale, with a dark ring round her eyes, and said she felt ill, and should she go away?'

Nobody realized how serious it was; Mary had a bad night, but when Miss Giberne called the next evening it was a great shock to learn from John that his sister was already dead. Presently she went upstairs to make a drawing of the dead girl, in her little frilled cap. John stood by her to look and said in a low voice, 'It is *very* like.' He could never again think of Mary without tears coming into his eyes.

3

CRISIS

The double shock of Mary's death and his own nervous collapse profoundly affected Newman; in his own words, it awakened him from a dream. 'I was beginning to prefer intellectual excellence to moral,' he noted in the *Apologia*; 'I was drifting in the direction of liberalism.' By the term liberalism Newman did not mean the idea of political freedom, but the notion that 'one opinion is as good as another' and that there can be no objective truth in religion. There is a difference between allowing men freedom to hold various opinions and denying that there is any standard by which to judge between them. But the tolerance advocated by political liberals in fact often led to general scepticism, and though the Oriel Noetics were all Christian clergymen, the next generation were those to feel the burden of doubt.

A common reaction among religious people was to oppose the corrosive effects of such 'liberal' reasoning merely with strong moral emotion; Francis Newman took this way and for a time became a member of a fanatical new sect, as usual attempting a primitive Christianity, which became known as the Plymouth Brethren. As he was a clever man, reason made a return, and in the forties, his own and the century's, he found himself rationalizing his way out of any form of Christian faith – each stage marked with a book.

But John, when Mary's death shocked him awake, just as he was emerging into the full vigour of maturity, did not react into either emotionalism or rationalism, but began to search more deeply into the actual world, the world of people and the world of history, to study the great fact of Christianity as it has existed, and the meaning of it. He began to approach the problem of reason and faith with a determination to include the demands both of head and heart, of consciousness and conscience. This was to be his personal lifework and the source of his enduring influence long after his death. It was slow work, and although he knew what he was doing, he did not know where he was going.

Although childhood and adolescence form a human being, his mind and personality often take their individual set in the years round about thirty, and this was so with Newman. He was just twenty-seven when Mary died and he became Vicar of St Mary's and he was thirty-two when he was brought near to death himself, by a fever in Sicily, and came back to Oxford to begin the Movement of the Catholic revival.

At the beginning of this crucial period two of his best friends got married. Pusey became Regius Professor of Hebrew, a post which carried a Canonry at Christ Church; and although his father contrived to die at the critical moment, Pusey did not put off his wedding, but took Orders and Maria Barker, leaving Oriel to settle at Christ Church for life. Newman liked Maria, especially after he had had 'a long gossip' with her alone, and she too became a devoted friend; he was a great favourite with the Pusey children when they arrived on the scene.

Bowden's wife, Elizabeth Swinburne, aunt of the poet Algernon Charles Swinburne, also became a lifelong friend, following Newman into the Catholic Church; two sons became Oratorians and one daughter a nun. The Bowdens lived in London, where Newman was a frequent visitor – they called him to each other 'Joannes Immortalis'. And he found their married life so happy and exemplary that for a long time it prevented his believing that a single life dedicated to God could be in any sense 'higher'.

It was in 1828 that Newman began to know Hurrell Froude well. Froude was elected a Fellow of Oriel in 1826 and wrote then to his father, 'Newman is a very nice fellow indeed, but very shy.' Froude himself was, if not shy, certainly lonely at first in that Noetic Common Room. 'I sat in the corner as I generally do, and said as little as I generally do.' That did not last long, but still he could say,

'Newman has foiled my analytical skill; I cannot make him out at all, but have got far enough to see that he is not my sort.'

No letters home remain to tell how he discovered that after all Newman was his sort; in the next, of 1830, the friendship is already established, and he was riding with Newman, and copying for his sister an anthem by Boyce which Newman had brought from St Mary's. Even by January 1829 Newman, travelling outside the coach to Oxford because it was cheaper on top, on changing with an under-graduate who wanted to smoke, wrote home that 'on tumbling into the coach I found Froude opposite me. He formed an agreeable companion "*in* course"' – so much so, that his gloomy prognostica-tions of loneliness were forgotten.

Much later Newman spoke of wanting to get a spark by collision with Froude; the metaphor exactly expresses the effect of the meeting of two such different yet congenial minds. Richard Hurrell Froude was two years younger than Newman and came from a very different background. Eldest son of an Archdeacon who lived like a cultured country gentleman in his comfortable house at Dartington in Devon, Hurrell grew up riding, shooting, fishing and sailing – but also sketching, with his father: the Archdeacon's water-colours are pleasing. Hurrell's Oxford friend Frederic Oakeley called him *riant*; evidently only a French word could express what he also spoke of as 'sunny cheerfulness'. Tom Mozley remembered him as 'tall, erect, thin' and a bold rider. 'He would take a good leap if he had the chance and would urge his friends to follow him, mostly in vain.' Hurrell was high-spirited. His eyes were bright, grey, ironic and keen. He enjoyed teasing the solemn.

Froude was utterly remote from the Protestant middle-class London in which Newman had grown up: he was never anywhere near Evangelicalism, which he laughed at, or Liberalism, which he hated. Keble, who had been his tutor, reinforced his High Church, High Tory character, but deepened his spiritual understanding and encouraged him to a self-discipline as severe and critical as Newman's, and also confided only to his journal. When extracts were published, after his death, people were shocked at what they considered a morbid preoccupation with taming vanity and greed; but nothing could be less morbid than Hurrell Froude as others knew him, always ready for a fight, and spurring Newman, who was more inclined to see the opposing point of view, to the attack.

Their first battle was a political one, when in 1829 Hawkins, an ardent Peelite, pledged the college to support Peel's re-election when he had changed views about Catholic Emancipation. Although Newman had no strong feelings against Roman Catholics being given votes, he resented State interference with the Church – and Oxford was still a clerical establishment. He and Froude campaigned against Peel so successfully that he lost his seat to Sir Robert Inglis and had to get back into Parliament by means of the close borough of Westbury.

Hawkins was furious at the young Fellows' success; so was Whately, who invited Newman to a party of 'two-bottle-orthodox' old Tories, sat him between 'Provost This and Principal That' and asked him how he liked his company. Although Newman treated this episode humorously in the *Apologia*, he admitted that Whately was 'considerably annoyed' at the defection of his protégé. The Noetics regarded themselves as avant-garde, and when their juniors took up a different position, it was understandable that they equated their views with those of the despised Tories. But Froude had no more use for what he called 'mere conservatism' than for the 'march of mind men'. His idea of the Church was of an autonomous body, a band of brothers, 'terrible as an army in battle array'.

Whately thought Newman abandoned the liberal cause for ortho-doxy because orthodoxy was in power, that his motive was worldly ambition; yet Newman's real motive was as unworldly as it could well be: he thought that liberalism in matters of religion betrayed the Church into the hands of the world – that is, human society so far as it is organized by self-will and against the will of God, as Christ has revealed it. In 1829 and 1830 his sermons at St Mary's were often directed to this theme of the Church and the world, and when he was eighty-five he quoted from them to make the same point to late Victorian society.

Although Newman probably felt the break with Whately more, because he liked him and owed much to his training, it was the break with Hawkins that immediately affected his position. In dealing with this, whether in the *Apologia* or in his private memoir of 1874, Newman's treatment is detached, and his judgments of others so lenient, of himself so severe, that few readers may guess how difficult the situation became. In his memoir Newman said that before his election Hawkins had been something of a Tribune of the People, advocating the participation of the tutors and Fellows in the government of the University, but once Provost he saw the advantages of the *status quo* and declared that the interests of the Fellows were sufficiently represented by the Head of the House. He used the authoritative 'we' so often that the younger Fellows nicknamed him 'the College'. He was a stiff, formal man. 'He could not endure free and easy ways,' Newman wrote in a passage which he did not, in the end, send to Anne Mozley, his sister-in-law, who edited his early letters for publication; 'and was disgusted with slang: what others only thought to be humour would instantly bring a strange rigid expression to his face.' Needless to say, Froude was frequently guilty of rigidifying the Provost.

After the Peel episode the Provost disliked the influence of Newman in the college and began to express disapproval of the reforms he was introducing into the tutorial system – or lack of system. Tutors had simply delivered lectures, and if any undergraduate wanted individual attention, he had to pay for it. Newman thought such private supervision was what the tutors were already paid to do; he also thought they had a duty to take a personal interest in the young men, a pastoral care. This, in fact, was what tutorship became in Oxford, and Oriel never recovered from the measures the Provost now took to ensure that it should not be so in *his* college. He forbade what he could put his finger on, the terminal tests; stiff letters were exchanged, but neither side would budge. Robert Wilberforce and Froude stuck by Newman; the other tutor, the eccentric Dornford, wavered. Finally the Provost crushed opposition by force. He sent no more pupils to the tutors who would not go along with him. Newman's were sent to his friend Renn Dickson Hampden, not then a Fellow, since he was married, but living in Oxford – a man who succeeded in being both a liberal and a pluralist.

Newman's remaining pupils came through Schools with flying colours, but in 1830 he had to resign the position which meant so much to him and several hundred pounds a year as well, as ever, needed for his family. 'All my plans fail,' he wrote gloomily to Froude in September 1830. 'When did I ever succeed in any exertion for others?' Yet out of the ruin of his hopes he made a sermon on 'Jeremiah, a Lesson for the Disappointed', meditating on a recurring theme, that Christians must expect disappointment in this world: to the world, Christ himself was a failure.

Just when Newman's income dropped, his mother and sisters determined to settle near him, and though he felt doubtful of the wisdom of this, knowing that he would be too busy to give them his full attention, as he could on holidays at Brighton, he fixed them, first at Rose Hill, and then at a small house, Rose Bank, in the village of Iffley. It is still there, an oasis in the midst of the hideous modern suburbs of Oxford. As usual, it was John who superintended the alterations, the painters and paperers, and the removal, admitting to Jemima in October, that he was 'supremely tired'.

At this critical moment Frank announced that he was going on a missionary expedition to Persia. Frank had been twenty-two in 1827 when he met J. N. Darby, the Evangelical clergyman of the Church of Ireland who became the magnetic leader of the Plymouth Brethren. Mr Mayers died soon after and Frank transferred his devotion to the Irish fanatic. Darby himself did not go to Persia; the party was a weird assortment, including mothers and wives – none of the women were to survive the expedition. Frank had fallen madly in love with Maria Giberne, but she refused his offer of marriage, faithful to an absent officer in India who was to die before he could return to claim her hand. Frank was the best-looking of the Newmans, with black hair, blue eyes and intense feelings, but of them all Miss Giberne obviously preferred John – 'Bless the Monk!!!'

she wrote in her enthusiastic way much later, describing the beginnings of her acquaintance with him.

Thwarted in love, Frank determined to be a missionary, without consulting his family, leaving them all to the care of John. As for Charles, he was no help but another liability; he was now bombarding John with letters attacking Christianity. John turned the tables by suggesting that instead he should try to prove the truth of atheism. For, he told Jemima, 'unbelievers took an unfair advantage in always *assailing* things, as if *they* had not also an hypothesis to maintain, and greater difficulties (as I think) to surmount.'

When Newman realized that his career as a tutor was already over, he put all his teaching energy into his sermons at St Mary's. When it came to publishing, he took more from 1831 than from any other year – twenty-seven in all. The theme of obedience runs through them, obedience to conscience as the path to the understanding of truth, and obedience to God in putting his commandments into practice. Many deal with the use and misuse of emotion in religion. He preached to his High Street parishioners on the dangers of emotion, but he preached to the University on the dangers of reason. His first university sermon was given on Act Sunday, 2 July 1826; he was twenty-five. His subject was 'The Philosophical Temper, first enjoined by the Gospel', and his text the words of Jesus: 'I am the light of the world.' Gracefully he introduced the motto of Oxford University: *Dominus Illuminatio Mea* – the Lord my light. Afterwards, he recorded, 'I lay on my sofa writhing, at the thought of what a fool I had made of myself.' It was a critical audience for these afternoon sermons to members of the university, all in their gowns, and the seniors all clerics.

From Advent 1831 to Advent 1832 Newman was appointed one of the Select Preachers; he was never appointed again. The most famous preacher in Oxford, perhaps in England, was deliberately excluded by the authorities. The six further sermons to the University (printed with the others in 1843) were preached at the appointment of friends, mostly on Saints' Days – two on Whit Tuesdays. The only two on Sundays were preached in the morning and before term began. Even in the year when he was Select Preacher efforts were made to prevent his turns falling in full term, and as an old man he noted that several of the set on Faith and Reason were preached to half-empty benches. Yet they contain some of Newman's deepest thought; he reissued them almost without alteration in 1871, the year after he had published his mature reflections on the same problems in the *Grammar of Assent*.

In the *Apologia* Newman tried to give Keble the credit for his theories on Reason and Faith, but he had to admit that it was partly dissatisfaction with Keble's approach that led him to elaborate his theory of assent. Keble was inclined to regard intellectual doubts as signs of moral failure; Newman, while always upholding the primacy of conscience, felt that reason must be given its due, and all through his life he was working out the reasonable justification for faith, with a psychological penetration and an imaginative understanding far removed from the bald abstractions of atheistic or theological rationalism.

Froude used to say he was like the murderer who had done one good deed in his life: he had brought Newman and Keble to understand each other. Newman owed less intellectually to Keble than he tried to make out, but he gained a friend whom he loved and admired and once compared to the saint who became his patron, the lovable eccentric, Philip Neri. Keble was small, bright-eyed, with a youthful look that lasted into old age, quirky, but full of real goodness. It was probably of Keble Newman was thinking when he wrote, in his sermon on 'Personal Influence, the Means of Propagating the Truth' of hidden saints, unknown to the world, who were yet the instruments God used to bring about his purposes for mankind. It was by this humble propagation of faith in Christ among the weak and oppressed that Christianity conquered the great Roman Empire. Newman was already meditating on the mysterious growth of the kingdom of Christ in the world of time.

As well as pouring his teaching energy into sermons, Newman during these two years was writing his first book. Rose and Lyall, editors of the new Theological Library, asked him to write the volume on the Councils of the Church. Hugh James Rose was a Cambridge man, the editor of the *British Magazine*, and it shows how promising Newman was already considered, that he was asked to contribute to this learned series. He had certainly read more than most in a field then little explored. Pusey had picked up for him in Germany folios of the Fathers at a shilling each – showing how little they were then prized. His ex-pupils gave him further volumes; all survive in the Oratory library today.

Newman soon realized that he could not tackle all the early Councils in one book; he contracted his view to the Nicene Council, but got so interested in the development of the Arian party and the activities of St Athanasius, the lonely champion of orthodoxy, that the Council itself was relegated to a summary at the end. Froude, when he heard of the length of the introductory portion, was afraid that Newman would never arrive at his subject. 'Recollect, my good sir,' Newman retorted, 'that every thought I think *is* thought, and every word I write *is* writing, and that thought tells, and that words take room, and that though I made the introduction the *whole* book, yet a book it is.' The only snag was that it was not the book he had been asked to write. And it was too long for inclusion in the series. In the end, he published it himself in 1834 as *The Arians of the Fourth Century*.

Newman worked so unrelentingly on this book that he had spells of faintness; sometimes he had to lie down till the dizziness went off. In the summer of 1832 there was an outbreak of cholera, but there were few cases in Oxford and none in Newman's parish, though he was afterwards accused of deserting it during an epidemic. His pupil and friend, Frederic Rogers, was afraid he might catch the disease, but Newman said he had a strong impression that he was destined for some work, as yet undone. 'Surely my time is not yet come. So much for the cholera.'

But someone else was beginning an illness that was to prove fatal – Hurrell Froude, at whose home in Devon Newman had spent some enchanted summer days in what he felt was an earthly paradise. 'Really I think I should dissolve into essence of roses, or be attenuated into an echo if I lived here.' He wrote verses in the albums of Froude's sisters:

> *There stray'd awhile, amid the woods of Dart,*
> *One who could love them but who durst not love.*
> *A vow had bound him, ne'er to give his heart ...*

It was not, strictly speaking, a vow, but nevertheless he and Froude had made up their minds to embrace the ideal of priestly celibacy. In a cancelled passage of the *Apologia* Newman later wrote that he 'was taught the Catholic belief of the moral superiority of the single life' by Froude. Already in 1827, before he knew Newman well, Froude was being teased by Sam Wilberforce, the first of that susceptible family to marry one of the beautiful Sargents, daughters of the Rector of Lavington. (Henry Edward Manning married another, Caroline, and succeeded the father in the living.) Newman gave the year 1829 as the date after which he had no doubts that he was called by God to live a single life. Before that he had sometimes wavered, 'with a break of a month now and a month then,' as he said in the *Apologia*, provoking one of the reviewers to remark, 'When, it may be, a pretty face, a gleaming eye, an ensnaring ankle, came between him and his resolution.' It was more likely to be the times when his married friends, the Bowdens, the Puseys, impressed him with the ideal of dedicated shared lives. In an unpublished sermon for Bowden's daughter Marianne, when she took her vows in the Visitation order, he spoke of the marriage ideal and compared it with the selfishness of singleness chosen for its own sake. 'Man is made for sympathy and for the interchange of love, for self-denial for the sake of another dearer to him than himself. The Virginity of the Christian soul is marriage with Christ.'

All the same, even Froude had some backslidings. In 1832 he wrote to Newman from Devonshire, 'I am getting to be a sawney (sentimentalist) and not to relish the dreary prospects which you and I have proposed to ourselves – but this is only a feeling – depend on it I will not shrink – if I buy my constancy at the expense of a permanent separation from home.'

Newman answered, 'What can you mean by your "feeling" against our dreary prospects? Were you myself, I should say you were falling in love – but I hardly suspect you of that. Your words are quite unintelligible, for what do you propose to stand to that you have not commenced already? and how can you ever be required to give up your friends of kin, where you do not now. Unriddle.'

Froude unriddled in his usual straightforward way, 'As to my sawney feelings – I own that home does make me a sawney ... but there is more fun in the prospect of becoming an ecclesiastical agitator ... and the rest may be regarded as irrelevant.'

It is interesting that Newman considered himself more liable to falling in love than Froude. His adoption of the ideal of celibacy was a psychologically positive, not a negative step; it was also a kind of protest against the comfortable life of the married clergy of the day, which Newman often made mild fun of, notably in his novel, *Loss and Gain*. Celibacy, for him, was always coupled with a life of penance, fasting and prayer.

Poor Froude would not have been able to marry in any case. The threat of the cholera was still in the air when, as Newman left Devon for Oxford in 1832, Froude told him that the doctors feared he had contracted a disease of the lungs – tuberculosis, then nearly always fatal. Long afterwards Newman wrote, 'I shook hands with him and gazed into his face with great affection,' and wrote some sad verses anticipating the worst.

But Archdeacon Froude, who had already lost his wife and a son to the scourge, determined to make a strong bid to keep his eldest. They would go to the Mediterranean for the winter, and Hurrell wrote to invite Newman to go with them. 'It would set you up,' said Froude, who thought his friend was overworking. Newman was made sleepless by the proposal; he had never dreamed of such a holiday. But if he was ever to travel, now was the time, when he had no pupils, had finished his book and had some money in hand – provided he did not spend more than £100. At last he made up his mind to it, preached his final sermon to the University in December, on 'Wilfulness, the Sin of Saul', and hurried off to Falmouth, riding on top of the coach to the west, through the frosty night. Typically, he became embroiled with someone 'called by courtesy a gentleman' who was making advances to 'a silly goose of a serving maid'. Newman, regarded as a rival for his interference, was called a damned fool, but the scene ended with a handshake. And so, hurrying away from his frustrations in Oxford, Newman met the Froudes at Falmouth and embarked on the *Hermes*, sailing out on the wild winter sea, image of the unknown.

The whole of this journey was to be for Newman a voyage into his own soul, ending with a death and resurrection in Sicily. This was why he wrote the detailed account of his illness there, and why he sent it to Anne Mozley when she was editing his letters. On advice from Dean Church she printed it entire, but with all Newman's references to the devil and to his bowels left out; the Victorian readers of 1890 were more prim than the Georgian Newman.

On the level of a holiday tour, one can only wonder that poor Froude survived at all. They started in storms. Newman turned out a fairly good sailor, better than Hurrell and much better than the unfortunate Archdeacon, who was prostrate for days. Newman burst into verse, as he frequently did when feeling slightly queasy. He wrote set after set of verses, as he called them, which were afterwards printed in the *British Magazine* and then in the collection *Lyra Apostolica* under the sign of the Greek letter delta. Newman shows his poetic qualities most strongly in his clear musical prose, but Matthew Arnold liked the plain diction of his verse, and some of his best lines have a sinewy muscularity, a ringing tone.

Gibraltar, and into the Mediterranean, more storms, Malta on Christmas Eve and all the bells pealing, but they could not land; on to Zante and Corfu – where they went to a ball. Froude and Newman went on long rides and visited Greek churches. He saw Ithaca, 'a barren huge rock' and could hardly believe it was the reality behind the Homeric dreams of his boyhood. 'I thought of Ham, and of all the various glimpses which memory barely retains and which fly from me when I pursue them, of that earliest time of life when one seems to realize the remnants of a pre-existing state.' He was writing home, long journal letters; in Corfu he collected seeds for his mother's garden at Iffley. The furthest reach of their voyage touched the earliest shore of memory.

Back to Malta, and a fortnight of quarantine in the Lazaret, with the Archdeacon and Hurrell touching up their sketches and Newman playing on a hired violin. Footsteps sounded in the great stone rooms but no one was visible. A crash woke Newman who cried 'Who's there ?' Prolonged silence, and he caught a fearful cold 'speaking to a ghost' as he put it. When they were allowed ashore he was too unwell to go out.

On to Palermo, and now Newman was carried away by the wonderful landscape of Sicily and the classic ruins on the desolate hills. It was the temple at Egesta (Segesta) which haunted him long after. 'Six gigantic pillars before and behind, twelve in length ... the whole place is one ruin except this in a waste of solitude ... Mountains around and Eryx in the distance! The past and the present! Once these hills were full of life!' All Sicily became to him a vision of the pagan world:

> So let the cliffs and seas of this fair place
> Be named man's tomb and splendid record stone.

On they went to Naples, arriving on 14 February in storms of rain which continued for days. Newman thought it a watering-place in comparison with Corfu and Palermo, which would be 'admired chiefly by watering-place people'. They visited Pompeii and Herculaneum and reached Rome on 2 March. 'And now, what can I say of Rome, but that it is the finest of cities, and that all I ever saw are but dust (even dear Oxford inclusive) compared with its majesty and glory? Is it possible that so serene and lofty a place is a cage of unclean creatures?' In spite of his already extensive discovery of early Catholicism Newman's imagination was still haunted by Protestant images of the Scarlet Woman. But his first experience of St Peter's was pleasant. 'Everything is so bright and clean, and the Sunday kept so decorously.'

In Rome they met English friends and caught up with English news, shocked to hear that the government was about to abolish several bishoprics of the (Anglican) Church of Ireland and adjust its revenues. Newman wrote to Tom Mozley: 'I hate the Whigs (of course, as Rowena says, in a Christian way) more bitterly than ever,' and longed to know what people in Oxford thought of 'the atrocious Irish sacrilege Bill'. Newman and Froude were going home burning with indignation at the State's interference with the Church. Hurrell and his father decided to return overland, having had enough of the sea on the *Hermes*, but Newman, why, he could not himself quite understand, determined to go back alone to Sicily. Everyone was against it, but nothing could put him off – not bugs, nor bandits, nor foreign food and foreign talk, not even loneliness. In fact, as he admitted to Jemima, he wanted to see what it was like to be 'solitary and a wanderer'.

First, going back to Naples, Newman climbed Vesuvius and went down some three hundred feet inside the crater, getting his shoes uncomfortably full of ashes. This descent into the underworld seemed a suitable beginning to his classical journey, and he repeated it, psychologically, by having nightmares in which he wanted to run away into the shrubberies at Ham but 'it was not allowed me.' Then, on 19 April 1833 he ended a letter: 'Half-past 7 a.m. the wind is fair. I am off suddenly.' This was the last anyone at home was to hear of him till June.

The servant he took, Gennaro, a Peninsular War veteran who had been sixteen years with one English family, proved very faithful, his one failing being a slight addiction to the bottle. They went by way of Taormina, which to Newman appeared like an earthly paradise, Etna magnificent in the distance. 'I like what I see of the people,' he told Jemima; 'dirt with simplicity and contentment.' These were shepherds and country people; in other places, the poverty had horrified him. He went on to Syracuse – storms again, so that he twice had to sleep, as well as he could, in an open boat at sea. The fleas at the inns were terrible and he got very sore with the long rides. Newman then decided to cut across country to Girgenti

(Agrigentum) on the southwest coast, but when they reached Leonforte, near Enna in the very middle of the island, Newman collapsed with a severe fever. Gennaro got him to an inn and made him camomile tea. 'As I lay in bed the first day, many thoughts came over me,' Newman wrote in the private memoir he called *My Illness in Sicily*. 'I felt God was fighting against me – and felt at last I knew *why* – it was for self-will ... Yet I felt and kept saying to myself "I have not sinned against light."' He had not seen his actions as following his own will against the will of God, though now he recognized that it had been so. On the next day Gennaro left him alone, locked into the room, and he felt his mind racing as it had in 1827; he tried to count the patterns on the wallpaper and was tormented by the whining of a beggar outside. 'I seemed to see more and more my utter hollowness.' He felt he had been developing Keble's convictions rather than his own; he had been self-willed about the tutorship and had blasphemed the Sacrament by going to it with resentment against the Provost. Perhaps this sickness was a punishment. Yet when Gennaro came back Newman insisted he was not going to die: 'God has still a work for me to do.' Gennaro was not so sure and got him to write down a home address; Newman gave Froude's.

The next day Newman was under the delusion that he had recovered and insisted on making a start, but soon he became so ill that Gennaro got him into a hut made of poles and there a doctor found him; Newman was slung across a mule and taken up the steep hill to Castro Giovanni, the ancient town of Enna, where Gennaro found him a large room in the house of one Luigi Restivo. Here he was well cared for but so delirious that he only knew the date again on 19 May, Jemima's birthday. Slowly, through fantastic dreams and hallucinations of armies marching, he came back to life; his skin began to peel, his hands were yellow, the nails discoloured. Later, his hair began to fall out. Gennaro made him tea for breakfast. 'How I longed for it! I could not help crying out from delight. I used to say, "It is life from the dead."'

As soon as he was well enough to move, Gennaro got him to Palermo, where he stayed at Page's hotel and was fed by Ann Page on sago and tapioca pudding. He began to move about with a stick, sat in churches and by the sea, longing for home – but no boat came. Gennaro got drunk in Palermo, but went back to his wife and family in Naples with £10 extra (quite a sum in those days) instead of the old blue cloak which was all he asked for. 'He was humanly speaking the preserver of my life,' Newman wrote in 1840, finishing his account at Littlemore, with the old cloak on his bed. 'He nursed me as a child. An English servant never could do what he did.'

At last, on 13 June, Newman embarked on an orange boat bound for Marseilles, and with his usual bad luck was becalmed off Sardinia in the Straits of Bonifacio. Here he wrote the famous poem which he called 'The Pillar of the Cloud' but which is generally known by its first words, 'Lead, Kindly Light'.

Newman associated his three feverish illnesses with three spiritual crises in his life. The first, when he was fifteen, 'made him a Christian', turning him away from scepticism; the second checked him, at twenty-six, when he was beginning to prefer intellectual excellence to moral. These are his own brief analyses, but he left none of the worst, which nearly killed him, and which he wrote down in such detail. This fever acted as a purge for his self-will, forcing him to realize his own hollowness as he lay helpless, struck down at the height of his powers, alone in the hands of strangers, and in the midst of the island which he had called man's tomb, the ruins of the greatest human civilization before the coming of Christ.

Beginning his account he wrote: 'Well, in an unlooked for way I come to Sicily and the devil thinks his time is come. I was given over into his hands … I could almost think the devil saw I am to be a means of usefulness and tried to destroy me. . . Now it certainly is remarkable that a new and large sphere of action has opened upon me from the very moment I returned.'

The fever burned up the past and released a tremendous spring of energy; Newman was going home possessed with the intuition that he 'had a work to do in England'. At last the wind blew and the boat sailed on; Newman disembarked at Marseilles, not forgetting to take some oranges for children in Oxford, and began hurrying northwards, by diligence. His feet swelled, he suffered from cold sweats, but nothing could stop him now. He travelled night and day and did not stop till he reached Oxford and his mother's house. It was 9 July 1833; Frank had arrived from Persia a few hours before.

On Sunday Keble preached the Assize sermon in St Mary's – on National Apostasy.

4

THE MOVEMENT

It was Newman who started the fashion for dating the beginning of the Oxford Movement from the delivery of Keble's sermon on National Apostasy – which in itself would not have started anything. Although he lamented 'fashionable liberality' and feared that duty to the Church might become irreconcilable with duty to the State, Keble's advice to 'the Church's children' was resignation. But Froude and Newman had come home burning for action and soon found like-minded men. There were hurried meetings and plans for a petition and an association. Froude went to the initial conference; Newman did not. He distrusted committees. Instead he sat down and wrote *A Tract for the Times*, addressed to the clergy in simple terms, set out under eye-catching headlines. In capitals appeared the caption: CHOOSE YOUR SIDE!

'I am but one of yourselves, a Presbyter; and therefore I conceal my name, lest I should take too much on myself by speaking in my own person. Yet speak I must; for the times are very evil, yet no one speaks against them … Should the Government and the country so far forget their God as to cast off the Church, to deprive it of its temporal honours and substance, *on what* will you rest the claim of respect and attention which you make upon your flocks? Hitherto you have been upheld by your birth and education, your wealth, your connections; should these secular advantages cease, on what must CHRIST'S ministers depend?' Having posed the question Newman answered it in terms which give the starting point of the Movement. 'CHRIST has not left his Church without claim of its own upon the attention of men. Surely not. Hard Master he cannot be, to bid us oppose the world, yet give us no credentials for so doing.

There are some who rest their divine mission on their own unsupported assertion; others rest it on their temporal distinctions. This last case has perhaps been too much our own; I fear we have neglected the real ground on which our authority is built – OUR APOSTOLICAL DESCENT.'

Essentially the Movement was the rediscovery of the Church as an autonomous community, organically one with the first disciples of Christ. Recognition of this actual visible body involved a new outlook on human society, so long accepted as 'Christian'. The first tract ended with the warning: 'Fear to be of those whose line is decided for them by chance circumstances, and who may perchance find themselves with the enemies of CHRIST, while they think but to remove themselves from worldly politics. Such abstinence is impossible in troublous times. HE THAT IS NOT WITH ME IS AGAINST ME AND HE THAT GATHERETH NOT WITH ME SCATTERETH ABROAD.' And the second tract demanded: 'Are we to speak when individuals sin, and not when a nation, which is but a collection of individuals? Must we speak to the poor and not to the rich and powerful? ... Are we content to be the mere creation of the State? ... Did the State make us? Can it unmake us?' Although the occasion of their protest was an attack on the Church's possessions, the founders of the Movement were not concerned with retaining secular power and privilege, but with spiritual authority. While Newman proclaimed, 'Exalt our holy Fathers the Bishops, as the Representatives of the Apostles and the Angels of the Churches,' he also kindly wished them 'the spoiling of their goods and martyrdom'.

As soon as the Tracts were written Newman had them printed and began to distribute them by the simple method of sending bundles to friends and ex-pupils. Even Miss Giberne in London was pressed into service, and while her mother paid calls she nervously handed packets to surprised maids for later delivery to the mistress of the house. As her mother's friends were all Evangelicals she had an uphill task, but some, like the Laprimaudayes, were to follow the lead all the way to Rome. Incidentally, it is interesting how many

Tractarians had Huguenot ancestry. Newman himself, shyness forgotten, rode round Oxfordshire and Northampton delivering his anonymous pamphlets to unsuspecting clergymen.

'Newman is becoming perfectly ferocious in the cause,' wrote James Mozley (Tom's younger brother) in September, to his sister Anne. '"We'll do them," he says, at least twenty times a day – meaning the present race of aristocrats and the liberal oppressors of the Church in general.' It was a battle, and Newman, at thirty-two, had become a leader. He had already offended some. 'Yet what can one do?' he wrote to Froude. 'Men are made of glass – the sooner we break them and get it over the better.' Froude agreed. He was campaigning in Devon: 'I think I have got my paw on another fellow.'

Newman's campaign notes, to assist his followers, are typical. 'Our object is to get together immediately as large a body as we can in defence of the *substance* of our spiritual rights and privileges, our creeds, etc. – but we wish to avoid technicalities and minutenesses as much as possible. The posture of affairs will not admit of delay. We wish to unite the clergy and create channels of correspondence among them.' But he had to issue a caution: 'Recollect we are *supporting* the Bishops – enlarge on the unfairness of leaving them to bear the brunt of the battle.'

It was hardly surprising that the Bishops, still rather eighteenth-century characters, did not know what to make of these ardent supporters; one spent hours trying to decide whether or not he believed himself to be a successor of the Apostles. Martyrdom was no aspiration of theirs. In the riots in Bristol before the passing of the Reform Bill the mob had burned down the Bishop's house, and the Bishop might have been burned with it if he had not made a hasty retreat from the back. The mob identified the Bishop not with the Apostles but with the Tories – so did most of the Bishops. To dissociate the temporal from the spiritual power of the Bishops, despising their alliance with the State while exalting their authority in the Church, was so novel as to puzzle both liberals and conservatives. But the Tracts made a stir and at first drew support from some establishment men.

But other people found them disturbing and Newman's old fear drove him to write to Froude on 13 November, 'My dear F, I so fear I may be self-willed in the matter of the Tracts – pray do advise me according to your light.' Froude was horrified. 'As to giving up the Tracts, the notion is odious ... we must throw the Zs overboard.' They called the establishment men the Zs; the Evangelicals were the Ys and the Xs their own Apostolicals. Froude was full of cheerful pugnacity. The Petition, as even the Archdeacon remarked, had turned out milk and water – 'Do make a Row about it.'

But Newman was soon to lose Froude's constant encouragement. In a desperate attempt to save his health he was going out this winter to Barbados. Newman signed a farewell letter, classically, *usque ad cineres* (till death, literally, to ashes) and Froude teasingly replied, 'why do you say *usque ad cineres* – if I am wrecked on Ash Wednesday you will be the cause of it.' Off he went, to a year and a half away from his friends and ecclesiastical agitation, with no one but Zs to talk to. 'Love to all Apostolicals,' he said, as he went. Newman was left to lead the battle without his chief aide.

Newman's letters and those of others to him give a vivid picture of the Movement as a campaign, with all the misunderstandings in the ranks, the rows with the opposition echoing in the newspapers, and the unwanted personal publicity. In the eighteen thirties the Church of England was still closely enmeshed with the nation and its rulers; the great majority of English people were Christian in the sense of never having thought they were anything else. Among the poor in the new cities there was a great deal of ignorance, and in intellectual circles some earnest disbelievers, but in general Christianity was accepted as the truth about things and its standards of morality assumed to be right, even if not lived up to. Except among the pious, who are always a minority, this adherence was vague, but it coloured the whole of society in a way which we can now hardly imagine.

Yet disbelief was on its way, was to become prevalent in intellectual circles in the eighteen forties and even more widespread later in the century. The Movement began with the authority of the Church, but this soon led to the question of the truth of the

Church's teaching. Newman was always aware of this more funda-mental question. The right of the successors of the Apostles to rule was secondary to their right – their duty – to teach; it was the truth of Christian teaching that Apostolic authority guaranteed. This belief, common in the Catholic and the Orthodox Church, had faded from the minds of Bible-based Protestants; the Oxford Apostles revived it in England about the time of the Catholic revival in the rest of Europe and both were haunted by the romantic idea of Gothic, or medieval, religious society – hence all those nineteenth-century spires and turrets, nostalgically restored monasticism and innumerable Guilds.

All this Gothic romantic life, which was already in the imagina-tion of English people, received from Oxford a strong intellectual organizing *idea*, the idea of the Church as the Apostolical society, not dependent on any one state or nation, teaching the revelation of God with the authority of Christ. The Catholic, universal, power of this idea appealed to the idealistic young, but to many it suggested what was Roman rather than Catholic: clerical power, obscurantism, oppression of conscience and the inquisition. Again and again the attacks on the Tractarians showed that this was what was feared and hated. People could not imagine a Catholicism that was not Roman, in this bad sense. And it was because he had maintained that there was a Catholicism that was not Roman that Newman, when he 'went over to Rome', was treated as a traitor by many who had been carried along with the Anglo-Catholic revival – which of course went on without him. Moreover, his life in the greater Catholic Church, with its reverses and ambiguities, was similarly misunderstood by those who identified the practices of the day with the necessary constitu-tion of the Church. Hence, Newman was thought a crypto-Romanist while he was in the Church of England, as a crypto-Protestant when he was in the Catholic and Roman communion.

Newman's idea of the Church was *not* medieval; it was patristic, founded on that of the Fathers of the early centuries. In some respects they were at first followed too closely; the belief that those who set up their own opinions in defiance of the Church must be shunned, for instance, led to Keble's embroiling himself unpleas-antly with dissenters in his parish, and to Newman's becoming involved in domestic contortions with his brothers, both of whom had become keenly heretical, Charles favouring atheistical socialism with Robert Owen as his prophet, and Francis the primitive gospel of J. N. Darby's Brethren.

While John was abroad Mrs Newman had rashly given Charles his thousand pounds from her dowry; he threw up his job in the Bank of England and rapidly ran through the lot. Charles was to be a permanent liability but Francis, as his faith leaked away, was to become more responsible and help John to support Charles. At present, however, he was lecturing John on the worldliness of keeping his mother and sisters in more comfort than was necessary – why should they have a manservant? John defended their ménage by saying that without them there would be no broth and rice for his poor outlying parish of Littlemore, just beyond Iffley. 'I suppose my money goes further than yours in journeying to Persia,' he added. Francis's mission to the east had converted no one to Christianity but had begun to undermine his own faith in the Trinity; the answers of Pope Darby proving unsatisfactory, he was moving towards Unitarianism.

In 1873, going through letters and thinking back to this time thirty years earlier, Newman wrote a note on his relations with his mother and sisters. Frank might think they made an idol of him, but he knew that his mother did not like what she felt to be his extreme opinions; they differed on the treatment of his brothers, they did not like all his friends, and they were not seeing as much of him as they had expected when they moved to Oxford. 'I got worried – I got worried by their affectionateness,' he noted. Harriett even wrote him lectures on his lack of affection. Family life was distracting to a missionary apostle.

This was a large part of his reason for believing in clerical celibacy. He thought country parsons should be married; it was the missionary type, at home or abroad who ought to remain single. It was because he felt Henry Wilberforce to be one of the chosen band at the heart of the Movement that he was annoyed and upset when Henry, always prone to fall in love, married Mary Sargent, one of the four beautiful but delicate daughters of the Rector of Lavington. Poor girls, all were to die young but Mary. There was quite a mis-understanding between Newman and Henry, not assisted by Newman's habit of writing explanatory letters which he did not send. He abhorred self-defence, but silence was often misinter-preted as anger. However, friendship stood the strain and he became godfather to the first baby.

Newman's first public row which attracted attention beyond Oxford was the case of Miss Jubber, daughter of a pastrycook who had refused to have her baptized but wished her to be married in church. Jubber thought the Vicar of St Mary's intolerant when he pointed out that to be a member of the Church she ought to be baptized. A paragraph appeared in an Oxford paper which accused Newman of saying: 'I will not marry her for she is an outcast!' It was useless for Newman to reply that he had not said it. It was the summer season of 1834 and the case was taken up in national papers, even in *The Times*. Questions were asked in the House. Newman was deluged with anonymous letters, threats of horse-whipping and rhymes:

> *'Who could affront a Lovely Woman?*
> *Who, why the Reverend Mr No Man*
> *A pretty Jesuit of a Vicar*
> *The Reverend Ruffian was in liquor.*
> 'An outcast!!! The unworthy priest should be cast out.'

He wrote to his mother that he felt like one man against a multitude; even the Bishop had pointed out that Miss Jubber, baptized or not, had a legal right to be married in church. But Keble and Pusey had written to support him: 'I seem as if I could bear anything now.' To Froude he scribbled cheerfully, 'K. and P. and Williams take my part, else I am solus, abused beyond measure by high and low – threatened with a pelting and prosecution – having anonymous letters – discountenanced by high church and low church. It should be you.' Later, answering Froude's request for further information, he told him 'nothing more came of it except some letters in the papers and plenty of most abusive articles in the vulgar town prints of Sunday.' England has not changed. And Miss Jubber, of course, was married in church just the same.

More private, but more painful to Newman was the rumour going round Oxford that he had absented himself from Oriel chapel so as not to receive communion with Whately, now Archbishop of Dublin. This shows how the Apostolical treatment of separatists was misunderstood; it was no part of their discipline to cut members of the Church with whom they disagreed. Whately himself wrote in October to find out the truth. This was that Newman had that day been administering the Sacrament in St Mary's, but a somewhat stiff correspondence ensued which Newman printed in later editions of the *Apologia*, because this particular slur on his conduct remained in circulation for many years. Whately's opinion that Newman was simply aiming at power never changed. He told Hawkins that the extracts from Newman's sermons which he had seen were 'very little different from Romanism except in not placing the Pope at *Rome*'. Twenty years later, when Newman went to Dublin to found a Catholic university, he approached a mutual friend to know if he might call on Whately. He was twice warned off. He told Henry Wilberforce what 'anguish' it caused him to pass Whately in the street without a greeting. But it was Whately who cut Newman, not *vice versa*. Yet in Newman's account of Whately in his memoir of 1874 there is no bitterness at all.

In the March of 1834 had appeared the first volume of Newman's *Parochial and Plain Sermons* (originally part of a series); eight were to appear in the next nine years, ending with two extra volumes, *University Sermons* and *Sermons on Subjects of the Day*. If the Tracts were the fighting front of the Movement, these sermons were the spiritual power behind it, and the real strength of Newman's leadership. He was not an ecclesiastical agitator but a prophet, in the Biblical sense of the term, a man who sees deep and sees far, inspired by the spirit of God. Newman read his sermons, then a common Anglican practice, and so they were carefully written, and surely there are few comparable writings of Christian devotion in the English language. The diction, as always with Newman, is marvellously clear, but the structure is complex, the sentences as delicately balanced as the thoughts they express. Few of Newman's sermons were controversial; they are psychologically penetrating applications of Christian teaching which could appeal to Christians of every tradition, and still do. They demand much from the hearer but morally, not intellectually, though the thinking in them is never superficial. Every one presents the call of Christ, to take up the Cross and follow him through the wilderness of this world.

Newman was not a good public speaker; he had a clear but not a resonant voice and it was inclined to go hoarse. His sermons gained nothing from oratory, though young hearers soon became spellbound by his personality, quiet and unrhetorical as it was. His habit of pausing between his fairly long sentences lent an intensity to his words when they came, though it was originally a mere pause for breath. This same year he imitated Keble in starting a daily reading of Matins in St Mary's, but the attendance was extremely poor, not more than half a dozen over a period of years according to notes he took of numbers, and it became increasingly 'dreary' to him – a favourite word. Far otherwise his own innovation, the services of Holy Communion held early on Sunday morning, to which many young dons and some undergraduates came. Newman loved the Eucharist and often preached on its central importance to the Christian; he was one of the pioneers of sacramental understanding in the Church of England, where for a long time this service, begun and commanded by Christ himself, had been celebrated only at rare intervals during the year.

The first volume of sermons was dedicated to Pusey, whom Newman wanted to gain for the Apostolicals, but who was at first reluctant to be identified with them. His first Tract, on fasting, was signed with his initials, EBP, in order to dissociate himself from the anonymous others. But as everyone knew EBP it was assumed that he was the leading spirit behind the Tracts. The Tractarians were immediately christened Puseyites, and in this typically roundabout way did Pusey become a Puseyite. His advent turned the Tracts from airy missiles to a heavy bombardment of scholarly tomes, and Newman himself wrote fewer and fewer, though he remained editor and sometimes suggested subjects to the earnest authors.

In the same month as the sermons appeared, March 1834, Newman failed to gain a Professorship in Moral Philosophy for which he stood. The election was a job, for Hawkins put up another candidate at the last moment – Renn Dickson Hampden, whom he had already used to get Newman out of his college tutorship. Old Martin Routh, the fabulous President of Magdalen, who was then about eighty and lived to be a hundred, was extremely annoyed, and said he would come down to vote for Newman, whose principles he regarded as truly descended from those of the seventeenth-century Caroline Divines. But Hampden, as James Mozley wrote home in disgust, 'being a Bampton lecturer, and an Aristotelian, and a Head of a House, and a Liberal, and, moreover, a stupid man in his way, was of course the successful candidate.'

Newman took his failure cheerfully, but it was soon after this that he made himself a lecture room of his own, in the chapel of Adam de Brome, the Oriel Founder, which at that time was partitioned off from the nave of St Mary's and used as a dump. A hundred men came to his first lecture, including William George Ward, a fat but very clever young man from Balliol, whose fixed stare so put Newman off that he had the benches arranged a different way. Ward, who had come to jeer, was converted and became the *enfant terrible* of the Movement.

Newman's lectures afterwards became his books on *The Prophetical Office of the Church* (1837) dedicated to Martin Routh, and on *Justification* (1838) – that theological hot subject, then still furiously dividing Christians three hundred years after Luther's traumatic break with Rome. Newman tried to show that the positive side of the conflicting positions on redemption from sin could both be recognized in the approach he had worked out from the New

Testament and the Fathers, starting from the Spirit of God indwelling the heart of man, through which salvation was effected. This eirenic method of theologizing has only recently come into its own. 'The Prophetical office' for Newman included theology, and covered the thinking, teaching side of the Church, as distinct from its sacramental and its practical ruling side: all three 'offices' were delegated from Christ, the Prophet, Priest and King. In 1877, when he reissued these lectures as the first volume of two entitled *The Via Media*, Newman wrote his mature reflections on the three functions of the Church as a preface, a magnificent analysis, calm and serene as the view from a mountain.

At the turn of the year 1834–5 Newman wrote eleven sermons for his second volume, published soon after. They were all on the theme of witnessing in word and deed to the objective Revelation lodged in the visible Church. About the same time he picked up his private account of what had happened to him in Sicily, begun in August, and wrote the passage on his own hollowness in failing to *be* what he *knew*. Thus he used the self-knowledge he had gained from that Sicilian death–and–resurrection to clear his mind when writing on this theme for others. Perhaps the reason for his taking up the account of Sicily was another attack of illness, of faintness and nervous exhaustion, from which he seems to have recovered with his usual resilience.

More trouble was blowing up with Dr Hampden, who in November 1834 had published a pamphlet advocating the admission of dissenters to the university on the ground that differences of theological opinion were not important among Christians. 'No communion as such can be the one Church of Christ, since the separation into distinct communions is an effect of discordant opinions; and the greatest disagreement of opinions may take place consequently, without any real violation of the Unity of the Church.' He sent a copy to Newman who replied that while he respected its tone of piety, he thought its principles would tend to 'make shipwreck of the Christian Faith'.

Hampden said he was ready to hear arguments against his views, but when Henry Wilberforce undertook the attack in an anonymous pamphlet, *The Foundations of the Faith Assailed at Oxford*, he became extremely angry, especially as it appeared in May 1835, just before the vote on the admission of Dissenters. Hampden took any attack as a personal one and boiled over when he got Newman's name, as editor not author, from the publisher. In June Newman copied his insulting letter and his own reply for Froude's benefit. 'Sir, I have heard with disgust of the dissimulation, falsehood and dark malignity of which you have been guilty,' Hampden wrote, accusing Newman of publishing calumnies. 'You have been among the "crafty firsts" who have sent their "silly seconds" to fight their mean and cowardly battles by their trumpery publications ... I charge you with malignity because you have no other ground of your assault on me but a fanatical persecuting spirit ... Would you have dared to act in such a way had you not taken advantage of the sacred profession?' Froude regarded this as the nearest thing to a challenge one clergyman could make to another. Duelling had not entirely died out, and the spirit of the duel is active behind much controversy in the first half of the nineteenth century. A gentleman was still considered responsible at the risk of his life for his words and actions.

Newman's reply was written in the third person, no doubt to keep passions at a distance; he insisted that he and Wilberforce were not attacking Hampden but his opinions, publicly put forward. This made no difference to Hampden, who illogically called another Tract writer a hypocrite when he signed his pamphlet and sent a personal letter to assure Hampden that no ill feeling was intended.

Newman's own letters are singularly free from personal attacks; he never ascribed unworthy motives to enemies, and it was rare that he even made a humorous critical comment, such as this to Froude on the Bishop of Winchester's chaplain: 'A specimen of donnishness grafted on to spiritual-mindedness, i.e. a constrained way of behaving which is redolent of both conceits. At confirmation he sprawled about like the statues in St John Lateran. Consider all this unsaid, *carissime*, and bury it in the folds of your mind: and really I reproach myself for my severity.'

Hampden became the centre-piece of the biggest row of the Oxford Movement and the last one in which the Apostolicals were accepted as allies by the establishment men, in 1836, when Lord Melbourne appointed him Regius Professor of Divinity at Oxford. 'We were electrified by the intelligence!' wrote Palmer in 1843, recapitulating the history of the Movement. Hampden, a liberal in politics as in religious opinion, united against himself both conservatives and evangelicals – the Apostolicals came in to provide the intellectual ammunition. Newman and Pusey were both on the committee called at Corpus Christi College to oppose the appointment, and they dissuaded the others from attacking Hampden in the newspapers, insisting that it was his theology which must be opposed, not him. Newman was asked to demonstrate Hampden's unorthodoxy, and sat up all night writing a pamphlet on his Bampton Lectures, known by the first word of its title as *Elucidations*, in which he proved to his own satisfaction that Hampden's principles, developed to logical conclusions, would end in unitarianism. 'It is not hereby insinuated that he agrees with them (Unitarians) in their peculiar errors,' he was careful to add, remembering the row last year.

The popular press thought Hampden a persecuted man; so did Hampden. He tried, without success, to get the Duke of Wellington (Oxford's Chancellor) and the Archbishop of Canterbury to intervene on his behalf, and then published his correspondence with the Archbishop under the impression that it showed his own injured innocence. He believed in God and the Church of England: how *could* anybody call his theological opinions heretical? Pamphlets were hurled to and fro. Whately was amused at a supposed papal encyclical addressed to Oxford collaborators. 'Softly, John!' was the title of another: 'or a word of caution to Calvin not to set up for Pope in a Protestant university.' The Hebdomadal Board, a Z institution with no Apostolicals on it, tried to carry a statute against Hampden which was vetoed by the Proctors. In March Hampden gave his inaugural sermon, good emotional stuff; St Mary's was crowded and copies circulated rapidly.

Hampden's most famous defender was Thomas Arnold, head-master of Rugby School, a keen reformer and liberal, who had already crossed swords with Newman in private correspondence through a third party – 'But is Arnold a Christian?' Newman was supposed to have said, laughing, in Rome in 1833. Of course he meant 'is he orthodox?' but Arnold took it as a personal affront to his moral character. Now he wrote an article for the *Edinburgh Review*, unsigned according to custom, entitled *Oxford Malignants*. Arnold stuck to his anonymity, but his authorship was an open secret. The article represented the modern liberals as the true heirs of the Reformation and the Revolution of 1688 – a view with which the Apostolicals concurred, repudiating all three parties alike. Arnold identified Newman and his friends with Laud and the later Non-jurors, and what angered him was the reason for their attack on Hampden – that his opinions were unorthodox. It was *moral wicked-ness*, it was 'the mingled fraud and baseness and cruelty of fanatical persecution'. The plea of conscience was not admissible, for it could only be a conscience 'so blinded by wilful neglect of highest truth, or so corrupted by the habitual indulgence of evil passions that it rather aggravates than excuses the guilt of those whom it misleads'.

In spite of Arnold the statute was put up again in Convocation on 5 May and carried by a large majority, many country clergymen coming up to record their votes against Hampden. However, like the Church of England, the University had no power to remove a Professor appointed by the State; Hampden was soon exercising his functions in the Divinity School and in December Newman himself came before him to sign the Articles on taking his BD. He had already done his disputation, curiously enough with Arnold, when the latter was hurriedly taking that degree after his appointment to Rugby in 1828. The disputations were formal displays of talent, not tests of orthodoxy, but Hampden later indulged in a little persecu-tion of his own by refusing approval to candidates who professed Apostolical opinions.

In the midst of this battle Newman's personal life was affected by several changes. His mother died, his sisters married, and he no longer had a home outside Oriel. An even greater loss came first, of the friend who would have been his companion and ally in all the conflicts to come.

Hurrell Froude came back to England in the spring of 1835 and travelled to Oxford to record his vote against the admission of Dissenters. Anne Mozley, who was staying with the Newmans, saw him 'as he alighted from the coach and was being greeted by his friends. He was terribly thin – his countenance dark and wasted, but with a brilliancy of expression and grace of outline which fully justified all his friends said of him. He was in the (Sheldonian) Theatre next day, entering into all the enthusiasm of the scenes, and shouting his *Non Placet* with all his friends about him. While he lived at all, he must *live* his life.' A day or two later he left Oxford, never to return. From Devon he wrote cheerfully to Newman, 'People don't look so horribly blank at me as they did, though perhaps that is only from being accustomed to my grim visage.' The sight of him had certainly been a shock to Newman. He wrote to Frederic Rogers, 'Dear fellow, long as I have anticipated what I suppose must come, I feel quite raw and unprepared.'

Letters went to and fro but sometimes Froude was too ill to put pen to paper, 'except yesterday,' he wrote once, 'when I began a letter to you upside down.' Newman was to go to Devon, but he was held up by parish work and lack of cash. Latin forms of address were the fashion among the Apostolicals. '*Dulcissime* …' Froude began; '*Carissime* …' Newman replied. '*Mi amicissime*, N has left me these lappets,' Keble wrote on the flap of one of Newman's letters. Newman scattered his '*Carissime*' lavishly among his friends. '*Antiquissime,*' said Rogers, whimsically.

Froude's letters, when he could write, were as forceful and amusing as ever. When Newman feared to go too far in an article on Monasticism for the *British Magazine*, Froude said, 'I cannot see the harm in losing influence with people when you can only retain it by sinking the points on which you differ from them. What is the good of influence except to influence people?' But he also protested against Newman's 'cursing and swearing' against Rome. 'What good can it do? I call it uncharitable to an excess. How mistaken we may ourselves be on many points that are only gradually opening on us.'

At last, on 15 September, Newman got to Dartington, and stayed till the last moment before term; indeed, as a coach was full, he arrived late for the first and only time. At the end of their correspondence Newman later noted: 'I took my last farewell of RHF on Sunday in the evening ... When I took leave of him his face lighted up and almost shone in the darkness, as if to say that in this world we were parting for ever.'

After he had gone Froude wrote, 'Don't be conceited if I tell you how much you are missed here ... Even I come in for my share of the benefit in finding myself partially extricated from the unenviable position hitherto held by me – that of a prophet in his own country.' In spite of his anxiety Newman responded with humour. Bunsen, the famous Lutheran, had been in Oxford. 'He says that if we succeed, we shall be introducing Popery without authority, Protestantism without liberty, Catholicism without universality and Evangelism without spirituality. In the greater part of which censure doubtless you agree.' Unable to get down at Christmas, he sent Rogers, and made both of them laugh with the things said of him – 'but somehow I wag on sluggishly.'

Froude's last letter came at the end of January 1836. 'I don't gain flesh in spite of all the milk.' The Archdeacon wrote to say that his son was free from pain. 'His thoughts turn continually to Oxford, to yourself and Mr Keble.' A few days later, 'Your friend is still alive ...' On 28 February the fatal news was sent: 'My dear son died this day.'

'Newman opened the letter in my room,' Tom Mozley wrote to his sister, 'and could only put it into my hand with no remark.' Newman wrote to Bowden, 'He was so very dear to me that it is an effort to me to reflect on my thoughts about him. I can never have a greater loss; for he was to me, and was likely to be ever, in the same degree of familiarity which I enjoyed with yourself in our Undergraduate days ... Everything was so bright and beautiful about him, that to think of him must always be a comfort.' To Miss Giberne he wrote, 'As to dear Froude, I cannot speak of him consistently with my own deep feelings about him, though they are all bright and pleasant ... I love to think and muse upon one who had the most angelic mind of any person I ever fell in with – the most unearthly, the most gifted. I have no painful thoughts in speaking of him (though I cannot trust myself to speak of him to many) but I feel the longer I live, the more I shall miss him.'

At the back of his diary in 1837, when he was preparing Froude's *Remains* for publication, are the scribbled lines: '*Vale, dilectissime, desideratissime, usque ad illum Diem qui te, paucissimis notum, omnibus patifaciet qui fueris.*' Farewell, most loved, so much missed, until that Day which shall make you, known to so few, manifest to all as you were.

Mrs Newman died on 17 May 1836, after a brief final illness, though she had been unwell for some time. Although John and Harriett were both with her, John, as usual after a sudden loss, was unhappy, remembering misunderstandings now that it was too late to clear them up. Yet there was no doubt that Mrs Newman had relied on her eldest son and he had done his best for her; to the last it had been financially a hard struggle. She was buried in St Mary's and a tablet was put up to her memory in the new church at Littlemore, of which she laid the foundation stone.

Three weeks before she died, her second daughter Jemima had married John Mozley who, although not the eldest of the many Mozley brothers, was the one who succeeded his father in the printing business in Derby. Square-faced and solid, he had not been sent to Oxford, but had visited it, and Rose Bank at Iffley. Jemima had the large Newman nose and was not beautiful, but she was gentle, and after Mary's death was the sister John was most fond of. After Mrs Newman's death Harriett went up to Derby to stay with the Mozleys, and the next thing was a proposal from the ebullient Tom, and letters arriving to ask Newman's consent.

At first he was not quite happy about it, consulting Jemima, because he had thought Harriett did not care for Tom – besides she was older than he was. However, Jemima had been teasing her sister for weeks, and John discovered that though Harriett might talk about duty, there was feeling as well. She was small and lively and very determined; Tom was good-humoured and impulsive, and in spite of the fact that he was in Holy Orders, Newman gave no hint of disapproval. He helped to get for Tom a college living at Cholderton, near Salisbury, sent Harriett £30 for her trousseau and gladly made over to them the furniture and plate of Rose Bank. He did not much like their being married so soon after their mother's death, but the wedding took place in Derby on 27 September 1836 and the happy pair went down to Cholderton, where the house was big but the church was tiny. Harriett was soon reporting to her sister that Tom had chased her all round the house and shut her in the pigsty; the treatment seemed to suit her. On Sunday the small church was so full that men sat on the altar and put their umbrellas in the font. High time for a Tractarian vicar, even such an unclerical one as boisterous Tom Mozley. He built a new Gothic church and was popular in the village; at the Coronation feast for the young Queen Victoria in the next year, someone chalked up on the wall: 'Long live Mr Mozley, Beef and Strong Beer.'

Newman now lived entirely at Oriel, in his two small rooms by the chapel, with a passage to its gallery where Whately had strung up dried herrings, but Newman used as an oratory, with a picture Miss Giberne had given him of saints praying round the throne of God. He told her that whenever he went in there he was 'tempted to say, "What, are you all at it still?" if that were a reverent and proper speech. It seems an impressive emblem of the perpetual intercession of the saints perfected, waiting for Christ's coming.'

5

APOSTLE IN ACTION

'Let everyone who hears me ask himself the question, what stake has *he* in the truth of Christ's promises?' Newman demanded in a sermon he called *The Ventures of Faith*, preached on his thirty-fifth birthday, 21 February 1836, a week before Hurrell Froude died. 'We know what it is to have a stake in any venture of this world. We venture our property in plans which promise a return; in plans which we trust, which we have faith in. What have we ventured for Christ? ... I really fear, when we come to examine it, it will be found that there is nothing we resolve, nothing we choose, nothing we give up, nothing we pursue, which we should not resolve, and do, and not do, and avoid, and choose, and give up, and pursue, if Christ had not died and heaven were not promised us.'

He went on to sketch a picture of the respectable men who called themselves Christians. 'When young they indulge their lusts, or at least pursue the world's vanities; as time goes on they get in a fair way of business, or other mode of making money; then they marry and settle; and their interest coinciding with their duty, they seem to be, and think themselves, respectable and religious men; they grow attached to things as they are; they begin to have a zeal against vice and error; and they follow after peace with all men. Such conduct indeed, as far as it goes, is right and praiseworthy. Only, I say, it has not necessarily anything to do with religion at all ...'

Newman's appeal to the young men of Oxford – mostly rich young men from rulers' houses – was that of a prophet, a John the Baptist in metal-framed spectacles. The twenty-year-old Richard Church heard this sermon, which fired him to make his venture for Christ and to become one of Newman's most devoted friends from now until almost the end of the century when, as Dean of St Paul's, he wrote the history of the Movement which had formed his youth.

The enemies of the Movement had no doubt as to who was its leader, jockeying Newman out of university posts, altering the hours of Hall so as to keep undergraduates from attending his afternoon sermons, and taking every means to prevent his influence. In vain; the young men were fascinated by someone who took Christ seriously enough to scorn advancement in this world, and devote his life to the ministry of word and sacrament, to fasting and prayer, and who yet lived a busy life in the midst of a busy town, with friends coming and going from London, always in the thick of some controversy.

In 1837 Newman started his Monday evening tea parties, at which the talk was general, not religious shop. James Anthony Froude, Hurrell's youngest brother, who was to shock the older generation by his novel *The Nemesis of Faith* in 1849, revealing his own lapse into doubt, in later years, when he was a respected historian who regarded Protestantism as part of patriotism, wrote of Newman in his essay on *The Oxford Counter Reformation*: 'He was never condescending with us, never didactive or authoritative … Ironical he could be but not ill-natured. Not a malicious anecdote was ever heard from him. Prosy he could not be. He was lightness itself – the lightness of elastic strength …' Froude thought his mind 'worldwide' in scope, and his head reminded him of Julius Caesar's. Even in his youthful novel Newman appears as Mr Mornington, a quietly dominant figure: 'that voice so keen, so preternaturally sweet … that calm grey eye; those features, so stern, yet so gentle.' It was a time of Gothic romance, and Newman himself was reading Manzoni's famous novel, *I Promessi Sposi*, the inspiration of the Catholic romantic revival in Italy, and remarked that 'the friar stuck in my heart like a dart.'

But Newman hated any kind of religious pretentiousness. Once a solemn oddity invited Newman to dine after he preached the university sermon on *Faith and Reason contrasted as Habits of Mind* which had annoyed the Heads of Houses. Eleven years later Faber reminded Newman, 'You scandalized him by making rabbits on the

wall; and when he scolded you, you went fast asleep in your chair.'
On another occasion two earnest Tractarians from Cambridge called
on Pusey and were shocked when Newman immediately retired to
an armchair, with little Lucy and Philip Pusey on his knees, putting
his spectacles first on one and then on the other, and telling them the
story of a magic broomstick.

Newman was often in high spirits during these peak years of the
Movement, his letters flowing in a legible but sprawling hand to
everyone. Miss Giberne was a constant correspondent; now in her
thirties, a handsome woman still receiving proposals of marriage,
her family teased her that she must want to marry Newman, whereupon she replied with hauteur that if she did, she would not write to
him. Anxious to contribute to the cause she suggested writing a
story for children. 'Your plan is the very thing I have been wishing,'
replied Newman. 'I am sure we shall do nothing till we get some
ladies to set to work to poison the younger generation – so I hope you
will begin at once.' Fired with enthusiasm, Miss Giberne (on her
knees) began the tale of Little Mary, which Newman got published
anonymously; some thought it was by him, some by his sister
Harriett, for she wrote several tales for children. Miss Giberne,
however, went back to her favourite art of painting and it was left to
Charlotte Yonge to be the great poisoner of the younger generation –
though it was a later generation, since at this time she was only
fifteen, preparing for confirmation under Keble. *The Heir of
Redclyffe*, best-selling Tractarian novel, did not appear till 1853 and
the stories for children later still.

It was in 1837 that Newman brought out *The Prophetical Office of
the Church*, setting out the ideal middle way for the Church of
England. 'I say nothing, I believe, without the highest authority
among our writers,' he told Jemima, 'yet it is so strong that everything I have yet said is milk and water to it and this makes me
anxious. It is all the difference between drifting snow and a hard
snowball.' The snowball was intended for the popular Protestantism
of the day, but because he also denounced Roman corruptions the
book became his biggest success so far.

But when Froude's *Remains* came out next year it excited horror and alarm by its downright dislike of the Reformation and all its works. Dead, Froude fulfilled his ambition to be an ecclesiastical agitator. The usually indolent Margaret Professor of Divinity, Faussett, was moved to write an attack on Froude's view of the Eucharist. 'He has been firing away at us in gallant style,' said Newman, and sat up all night to write a reply – which sold more copies than Faussett's pamphlet. To Froude, indirectly, Oxford owes the Martyrs' Memorial, for it was raised to the heroes of the Reformation by public subscription, largely through the exertions of the Reverend C. Portales Golightly, once a curate of Newman's, whose oddities had been a joke with Froude and Rogers. Newman called him Golius and could not take his attacks seriously; yet Golightly was to do him a lot of harm by his busy agitating.

Newman took his bishop, Bagot, very much more seriously than that gentleman of the old school expected. When Bagot made a mild grumble against the Tracts in his Charge, Newman at once offered to withdraw them from publication. Nothing as definite as that need be done, said Bagot, alarmed by such Apostolical submission. His own daughters were keen admirers of Newman's, as their friend Emily Bowles afterwards recalled. Nor did Newman's friends in the Movement relish his early Christian reverence for episcopal authority: to them the doctrine of the Apostolic Succession was more important than a mere Bagot. The Anglo-Catholic tradition of disobeying bishops for their own good had begun. But Newman could not divorce the idea from the person. 'My dear fellows,' he said, '*you* make me the head of a party – that is your external view – but I *know* what I am – a clergyman under the Bishop of Oxford, and anything more is accidental.' Maybe it was, but Newman's personal influence was to make him, all his life, far more important than any bishop, Anglican or Catholic, under whom he acted as a simple clergyman. It was like having an unexploded bomb in your diocese.

Troubles did not come singly and in the autumn of 1838 there was a row within the Movement, significantly caused by a proposal to translate the Roman Breviary. Newman, asked to choose one of

Froude's books by his father, had wanted the works of Bishop Butler but they were bespoken; Rogers had suggested that he took the four volumes of the Breviary and since he had begun the daily use of them, Newman had become impressed with the riches of the office. But powerful opposition was aroused among the high churchmen, among them Keble's brother Tom, Rector of Bisley, and the Reverend Sir George Prevost, an influential 'squarson'. They did not want the Breviary translated at all, but if it was, it must be cut and altered to suit Reformed ears. Even Rogers took the Prevost side and Newman felt harassed. 'It is just like walking on treacherous ice,' he wrote to his old friend Bowden; 'one cannot say a thing but one offends someone or other – I don't mean foe, for that one could bear, but friend. You cannot conceive what unpleasant tendencies to split are developing themselves on all sides, and how one suffers because one wishes to keep well with all, or at least because one cannot go wholly with this man or that.'

It was always to be Newman's difficulty that while he liked to be a moving spirit among a band of brothers freely acting together, others expected him to direct operations like a general or be as adroit as a politician at internal party manoeuvres. It is significant that when he chose a leader, it was Philip Neri, the sixteenth-century Florentine whose method was almost exactly his own – a non-authoritarian inspiration of others.

Meanwhile, as well as editing the Tracts, Newman became in 1838 the editor of the *British Critic* – by accident, as with most of his journalistic ventures. But as Rose had to give up the *British Magazine*, owing to ill health, Newman took on the other magazine so that the Movement should continue to have its periodical – for he realized the immense importance of such a vehicle for ideas. He was a good editor, insisting on readability, but allowing great freedom to contributors. It meant extra work, however, and identified him even further, in the public mind, with ecclesiastical agitation.

People later got the idea that Newman at Oxford was an intellectual recluse, partly because the *Apologia* gave no account of his day-to-day life. As well as editing the Tracts and the *British Critic*, delivering his lectures in Adam de Brome's chapel, writing his sermons, preparing his next book, entertaining all and sundry in his rooms and keeping up with his correspondence, Newman was one of the most active of parish priests. His diaries are like graphs of the endless business of his daily life, with the spare pages at the end a shore on which flotsam and jetsam were cast. Baptisms, burials, weddings ('married the waiter at the Star'); duties as Rural Dean ('went over St Peter-le-Bailey'); visiting the sick, week after week ('sat with so-and-so'); confirmation classes; daily Matins at St Mary's and the weekly early communion; walking out to Littlemore and back ... all this had to be fitted in with lists of 'people I must be civil to' – invitations, all ticked but two. Notes on Antichrist and Pantheism follow hard on jotted accounts: umbrella, washing, charity, medicine, letters, parcels, the early communion collections which went to clergy charities, and a memo for powder for toothache. Newman endured a lot with his teeth: 'they have been my penance for thirty years,' he once remarked.

Yet he was supremely confident in his cause and this was all that mattered to him. 'I love our Church as a portion and a realizing of the Church Catholic among us,' he had written to Rose in 1836, after the Hampden affair. But he did not love it 'right or wrong'. Three years later, in the summer of 1839, he received what he called 'the first hit from Rome', and after that nothing was quite the same again. That summer he settled down to study the doctrine of the Incarnation and the theological conflicts which led to the conciliar definitions, particularly those which condemned the Monophysite (one-nature) view of Christ. It was theology he had set out to study, but it was history which rose up and hit him. The truth of the teaching about Christ had been settled at the Councils, and had often been settled by adopting a new formula to express more clearly the faith which had always been held. These 'innovations' were often resisted by large parties, backed by the civil power, who claimed to be 'primitive' but often proved to be on a sidetrack from the main Christian tradition. Looking back at the fifth century Newman saw the Via Media – and it was on the wrong side. Years later he wrote in the *Apologia*, 'My stronghold was Antiquity; now here, in the middle of the fifth century, I found, as it seemed to me, the Christendom of the sixteenth and the nineteenth centuries reflected. I saw my face in that mirror, and I was a Monophysite.'

On top of this shock – for it is a shock to believe you are a defender of the universal truth and see yourself instead as a member of the party in error and broken off from communion – a worried friend pressed into Newman's hand a Copy of the *Dublin Review*, a Catholic quarterly recently founded by Nicholas Wiseman, which contained an article of his on the schism of the Donatists in Africa, in the days when St Augustine was Bishop of Hippo. Newman was not particularly interested, for he saw no Via Media parallel in this situation. But the friend kept repeating the old maxim to which St Augustine had appealed, and which Wiseman quoted: *securus iudicat orbis terrarum* – the whole world is a safe judge. It was the principle on which all Church councils worked: what was accepted as true by the majority of the Church was to be held by all, and to prefer your own view against this consensus was the way to error, heresy, which is the choosing of your own will.

The Via Media position, that the Church of England was Catholic because it held the Catholic faith, rested on the belief that the Catholic faith is what is held by the whole Church; Anglo-Catholics believed that Roman Catholics had erred by adding to the original teaching. But now Newman had just seen that in the ancient world it was the new formulation which safeguarded truth and the ambiguities of the old which left the way open for misinterpretations. Moreover, although the contenders were mostly Greek-speakers, the Roman See not only upheld these conciliar decisions but regarded its endorsement as essential, part of the office entrusted to St Peter and his successors as chief of the Apostles and shepherd of Christ's flock on earth. 'Rome was where she now is.' Could it be possible that the *orbis terrarum* was on the side of Rome, after all? And was the Church of England cut off from that *orbis terrarum* by actions taken in the sixteenth century?

Back in Oxford after the vacation Newman found Wiseman's article was causing him alarm and despondency; it was a new thing to have a Catholic of his intelligence and learning taking part in their controversies. He had been Rector of the English College in Rome, where Newman and Froude had met him in 1833, but he had now come to England as a bishop, for the Midland District, and was living at Oscott, near Birmingham, where Pugin had recently been building a splendid Gothic college in red brick, with quadrangles and halls, a tower and a chapel.

Newman pulled himself together and wrote an essay for the *British Critic* which he prefaced with a pithy dialogue. The Anglo-Catholic says, 'Our teaching is the true, because it is the primitive; yours is not true because it is novel.' The Roman Catholic replies, 'Our teaching is true, for it is everywhere the same; yours has no warrant, for it is but local and private.' 'We go by Antiquity,' says the Anglo-Catholic. 'We go by Catholicity,' says the Roman. Newman was trying to prove that Rome was at least no more likely to be right than Canterbury. But the Monophysite ghosts were not to be laid so easily; they too had said their teaching was right because it was primitive. But if new terms had been elucidations of truth and safeguards of orthodoxy in the fifth century, why not in the sixteenth, at that 'wretched Tridentine Council'?

But Newman's deepest reaction to this first hit from Rome was that of a man who above all wants to find out the will of God, not his own. In Lent 1840 he retired to Littlemore for a period of fasting and prayer. The opportunity offered when John Rouse Bloxam, a Magdalen man who had been acting as Newman's curate for three years, had to go home to a sick father. Littlemore was a neglected outlying adjunct of St Mary's, once containing a nunnery (long since become a farm and now derelict); it was a mere conglomerate of cottages with no big house and no church till Newman built one, dedicating it on 22 September 1836. It was a simple barn-like building with lancet windows and a steeply pitched roof; the present sanctuary was added after Newman left. In his day there was stone arcading behind the altar and he put a stone cross there – he was just trying its position when Bloxam happened to look in at the door, and was asked his opinion. Bloxam, a timid soul, who had long wished to know Newman, became a devoted friend, collecting snippets of information about him in large scrapbooks which now repose in the library of his old college.

Instead of sending one of his other disciples to Littlemore, Newman went himself. He was feeling lonely; Rogers had just departed for London, after seven years of *contubernium*, as Newman called the companionship of daily life under the same roof – just the span of his time with Froude. And at Christmas there had been an uncomfortable episode, when Rogers had rejected the proposed dedication to him of *The Church of the Fathers*, in which Newman had collected the pieces he had written for the *British Magazine* on the theologian saints of the early centuries. Rogers was embarrassed by the terms Newman used in his dedication and thought ordinary society would 'think it a conclusion on the mooted sanity of Oxford divines'. The book was eventually dedicated to Isaac Williams, the Tractarian poet: 'the sight of whom carries back his friends to ancient, holy and happy times.' Isaac was surprised, but delighted. This book had a very wide influence and inspired many enthusiastic young people with the ideal of holiness – sometimes with more romantic fervour than common sense, as Newman recognized, when he made mild fun of it all in *Loss and Gain*.

Newman's Lent was severe but he did not cut himself off from ordinary life, only from the distractions of Oxford. A school had been started at Littlemore but Newman wrote in a private note that the schoolmistress was 'a dawdle and a do-nothing – and what was worse, she attempted to be obsequious to me.' He told Tom Mozley he was afraid she drank and later admitted, 'She does drink, badly.' The children were dirty and ill-behaved and came in all sizes from three years old. 'I find I am not deep in the philosophy of schoolgirl tidiness,' he wrote to Jemima. But he got Mrs Henry Wilberforce to send pinafore patterns and told Jemima that he had 'lectured with unblushing effrontery on the necessity of their keeping their work clean and set them to knit stockings with all their might.' At Easter the white pinafores were to be set off prettily with pink bonnets and white tippets which he gave them.

Meanwhile, he told Jemima, 'I have rummaged out an old violin and strung it, and on Mondays and Thursdays have begun to lead them in it' – the psalms, in 'Gregorians' – 'a party of between twenty and thirty great and little in the schoolroom'. The children seemed to take to the chant, 'though they have not learned it yet – for I see it makes them smile – though that may be at me.' On Sundays in the church he taught them their faith. 'Newman's catechizing has been the great attraction this Lent,' James Mozley wrote home, 'and men have gone out of Oxford every Sunday to hear it. I thought it very striking, done with such spirit, and the children so up to it ... all unanimous on the point of the nine orders of angels.'

Newman himself wrote to Bloxam with unwonted enthusiasm: 'The children are vastly improved in singing and now that the organ is mute, their voices are so thrilling as to make one sick with love. You will think I am in a rapture.' It was such a contrast with St Mary's – 'Everything is so cold at St Mary's. I have felt it for years.' And to his aunt he wrote later, 'I came up here as a sort of penance during Lent. But though without friends or books, I have as yet had nothing but pleasure. So that it seems a shame to spend Lent so happily.'

Yet all the time he was fasting rigorously. He did not dine out, did not read the newspapers and, a nineteenth-century touch, did not wear gloves. He breakfasted on bread and milk and an egg; dined on cold bacon, bread, cheese and water; supped on barley water, bread, and an egg. Bacon was his only meat. This sugarless, butterless diet, without fruit or pastry or even fish, he kept up throughout Lent. On Wednesdays and Fridays he ate nothing at all till 6 p.m. and then had an extra egg for supper. On Sundays he allowed himself tea and a glass of wine. All Holy Week he fasted till six and on Maundy Thursday and Good Friday ate nothing till he took some bread and water in the evening. 'I have felt rather weak in the limbs,' he noted calmly at the end, 'I have been able to think, write and read as usual.' He used the full Breviary office, in private, daily.

It snowed on 25 March, the feast of the Annunciation, and Newman, alone at Littlemore, took out the old exercise book in which he had written his account of his illness in Sicily and suddenly finished it. He remembered the faithfulness of Gennaro, who had asked only his cloak. Newman gave him more than its worth, but kept it. 'I have it still. I have brought it up here to Littlemore, and on some nights I have had it on my bed. I have so few things to sympathize with me, that I take to clokes.'

He was feeling lonely and began to wonder why he had written down all these details – who would be interested? 'This is the sort of interest a wife takes, and none but she – it is a woman's interest – and that interest, so be it, shall never be taken in me.' He was thirty-nine, but felt he could not now take that interest in the world which marriage required. 'I am too disgusted with this world – and, above all, call it what one will, I have a repugnance to a clergyman's marrying. I do not say it is not lawful – I cannot deny the right – but, whether prejudice or not, it shocks me. And therefore I willingly give up the possession of that sympathy, which I feel is not, and cannot be, granted to me. Yet, not the less do I feel the need of it ... Shall I ever have in my old age spiritual children who will take an interest such as a wife does?' He was to have very many indeed.

It was snowing, he was half starving himself, Froude had died, Keble and Henry Wilberforce had married, Rogers had gone away. Newman had a heavy cold and lost his voice. 'I have been sucking liquorice all day to my great disgust and without any perceptible benefit,' he told Jemima. But on Easter Eve Bloxam came to tea and Newman broke his fast after three days on nothing but bread and water. They got out the altar cloth which Jemima and the Mozley women had been working in Derby and arranged it in the little church. 'We have got some roses, wallflowers and sweet-briar, and the chapel smells as if to remind one of the Holy Sepulchre,' he wrote to Jemima. And the next day there were the children in their new pink bonnets and white pinafores, singing the Psalms in Gregorians, and Newman was so happy he was afraid of being too happy.

Peace and happiness were to be found in the simplicities of Littlemore, but back in Oxford the controversies began again, and culminated the next year in the great row over Tract 90. Curiously enough, while he was making this vain attempt to reconcile the Thirty-Nine Articles with Catholic doctrine, Newman was making a hit in *The Times* with a series of articles, signed 'Catholicus', commissioned by the editor John Walter, whose son, another John Walter, had just gone down from Oxford full of enthusiasm for Newman. Seven letters were written, appearing in February 1841, and published much later under the title of *The Tamworth Reading Room*, for they began as an attack on Sir Robert Peel's speech at the opening of that admirable institution. Peel had praised education; knowledge refined people, improved their character, raised their standards. Newman referred these views to Lord Brougham's philosophy, which so annoyed Peel that the series was nearly stopped at the third letter. But since everyone was talking of these brilliant essays they were eventually continued, with a leading article 'to satisfy people that they are not intended to serve political purposes'. Newman certainly only wished to attack the notion that education makes people morally better. He did it with ridicule and was at the top of his form.

'It seems that all "virtuous women" may be members of the Library. A very emphatic silence is maintained about women not virtuous. What does this mean? Does it mean to exclude them while bad *men* are admitted? Is this accident or design, sinister and insidious, against a portion of the community? What has virtue to do with a Reading Room? It is to make its members virtuous; it is to "exalt the moral dignity of their nature"; it is to provide "charms and temptations" to allure them from sensuality and riot. To whom but to the vicious ought Sir Robert to discourse about "opportunities" and "access" and "moral improvement"; and who else would prove a fitter experiment, and a more glorious triumph of scientific influence?'

Man could not improve himself morally by increasing his knowledge; his sins would only become more subtle. 'You do but play "hunt the slipper" with the fault of our nature till you go to

Christianity ... If we attempt to effect a moral improvement by means of poetry, we shall but mature into a mawkish, frivolous and fastidious sentimentalism; – if by means of argument, into a dry, unamiable longheadedness; – if by good society, into a polished outside, with hollowness within, in which vice has lost its grossness and perhaps increased its malignity; – if by experimental science, into an uppish, supercilious temper, much inclined to scepticism.' Some may think that since Newman's day we have the results of just such an education.

Fascinated by the results of scientific investigation, some people imagined that better knowledge of nature would bring better knowledge of God. Newman retorted: 'The truth is that the system of Nature is just as much connected with Religion, where minds are not religious, as a watch or a steam-carriage. The material world, indeed, is infinitely more wonderful than any human contrivance; but wonder is not religion, or we should be worshipping our railroads.' Many were to cease believing in God when science found no direct evidence for his action in nature. 'Religion,' Newman said in 1841, 'never has been a deduction from what we know; it has ever been an assertion of what we are to believe ... Christianity is a history supernatural, and almost scenic; it tells us what its Author is, by telling us what He has done.'

The identity of Catholicus was kept secret, but liberals grew very angry with him. 'Puseyism claims to be a god upon earth and commands intelligence like a slave,' said the *Morning Chronicle*. Newman wrote to HW (Henry Wilberforce: he often used initials for intimates): 'You should have seen the late article in the *Globe* silently alluding to Catholicus. It seems as if hitherto they had thought Puseyism a thing of copes and lighted tapers. Geese, they never read a word till the fist is shaken in their face.'

Richard Church told Rogers that in the House Lord Morpeth had made 'a savage attack on Oxford as being a place where people who were paid for teaching Protestantism were doing all they could to bring things nearer to Rome.' Right in the middle of this excitement Tract 90 was published.

It appeared on 27 February 1841; Newman; had recently written to his sister, 'I never had such dreary thoughts as on finding myself forty.' He had not expected the storm that now burst over his head. The Tract was not a polemic but a short treatise in which the author began by stating that he was not concerned with the intentions of those who had framed the Articles but with interpreting them according to the faith of the Church Universal. The Articles were not on a level with the Creeds; they were protests against abuses, not against the true Catholic doctrine. The Evangelicals had already adopted doctrines of Justification difficult to reconcile with the Articles; for this very reason Francis Newman had refused to sign and consequently, in spite of his first class degree, was teaching at Manchester College and not at Oxford. But Newman was to find that the latitude allowed to Protestants within the establishment was refused to Catholics.

He called his ex-curate Golightly the 'Tony-fire-the-faggot' of the subsequent agitation. Golightly bought up dozens of copies and sent them round to Bishops and influential people, with the popery suitably underlined. A week after publication, on 8 March, the four senior tutors of the University issued a public letter demanding the name of the author. 'Do you know I am in a regular scrape about that Tract 90?' Newman wrote to HW. To Harriett, on 12 March, he wrote, 'I fear I am clean dished. The Heads of Houses are at this moment concocting a manifesto against me. Do not think I fear for my cause. We have had too great a run of luck.'

He began an explanatory letter to Dr Jelf (a senior, and an Oriel man) but before it was done, on 15 March, the Heads promulgated a resolution which was printed under the University Arms and signed by the Vice-Chancellor, in which it was stated that the Tract, 'evading rather than explaining the sense of the Thirty-Nine Articles and reconciling subscription to them with the adoption of errors, which they were designed to counteract', was inconsistent with the due observance of the University Statutes. This was to declare that Anglo-Catholicism was not the religion of the Church of England, and its universities.

On the same day Newman sent a dignified reply, admitting that he was the author of the Tract. 'I hope it will not surprise you if I say, that my opinion remains unchanged of the truth and honesty of the principle maintained in the Tract, and of the necessity of putting it forth.' He added that no doubt it might have been done in a better way, but that while he was sorry for the trouble he had given to the Board, he thanked them 'for an act, which, even though founded on a misapprehension, may be made as profitable to myself, as it is religiously and charitably intended.'

Church, who was keeping up a running commentary for the benefit of Rogers in London, thought this 'must have let new light into these excellent old gentlemen ... It softened many people: even the Provost, who is very strong, thought it necessary to butter a little ...' James Mozley, however, thought it too meek, and that the Heads would call it humbug. His sister Anne disagreed. 'There is a Catholic spirit of humility in it that one finds in some books and longs to see practised,' she said.

Newman wrote to Bowden: 'Do not think all this will pain me. You see no *doctrine* is censured, and my shoulders shall manage to bear the charge.' On the flap of Church's long letter to Rogers he wrote: 'I am now in my right place, which I have long wished to be in, which I did not know how to attain, and which has been brought about without my intention, I hope I may say providentially, though I am perfectly aware at the same time that it is a rebuke and punishment for my secret pride and sloth ... I cannot anticipate what will be the result of it in this place or elsewhere as regards *myself*. Somehow I do not fear for the *cause*.'

Here he was wrong; in the usual Anglican way nothing much was to happen to him, but the cause was to founder on the rock of episcopal opposition to Tract 90 and all that it stood for.

The *Letter to Dr Jelf* came out and Newman was attacked and caricatured in the newspapers; his sister Harriett, when she visited him, thought him shockingly thin, and as old as the caricatures made him look. He was fasting again, spending Lent at Littlemore, though he had to be a good deal in Oxford and lost his voice with all the talking. But he minded nothing till the Bishop came in.

Bagot could not help it; he was inundated with furious letters from Evangelicals. He used Pusey as his intermediary and asked that Tract 90 be withdrawn and the series discontinued. Notes passed to and fro. Newman felt he was being driven into a corner where he must either defy his Bishop or deny his principles – for to suppress the Tract would imply its censure. He told Pusey that he would have to give up his living. 'I should not be signing the Articles in the sense he meant them to be signed.' Two days later he said sadly, 'It is vain to deny that I shall be hurt and discouraged beyond measure if the Tract is suppressed at all.' Bagot melted and a compromise was effected. Tract 90 was to remain in print but the series must end with it. Newman was to make no further comments on the Articles and write a public letter to his Bishop in which he repudiated the claims of Rome. On his side the Bishop gave Newman to understand that if this was done, Tract 90 would not be censured.

Newman dated his *Letter* to the Bishop from Oriel, 29 March, and wrote it in such a hurry that the first sheets were in the press before he had finished the last. It was already distasteful to him to speak of Roman 'corruptions' but it was the only way to prove that he was a *bona fide* member of the Church of England. His positive view was expressed thus: 'I think that to belong to the Catholic Church is the first of all privileges here below, as involving heavenly privileges ... and ... I consider the Church over which you preside to be the Catholic Church in this country.' The Bishop was pleased and said he would never regret it. Newman wrote to Keble, whom he had of course consulted all along. 'We are all in very good spirits here.' Catholic doctrine was not censured, the Bishop was obeyed, and the Tract was selling like hot cakes. Newman added, 'Pusey is writing; I wish he were not.'

Not only Pusey but everyone seemed to be writing: Golightly was making popish extracts from Newman's works; Ward, on the other side, was startling the Balliol Senior Common Room with his assertion: 'I believe all Roman doctrine.' Hook, the respected High

Church Vicar of Leeds, was addressing his Bishop; but Pusey's *Letter to Dr Jelf* (everybody's favourite public correspondent, perhaps because he did not reply) took the prize for length with 186 pages plus 41 of appendix. Newman wrote to George Ryder, son of the Bishop of Lichfield, 'Pusey has just discovered that I dislike the Reformers.' Typically, Pusey had not even read Keble's preface to Froude's *Remains*, but in spite of the shock he loyally defended Tract 90 and its author. Most of the Tractarians enjoyed the battle. 'What a glorious clamour it has made!' wrote Miss Giberne. 'As the Blessed Froude says somewhere, "I deprecate a calm."'

On 9 April, which was Good Friday, after an even more severe Holy Week fast than the year before, Newman preached on *The Cross of Christ the Measure of the World*. 'It is the death of the eternal Word of God made flesh, which is our great lesson how to think and how to speak of this world. His Cross has put its due value upon everything which we see, upon all fortune, all advantages, all ranks, all dignities, all pleasures; upon the lust of the flesh and the lust of the eyes and the pride of life. It has set a price upon the excitements, the rivalries, the hopes, the fears, the desires, the efforts, the triumphs of mortal men. It has given a meaning to the various, shifting course, the trials, the temptations, the sufferings, of his earthly -state. It has brought together and made consistent all that seemed discordant and aimless. It has taught us how to live, how to use this world, what to expect, what to desire, what to hope. It is the tone into which all the strains of this world's music are ultimately to be resolved ... Thus in the Cross, and Him who hung upon it, all things meet; all things subserve it, all things need it. It is their centre and their interpretation. For He was lifted upon it, that He might draw all men and all things unto Him.'

What could the world do to one whose standard, in fact as in word, was the Cross? It could make him carry it.

6

TRANSITION

Newman was content with his bargain and was so scrupulous in carrying it out that he resigned the editorship of the *British Critic* to Tom Mozley. This was not a good move, as Tom did not always take his advice but, as he was a relation, Newman was still held responsible. The rows over Tract 90 and Romishness at Oxford continued unabated and Newman moved out to Littlemore again that summer, with a view to settling there. This time he stayed in an old house called St George's, which had once belonged to recusant Catholics, and still survives amidst the housing estates. For himself he bought an L-shaped block of stabling just across the road, which had belonged to the man who ran the Oxford and Cambridge coach. The loose boxes were to be turned into rooms and the barn into a library. But even these simple operations took time, and the place was not ready till the spring of 1842.

In 1841, however, when Newman settled down to the translation of the works of St Athanasius, which he was doing for the Library of the Fathers, he found, as he was to write in the *Apologia*, that 'The ghost had come a second time.' He was again thrown back to the days of the Arians and wondered how he had not seen before the parallel to the modern situation. 'The pure Arians were the Protestants, the semi-Arians were the Anglicans, and Rome now was what it was then. The truth lay, not with the Via Media, but with what was called "the extreme party".'

That year, too, the Church of England seemed bent on showing its Protestant rather than its Catholic face. A plan of Count Bunsen's, to send a bishop to Jerusalem to preside over the English and Prussian residents, was taken up in high quarters in order to provide official footing for Protestants in Palestine, where France and Russia had established themselves as protectors of the Catholics and the Orthodox. Most Tractarians were horrified at this compromise with heresy, though Pusey, optimistic as ever, hoped that the introduction of an Anglican bishop among the Lutherans would soon Catholicize the whole system. Protests were published, but made no difference; the Jerusalem bishop (a Lutheran as it turned out) was sent off with the blessing of State and Church.

The tide had set against the Tractarians; a campaign was got up against the inoffensive Isaac Williams who was standing for election to the Professorship of Poetry – that casual post which has provided so many excitements in its day. When the opposition cunningly got the Bishop to ask Williams to retire, of course he did. 'We are hit because we are dutiful,' Newman observed after the defeat, in January 1842. Even Keble was in trouble, for his Bishop (of Winchester) had twice refused to ordain his curate, Peter Young, for holding exactly the same Eucharistic views as Keble himself held. It looked as if *Keble* would have to resign his living. (What would have happened if he had?) Newman wrote, to cheer him up, that the Bishops had always lagged behind the clergy: 'Recollect the clergy left off their wigs before the Bishops did.'

Newman was suffering from bishops himself, and in a way that eventually convinced him that he had the full episcopal authority of the Church of England against him. At that time, as Convocation had been suspended (by the State) for over a century, the Bishops could only act publicly by means of their triennial Charges, which were widely reported in the newspapers, especially on the hot subject of popery at Oxford. It was an individual means of censure, but against Tract 90 and its author there was an unprecedented unanimity. Seven Charges against the Tract came out in 1841, more the following year, and by 1844 a hostile pamphleteer could print the names of twenty-four bishops who had anathematized it, and often its author as well.

Newman copied out extracts from these Charges. 'At first I intended to protest,' he wrote in the Apologia. 'But I gave up the thought in despair.' He had insisted on the apostolic authority of bishops and when that authority condemned him, he was defenceless. And now Catholic doctrine as well as the Tract was condemned; the Church of England showed itself Reformed. The unkindest cut came late in 1842 when Bagot joined the chorus, though in the mildest terms.

Newman could not reply; he had promised to write no more on the Articles, he had stopped the Tracts, he was no longer editor of the *British Critic*. But he could still speak from the pulpit of St Mary's, and it was now that he delivered the *Sermons on Subjects of the Day*. They are not as controversial as they sound but Newman compared the Church of England to Samaria, and pointed out that the Prophet Elijah did not command the Samaritans to worship at Jerusalem. This theory appealed to Keble, who could never believe that God intended anyone to move from the place in which he had been born. Newman was later forced to point out that in that case none of the Jewish apostles could ever have become Christian; but at the time the theory comforted him. Even Keble, however, was puzzled by the Advent series of 1841, which Tractarians considered 'methodistical' because of their emphasis on religious experience. Newman fell back on the experience of grace in the sacraments as a proof of the Catholicity of the Church of England. He was afterwards scornful of this lapse into reliance on feeling, but something had happened which for the moment overwhelmed him.

What exactly it was we cannot know, for Newman was always reticent about his own religious experience. But he did, in a guarded way, admit to several friends that 'something that had happened in connection with the Most Holy Sacrament' could be taken as an encouragement to stay in their Church. Lord Shrewsbury wrote to Ambrose Phillipps de Lisle, as one Catholic convert to another: 'Does not this sufficiently prove Newman's Vision to be an illusion of the Father of Lies, since they take it in evidence of the truth of their system and in Justification of Schism?' Newman was soon getting James Mozley to write to Phillipps to deny rumours of supernatural visitations; yet something must have happened to inspire his sermon on *The Invisible Presence of Christ*: '… if your soul has been, as it were, transfigured within you, when you came to the Most Holy Sacrament … O! pause ere you doubt that we have a Divine Presence among us still, and have not to seek it …'

Ambrose Phillipps, who later took the name of de Lisle, was the heir of a wealthy family who had become a Catholic at fifteen, married Laura Clifford, of an old Catholic family, and settled down in Leicestershire to create a Gothic estate, with Pugin to design a chapel and the 'right' vestments, and Trappist monks imported from France to chant in the monastery he built for them. (The monks survived his patronage and still flourish.) Disraeli drew his portrait in *Coningsby* as Sir Eustace Lyle, and called his Gothic residence 'St Genevieve', thus underlining the foreignness of Roman Catholicism, as it then appeared. Phillipps was delighted with 'the Oxford men' and had visions of High Mass in Westminster Abbey, celebrated by Dr Wiseman. For Wiseman was making the new Oscott college, with the chapel where Pugin had for once been allowed to let himself go, rich in the Gothic detail he loved, into a centre of renewed Catholic life. A steady stream of interested Oxford men came over to view this Roman stronghold.

Newman himself never went. Nor was he encouraging about reunion when the eager Phillipps conducted a three-cornered correspondence through Bloxam. 'While Rome is what she is, union is impossible,' Newman wrote. 'That we too must change I do not deny.' He saw only the politics of the Roman Church, no signs of sanctity. 'Never can I think such ways the footsteps of Christ. If they want to convert England, let them go barefooted into our manufacturing towns – let them preach to the people like St Francis Xavier – let them be pelted and trampled on – and I will admit that they can do what we cannot … Let them use the proper arms of the Church, and they will prove that they are the Church by using them.'

Through Bloxam, Phillipps replied that it was true that a reformation was needed in 'the English R. Catholick body' but pointed out that Newman knew little of it. 'In the Cistercian monastery here, in the Benedictine Nunneries generally throughout England, at

Stonyhurst among the Jesuits, I could show him individuals of solid piety, of heroick virtue, who live only for God, and whose hearts are truly on fire with the charity of Christ.' It was true that Newman did not know them; he did not know that on Guy Fawkes day in 1840 a little Italian friar, Fr Dominic Barberi of the Passionist Order, had landed in England, and was doing just what Newman had suggested – going barefoot and in his habit into the industrial towns, enduring mockery and pelting, but preaching in his broken English to anyone who would listen, with surprising success.

The only Catholic at this time who made real contact with Newman was Dr Russell of Maynooth, the chief seminary of Ireland; ten years his junior, he wrote to disabuse Newman of the gross notions of the Real Presence which Catholics were believed to hold. Writing on Holy Thursday, not only showing his own deep love of Christ in the Eucharist but assuming that Newman felt the same, he reached his heart. But even to Russell Newman could write, 'That your communion was unassailable would not prove mine was indefensible.' And he added, 'I wish to go by reason, not by feeling.'

In that agitated aftermath of Tract 90 Bloxam was reported to the Bishop for 'bowing down' at High Mass at Oscott – he loved visiting Pugin's Gothic chapel and looking through their vestments. Newman wrote to Bagot on his behalf, giving the assurance that he had only been in the gallery, saying his own prayers, but Bloxam was much cast down at being accused of idolatry. Newman scribbled a note to him. 'My dear Bloxam – they tell me you are at present performing the character of mope – and that the due maintenance of that character forbids your coming so far as Littlemore. If you have nothing better to do I would come and mope with you at your rooms at dinner on St Peter's day (Thurs.) at any time you please. I am, my dear Bloxam, your sympathetic mope, John H. Newman.' It must have been difficult to mope after that.

Not only Oxford was agitated, but the whole country. Petitions were sent to the Archbishop of Canterbury, meetings were held and reported in the newspapers, and after Pusey had preached at St

Mary Redcliffe, Bristol, he was denounced the next Sunday from the same pulpit as 'the hellborn heresy of Puseyism which has lately appeared in bodily form among you.' Travelling by coach Pusey once heard a lady telling the company that Dr Pusey sacrificed a lamb each Friday. 'Madam, I am Dr Pusey, and I assure you I do not know how to kill a lamb.' Newman also came in for these tales – lamps were burning night and day at Littlemore and he wore 'a cross down his back' when he celebrated Holy Communion. In fact, Newman was no ritualist; he celebrated from the north end of the altar and never wore vestments.

Thomas Arnold, who had supported Catholic Emancipation in 1829 when Newman opposed it, was too true a liberal to believe such nonsense, but he disapproved very strongly of the Catholic revival because he thought it was introducing clericalism into England. In 1841 he had been appointed Regius Professor of Modern History at Oxford, and his series of lectures on that extra-curricular subject was popular and crowded. He was invited to the Oriel Gaudy, on 2 February 1842, and when Newman realized that as Senior Fellow he would have to sit next to him and entertain him, he at first thought of getting out of it, but decided that would be cowardly. Arnold was five years older than Newman and had forgotten that he had disputed with him for his BD in 1828.

In 1844 in answer to an inquiry of Jemima's, Newman told her at length of the meeting, of his own self-consciousness at first, his exertions to talk on safe subjects, and success. 'In the Common Room I had to take a still more prominent part and the contrast was very marked between Arnold and the Provost – the Provost so dry and unbending, and seeming to shrink from whatever I said, and Arnold, who was natural and easy.' Others were watching with fascination and told Newman afterwards how they had been amused, after someone had made an irreverent remark, 'to see how Arnold and myself, in different ways, retired from it.'

The meeting ended well. 'At last the Provost and Arnold rose up to go, and I held out my hand, which he took, and we parted.' News later reached him that Arnold had been surprised to find Newman was not the sham-meek fanatic he fancied. It would not do to meet Newman often, he told Arthur Stanley, his prize ex-pupil, later the liberal Dean of Westminster; it was not desirable to meet often people one disagreed with. Polemical though he might be, Arnold was a man without malice. In June 1842 he died suddenly of angina pectoris, and passed into legend through the medium of Stanley's life of him and the influence of his old pupils. Keble, a friend of Arnold's youth, was distressed when his books were reissued but Newman thought there was so little system in his ideas that they would not have much effect, while his influence as a man and as a headmaster was all for good. So the radical reformer and the Oxford Malignant shook hands before death took one and Rome the other.

Newman's sixth volume of sermons, the first to appear since Tract 90, came out in February 1842 and caused, as Jemima put it, 'a hubbub'. What really annoyed those who ransacked the book for papistry was that Newman's instances were taken from Scripture. His was a Biblical Catholicism. It was too bad, since it was well known that Protestantism was the Bible religion. The Tract, too, was still in print, and still selling. But Newman did not dedicate this book of sermons; he felt himself under censure and did not wish to involve others by association.

The stables at Littlemore were now nearly fit to be lived in and Newman moved up there, transporting all his books and injuring his thumb moving the heavy folios. It affected his writing and this made his friends think he must be ill. But on the whole he was happy, and as the summer went on, even light-hearted in spite of some harassing publicity. He had spent Lent in lodgings but moved in after Easter and already in April there were reports in the papers that 'a so-called Anglo-Catholic monastery is in process of erection at Littlemore.' Poor old Bishop Bagot was forced into action again, writing to Newman 'to afford him the opportunity of making an explanation'. Newman was aggrieved. 'What have I done that I am to be called to account by the world for my private actions in a way in which no one else is called?' he wrote to the Bishop. '... I am often accused of being underhand and uncandid ... but no one likes his good resolutions noised about, both from mere common delicacy and from fear lest he should not be able to fulfil them.' After all, he was only providing a parsonage house for Littlemore. 'The "cloisters" are my shed connecting the cottages ... I am attempting nothing ecclesiastical but something personal and private and which can only be made public and not private by newspapers and letter writers.'

Bagot was satisfied, though he might have been surprised by the primitive nature of the parsonage house. After Newman left, the converted stables were let to the poor and a comfortable house was built for the new clergyman and his family. It was just this social ease that Newman wished to free himself from; hence he rejoiced in the uneven brick floors, the straw mattresses and comfortless simplicity of his new dwelling. His own two rooms were at the end of the long arm of the L; he later gave up his bedroom to be the chapel, when the loose boxes filled up with visitors. For Newman did not remain alone for long.

He did not choose those who came; they were young men made restless in the search for a Catholic life, some refused positions because of their views, some sent by families in the hope that Newman would persuade them not to 'go over to Rome'. The Littlemore community was never an attempt at a monastic order, but those who stayed conformed to a simple routine of life, with regular times for common prayer and silence kept except in the afternoons. They did their own housework except for the fires, which were dealt with by a man from the village. Meals were simple and breakfast was taken standing at a sideboard which the young men called the pig-trough. After dinner there was talk and laughter; Newman got out his violin and played sonatas with anyone willing.

The first to come was John Dobree Dalgairns, a Guernsey man of twenty-three, unable to get a Fellowship because of his Catholic views. He was clever, enthusiastic and immature – his handwriting like a boy's. In July William Lockhart arrived, a connection of Sir Walter Scott's, already ambitious to be a 'Brother of Charity'. He promised Newman to wait three years, but that was an eternity at twenty-two – he was the first to go. In December came Frederick Bowles, musical, nervous and delicate; his family lived at Abingdon and he caused Newman some embarrassment by taking lily bulbs from his mother's garden.

Henry Wilberforce's favourite curate, Ambrose St John, did not come till the summer of 1843. Henry had got a good living in Kent and Newman had teased him: 'I only hope your new preferment will not make you a shovel-hatted humbug. Beware of the Lambeth Livery.' Henry had called his new baby Ambrose Newman, after his old and his new friend. 'I wish Newman had been a prettier name,' wrote the owner of it, ' "Melville" e.g.' In 1843 Ambrose St John was twenty-eight, though he looked younger; in character he was more mature than the others. Newman took to him at once and wrote to Henry: 'St John goes tomorrow and I ought to thank you for letting me have the great pleasure of making his acquaintance. He wishes to pay me a longer visit – and I assure you *I* do.' St John's longer visit lasted the rest of his life. He was practical and brisk, rather blunt and tactless but ready to admit he had been wrong. A keen gardener, he had a pet rose even at Littlemore; wherever he lived directions about plants went to and fro while he was away. He was a good linguist and had studied Hebrew and Syriac; a Student of Christ Church he had worked under Pusey and was always fond of him.

It was to become a common jibe that Newman surrounded himself with 'inferior men' but he did not choose them, and it was not his fault if they were less brilliant than his old friends, most of whom were now either married or dead. Samuel Wood, who had helped to buy the Littlemore stables, died in April 1843 and Newman wrote to Jemima: 'But really I ought to be very thankful, or rather, I cannot be as thankful as I ought to be, for the wonderful way in which God makes to me new friends, when I lose old; to be sure they are younger, which is a drawback, as making me feel so very antique; but there are compensations even then.'

The young men were set to work on a new project: *Lives of the British Saints*, to follow up the success of the *Church of the Fathers*, which had set the enthusiasts trying to be saints. Of course they imagined Newman to be one and were surprised when they met him, to find him behaving like a nineteenth-century person. Mary Holmes, who first wrote to Newman in 1840, was a clever, emotional girl, forced to be a governess though she longed for an artistic life: a real Brontë type. She was related to Thackeray and corresponded with him; alas, when he met her, he thought her plain and her nose was red – he lost interest. In 1842, passing through Oxford, she begged to meet Newman; she had evidently imagined him a father figure and must have let her disappointment show, for Newman wrote, 'As for myself, you are not the first person who has been disappointed in me. Romantic people always will be. I am, in all my ways of going on, a very ordinary person.' Miss Holmes was soon trying to put her idol back in his shrine but he said firmly, 'I am *not* venerable and nothing can make me so … I cannot speak words of wisdom; to some it comes naturally …' But he gave her good advice, though she did not always take it, and did not abandon her even when her letters became frenzied. ('Oh Mr Newman you do not know what the torture of being a waverer is? … Oh Mr Newman, do you wish me to die before your eyes?') She nerved herself to become a Catholic, in spite of his influence, in November 1844 – 'Oh Mr Newman, why will you be so long in coming over?' She felt *almost* willing to be run over on the railroad if that would make her a martyr and bring him in.

Emily Bowles, Frederick's sister, was another young lady who became his devoted disciple about this time; in her private memoir she dated their first meeting to 1840, but as she mentions the 'monastery' it was probably a couple of years later. She came to the church's September feast and remembered the flowers, the procession of singing children, and 'one face, grand, reticent, powerful, both in speaking and at rest and slightly forbidding … At his voice I trembled all over and at last tears began to flow for no other cause but that of the awful sense of the Invisible Presence which he brought among us.' Afterwards Newman entertained his guests at the monastery and Emily was quite overcome when this prophetic sage bent down with a kind smile and said, 'Will you have some cold chicken?' Her mother had to answer for her.

Newman was in high spirits this summer. Miss Giberne wanted to draw him, disgusted with the caricatures. 'How do you know that many persons would not think *me* a scarecrow and my caricature an improvement?' Newman said. He reminded her of Westmacott's bust (for which he had taken Newman's measurements by subterfuge). 'I suspect it is flattered enough to please the most indulgent friend.' But he pretended that if his portrait were done he would be 'represented in an elegant dress and attitude, with my hand between the buttons of my waistcoat.' Two years later Henry Wilberforce persuaded him to have his head drawn by George Richmond, and thought the result lifelike, except that he missed the spectacles. The original is now in the small Common Room at Oriel, and at Littlemore is the miniature by Sir William Ross, a full face threequarter portrait, with spectacles, simple and almost smiling, with hands loosely clasped on his lap. The pictures were all done at the request of others and except for Miss Giberne's efforts there are few till the photographs that followed the fame of *Apologia*, when he was over sixty.

Meanwhile that enthusiastic 'R. Catholick', Ambrose Phillipps, brought to Oxford the Italian priest Luigi Gentili, a member of the new Institute of Charity founded by Rosmini, a remarkable and liberal-minded Catholic, always in trouble with the Holy Office. 'We were quite enchanted with Newman,' wrote Phillipps, 'whose amiable manners are only equalled by his gigantick learning and talents.' Newman had just brought out a translation of Fleury's Church History with an introductory essay on Miracles. 'It is quite magnificent,' Phillipps told the suspicious Lord Shrewsbury. 'Not only Catholick and orthodox, but written with a power of argument perfectly *tremendous*. Newman has the intellect of the cherubim — forcible like the lightning flash, clear as crystal.'

Newman might have the intellect of the cherubim but he had none of the craft popularly attributed to him, and in January 1843 got himself into hot water again by publishing a Retractation of his attacks on the Roman Church, which he sent to the *Conservative Journal*. It was so worded that people thought he was admitting to having used abusive terms which he did not believe; in fact, he meant that he had adopted the views of respected Anglican divines on Roman corruptions and now no longer thought them well-founded. As a result, he was very generally called a hypocrite and a deceiver, and the Evangelical Dean Close of Cheltenham said at a public dinner in March that he would not trust the author of Tract 90 with his purse. In a private letter to Hawkins, Whately said that Newman had nothing to learn from 'the *Slanderer* himself'. It was at this point that Newman preached the sermon on *Wisdom and Innocence* which Charles Kingsley later thought was teaching that lying and cunning were the Christian's weapons against the world. What Newman actually said was that the world only recognizes two reasons for success: force or guile. As Christianity had not conquered the Roman Empire by force, its success was put down to guile, not to the power of truth. So with the Movement, he implied. Kingsley proved him right by suspecting him of guile himself.

But now Newman was beginning to feel that he was, though unintentionally, deceiving people by remaining in the ministry of the Church of England. 'I am a Roman in my heart,' he confessed to Henry Wilberforce. But his reason had not yet caught up with his heart. 'It is so very difficult to steer between being hypocritical and revolutionary.' There was, too, an unhappy misunderstanding with Rogers, who came down for the Gaudy and when Newman wished to consult him about resigning his living, refused to listen. From London he wrote a farewell-this-is-the-end kind of letter, which Newman tried to answer, discarding several attempts. In vain, for Rogers was determined to cut himself off from Newman's influence and did not see him again for twenty years.

His final letter came when Newman was making his first retreat with his Littlemore companions, in the Lent of 1843, using a Catholic manual; he found it difficult to concentrate when they were all together in the tiny chapel made out of his bedroom, with the window filled up to prevent the curious from peering in. They did not have an altar but a narrow shelf, with hangings behind and a crucifix on it. Down the centre of the room was a board with candles.

But despite his discomfort in the exercise, Newman's self-examination was even more rigorous than of old. He feared that his motive in all his exertions during the last ten years had been 'the pleasure of energizing intellectually'. It was certainly not his *only* motive.

At the beginning of Lent Newman had written to Keble to ask his advice on resigning St Mary's; he sent a further note on Easter Eve and at last in May Keble answered that he thought it permissible. But by then Newman felt that he must unburden his conscience still further. 'Oh forgive me, my dear Keble,' he began, and told the story of his doubts, since 1839, that the Church of England was in schism from the Catholic Church. Keble read Newman's confession, as he recalled next year, 'in a deserted old chalk pit. I cannot tell you with what sort of fancy I look at the place now.' He did not answer till *ten days* had elapsed, but then he said, 'Believe me, my very dear Newman, that any thought of wilful insincerity in you can find no place in my mind.' But knowing what he now knew, Keble regarded resignation as a 'perilous step', as bringing Newman nearer to 'the temptation of going over'. And his loss would be a 'grievous event' just when there were signs of renewal in the English Church. Newman was greatly relieved not to incur Keble's condemnation, and letters continued, but he had already followed the only advice Keble could give, to wait and test his views. 'My present feelings have arisen naturally and gradually, and have been resisted. It is true, that I have now laid down my arms rather suddenly.'

In August 1843 came the pretext for resigning St Mary's – young Lockhart went to visit Gentili at Loughborough and was received by him into the Catholic Church. Gentili wrote Newman a letter full of understanding, said he hoped to have the *Lives of the British Saints* read aloud in his refectory, and urged Newman to write against State appointments in religion, which he deprecated just as much for Catholics. Years later Lockhart wrote in his memoir how he had gone to Newman for confession and had suddenly asked him '"Are you sure you can give me absolution?" He did not speak for a few moments, then said in a tone of deep distress, "Why will you ask me? Ask Pusey."' He often sent the doubtful to Pusey, who had no doubts. But Pusey himself was in trouble this year, suspended from preaching for his views on the Eucharist.

Just as Newman was drafting his letter of resignation to the Bishop, he received an excited communication from Tom Mozley, who had rushed back from a holiday in Normandy (leaving Harriett and the baby, Grace, over there) to say he must at once join the Church of Rome. Newman hurried over to Cholderton, spent the day walking the country with Tom and persuaded him to wait by telling him his own doubts, though binding him to secrecy. But Tom could not keep a secret; he told Jemima and set the Derby household in an uproar, and then Harriett found out. She never forgave her brother but she soon got Tom back where she wanted him. He gave up his editorship of the *British Critic* and later his pastoral charge to be a journalist on *The Times*, but he never became a Catholic. Harriett told Newman that Catholics in France were not all they should be. He replied by reminding her of his studies of ancient controversies. 'I saw from them that Rome was the centre of unity and judge of controversies. My views would not be influenced by the surface or the interior of the French Church or of any other.'

While Tom's 'indiscretion' ran its course, Newman had taken the step he had hesitated over so long. He wrote to the Bishop to resign his living, apologizing for adding to his anxieties about the Church. 'I am not relaxing my zeal till it has been disowned by her rulers. I have not retired from her service till I have lost or forfeited her confidence.' Reluctantly, Bagot accepted his resignation and Newman went up to London on Monday, 18 September 1843 and signed away, before a notary, St Mary's and Littlemore, and all that they had been to him for fifteen years. The night before, he noted in his diary, he could not sleep.

Newman preached his last sermon at St Mary's on Sunday, 25 September, and at Littlemore, on the Monday, gave his farewell, the sermon he called *The Parting of Friends*. Pusey took the service; there were a hundred and forty communicants; the church was full of fuchsias, dahlias and passion-flowers; the children were all in new frocks and bonnets, Newman's parting gift. Many London friends were present and the lawyer, Serjeant Bellasis, wrote to his wife that he would never forget the sermon, with its long pauses. 'Newman's voice was low, but distinct and clear.' He did not break down, though everyone else seemed to be in tears.

'O my mother,' he addressed the Church of England, '... Who hath put this note upon thee, to have "a miscarrying womb and dry breasts", to be strange to thine own flesh, and thine eye cruel to thy little ones?' The Church had rejected him and his theory that it was an integral part of the visible Catholic Church, and so he must resign his cure of souls. 'And O my brethren, O kind and affectionate hearts, O loving friends,' he said to the listeners, if they knew of one who 'encouraged you, or sobered you, or opened a way to the inquiring, or soothed the perplexed,' if they had taken an interest in him, 'remember such a one in time to come, though you hear him not, and pray for him, that in all things he may know God's will, and at all times he may be ready to fulfil it.'

When he left the pulpit he threw his gown and hood over the altar rails, as a gesture of finality. He received communion but took no further part in officiating.

Newman's successor at St Mary's was a man called Eden; Dean Burgon, in his *Twelve Good Men*, recorded his aggressive manners – he slanged servants in public and was rude to foreigners. But though he was brusque and patronizing to Newman, he allowed William Copeland to stay on at Littlemore as curate, and this meant much to the community in the stable monastery. Since this belonged to Newman and since he was still a Fellow of Oriel, he was able to remain there. By Eden's permission he was allowed to continue to visit a parishioner, Elizabeth Lenthall, who was ill with cancer, and this he faithfully did till her death two years later.

The news of Newman's resignation brought him many letters from anxious members of the Movement, among them Henry Edward Manning, at this time an Anglican Archdeacon. To him Newman replied: 'It seems a dream to call a Communion Catholic when one can neither appeal to any clear statement of Catholic doctrine in its formularies, nor interpret ambiguous formularies by the received and living sense, past or present.' Of himself, he added: 'It is felt, I am far from denying, justly felt, that I am a foreign material and cannot assimilate with the Church of England.' It was typical of him to use an image relating to living bodies.

Manning administered some polite admonishment and Newman replied straight out: 'I think the Church of Rome the Catholic Church.' Manning sent this letter to Gladstone, who said it made him stagger to and fro like a drunken man; he thought if it came out Newman would be disgraced and the Movement discredited. Manning wrote a soft answer to Newman but then came down to preach from the pulpit of St Mary's the anti-papist sermon prescribed for 5 November, but omitted by Newman for years. 'Manning has delivered a No Popery bark,' said Church, scornfully. Yet Manning walked out next day to call on Newman, and was surprised at a cool reception. But by December, when he read in Newman's sermon of Orpah, who in contrast to the faithful Ruth, kissed Naomi and left her, he immediately thought it meant for him. Newman answered that such a thing had never crossed his mind: 'Really, unless it were so sad a matter, I should smile ... Rather I am the person who to myself always seem, and reasonably, the criminal ... It is no pleasure to me to differ from friends – no comfort to be estranged from them – no satisfaction or boast to have said things which I must unsay. Surely I will remain where I am as long as I can. I think it right to do so. If my misgivings are from above, I shall be carried on in spite of my resistance.'

He was to remain where he was – in lay communion in the Church of England – for two years. There were deep reasons for this; one was distrust of what he called 'paper logic', his conviction that 'the whole man' must move; but he equally distrusted a merely emotional motive. He tested his conclusions by living with them, by prayer, self-examination and penance. He asked himself, 'Am I in a delusion?' The fact that Keble did not see things as he did weighed heavily against him. But there was also an uneasiness of mind; from this was to spring his theory on the Development of Christian

Doctrine. It was germinating all through the painful year that followed his resignation.

Bowden was dying. He died of tuberculosis, like Froude, and like Froude, by inches. Newman could not share with this oldest friend his doubts and growing convictions; and to Bowden he continued to administer Holy Communion, so as not to unsettle the peace of that good man, as he went slowly down the hill. The last birthday they shared fell on Ash Wednesday in 1844. 'One forgets past feelings, else I would say that I never had pain like the present,' Newman wrote in September, when Bowden was on his death-bed. He went up to London to see him and noted afterwards, 'I sobbed bitterly over his coffin to think that he had left me still in the dark as to what the way of truth was, and what I ought to do in order to please God and fulfil his will.'

Bowden had told his wife to be guided by Newman, and though he had to begin by telling her of his own uncertainty, she soon got over the shock and welcomed his continuing friendship; visiting her and the children and writing to them took much of his attention during the next few months. He was glad he had told her, and all his friends, before November 1844, when a false report that he had already been received by Rome got into the papers and an avalanche of letters descended on him, from known and unknown, many abusive, but many more anguished and hurt. Perhaps no one who has not read through this box full of letters, still preserved, can realize what a terrible experience it must have been to receive them. 'On Saturday for some time my heart literally ached,' he wrote to Edward Coleridge, then an Eton master. Pusey realized something of what he was suffering. 'It even seems to affect his whole frame as one might imagine "a sword piercing", a pain shooting through every part.' His distress was the result of the distress of others, who felt betrayed and abandoned by hearing that their prophet and guide had given up the cause. 'The one predominant distress upon me has been this unsettlement of mind I am causing,' he told Jemima, and yet at the end of that terrible month he could say to her, 'I am not unwilling to be in trouble now, nor for others to be – and the more of it, the sooner over. It is like drinking a cup out.'

The strain made him ill, with headaches, pains and influenza, but through it all he was working on the proofs of *St Athanasius*, who always seemed to be in a critical state at times of stress. And at the end of that death of the heart (he often at this time called himself a dead man) suddenly he was possessed by the idea of development, so strongly that he had to begin his book at once. It was Lent when he got back to Oxford after a visit to the Bowdens at St Leonard's (where he had not been since 1810). Ash Wednesday fell on 5 February in 1845 and on that day he heard, hardly caring whether he heard it or not, that the Hebdomadal Board proposed to introduce into Convocation a formal censure on Tract 90.

This was the last big row the Movement made in Oxford, and great was the excitement in the nine days before the occasion. The only person who was not upset was Newman, half hoping for a formal condemnation as a sign that it was time to act. Pamphlets were flying as usual, but he meant to keep silence, he told Jemima, 'for really I am not bound to come forward and play the Scaramouch for the amusement of the *Standard* and *Record* papers.' He did not go to the theatre on 13 February.

It was a cold snowy day and the main event was the proposal to condemn W. G. Ward's book, *The Ideal of a Christian Church*, in which the ideal was plainly fulfilled rather by Rome than Canterbury. Ward spoke for an hour and a half, declaring 'I hold all Roman doctrine.' There was a large majority in favour of condemning his book, a much smaller one for depriving him of his degrees, but both measures were passed. Then the proposed censure of Tract 90 was brought forward and pandemonium broke loose. In the turmoil the two proctors, Guillemard and Church, rose to impose the veto: Guillemard, the senior, had to shout above the din: *Non Placet!* Jubilation from the Tractarians, groans from the opposition! Outside a crowd of undergraduates snowballed the Vice-Chancellor but cheered Ward, as the fat philosopher slipped in the snow, scattering the papers of his speech broadcast.

Ward was condemned, and was soon to go over to Rome, announcing it, and his marriage, in *The Times*; Tract 90 was spared. But Newman knew that without the veto the university would almost certainly have rejected him as well as Ward. He was past caring. He was hard at work now, standing at the desk Henry Wilberforce had given him, composing his book on *The Development of Christian Doctrine*. All through the spring and summer he worked at it, but it was to be left unfinished in the autumn, for it carried him at last beyond theory into action, into communion with the Church of the Fathers, in which the centre of unity was the See of St Peter at Rome.

7

ROME AND THE ORATORY

It was the idea of development which finally brought Newman to the point of action. From his studies of antiquity he had come to see Rome as the centre of unity, and the Church of England as deliberately out of communion with Rome, which was believed to have corrupted the faith. Newman himself was well aware that the modern Catholic Church was very different from what it had been in the fifth century. What would St Athanasius have made of it? It was easy for Protestants, who wished to ignore history and live as if they were St Paul's converts, to condemn everything after the New Testament as a corruption. But Newman, as an Anglican, had long since accepted the fact that Christianity not only had a history, but *was* a history. Christ was a person, not an idea. Similarly the Church was a collective person, a personal community in which the Spirit of God was the unifying bond, the life of mind and heart. And because human beings think, there must be a community of thought as well as a community of love.

Christ compared his kingdom to a seed which becomes a tree. This image was commonly used of the expansion of the Church and the elaboration of its structure as the peoples were gathered into its fold. But it can also be used as an image of living growth, from source to maturity. Newman's originality was that he saw how *ideas* as well as organization develop in time.

Because we are so familiar with the idea of evolution it is quite difficult to imagine the time when even highly educated men believed that the world had come into existence more or less as they found it. During Newman's Oxford years there was much talk of the speculations of geologists as to the age of the earth but it was not till the appearance in 1859 of Darwin's book, *The Origin of Species*, that the general public became aware of the possibility of biological evolution and the development of the human from an animal stock. The discovery of the slow changes of living forms has been the greatest mental revolution since the discovery in the sixteenth century that the earth was not the fixed centre of the universe. And just as the fact that the earth was a moving sphere seemed to unseat heaven and hell, those moral realities then polarized in space, so the idea of biological evolution seemed to contradict man's God-given soul, his supremacy over nature and destination to eternal life.

Darwin's theory did not shock Newman; he told a correspondent he was willing 'to go the whole hog with Darwin'. Sixteen years before the famous book appeared he preached his last university sermon on 2 February 1843, Oriel's foundation feast of the Purification of the Blessed Virgin Mary, on the text: 'And Mary kept all these things and pondered them in her heart.' She was the pattern of all Christians who ponder the mysteries of the divine revelation in Christ. The sermon was Newman's first public formulation of his theory of development of doctrine; the book written in 1845 was the formal exposition of it. Circumstances had forced him to ponder on the formation of the ruling ideas of Christianity and in the century when history became an academic and almost a scientific discipline, Newman pioneered an approach which became common later. The historical development of ideas, of institutions, the action of many minds working over long periods of time, the importance of the conditions which limited their understanding, and the way in which a central idea can change without losing its identity, how associated ideas can bring out or obscure the main reality, how a new formulation may preserve the old meaning better than outdated terms – all this was very new thinking when Newman composed his essay. It was new to Anglicans, who rejected it as betraying the everlasting revelation in the interests of an innovating Romanism; it was new to Catholics, and though welcomed by some, not properly assimilated by those whose minds were formed by the static philosophy worked out by lesser men from the great Thomas Aquinas.

Newman had passed from a static to a dynamic view of the universe before the doctrine of evolution convulsed his contemporaries.

He wrote himself into final conviction; he wrote himself into action. The essay was an exploration but he came to feel that the idea of development was essential to the Church and it enabled him to see how, and sometimes why, ideas had grown up about the mother of Jesus, for instance, or the Eucharist, or the papal office, which were not corruptions but the result of collective pondering on what happened in Jesus the Christ. And because it was necessary to draw the line between reality and superstition, the need for such judgment had gradually defined the apostolic office of the bishops, with the Pope at their head – a collective responsibility, whether exercised in Council or individually. The Church was not a changeless idea; it was a living community. Christ was one and the same, but the understanding of him must grow as the collective mind of the human race grows in the search for truth; the guidance of the Spirit was promised to, and mediated through, the united body. And St Peter's successor was the divinely appointed centre of unity.

That summer, while he was writing on Development, Newman had many visitors, among them his sister Jemima and her eldest boy, Herbert. At the end of Lent he had been telling his intentions to all his friends and relations. 'What can be worse than this?' Jemima had lamented. 'It is like hearing that some dear friend must die.' In his reply Newman tried to make her understand that it was only the compulsion of truth which could force him to break the ties which held him, giving up home, work and income, just as he was approaching middle age, and distressing all he loved. 'Oh what can it be but a stern necessity which causes this? Pity me, my dear Jemima.' But next morning, on Palm Sunday, his mood was calmer. No one had the right to judge him, not even Jemima, since he was doing his best: 'May we not trust it will turn to the best?' But though Jemima came to see him, she could not understand.

Nor could Frank, who urged Newman to start a sect of his own if he was dissatisfied with the Church of England. John commented in a private note: 'That I could be contemplating questions of Truth and Falsehood never entered into his imagination!' But he was on fairly good terms with Frank now, and they were already sharing the responsibility for Charles, whom the doctors had just pronounced sane, though Frank felt he suffered from a moral insanity. Charles had recently pursued an erratic course at Bonn University, but now he was persuaded to settle in lodgings at Tenby, supported by his brothers and happily writing pamphlets on Owenite socialism. As for Harriett she had become distant to John since Tom Mozley's abortive conversion and scarcely ever wrote to her brother now.

Newman's young friends at Littlemore were not suffering, as he was, a tearing apart of affections; as the year turned he allowed them to have their way. Dalgairns went off to Fr Dominic Barberi at Stone and was received on the feast of St Michael and All Angels, 29 September. When he came back, Newman wrote to Mrs Bowden, 'If you could see how happy and altered D is, you would wonder – I cannot describe it, but it is the manner of a person entrusted with a great gift.' Ambrose St John resigned his Studentship at Christ Church and went to Prior Park, near Bath, where he was received on 2 October, the feast of the Holy Guardian Angels. The next day Newman sent in his resignation to the Provost. He was no longer a Fellow of Oriel.

And suddenly now he acted. The book was left in the middle of a sentence. Fr Dominic was passing through Oxford on his way abroad and Dalgairns had asked him to visit Littlemore again – he had been there once before, now dressed *à l'anglais* in boots, a scratch lot of clothes and an odd hat. Newman had not only liked him, but felt at once that he was a man of true holiness. Dalgairns later recorded that as he was going to meet the coach Newman said to him, 'in a very low and quiet tone: "When you see your friend, will you tell him that I wish him to receive me into the Church of Christ?"' Dalgairns told Fr Dominic as he was dismounting, soaked through after five hours on top of the coach, delayed by the appalling weather. 'He said, "God be praised" and neither of us spoke again till we reached Littlemore.' They took a chaise there, arriving at eleven at night in pouring rain. 'I took up my position by the fire to dry myself,' Fr Dominic later wrote to his superiors. 'The door opened and what a spectacle it was for me to see at my feet John Henry Newman begging me to hear his confession and admit him into the bosom of the Catholic Church! And there by the fire he began his general confession with extraordinary humility and devotion.'

It had to be finished next day. Something of what Newman felt on this occasion, which seems to have been described by everyone except himself, can be gathered from a letter to Mrs Bowden next spring, advising her how to meet last-minute trials. 'The moment before acting may be, as can easily be imagined, peculiarly dreary – the mind may be confused – no reason for acting may be forthcoming to our mind – and the awful greatness of the step itself, and without any distinct apprehension of its consequences, may weigh on us. Some persons like to be left to themselves in such a crisis – others find comfort in the presence of others – I could do nothing but shut myself up in my room and lie down on my bed.'

The next morning – it was 9 October 1845 – Fr Dominic walked down to the Catholic chapel in St Clement's to acquaint the priest, Mr Newsham, with the situation and to say mass. He returned, still in pouring rain, heard the rest of Newman's confession and those of Frederick Bowles and Richard Stanton, who had joined the group that summer. In the evening at six o'clock, as Fr Dominic reported, 'They made their profession of faith in the usual form in their private Oratory, one after another, with such fervour and piety that I was almost out of myself with joy.' He gave them conditional baptism (in case it had not been properly administered) and the next morning he said mass in the tiny chapel, using as altar the writing desk Henry Wilberforce had given Newman, at which he had written the *Essay on Development*, and which is there again today, in the restored chapel. All received communion: Newman, St John, Dalgairns, Bowles and Stanton. Newman marked the occasion in his diary with a little cross.

Fr Dominic had to leave next day, Saturday; he wrote to his superiors that Newman was 'one of the most humble and lovable men I have met in my life'. And Newman was writing of him to Mrs

Bowden, 'I wish all persons were as charitable as he. I believe he is a very holy man.' All persons were not as charitable as Fr Dominic; when the news broke letters came pouring in, but the newspapers only became violent as the weeks went on and it became plain that Newman's conversion had started a landslide. A few individuals had already 'gone over' but now the family and professional men began to move. It was this that caused the alarm; conversion could not be put down to the instability of youth. 'More Perversions!!!' the newspapers cried, in fury.

Newman and his companions went to Oscott for confirmation at the feast of All Saints, 1 November. He met Wiseman for the first time since 1833 in a small upstairs room with a distant view of the red roofs of Birmingham. Wiseman was embarrassed and Newman had a fit of his disabling shyness; however, things went better after the ceremony in Pugin's Gothic chapel next day, when Newman, taking a patron saint according to custom, took the name of Mary. Newman offered up his book to his new bishop, promising to do with it whatever he said. Wiseman had the breadth of mind to insist that it should be published as it stood; Newman therefore brought it out on his own responsibility.

Apart from publishing *Development*, Newman had to decide what to do with his life, and it was Wiseman who persuaded him that he should become a Catholic priest. He hesitated, because he felt he had been so long a teacher in a Church he now felt to be in schism. He saw the ministry as a corporate authority, for at this time he had no doubt but that his Anglican ordination was valid. It was the Bishop in London who was to remove his scruple about a second ordination ceremony, by pointing out that it would be done for Catholics if there had been any doubt of authenticity. The validity of orders always seemed to Newman a secondary question just because it was the corporate unity of the Church which was primary.

His younger disciples wished to stay with him, thinking they could all join some religious order as a group, and when Wiseman offered them old Oscott college, down in the valley, to be 'Littlemore continued' till they found their feet in the Church, Newman accepted. They walked down the hill to look at the house, of red brick, rather like Sandford Mill, on the river near Littlemore, Newman thought. Inside the forbidding high wall, built as a protection from hostile Protestants in penal days, there was a semicircular pillared ambulatory with a vine growing over it, and a big garden. Newman called the place Maryvale, a name it has kept to this day.

They were not to move there till the new year; meanwhile, Newman had received many invitations from Catholic bishops and colleges, and went off on a kind of tour. 'We must throw ourselves into the system,' he said to Ambrose St John, usually his companion. It was a surprise to find how indomitably English the Catholics were, and not the politically minded liberals Newman had feared. He was impressed with the simplicity of everything.

While he was in London Newman gave Miss Giberne a helping hand over the threshold, putting her into a cab and taking her to Fr Brownbill, a 'terrible Jesuit', who reassured her by shaking hands, and into whose large red ear she summoned up courage to make her confession, relieved to find it was not the ordeal she had imagined. She had difficulties with her Evangelical family and in the end had to leave home, arriving at Maryvale in tears. Newman gave her a cup of tea and took her up to Oscott for Benediction; in Pugin's chapel she felt she was in heaven.

Miss Giberne and many others followed Newman, but not his nearest friends, Pusey and Keble, though both remained kindly to him and Pusey wrote of his going to labour 'in another part of the vineyard'. Everyone was now reading the *Development* (so rapid was the process of publication in those days) and, for the most part, failing to grasp what it was about. Protestants fastened on the fact that Newman believed miracles possible, as evidence for his credulity. Whately, writing to Hawkins, expressed the feeling of many: 'My own suspicion is that N himself is only seeking to escape Infidelity by a violent plunge into credulity.' James Mozley, now part owner and co-editor of the *Christian Remembrancer* (successor to the *British Critic*) wrote for it an article 'On the Recent Schism' for the January number which hurt Newman because he felt James had used private knowledge merely to misrepresent his motives. He was annoyed at the notion that it was his 'sensitiveness' to hostility which had driven him out of the Church of England. To have endured hostility so long only to have his conversion put down to cowardice in the face of it, was not only galling but gave people an excuse for sidestepping his arguments.

In February 1846 Newman was back at Littlemore to pack up, an exhausting and melancholy task, after twenty-five years in Oxford. 'It is like going out on the open sea,' he told St John, who had gone ahead to Maryvale. The others all preceded him, so that Newman was left alone in the house by 21 February, his forty-fifth birthday. 'I came into this bower by myself,' he wrote to HW – 'I quit it by myself.' How happy he had been there! He ended a letter to Mrs Bowden, 'I must once more go over to the poor house before the fly comes.' The people at Littlemore, understanding little of what had gone on in his mind, always remembered his kindness in visiting them, his faith which upheld them in distress.

To Copeland Newman wrote, 'I quite tore myself away, and could not help kissing my bed, and mantelpiece and other parts of the house. I have been most happy there, though in a state of suspense. And there it has been that I have both been taught my way and received an answer to my prayers.' The last day, 22 February, began with walking to mass at the chapel in St Clement's; it ended with dinner at the Radcliffe Observatory, where Newman stayed the night with the Observer, who was his old friend Manuel Johnson, a relative of Bowden's. Others came there to say good-bye, Pusey last of all, late at night. Newman left Oxford next morning at half-past eight and did not see it again, except from the train, for thirty-two years.

This first sojourn at Maryvale lasted only six months, for Wiseman decided that Newman ought to go to Rome. It was a difficult time, for Oscott was the show-place of English Catholics and the illustrious convert the showpiece. In 1863, struggling to understand his personal position after many failures, Newman was to write in a private journal: 'How dreary my first year at Maryvale, when I was the gaze of so many eyes at Oscott, as if some wild incomprehensible beast, caught by the hunter, and a spectacle for Dr Wiseman to exhibit to strangers, as himself being the hunter who captured it! I did not realize this at the time, except in its discomfort.'

Emily Bowles, from the gallery of the chapel, once saw Newman 'catechized by an Italian priest'. In her memoir, written many years later, she said, 'It was almost more than I could bear to see the great teacher come out to be questioned and taught as a little child ... The beauty of his voice and singular lowliness and unself-consciousness of his whole bearing so overwhelmed me with emotion that I have little recollection of what he said, except that it was about the Magi.'

Newman himself noted two such occasions, in 1863: 'I was made an humiliation at my minor orders and at the examination for them; and I had to stand at Dr Wiseman's door for Confession amid the Oscott boys. I did not realize these as indignities at the time, though, as I have said, I felt their dreariness.'

Someone who demands no special consideration rarely receives it. Had Newman stalked about looking important, people would not have treated him like an exhibit or a truant schoolboy. A few years later Wiseman ordained Manning within a few weeks of his reception and when he went to Rome it was to the Accademia, the college for priests of noble birth and the nursery of ecclesiastical diplomats. Manning was a person nobody dreamed of snubbing, yet he had not, like Newman, an international reputation.

Nevertheless, in spite of snubs and stares, and the unfamiliar ways of modern Catholic devotion, Newman's heart was at peace. He wrote to HW, 'It is such an incomprehensible blessing to have Christ's bodily presence in one's house, within one's walls, as swallows up and destroys, or should destroy, every pain. To know that He is close by – to be able again and again to go in to Him; and be sure, my dearest W, when I am thus in His Presence you are not forgotten ... Thus Abraham, our father, pleaded before his hidden Lord and God in the valley.'

He was praying for many friends just now. Henry did not yet move, but Mrs Bowden and her children were received in London at the chapel in Warwick Street, off Piccadilly, once an Embassy chapel where Catholics could safely attend mass, by old Mr Wilds, the priest, in Newman's presence. John Bowden, at Eton, was held back for a time by relations; but Charlie, Newman's godson, was a keen convert. 'The very first day he went to mass with Newman he set him right,' St John told Dalgairns, in September, before they left for Rome.

Hastily collecting clothes for his year abroad Newman had been warned that 'knit woollen shirts are the *very things* they seize in France and Italy', and soused them all in water – how did they survive such treatment? But they may not have been woollen, for a few years later Newman discovered from his friend Lady Olivia Acheson that what he had always thought was 'knit wool' was really 'knit cotton'. That, he decided, must be why he had always felt so cold in winter.

They crossed the Channel early in September, slept the night at Dieppe and went on to Paris next day. Newman was now famous abroad and M. Gondon, the French impresario of the Movement, who was translating *Development*, presided over a festive welcome, and Newman was embraced by the Archbishop, the same who was later assassinated. From Paris they went on to Langres where Dalgairns had gone to study for the priesthood, and there were more receptions with formal bows, 'and for me, who hardly ever made a formal bow in my life,' wrote Newman to Bowles, left at Maryvale, 'I can hardly keep my countenance as I put my elbows on my hips and make a segment of a circle, the lower vertebrae being the centre and my head the circumference.' His French was so poor he was reduced to conversing in Latin. Meals cooked in oil, cold wine instead of hot tea, fricasseed frogs and feather beds, left Newman exhausted, and glad, when they had crossed the Alps, to find rest in a retreat house next to the church of S. Fidelis, 'lofty, cool and quiet in the heart of Milan'. Newman loved the classical style, which he called 'Grecian', of this church. 'It has such a sweet, smiling, open countenance, and the altar is so gracious and winning – standing out for all to see and approach.'

Indeed, he loved Milan, and the Duomo – 'its pinnacles are like bright snow against the blue sky' – though not the spitting, which was done everywhere, even in church, or the 'tyranny of the Austrian Government' which, he told Jemima, was 'inconceivable'. They went on to Rome at the end of October, a hazardous journey owing to floods and the threat of bandits, but arrived safely and went 'to say the Apostles' Creed at St Peter's tomb, the first thing – and there was the Pope at the tomb saying Mass – so that he was the first person I saw in Rome and I was quite close to him.' This was not Gregory XVI, who had sent Newman an Apostolic blessing and a relic of the True Cross, but his successor, Pius IX, destined for a long and stormy pontificate.

The College of Propaganda, where students from all over the world were prepared for the priesthood, and which in those days was still housed in a large building in the Piazza di Spagna, near the famous Spanish Steps, was not ready to receive them and they stayed a week in a hotel, appalled at the dirt and tormented by the clerical clothes they had to wear 'Buckles at the knees, buckles on the shoes,' wrote Newman to Stanton, 'a dress coat with a sort of under-graduate's gown hanging behind, black stockings which must be without a wrinkle, and a large heavy cocked hat; that I should have lived so long to be so dressed up!' The hat had no brim to keep off rain and blew off at every gust of wind. When they did get to Propaganda there were more clothes to buy. Newman groaning at the expense, but glad 'to shrink into a cassock'. Here they were given such special treatment as to make them laugh; after the austerities of Littlemore they hardly needed 'worked muslin curtains to their beds'. They begged off carpets and butter, because the other students did not have them, but the Rector insisted on their having tea, for he had installed a wonderful machine in their rooms to make it. St John had to make all the conversation to the Jesuit Fathers who ran the place; Newman was reduced to silence by shyness and inability to master Italian, though he took lessons in it.

Lectures were fortunately given in Latin but they were intended for beginners and St John was soon accusing Newman of going to sleep in morals and dogmatics. He gave it up and spent the time turning some of his work on St Athanasius into Latin dissertations. They were hardly a success, but when he met the Roman theologians he got on better.

Meanwhile the weather was terrible, it rained incessantly, and the streets were filthy. On coming in from a visit to Miss Giberne, now also in Rome, they were summoned to meet the Pope at once – and their cloaks 'had a deep fringe of the nastiest stuff I ever saw', Newman told Bowles. However, the cloaks were dipped in water by the resourceful Italians, hiding rather than removing the dirt, and off they hurried – only to have to wait an hour and a half before they saw the Pope. Newman, awkwardly kneeling to kiss the Pope's foot (then still *de rigueur*), managed to knock his head on his knee, as he afterwards related with amusement. The Pope was 'a vigorous man with a very pleasant countenance, and was most kind,' said Newman.

Here, as at Oscott, people wanted to show off the famous convert, but Newman's first public appearance in Rome was, typically, a social fiasco. 'O I was a sort of sucking child,' he wrote of this incident in 1863, 'just as much knowing what I should say, what I should not say, and saying nothing right, not from want of tact so much as from sheer ignorance.' Prince Borghese, who had been married to a daughter of Lord Shrewsbury's, came to ask Newman to preach at the funeral of Miss Bryan, a niece of Lady Shrewsbury's. Newman tried to get out of it but was forced to accept and then annoyed the fashionable congregation very much, partly by saying: 'We all need conversion.' What he had said was much exaggerated by gossip and Ambrose recorded in his diary that on Christmas Day, when they were in the great church of Ara Coeli, there were lots of Protestants present 'looking as if they would eat Newman'. In January Newman told Mrs Bowden that 'Miss Ryder heard a man express the sentiment in a party, that I ought to be thrown into the Tyber.' (George Ryder, son of the Bishop of Lichfield, who had married one of the beautiful Sargent sisters, had come over to Rome – literally – with all his family.) Even the Pope remarked that on such occasions honey was more suitable than vinegar, and that Newman must be more of a philosopher than an orator.

Just about this time Newman was hearing Catholic criticisms of his theory of Development, though he won round the chief Roman theologian Perrone, when he was able to meet him and talk. He had been disappointed to find that in Rome theology was taught from second-rate manuals; not merely was St Augustine virtually unknown but even St Thomas Aquinas was not read. Catholic theology was at its nadir; the Revolution had closed the great schools of France and disrupted the traditional learning in many parts of Europe. In Germany a revival was beginning, but scarcely as yet recognized in Rome. Newman could have little real discussion and wrote somewhat despondently to Dalgairns that he felt he had not been done justice to – though God knew what he was doing. It was always Newman's faith that his work was in the hands of God, to be used according to his will. 'Yet sometimes it is marvellous to me how my life is going and I have never been brought out prominently – and now I am less likely than ever – for there seems something of an iron form here, though I may be wrong – but I mean, people are at no trouble to deepen their views. It is natural.'

It might be natural for Catholics to live off inherited capital in theology, but it was not wise. It was Newman, not the Roman theologians of the day, who was aware of the fundamental questions which were coming up for answer in the modern world.

And it snowed, a rare occurrence in Rome. But apart from these failures in communication, Newman was happy, as he told Henry Wilberforce then, and repeated in his journal in 1863: 'the happy days, thank God, at Propaganda.' The happiness came from the knowledge that he was doing God's will and from the life that flowed from the sacraments into his prayer-filled days. For he did not go out into society but only to visit shrines or to see that Miss Giberne was keeping warm, and otherwise stayed at home, trying to settle the question of his vocation.

It was not easy, for it involved so many others besides himself. Dalgairns was drawn to the Dominicans, St John to the Jesuits.

Wiseman had already suggested the lesser known Congregation of the Oratory. Newman thought the Dominicans of the day inclined to rigorism: 'I shall be of a (so-called) lax school.' The revival of the order begun by Lacordaire in Paris had then only just started. As for the Jesuits, Newman told Jemima that they were like first-class Oxford men but, judging from those he met in Rome, he thought them 'suspicious of *change*, with a perfect incapacity to create anything *positive* for the wants of the times'.

By the middle of January he was writing to Dalgairns about their visit to the Roman Oratory, a splendid building by Borromini alongside the Chiesa Nuova, 'the new church' which St Philip Neri had built in the late sixteenth century. Newman thought the house beautiful, 'rather too comfortable', with its galleries, sets of rooms, orange trees and fine library. 'It is like a college with barely any rule. They keep their own property and furnish their own rooms.' But the more he heard about the Oratory the more he felt it was what they needed. It was not a religious order, since its members did not take vows; but they lived together according to a simple rule like a small republic, with a Father Superior, or Provost, elected every three years and assisted by a council of four Deputies, elected from among the Decennial Fathers – those who had been over ten years in the community. Keeping their own property gave the members a relative independence and enabled them to leave, if they wished. They worked independently too, each based on his own room, but lived together as a team or group of friends. Oratories were intended as centres in large towns, rather than as monasteries or parishes.

The original Oratory had been simply Philip Neri's way of organizing an evening's prayer, Bible study and meditation, for anyone who cared to come, and in the early days most of them were laymen, as Philip himself had been till he was forty. Born in Florence in 1515, he had come to Rome at eighteen and stayed till he died, at eighty. At first he spent nights praying in the catacombs, and days helping in the public hospitals; as a priest he was at one time suspected of heresy but lived to count many Cardinals among his disciples, who called his room 'the School of Christian Joy'. Philip was the most original of saints, a visionary and a clairvoyant, with a shrewd sense of humour and a great gift for communicating the Spirit of love.

'This great saint,' Newman told Jemima, 'reminds me in so many ways of Keble ... he was formed on the same type of extreme hatred of humbug, playfulness, nay, oddity, tender love for others, and severity, which are the lineaments of Keble.' The humour and hatred of humbug were Newman's lineaments too; he had more in common with his patron than might be supposed at first sight.

In January, in what is now kept as the week of prayer for Christian unity, between the feasts of St Peter's Chair and the Conversion of St Paul, Newman and St John made a novena of prayer at St Peter's tomb for light on their vocation and studied the Rule and history of the Congregation. The Rule was more like a list of customs in the Roman Oratory of the sixteenth century, and some were unsuitable for England in the nineteenth. Newman was allowed to revise the Rule for England, which he did principally by distinguishing decrees from customs. He saw great possibilities in this free form of association, especially suitable for modern cities and for men of different capabilities. Once the decision was made, he wrote at once to Wiseman, anxious for ground to be bought before the newspapers got wind of it, 'in a populous part of Birmingham in the midst of the mechanics'. As to the church he proposed to build, 'I'm afraid I shall shock Pugin.' He did shock Pugin, whom he met in Rome. Pugin cried out that he would as soon build a Mechanics' Institute as an Oratory. To Pugin the classic style was Pagan – and the war between the Goths and the Pagans was in full swing!

The Pope wanted them to make their novitiate together in Rome and so the others were hastily sent for, Newman in high spirits telling Dalgairns he wanted 'men with a good deal of fun in them ... I should like a good mimic to take off the great Exeter Hall guns. What stuff I am writing. If we have not spirit it will be like bottled beer with the cork out.' Exeter Hall was the London headquarters of the Protestant Evangelical Alliance and the scene of excited No

Popery meetings. Richard Stanton and William Penny, a new recruit, turned up in March; the others came later, even Bowles, though Newman rather wished he would not, because, nervy and unpredictable, he needed so much looking after.

In Rome for Holy Week, Newman and St John washed the feet of pilgrims on Good Friday – some years later Newman mentioned it as a task unpleasant in itself but with a romantic halo about it, unlike less spectacular services of charity. Then, after Easter, he made a retreat in preparation for ordination. His retreat notes, made in Latin, were even more self-critical than usual. He felt he was lacking in fervour, that he would like a comfortable life among books and friends rather than bind himself to a rule, that things he had done willingly as an Anglican, fasting and penance, now seemed a burden. Meditation made his head ache. 'I am always languid in the contemplation of divine things, like a man walking with his feet bound together.' He felt this to be an almost physical limitation of his personality, and certainly he was one whose feelings were deep and tenacious rather than strong and intense. Newman was emotionally exhausted by the long strain of the years of indecision and the calumny he had had to bear; he was no longer young and yet had to begin a new life and in unfamiliar surroundings.

But now the decision was made, courage returned. After the retreat came a holiday at Mount Cavo, with wild jonquils 'smelling most piercingly sweet'. The country was wonderful; he told Jemima that he liked 'an extensive view with tracts bold and barren in it, such as Beethoven' s music represents'. And he was reminded once more of Sicily and that earlier return to life.

On 26 May, St Philip Neri's day, Newman and St John were ordained subdeacons by Cardinal Fransoni in his private chapel; on the Saturday they were made deacons at St John Lateran, the cathedral church of the Bishop of Rome, and on Trinity Sunday, 1 June 1847, priests in the church at the Propaganda College. In a small chapel there Newman said his first mass on the following Thursday, Corpus Christi day. He wrote nothing on these events at the time, and for once no one else seems to have done so.

At the end of June they all moved out to Santa Croce to learn how to be Oratorians under Fr Rossi, a member of the Roman Oratory. In tracing the origins of his troubles as a Catholic Newman wrote in 1863: 'How dreary Fr Rossi and Santa Croce' – but did not say why. Rossi seems to have been excitable and opinionated and in 1859 Newman told Miss Bowles that 'at Rome Dalgairns and Coffin took part against me.' (Robert Coffin, erstwhile Vicar of St Mary Magdalene's, Oxford, had recently joined them.) This was a significant presage of things to come. After the month of novitiate they visited the Naples Oratory. Newman still thought the hills there 'lumpish' but was enchanted by the vines and figs and the 'splendour of the sun and its light,' as he told Jemima.

Back in Rome, while the younger members were going out to Frascati in pairs, to the Prop. Villa, as they called the college's summer retreat, Newman suddenly began writing a novel. It was conceived as an answer to a novel called *From Oxford to Rome* by a young lady who had actually taken a return ticket, and involved Frederick Oakeley, then the Tractarian Vicar of Margaret Chapel (All Saints, Margaret Street) in a shattering newspaper scandal. Miss Harris's brother wrote darkly that 'Mr Oakeley *was* an English gentleman before he was a Romish deacon.' Newman thought his own novel might help 'poor Burns' – the convert founder of the publishing firm of Burns and Oates. He called it *Loss and Gain*, a dull title for such an amusing book – it made Newman himself laugh while he was writing it. But as coming directly after *The Development of Christian Doctrine* it surprised some people. Earnest Puseyites, as Faber later informed Newman, were saying he had 'sunk below Dickens'. Newman put in no real persons except himself as 'Smith – he never speaks decidedly on difficult questions.'

At last he was free to leave Rome and made a typical dash for home, amused at St John's having to get his holy relics through the customs as a mummy, stopping only at shrines and to visit Wiseman's old mother and the German scholar Ignaz Döllinger, crossing from Ostend in fog and snow and arriving in London on Christmas Eve. 'So we began our English life with the Nativity,'

Newman wrote to Henry, 'saying mass first in England on that blessed day, as I had said it first in Rome on the feast of Corpus Christi. They are cognate feasts.' His last mass, too, would be said on Christmas Day.

8

BIRMINGHAM AND FABER

Newman reached Maryvale in time to say mass there on New Year's day, 1848. But before he left London, Wiseman, who had recently been transferred there from the Midland District, had told him that Father Faber and his community wished to join the Oratory.

Frederick Faber had been up at Balliol with W. G. Ward, and was known as a poet – Wordsworth thought well of his early verses. He was the youngest son in a family with many clerical connections; his father was secretary to the Bishop of Durham and his uncle, Stanley Faber, a well-known pamphleteering clergyman. Frederick, the favourite of his mother, lost her when he was at Harrow, and his father died just after he had gone up to Oxford in 1833. Born in 1814, Faber was thirteen years younger than Newman. As a young don he became a keen Anglo-Catholic and in 1843, as vicar of Elton in Huntingdonshire, a notorious Romanizer. He was one of those kept back by Newman's advice, who 'went over' in November 1845, taking with him a flock of lads from his country parish, whom he began to form into a religious community, romantically medieval in spirit. Faber, who made several trips to Rome during these years, was ordained priest by Wiseman on Holy Saturday, 1847, but even before that he had been Superior of his 'Brothers of the Will of God' and so much were they under his influence that shrewd Fr Dominic Barberi called them 'Brothers of the Will of Faber'.

Faber had begun a series of translations of Italian lives of saints, and had done one on St Philip Neri, for whom he conceived a great veneration, and when he heard of Newman's decision to form an Oratory in England he wrote to Rome in some agitation. 'Some say you craftily got ye Bishop to remove us from Birmingham that we might not stand in your way.' Faber's small decorative handwriting, with its deliberate archaisms (neither Newman nor Keble, much older men, used the old form 'ye'), was soon to become all too familiar. Since Faber had not been removed, but had moved himself to undertake the country mission near Alton Towers, Lord Shrewsbury's seat, where he was already Gothicizing the old Cotton College, rechristened St Wilfrid's after the patron whose name he had taken – Newman did not think their spheres would 'intersect' as Faber feared. But Faber talked a lot about 'Santo Padre, as we call St Philip', to show that St Philip, no less than St Wilfrid, really belonged to him.

Faber's decision to join Newman came to him as an inspiration before mass one morning early in December 1847, when he and his friend Fr Antony Hutchison, the only two priests among the Brothers, were preparing to take their vows in Wiseman's presence. He went out, as he told his friend Michael Watts Russell, a married convert clergyman who had once been his confessor, in a mood of 'calm broken-heartedness ... everything had ceased to be mine: the rising spire of our magnificent church, the young trees, all seemed buried in one thing, God.' The three young Cambridge converts who aspired to be priests did not care for the idea at all, but Faber soon won them round and rushed up to London to gain Wiseman's approval. Wiseman was enthusiastic and rashly assured Faber that St Wilfrid's could be kept as an Oratorian house.

So here was Newman, arriving to set up his Oratory, with five newly ordained priests (and Bowles and Francis Knox to come), faced with the prospect of seventeen Wilfridians who had been living several years under Faber's command and had just settled themselves in a place quite unsuited to an Oratory, which was intended to function in large towns. Newman envisaged Oratories in all the great towns as centres of religious education in the broad sense – Pugin had reason to compare them to Mechanics' Institutes. In writing to Faber Newman was anxious that he should understand '*what* Oratorianism is'. It was not like Faber's monastically conceived community, nor designed for lay brothers under strict authority; it was not particularly ascetic. 'It is not poetic – it is not very devotional … An Oratorian ought, like a Roman legionary, to stand in his place and fight by himself though in company – instead of being a mere instrument of another, or a member of a phalanx.'

But Faber would not listen. 'Consider us as giving ourselves over to you in ye spirit of surrender,' he replied. Yet in spite of much talk of 'blind obedience' he was groaning to Watts Russell at the prospect of losing everything and complaining that 'the Oratory has been a bloody husband to me because of the circumcision … I have had a house full of temptations and repugnance to govern for some weeks past, but by the grace of God and dear Mama's help I hope to steer my little crew into the port of San Filippo without a loss.' Dear Mama was Faber's name for the Mother of God.

Newman set up the Oratory in England at Maryvale on the feast of the Purification, 2 February 1848, Oriel Gaudy and now that of the English Oratory too. He admitted five fathers, one novice (Knox) and three lay brothers on the eve, and distributed the blessed candles at the mass on Candlemas day itself, a duty and honour he carried out for almost the rest of his life. Ten days later he went to St Wilfrid's to receive Faber and his Brothers.

Faber recovered his spirits at a bound, writing to Watts Russell, 'Father Superior has now left us, all in our Philippine habits with turndown collars, like so many good boys brought in after dinner.' (The Oratorians wear a long cassock with a sash, and a divided, not a Roman collar.) 'In the solemn admission on Monday morning,' Faber continued, 'he gave a most wonderful address, full of those marvellous pauses which you know of. He showed how wonderfully we had all been brought together from different parts, and how, in his case and ours, St Philip seemed to have laid hands on us and taken us for his own, whether we would or not. Since my admission I seem to have lost all attachment to everything but obedience; I could dance and sing all day, because I am so joyous.'

Even before he received the Wilfridians Newman discovered that he had been landed with more than the responsibility for Faber and seventeen young men. Beautiful as it was, St Wilfrid's could be no use to the Oratory and he proposed to put in a secular priest to run the village mission. But Lord Shrewsbury (though he had his own chaplain) was extremely annoyed; he had given his financial assistance on condition that the church was served by a religious community. Newman then discovered that the Wilfridians had spent all their money; even Hutchison, the rich man among them, had come to the end of his resources, having sunk a large sum in the new Gothic church. All Faber could suggest was that Hutchison's aunt would leave him her money, and as she was over ninety she could hardly last much longer. All through March Newman was trying to pacify the Earl and come to some arrangement which would satisfy all parties.

Meanwhile, he had been persuaded to deliver sermons at St Chad's cathedral, Pugin's Gothic gesture thrown down like a gauntlet in the midst of industrial Birmingham. Newman preached there eight times, nearly always walking the six miles from Maryvale and sometimes back as well, across a wild common which was then the haunt of thieves. On Sexagesima Sunday, 27 February, a youth of nineteen slipped into St Chad's to see the famous turncoat; he was Edward White Benson, future Archbishop of Canterbury, and he wrote to his friend Lightfoot: 'He was very much emaciated, and when he began his voice was very feeble and he spoke with great difficulty, nay sometimes he gasped for breath; but his voice was very sweet ... But oh, Lightfoot, never you turn Romanist if you are to have a face like that – it was awful – the terrible lines deeply ploughed all over his face, and the craft that sat upon his retreating forehead and sunken eyes ... to think of that timid looking, little, weak-voiced man having served old England as he has done.' Yet when Newman spoke the name of Christ, lifting his 'priest's cap' and bowing to the altar, Benson felt his heart yearn towards him.

Wiseman persuaded the Oratorians to undertake a mission in London at Passiontide; Newman took part himself but few people came and he felt it was a blunder. He hurried back for Easter Sunday at Maryvale and for the opening of the church at St Wilfrid's on the Monday. After Easter Faber was supposed to come for his novitiate but he had one of his attacks, writing a detailed account of his vomiting, diarrhoea and other miseries to Newman, all in his neat little handwriting. 'I thought I was going; it was ye anodyne, ye sufferings were very dreadful, besides being half drunk so that I could not pray and had horrid temptations to blaspheme Almighty God. I have had another night without sleep and have been screaming for several hours.' Recovering from this, he then had to stay longer because one of the young Brothers was dying. The day after his death, Faber had the bright idea, culled from his reading of hagiography, of swallowing three of the Brother's hairs in a glass of water. Whether or not this effected a miraculous cure, Faber was certainly well enough a week later to indulge in a tremendous row with Pugin and Phillipps, who were staying at the Towers.

Faber's battle with the two eminent Goths took place near 'Mama's statue' outside St Wilfrid's, as he told Newman, giving an account in vivid dialogue form. Phillipps asked why there was no screen in the new church; Faber replied that Newman did not wish it, and when Pugin asked what he would do with the sixteenth-century screens, Faber said, 'Burn 'em all.' Phillipps cried, 'Father Faber, God for your pride destroyed and brought to naught your first effort (stamp, fist to heaven). He will curse and destroy your order and it will perish if you go on thus.' Pugin was upset. 'Now come, my dear sir, come, hold your tongue, my gracious what a thing upon my life – really – well, I always thought I was ye only moderate man in ye world.' The Goths ended by dining with Faber, but Newman became involved in correspondence with Phillipps. His own view was that architecture ought to be contemporary: 'Gothic is like an old dress which fitted a man well twenty years back but must be altered to fit him now.' And for the Oratorians, founded at the end of the sixteenth century, 'to assume the architecture simply and unconditionally of the thirteenth would be as absurd as their putting on them the cowl of the Dominican or the tonsure of the Carthusian.' Phillipps was pacified but not convinced.

Time went on and still Faber did not come for his novitiate. He went up to Scarborough for a holiday but began preaching in crowded churches and holding 'Oratories' for ladies in drawing-rooms – even he realized that this had not been a custom of St Philip's. At last Newman said he must come by Corpus Christi – and finally he arrived. The novitiate he had so much dreaded lasted only a month and Newman made him novice-master. It was a great mistake. Among such a large collection of young men, some Faber's own village boys, others university converts, there were bound to be grumbles, but Faber, instead of dealing with these himself, repeated them all to Newman, often exaggerating them, and indeed began to use the supposed dissatisfactions of the novices to make known his own. Newman did not realize this till much later; at the time, continual complaints that he was 'cold' depressed him. He felt he had lost his touch with young men. But they, or Faber for them, wanted an emotional relationship with him, rather as Miss Holmes had done, casting him in the role of father and yearning, now for affection and now for dominance.

This situation became worse when Newman, finding it impossible to run two country houses, and unable to give up St Wilfrid's, decided to transfer the whole community there for the present; it was done by October. Meanwhile they would take sites in Birmingham and in London for two Oratories. He had already found one in the back-streets of Birmingham; it was a gin distillery. But the London site in Bayswater, then right at the edge of the town, fell through, and so Faber and the novices had nothing to do except worry Newman and blame him for everything they did not like. And now that Faber was back on his own ground he threw himself into his old mission, easily managing Hutchison, who was officially in charge of the little parish. Before Newman moved to Birmingham he made a private memorandum, dated 14 January 1849, in which he noted how Faber had gradually forced them to give up the specific Oratorian exercise of daily prayer together because it interfered with his mission services; the Sunday Vespers, in particular, suffered. 'At this moment the mission is supreme in the Church and the Oratory is nothing.' Newman's conclusion was that he must make the Birmingham experiment primarily an Oratory, and found a house in London from there.

Newman arrived at Alcester Street on Friday, 26 January 1849 and on Sunday described his removal to Coffin, whom he had left in charge at St Wilfrid's as rector, giving a list of the books gallipots, violins, crucifixes and 'rattletraps loose' with which his fly was loaded. The gin distillery contained a hall a hundred feet long, full of vats when he had first seen it, which was made into a chapel, and the room over it was to be the library. It was in Deritend, then on the outskirts of the growing town, among the small press factories where the cheap Birmingham ware was turned out. So far as it was religious, the town was more Nonconformist than anything, and Newman's arrival was watched by many hostile eyes.

The chapel was opened on 2 February, the first anniversary of the Oratory in England; it was a Friday, and all was quiet. But on Sunday evening they expected trouble and sent for two policemen. Five or six hundred people crammed in, but there was no disturbance. Newman's simple sermon held them.

The next week they started talks in the evenings and were astonished when forty children turned up to the first. 'Boys and girls flow in for instruction as herrings in season,' Newman told a convert friend, John Moore Capes, who had bought the *Rambler* Magazine and kept him in touch with London news. He did not expect the flood to last, but it did. They had hoped to start a school for the children but there was no chance of it, for all from the age of seven went out to work from early morning till seven or eight in the evening. 'The poor factory boys seem to have no prejudice against us,' Newman told Miss Giberne, ' many of them literally profess no religion and numbers of them have not been baptized.' Girls came too and their new religion did not make life easier as they grew up. 'It is a dreadful trial for the poor girls – they don't get places, they don't get married.' But out of these unwanted waifs of industrialism Newman and his colleagues built up a sturdy Catholic community which took root and endured.

It was exhausting work, but simple and rewarding. But at the same time Newman was trying to solve the problem of the Oratory's future, which he was forced to grapple with immediately, for scarcely had he arrived in Birmingham when Faber let loose a flood of complaints. First it was the novices, set on complaining of his 'coldness' – Newman had to write to them all by turns to assure them of his personal interest and affection; then Faber suddenly complained of his 'particular friendship' with Ambrose St John, who was supposed to influence him. Newman disliked the jargon phrase and wrote some sensible remarks on friendship, recognizing that nobody can feel the same about everyone, but the Christian's duty is to be as friendly as possible to all; he denied that he was influenced by Ambrose and was goaded to remark on Faber's influence over Antony Hutchison. That seemed quite different to Faber, since *he* was doing the influencing, not Hutchison. He quickly wriggled out of that question into another – who was to go to London?

Newman, always a believer in natural growth, wished to leave the final sorting to time but Faber insisted that people wanted their future settled at once and then proceeded to complicate it by vowing that he himself would never leave Newman. Although this ensured his being in a secondary position and so seemed 'humble', it was more of a nuisance than a help, because Faber also felt that Newman (and therefore he too) should be in London. He imagined Newman in a book-lined room upstairs, receiving educated converts, while he carried out his popular missions in the church. Newman, however, was convinced that if he did not stay in Birmingham, nobody would; and he would be able to combine pastoral work and writing there as he could not in London; moreover, the papal brief had fixed him there, before Wiseman had been moved to London, and he did not want to desert the bishop who had taken Wiseman's place, a sturdy little Yorkshireman, William Bernard Ullathorne, who had started life as a cabin boy and was very suspicious of the Oxford intellectuals, but needed their assistance.

After a gruelling day-to-day exchange Faber was at last persuaded that he 'ought to throw in his lot with the London group, even though Newman remained in Birmingham. Then there was another upset when Faber realized that not he but Coffin was to be appointed rector in London. Letters about Coffin's deficiencies were posted off to Birmingham one after the other – how he antagonized everyone, how difficult he was: 'He is childish; power is a pleasure to him and he cannot conceal it.' Faber was also horrified at the suggestion that Robert Whitty, a clever Irishman whom Newman had met at St Edmund's College, Ware, should go with them; 'he must be under you,' said Faber, 'for he respects nobody else.'

'Precious cadavera!' cried Newman, taking up Faber's repeated wish to be a corpse in his hands. 'And you lecture me and say, "My dear F. Superior, do take us at our word – you can make minced meat of us – you can turn us into Bolognas and Germans – don't be consulting for us – speak, speak out what you think and all difficulty is at an end."' Even Faber had to eat humble pie then, as he admitted. But unable to move Newman about Coffin, he took to his bed with spasms.

Faber's collapses sound like migraine, for attacks, with acute sickness, can be brought on by stress and excitement, unfortunately he was so excitable as to be almost unbalanced, and certainly had very little self-control, so that he was always making his condition worse. He became more erratic, not less, as he grew older, but he must have had considerable charm, for he attracted many, not only to the faith but to himself. His latest friend was Lord Arundel, heir to the Duke of Norfolk, and it was he who solved Faber's present problem by pressing him to come to London and offering him every assistance. By this time Newman had succeeded in getting his precious 'cadavera' to give their real wishes, and had divided the Oratory into two teams, giving three of his own best men to London: Coffin, Stanton and Dalgairns. He now told Faber he might take Hutchison and Dalgairns and go prospecting in London; Coffin was to remain temporarily at St Wilfrid's and Whitty was to join the Birmingham team. Newman in fact kept all those nobody else wanted: eccentric Penny, unpredictable Bowles, and another Irishman, John Stanislas Flanagan, who, Faber scornfully said, might make a good vulgar preacher. But he also kept Ambrose St John, who, though he annoyed some by his brusque manner, was at least reliable.

Dalgairns went off uneasily and was soon asking the reason for Newman's recent 'coldness'. For answer, Newman wrote him a very careful and searching account of his conduct, from which it was clear that he had allowed his own group of convert factory lads to make themselves a nuisance to everyone else, and had laughed at other people's efforts; his great fault 'put harshly' was 'contempt of others'. Newman blamed himself for not being the guide he should have been; 'I have not the self-confidence and self-possession necessary for exciting confidence in others; I am old; and you have fits of reliance on me and fits of mistrust and suspicion.' Alas, this pattern was to repeat itself. He ended, 'Just write a word to me to say you do not think me unkind ... ' Dalgairns had lived seven years in Newman's company, the time of *contubernium* shared with Froude and Rogers, and Newman felt his departure, even though he had never been an equal, like Froude.

The Oratory was offered another gin shop in London, not a distillery, like Newman's, but a place of entertainment in King William Street, Strand. It was central, and they took it. Faber was now in his element and managed to move in, with hardly any furniture and a great shortage of cutlery, by 28 April, less than a fortnight after leaving Birmingham. John and Charlie Bowden were now youthful novices and Faber wrote that Mrs Bowden 'flits about ye house, visits me in my bedroom, inundates us with floods of devout Irish charwomen, groans over ye dirt and is a positive mother and St Elizabeth of our Chiesa Nuova.'

In spite of spasms brought on by battles with builders, Protestants, 'old' Catholics, and, at a distance, with Bishop Ullathorne over St Wilfrid's, Faber was determined to open the new Oratory in June and to do it in style – inviting everyone to come and hear Newman preach, a prospect which so alarmed Newman that *he* was driven to talk of being given a headache by the railroad, an excuse he otherwise never made in his travelling days. Faber had before now pleaded 'ye horrid motion of a railway' to avoid an uncongenial task.

The newspapers were already jeering: 'Here is Mr Newman just clothed in St Philip's mantle and coming over from the Pope to convert the English. Only let him rise "several yards high in the air" in Lincoln's Inn Fields and remain there a proper time "his countenance shining with a bright light" – and we will promise him a large harvest of converts'. They had been reading Faber's Italian life of St Philip, which made much of his levitation (fairly well authenticated, though for a matter of inches, not yards). Newman was to preach in the evening and he wrote to St John, 'It is now close upon 5 and the carriages are setting down their burdens. Birmingham is a place of peace. O that I had wings like a dove – for I do dislike this preaching so much. Some Frenchman gave his feelings up (to) the last moment under the influence of charcoal – I am giving mine till F. Richard (Stanton) calls me.' In fact, it went off well. 'Prospects of a Catholic Missioner' was printed in his volume *Discourses to Mixed Congregations*, published at the end of that year, 1849. Newman's main line, as always, was the battle of the spirit of Christ against the selfish world.

He went straight back to Birmingham, leaving the London Oratory playing to crowded houses and Faber converting high society, including Lord Arundel's wife. In Birmingham they formed a choir out of the factory girls who sang Compline in English, making the best of such Catholic translations as 'the business which walketh in darkness'. Newman gave what he called 'a flash lecture on Poetry' in St Chad's school hall, which was applauded and reported in the local papers. Miss Giberne had heard that Newman had been denounced as an idolater by two ladies. 'Not two *ladies*,' said Newman, '(for *entre nous* we have not yet found a lady in Birmingham) but two well-meaning Methodists came in … and horror-struck at seeing the real thing, which they thought we only kept in our pockets and dared not produce, viz., an image of our Lady, they certainly did ask me, in a fit of enthusiasm, what I could mean by such idolatry or the like.' Had they known it, Newman had a particular dislike of this statue. Miss Giberne had wondered at St Philip's dancing before his pious admirers and Newman thought it was done out of 'his intense dislike of hollow pompous pretence'. And he added, mischievously, 'What a thing it would be to extirpate donnishness in England!'

He was generally in good spirits all through this period of hard work in the backstreets of Birmingham, in spite of bugs in the confessionals, smells in the passages, tensions within the community and his own poverty, which led him once to cry, in this year of the Gold Rush, 'O for a private California!' The greatest problem on his hands was the property and mission at St Wilfrid's, and many were the letters which passed to and fro about it. Now that he was evangelizing in London Faber had lost interest in St Wilfrid's, and all Newman's efforts to keep it going as a holiday home for both Oratories, or as a school, fell through. Yet he could not simply give up the charge, for Bishop Ullathorne was touchy about every suggestion he made. Faber's *Lives of the Saints* had got into trouble with some of the 'old' Catholics, and Newman, defending Faber, got on the wrong side of Ullathorne at the start of their relationship. Meanwhile Faber had not got over his aversion to Coffin; he did not want Coffin stepping in above him in London. Coffin had to be left at St Wilfrid's, where he became more and more disillusioned with the Oratory.

1849 was a cholera year and though Birmingham remained free of it, at near-by Bilston the situation was so bad that Ullathorne asked Newman to send someone to assist the priest there. Newman at once set off himself, with St John, leaving everyone in the parish 'crying out as if we were going to be killed', he told John Bowden afterwards, feeling that in this they excelled the London house. 'A parish is an onus, but it creates a *local mass* of affection.' The cholera was abating when he reached Bilston and he did not have to stay long, going on for a brief holiday at St Wilfrid's. While there, enjoying the beauty of the countryside, he heard from a convert clergymen friend, Edward Caswall, whose wife had been carried off by the plague in fourteen hours of acute illness. Caswall had been at Oxford in the thirties, he had read *Development* four times, called on Newman at Propaganda and was received in Rome by Cardinal Acton. He had no children, and within a few months he was to join the Birmingham Oratory and remained one of its chief supports till his death, nearly thirty years later. A gentle, stammering man, his name still appears in hymn-books, for he wrote and translated hymns which have long retained their appeal.

The same visitation of the cholera had a profound effect on Henry Wilberforce and his wife in Kent, where it struck the London hop-pickers on holiday work in his parish. So many were Catholics that he sent to the London Oratory for help. Newman was half expecting Henry to ask him to come and receive him into the Church but Henry was not yet ready to make the move, and Newman went back to Alcester Street, where he was rapturously received, and the chapel was so crowded that, as he told Miss Giberne, 'we give Benediction right into the street, people kneeling on the opposite pavement.'

Their popularity with their parishioners did not altogether please Bishop Ullathorne, who had heard a report, as Newman wrote with amusement to Faber, 'that we were so familiar with our female peni-tents that they said they could marry us next morning – and that I was so reserved and had such notions about the line of delicacy, that he did not know how to come here and judge for himself'. At this period Ullathorne, unable to believe that the converts were a real religious community, never called Newman 'Father'. Newman said cheerfully, 'I suppose he speaks of Mr Dominic.' Fr Dominic Barberi, so good a friend to them, died suddenly at the end of August, struck down on a railway journey, at Reading station. Newman was sure he was a saint and later gave testimony for his process of canonization, completed only recently: he is now St Dominic Barberi.

Christmas 1849 was the first in Birmingham. Not having crib figures they used a picture copied by Miss Giberne, 'beflowered and belighted', as he told her. Newman was playing the organ himself, as they could not afford to pay an organist. The violin lay unused; there was no time for Beethoven. Newman was personally so poor that he had not been able to buy himself new shoes or stockings for a year. Because of this, he owned he was quite interested that his sermons should 'sell' as well as 'tell'. Dalgairns thought them too stern. Newman wondered why, in that case, his Anglican sermons, which were not less so, 'were so liked by a lot of women'? His sternness was a matter of pointing out to self-satisfied Christians that they were 'in danger of hell' – in danger of being found lacking in that love without which, as St Paul insisted to the Corinthians, we are lost, however virtuous we think we are.

Certainly the women in Birmingham, whatever they thought of the sermons, thought the preacher a saint. A pious lady passed on this information to him: Newman did not, like St Philip, do a dance to destroy the image, but his reply is very like one. 'I have no tendency to be a saint – it is a sad thing to say so. Saints are not literary men, they do not love the classics, they do not write Tales. I may be well enough in my way, but it is not "the high line". People ought to feel this, most people do. But those who are at a distance have fee-fa-fum notions about me. It is enough for me to black the saints' shoes – if St Philip uses blacking, in heaven.'

9

TRIAL BY FURY

In May 1850 Newman delivered a course of lectures in London which he published under the title *Certain Difficulties felt by Anglicans in Catholic Teaching*. It was Wiseman who persuaded him; he was extremely reluctant, not wishing to offend old friends or to stir up useless recrimination. In the end he addressed them specifically 'to the Party of the Religious Movement of 1833', with the intention of showing that the Catholic principles of the revival found their natural place in the Roman communion. In the first seven lectures he traced the origin and development of the Movement, showing how far removed were its ideas from those which actually animated the Church of England as a living institution; in the last five he defended the Sanctity, Unity, Catholicity and Apostolicity of the Roman Catholic Church against the dissuasives urged by Anglicans. He took care not to sneer at the religion of individuals and wherever he could he inserted a tribute, to some Caroline divine or to his old bishop, Bagot; but he allowed himself to make fun at the expense of the Protestant Establishment, which the Anglo-Catholics had been doing ever since Froude was alive and kicking.

The lectures were given in the lower chapel at King William Street, so that Newman was saved 'from being satirical etc. before the Blessed Sacrament' – which was reserved in the chapel upstairs. He sat at a reading desk on a platform before a crowded audience in this, the former assembly and whisky room of the gin palace. Wiseman was present, and rocked in his episcopal chair at the picture Newman drew of the helpless Tractarian, tied to his apostolic post while the bishops executed a war dance round him. Among the listening crowd was Doyle, the *Punch* artist, the novelist

129

Thackeray and a journalist who was shocked at the 'unseemly mirth' displayed – 'the Fathers of the Oratory were heard to titter, the Romish ladies to giggle, while a scarcely suppressed laughter arose from the *heretical* Protestants.' He thought Newman's appearance the embodiment of Romanizing guile and suspected he *put on* his simple and untheatrical manner. R. H. Hutton, afterwards editor of the Spectator, thought otherwise: 'Never did a voice seem better adapted to persuade without irritating.'

Miss Giberne, back from Rome, made a picture of Newman at these lectures, thin and beaky, with his hair still thick and dark. Some Tractarians were influenced to make the final move. Henry Wilberforce attended once, but he and his brothers were so well known as to attract notice; his wife was received in June but he himself not till the autumn, and in Brussels. Sam Wilberforce, now the Bishop of Oxford, had seen Newman that March at the funeral of George Ryder's wife Sophia, the third of the beautiful Sargent sisters to die young. Manning had lost his Caroline in 1837, Sam his Emily in 1841; now Henry's Mary was the only survivor. Sam wrote to his brother Robert, the theologian of the family, that Newman was there, 'But I thought it best not to see him; I heard that unmistakable voice, like a volcano's roar tamed to the softness of a flute-stop, and got a glimpse (may I say it to you?) of a serpentine form through an open door "the Father Superior".'

George Ryder wrote often to Newman for comfort and advice and was soon to send his two eldest sons, Lisle and Harry, for tuition at the Oratory.

It was during this summer that Newman at last succeeded in handing over St Wilfrid's to the diocese. At about the same time he lost Coffin to the Redemptorists; Fr Lans, staying at St Wilfrid's, persuaded him that he would never get real spiritual discipline in the Oratory. Before he left, Coffin accused Newman of diplomacy, a charge which puzzled him. 'I suppose the word means either having some secret end, or using some underhand means,' he wrote to Faber, repudiating any such design. 'But I am quite conscious *always* of not liking to tell people how keenly I feel things, both from tenderness to them, and again from the consciousness that, when once I begin, I am apt to let out and blow them out of the water.' People are apt to think that there are only two reasons for self-control: either there are no emotions to control or they are controlled in order to manipulate others. So some thought Newman cold and others calculating. Coffin stayed with the Redemptorists and later became Provincial in England. Newman said that St Philip no doubt meant this unhappy defection to teach them 'greater personal exactness and devotedness to God'. Indeed, the times themselves impressed on them 'the necessity of being men, of pruning luxuriances, lest we get thin and shabby about the roots'.

For the times had suddenly become dangerous; a storm had been let loose by the restoration of the Roman Catholic hierarchy in England, which the newspapers called the Papal Aggression. Fury was roused when Wiseman sent a pastoral letter from Rome as he was returning to take his place as Cardinal Archbishop of Westminster. 'From out the Flaminian Gate,' he dated it, and triumphantly announced that 'Catholic England had been restored to its orbit in the ecclesiastical firmament.' Naturally *The Times* resented such language as a personal insult to Queen Victoria and a Protestant nation. Lord John Russell, the Prime Minister, added fuel to the fire by writing a public letter, printed just in time for Guy Fawkes day, indignant against this 'pretension of supremacy over the realm of England'.

The mob burst into No Popery rioting, burning effigies of the Pope and Cardinal (in red hat) all over the country, and what was worse, breaking windows in chapels and convents and pelting any Romish priests they could find with dirt and stones. Big meetings, with hysterical orators, went on all through the winter. *Punch* became so violently anti-papist that Doyle left its staff. In the cartoons Newman appeared almost as frequently as Wiseman – the cadaverous monk and the fat hypocritical Cardinal. Poor Wiseman, a keen *Punch* fan, was very upset. As soon as he came back he published 'An Appeal to the English People', which was printed in all the leading newspapers, making it clear that he was claiming no sort of temporal power, but only the spiritual care of the Catholics in London, mostly the very poor. This had a pacifying effect but the popular agitation continued for a long time, the Puseyites often getting the worst of it, as traitors within the gates. The English people, who had welcomed the fugitive nuns and priests from the French Revolution, a generation earlier, with such kindness, now lapped up all the scandal they could get and enjoyed an orgy of moral indignation.

The London Oratorians were in the thick of it. At that time they were wearing the Oratorian distinctive cassock in the street, and Faber told a friend that 'even *gentlemen* shout from their carriage windows at us.' Placards appeared everywhere; Faber's favourite was one in Leicester Square which read: 'No Popery! Down with the Oratorians! No religion at all!' On Guy Fawkes day there were threats of burning down the house, but in the end it was only effigies that were burned. 'Crackers were thrown on ye roof of ye chapel, and ye like,' Faber told Newman. 'We gave our policemen supper.'

Birmingham too was not without its excitements. At the height of the public fury Fr John Cooke, a young priest who had joined Newman, and had been ill a long time with consumption, suddenly died, and a mob surrounded the Oratory shouting that he had been murdered. Police had to be sent for, but Newman calmly proceeded with the prayers for the dead, and no harm was done. The grand protest meeting in the Town Hall was a flop, owing to the firm stand taken by the Quaker Joseph Sturge and other Nonconformist leaders, and suddenly 'Hurrah for the Catholics!' was heard in the streets. Newman himself continued to be a target for rumour. 'The report grows stronger and stronger here that I am married,' he wrote to Faber, 'and have shut up my wife in a convent.'

About this time both houses decided to introduce the exercise of the discipline, as practised in St Philip's day, when on three evenings a week, after their half-hour of prayer together, the members practised this form of penance, more or less in the dark. Faber wrote a graphic account of the first attempt in London, making it sound like a comic turn: 'The sound was horrid, like hailstones on flesh.' But with his usual rash enthusiasm he wanted to introduce the exercise among the lay associates, the Brothers of the Little Oratory. Newman wrote, 'Are you not afraid of this getting into *Punch*, with a picture of Father Faber in the act?' But next April, 1851, Faber was able to retort triumphantly, 'You prophesied *we Londoners* should be there *cum disciplina* instead of which it is *you*.' A recognizable long-nosed Newman drooped, whip in hand, in a corner of *Punch*. Yet though the Birmingham house also undertook the exercise, Newman wrote about mortifications to George Ryder: 'I will tell you what is the greatest viz. to do well the duties of the day.' In this he was following St Philip, who always maintained that mortification of the *razionale* was what mattered most – the submission of our own opinions to the will of God. Physical discipline should be a means to mental discipline.

It was inexplicable to Englishmen that conversions still continued. In April 1851 Newman was summoned to Leeds to receive nearly all the clergy of Pusey's church of St Saviour's, built as a memorial to his wife and daughter Lucy, who had died young when Newman was at Littlemore – 'she was a saint' he said. Newman hoped that these clergy, who had lived and worked together as a group, might form another Oratory, perhaps in Leeds itself, but in the end they separated. Only one joined Newman, William Paine Neville, a nervous, anxious young man who was to remain with him for the rest of his life, acting as his secretary and infirmarian in his old age.

This year Newman delivered another series of lectures, in the Birmingham Corn Exchange, on *The Present Position of Catholics in England* – some of the most amusing and lively pieces he ever wrote. Ladies were not admitted and Miss Giberne, prowling outside, heard the laughter from within with frustration. Among the audience was Henry Edward Manning, who had submitted to Rome at Easter, drawn in at last after the inconsistencies of the Gorham case, when the courts supported a clergyman who did not believe in baptismal regeneration against his orthodox bishop.

Newman used ridicule to shame Protestants out of their more absurd prejudices, but when he learned that the Evangelical Alliance had sent an ex-priest, Giacomo Achilli, to speak in Birmingham, he used a later lecture to attack him, revealing that he had not fled from the Inquisition to escape persecution for conscience sake, as he maintained, but the penalties for sexual misdemeanours. Newman, basing himself on an article in Wiseman's *Dublin Review*, referred to Achilli's seductions of young girls in no uncertain terms and asked if such a proven liar should be believed when he spoke scandal of other priests.

There were soon rumours of a prosecution for libel, but Newman's friends, even the lawyers, did not think Achilli would act, since in bringing a criminal information he would have to swear on oath to the falsity of each charge. But as he was making a good thing out of his tirades against Rome, Achilli allowed his respectable but fanatical backers to push him into action. On 27 October 1851 he urged a criminal information of libel against the publishers and Newman's name was substituted on 5 November – a suitable date. Legally, Newman knew he would have a hard battle, since he would have to prove the truth of each charge, but after taking advice from many, including the Cardinal, it was decided that to give in now would be a scandal to the Church. The problem of expenses was solved by opening a defence fund, to which Wiseman contributed £100. But he still did not expect things to come to a trial and did not produce for Newman the documents on which the article in the *Dublin* had been based.

Newman was 'called up to town by Electric Telegraph' to appear in court on 21 November, as St John informed Joseph Gordon, one of the Birmingham Oratorians who had already been sent off to Italy to collect evidence. The same day Newman was reporting to St John, 'The Judges are clean against – will grant nothing – determined to bring on a trial and have witnesses in the box instead of affidavits – the people present humming assent ... Badeley last night thought I should have a year in prison.' Badeley was a Tractarian lawyer who was to become a Catholic in the course of the case. His forecast was no idle scare; a lord had recently been sent to gaol for libel – it could happen much more easily to a Romish priest.

Newman could still have submitted before the Rule was made absolute, but on learning that he could only do so by retractations, he decided to fight it out. He was writing round for evidence, and also for prayers, especially to Mother Margaret Hallahan, whose community was about to move from Clifton to Stone, following Ullathorne from the Western to the Midland District. The tough little Yorkshireman had been a great ally to the ex-servant girl Margaret Hallahan, and it was she who eventually got him to trust Newman, for whom she already had a great and affectionate admiration. Her nuns were Third Order Dominicans and several convert friends of Newman's had joined her; Sister Imelda Poole carried on most of the correspondence and to her Newman confessed his presentiment that the case would go on, and go hard for him – 'anyhow it is no harm to offer myself in expectation and in will, a sacrifice to Him who bore the judgement seat and the prison of the unbeliever ... He has let me be bound as in a net ... nothing but prayer can break the bond.'

To Capes he used a still more vivid image: 'If the devil raised a physical whirlwind, rolled me up in sand, whirled me round and then transported me some thousands of miles, it would not be more strange, though it would be more imposing a visitation. I have been kept in ignorance and suspense, incomprehensibly every now and then a burst of malignant light showing some new and unexpected prospect.' He had written to Talbot, a convert who had become a Papal Chamberlain, for papers from the Inquisition on 27 October; nothing had come a month later, not even a letter to say they were coming. Newman told Ward that one of the sources of his trouble was 'the Cardinal, who *did not look* for his documents till the hour when the Rule was made absolute and it was too late. In that hour he looked and he found. Fr Hutchison brought them to me. I took up my hat and went to Lewin. He had just returned from Westminster. It was all over.'

The Rule was made absolute at the end of November and the trial was fixed for February, the earliest possible date. There began a frantic chase after witnesses. Miss Giberne was requisitioned. At this time she was living with some other 'nunnish ladies' as Newman called them, helping in the parish; a year later she wrote an account of her adventures. She had been to confession in the guest room and afterwards 'the Father, leaning against the mantelpiece, said to me "I think you can be very useful to us in this affair."' He wanted her to go to Italy and escort back some of the women witnesses. 'I am ready at your service,' said the intrepid Miss Giberne, and off she went, a single lady of fifty, in the middle of winter, carrying one bag. She had a terrible journey, with the steam boiler on the boat blowing up and killing several people; she continued on her way by another boat – the captain thought she must be a relative of Napoleon's, she looked so like him!

At this critical moment in Newman's affairs there was a serious crisis in the London Oratory, which had recently been given its autonomy, though still bound to consult Newman on important matters. Faber had been elected its head and was now set on leaving King William Street for Brompton, then a village at the end of a miry road, even further out of town than Bayswater. After a bad spell of headaches and illness he was sent abroad in October by his doctors, for six months' rest. As soon as they were relieved of his presence the senior members of his community began writing to Newman with complaints, and wanted to depose him. Dalgairns, who was rector in his absence, voiced this request.

'Everything will go wrong, even as a matter of human calculation, if you depose F. Wilfrid,' Newman wrote, pointing out that like all Oratorian Provosts, he was only elected for three years. 'You must not droop,' he told Dalgairns, whom he knew so well. 'You tend to make matters worse than they are.' This was too bracing for Dalgairns; after Christmas he poured out his complaints of Faber. 'He brooks no opposition. If there be any he goes from room to room, painting the opponent's conduct in the most extravagant colours ... He governs the house by sarcasms.' Dalgairns was in the mood to exaggerate but Faber certainly had behaved like this at St Wilfrid's. He did not show sarcasm to Newman, but his letters to Hutchison often reveal it. Dalgairns went on to criticize the other members of the house, which induced Newman to defend them and to encourage Dalgairns to persevere. 'All acclimation is painful,' he reminded him; all who joined religious orders had to go through it – so did women who married. But even if Dalgairns might have pulled himself together in Faber's absence, his sudden return from abroad, months before his rest cure was finished, struck panic into his deputies. 'He will go wild unless you come and help us.'

Newman wrote to Faber that he should obey his doctor's orders, provoking a wail of despair; Faber had arrived on a wave of high spirits and did not want to be sent off again. 'I can't get well while I am unhappy – I am unhappy abroad.' Newman, thinking that London would bring on 'excitement of the brain', arranged for him to spend his leave near by, in a house at Hither Green, where he had a fat housekeeper to look after him and clandestine visits from his friends. 'I am well, quite well, but they won't believe me,' he told Lady Arundel cheerfully, little knowing what his colleagues had been saying in his absence. To Stanton he retailed gossip about the Roman Oratory and remarked in passing, 'The Padre (Newman) has lost a front tooth and is looking old. He has clearly suffered greatly about ye trial and he is like a regular quaint old saint about it now.' But Faber's high spirits had completed Dalgairns's collapse and *he* had to go and rest, not at Hither Green, needless to say, but in Norwood. London Oratorians were dotted about, recovering from each other.

All this happened in January 1852; at the end of that month, Achilli's supporters, hearing that witnesses were on their way, changed their tactics from hurry to delay, well knowing that it would be difficult to keep poor Italians in England without bribery. So when the Defendant's Pleas were lodged, they put in a Demurrer. The Pleas were amended but the trial was postponed. 'Cowardly curs as they are,' Newman wrote to Stanton, – who fly at one's heels, and then scour away as one looks round … '

Miss Giberne was in Paris with her witnesses, one woman with her husband Vincenzo, and another with grandmother and baby — this was the girl seduced at fifteen, and in a sacristy. Miss Giberne bathed the baby and joked about bugs and fleas, but how was Vincenzo to be entertained? Newman replied, 'Is there no equestrial exhibition? no harmless play? no giant or dwarf? no panorama, cosmorama, diorama, dissolving views, steam incubation of chickens, or *menagerie* (the jardin des plantes !) which he would like to see? Surely beasts are just the thing for him.' He sent Ambrose over to assist her and bring them all to England, where they had to be kept secretly.

This Lent Newman effected the transfer from Alcester Street to the new house in the suburb of Edgbaston which he had been building; a large part of the money came from Edward Caswall. During the No Popery scare it was said in the papers that dungeons were being built and Newman shocked as many people as he amused when he wrote to declare that they were beer cellars. The mission at Alcester Street had to be run as well and it was there that the saintly Brother Aloysius died in March, and Lady Olivia Acheson, one of the 'nunnish ladies', within a few days of each other. Newman watched by both of these death-beds; he was still taking his turn with all the other pastoral duties, and he was trying to write the series of lectures which were to become one of his most famous books: *The Idea of a University*. When he heard that the trial, fixed for May, had been postponed again, he crossed over to Dublin to deliver the first, on 10 May 1852, in the Rotunda.

Newman had been persuaded by Wiseman to undertake this project, which at first was envisaged as a university for all English-speaking Catholics. He had little idea of the difficulties he would encounter, not from Protestants but from other Catholics. The lectures were a great success, though he was so nervous beforehand that he was reminded of his examination for the Fellowship at Oriel. He came back to Birmingham for St Philip's day and then returned to Dublin, but he had to leave without completing the course when he heard that his trial was fixed for 21 June. Badeley had now decided to become a Catholic. 'I take it as an omen of success,' said Newman.

He was unlikely to be called into court but he had to be at hand, so he spent most of the time in the chapel at King William Street, praying before the Blessed Sacrament, in the tribune, where he could not be seen. The case was tried before Lord Chief Justice Campbell, who showed his anti-papist bias throughout; and the jury was 'a set of pothouse fellows' as Newman had surmised. But the witnesses and their stories created a bad impression against Achilli, which he hardly improved when he appeared; he denied everything, but looked capable of anything. Yet, after such a summing up as Campbell gave, the lawyers at least were not surprised when the verdict went against Newman. Only one of his charges was regarded as proved – that Achilli had been deprived of his lectureship! Vigorous cheers greeted this decision.

Newman had expected it all along and refused to feel 'floored'. He wrote cheerfully to his friends, encouraging the downcast. There was now another wait for judgment, but meanwhile life went on, and it was in this July that, at the first Synod of the reconstituted Catholic hierarchy in England, held at Oscott, he preached his famous sermon on *The Second Spring* – 'The world grows old but the Church is ever young.' The Church was rising again, but people must not be surprised if the spring was a cold English one. He went home to receive the news of his sister Harriett's sudden death; he had seen and heard little of her since 1843, but it was a shock. A few weeks later poor old Aunt died, taking his mind back to his earliest childhood, in memories of her kindness and affection.

Newman was already tired when he went over to Ireland to find himself the reluctant hero of many celebrations, and these nearly caused him to break down completely, but a week quite alone in a friend's country house restored him sufficiently to face renewed harassment on his return to England. His lawyers wanted medical affidavits to lessen the chance of imprisonment, and the doctors he saw predicted an early death if he continued to live at the present pressure. But what upset him far more was his lawyers' wish to ask for a retrial. Newman felt anything, even prison, was better than more suspense, but at the last minute he agreed, persuaded by his old friend, Serjeant Bellasis. It was 22 November, St Cecilia's day (an Oratorian feast) and quite a crowd was in court to see Newman sentenced. Instead, they heard the request for a new trial, which caused quite a sensation.

In the interval before the decision Newman was persuaded to take a holiday at Abbotsford, with his Oxford friend James Hope, who had taken the name of Scott when he married Charlotte Lockhart, Sir Walter Scott's granddaughter and heir. Although he had gone down with influenza after St Cecilia's day, it took two bishops and the Cardinal to get him to agree to the holiday. He wrote an amusing account of his train journey to Scotland and of the dark corridors and smoking fires of Abbotsford, but he was fond of its inhabitants and they loved having him. Unfortunately the end of the visit was spoiled by having to deal at a distance with a crisis in the Birmingham Oratory – Brother Bernard Henin had been trying to kiss Mrs Wootten, one of the 'nunnish ladies' and the widow of Newman's Oxford doctor. From the way the episode was told Newman at first thought somebody had been raped; there was a misunderstanding as to how to deal with the young man and he was sent away before Newman got home; the precipitate and excitable actions of his community upset him as much as the Brother's behaviour. Henin later married (the Brothers were not under vows) and brought his wife to see Newman, but at the time the crisis was a painful revelation of the instability of his community.

The new trial was not allowed and Newman went up to London to be sentenced on 31 January 1853. He had written a memorandum but was not allowed to read it. The newspapers reported that he stood with arms folded on the floor of the court while Mr Justice Coleridge (Keble's great friend) addressed him, delivering what Newman called a lecture or a 'horrible jobation ... the theme of which was deterioration'. The Judge was shocked at Newman's bad taste and 'ferocious merriment' in detailing Achilli's crimes. 'Poor fellow, I think he seemed hurt I was not moved,' observed Newman to Henry Wilberforce afterwards. Coleridge himself was moved, however, for he wrote in his diary: 'But I was overpowered. The immense crowd, the anxious and critical audience, his slender figure, and strange mysterious cloudy face ... Oh! what a sweet musical almost unearthly voice it was, so unlike any other we had heard ...' But he felt Newman was 'an *overpraised* man, he is made an idol of.'

The sentence, when at last it came, was light: a hundred-pound fine and imprisonment till it was paid. Of course it was paid at once by Newman's friends and he left the court a free man, 'amid the hurrahs of 200 Paddies', St John wrote to Birmingham.

Newman's friends were indignant at Coleridge's moral lecture and wanted him to answer it publicly but he would not. He felt that in the end he had come off best. Achilli left soon afterwards for America, with the smart young wife he had brought to the trial, but leaving a further trail of seduced servant girls behind him. His future career was not an improvement on the past. When all expenses were paid Newman had money left from the fund and later used it to build his university church on Stephen's Green. And for years he prayed for his benefactors in this trial.

He went back to Birmingham to find that Joseph Gordon, who had been ill a long time, was now dying. Gordon was one of the firmest supporters of his Oratory and had been of great assistance in collecting evidence and witnesses. He died at his home in Bath, where Newman saw him just before his death, giving him much needed help at the last, but his body was eventually brought to the burial ground of the Oratory at Rednal, the little country retreat Newman built on the Lickey Hills. In 1865, twelve years after Gordon's death, Newman dedicated to his memory *The Dream of Gerontius*.

This loss, coming after the long suspense of the trial, made Newman feel that he had come to the end of a season in his life. He remembered a summer in his youth, interrupted by a week of rain which had divided the seasons like a river – for afterwards it was autumn. 'And so I think I have now passed into my autumn, though I trust grace will more than make up to me what nature takes away.' It was to be a long and stormy autumn, and a dark cold winter before the unexpected gleam of a second spring.

10

THE FACT OF A UNIVERSITY

After the Achilli trial Newman's influence was at its lowest ebb with most of his fellow-countrymen but high with the Catholic minority, who regarded him as a champion and near-martyr in their cause. During the rest of the fifties, his own and the century's, Newman was losing his prestige with the Catholic authorities in London and Rome, so that by 1863, ruminating in his journal, he could feel that his work had been wasted and himself regarded as a crypto-heretic and disloyal to the Pope, while among Protestants he was almost forgotten, a fanatic who had outlived his reputation. This strange reversal of fortune is the critical period of Newman's life, for the understanding of his mature character and the nature of the influence he was to exercise after the success of his *Apologia* in 1864, which still continues.

For most of this crucial decade Newman was living a double life, as founding father not only of the Congregation of the Oratory in England, but of the Catholic university in Ireland. In both situations he was involved with a multitude of people and a great deal of administrative work in two dissimilar fields, but both out of sight as far as London and Rome were concerned. Legends grew up which persisted long after his death, about his character and abilities – or lack of them. The eventual split between the two Oratories and the frustration of the Catholic university were both attributed largely to his mismanagement of men and his own supposedly difficult temperament; at the same time, because of his association with the liberal Catholics who ran the *Rambler* Magazine, notably Sir John, later Lord Acton, Newman came to be regarded with suspicion by papalist Ultramontanes as a centre of disaffection. These men were dominant in the Church for a generation, their devotion to the Pope increasing as his temporal power decreased, the campaign for his sovereignty merging into the campaign for the recognition of his infallibility in matters of faith and morals. In England, the most fanatical papalists were nearly all converts; the chief of them, Manning and W. G. Ward, did not reach their full power till the sixties, but were at work before that in the cause, and against the liberals, whom they considered as traitors to the Church. The Church was almost identified with the Pope, for the Ultramontanes.

Newman's position was complicated by his past leadership of the Oxford Movement which had brought so many into the Church and by the fact that he did not understand what was happening to him till the beginning of the sixties, when it was too late to alter the image he had acquired in the minds of the authorities. As in the Movement, he followed where his principles led without foreseeing how things would turn out for him, trusting in God and the truth. This way of living, in fact so simple and straightforward, earned him an unenviable reputation as a subtle, diplomatic and even devious man, because other people, judging him by themselves, imagined he was always working to attain definite objects of his own.

Certainly, Newman was not an organization man; he was a sower of the word and like the one in the Gospel believed that God gave the growth. Thus in starting both the Oratory and the University he made it his business to plant the right ideas in the basic minimum of structures which should ensure freedom of development; he did not create or try to maintain a detailed plan for the future. It is possible that such a man is not the ideal founder of an institution – nevertheless, most institutions which remain alive are those which find their origin in someone of creative imagination, the artist of life rather than the politician. As for dealing with men, Newman was not a commander or director; he treated others as equals, as capable of a responsibility they did not always show. The younger clerical converts saw him as a father figure, but he did not behave like one. In an era strong in father figures, Newman preferred brotherhood, though because of his age and prestige it was perhaps *elder*-brotherhood, the position he had filled so long in his own family.

The year 1853 was one of merely irritating frustration for Newman, since most of it was spent waiting, bags packed, to be summoned to Dublin for consultations on the proposed university. But the Irish bishops promised and then deferred till October, by which time Newman was immersed in other activities. An extraordinarily wet summer, with floods in April, gales in May, fog in June and storms in July, was punctuated for Newman by heavy colds, visits to the dentist and weekly journeys to Liverpool to deliver lectures on the history of the Turks; the only originality in these lay in Newman's reflections on the history he surveyed. There was some hope of a third Oratory being started in Liverpool, which he thought a better place for one than Birmingham.

In September Newman went up to London to be 'in at the death of King William Street'. Faber, with the aid of his noble friends, had bought a site in Brompton next to the Anglican parish church of Holy Trinity, and in spite of the protests of the incumbent (the Bonze, as the London Oratorians cheekily called him) a large house in the classical style was built and a temporary church, enriched with gifts of altars, statues, and pictures. Until the house was finished the members of the community spent much time at Sydenham, then a fashionable country place near London, where Newman stayed several times when he went to visit his dentist and to sort out misunderstandings already in evidence between the two groups. Faber's first book, *All for Jesus*, had proved an instant success, and he gave the next a flowery dedication to Newman, but by the time that the Birmingham church was ready for opening, Faber was so annoyed and upset over the transfer of Dalgairns that he refused to come.

Dalgairns had for some time felt unhappy in London; Faber and Hutchison teased him unmercifully and his earnest kind of enthusiasm did not harmonize with Faber's unstable exuberance. He wanted to return to Newman, but the request for him to do so was mismanaged, as Newman afterwards admitted, and confused with a young novice's going from Birmingham to London, with the unfortunate result that there was a great emotional scene over Dalgairns's leaving, which Faber resented. More unfortunate still, the London house was just entering on a new period of success in its permanent home, so that Dalgairns left a flourishing concern at the point when he himself was getting over his feeling of being despised by the others. He was to prove an unassimilable element in the Birmingham community, which he judged by the standards he had learned from Faber. Used to ardent emotionalism, the Birmingham house seemed to him lacking in fervour, spiritual devotion and enthusiasm for the latest Ultramontane ideas; while Ambrose St John found Dalgairns's preaching 'ranting' and it was felt that his criticisms proceeded more from self-conceit than genuine moral superiority.

The Oratory church in Birmingham was opened on St Cecilia's day, 22 November; the patron of music, she had been a patron of the Oratory ever since St Philip's friends in the papal choir had sung without charge at his services. Music and poetry were very much part of 'the School of Christian Love' – Philip Neri's idea was always to use the best of human arts and skills in living a Christian life. Newman's church had to be built on the cheap, with a roof bought second-hand from a factory – 'in style something between a Basilica and a Tithe Barn,' St John told Lady Arundel. But with painting and music he tried to make it as fine as he could. He had to get up from a bed of sickness for the occasion, driven there after an arduous visit to Ireland.

For the Irish bishops had suddenly summoned him. He had gone to Liverpool, running two lectures together and speaking for nearly three hours, on 3 November, went straight on to Dublin, arriving in the middle of the night, and then spent a hectic day seeing all kinds of people about the proposed university. Then he crossed the sea again to preach, at Ullathorne's request, at the first diocesan Synod of Birmingham – the sermon, 'Order, the Witness and Instrument of Unity' was later published in *Sermons on Various Occasions*. As soon as the Synod was over he had to go to Clifton, calling on seven or eight people in the short time he was there. Pouring rain, ice and snow, accompanied these travels, so it was hardly surprising that he caught such a severe cold as to be unable to say mass – a rare thing for him – for two days before the opening. He managed to preach at it, though with difficulty. 'People *won't* believe me,' he told Mrs Bowden, blaming his weakness on the strain of composing. 'Because I seem to do things easy, they say "O Dr Newman writes so easily, it gives him no trouble – he writes things off – he can sit up and write a sermon for next morning – he merely talks, he does not exert himself" and they simply discredit me.' Writing, composition, was always hard work to him, and he compared the revision of sermons or lectures for publication to hedging and ditching.

In October 1853 the Irish bishops had summoned Newman to begin the University but almost at once they told him 'to do nothing publicly'. This was, in effect, to prevent his acting at all, as he said to Wiseman, who was in Rome, in January 1854. He wondered whether he should not resign unless he were given public authority as Rector. He said he had been trying to act for two years, he knew he had even been blamed in Rome for doing nothing, but he could not act without official authority. Wiseman replied that he had suggested to the Pope that Newman should be made a bishop – not a diocesan bishop but, according to the custom then obtaining, of a defunct see in *partibus infidelium*, so that he would have a status equal to that of the bishops on the university committee. At earlier rumours of a bishopric (at the time of the hierarchy's restoration) Newman had been alarmed – he had no gifts for administering a diocese and could not have combined such work with the Oratory; but this titular bishopric would simply give him the necessary standing for founding the university, so he sent Wiseman a grateful acceptance.

Newman felt it right to tell his own bishop, and Ullathorne, who had by now become friendly towards Newman, proudly announced it at a public dinner, so that the news went rapidly round, and Newman's friends began sending congratulations and presents – even a pectoral cross. The next weeks were full of activity, including an arduous tour of Irish bishops and colleges begun in February

1854, of which Newman wrote an amusing account to his community, making fun of his own mistakes and misadventures. He got on well with most of the bishops, even the tough ones – only one was 'donnish'. But he discovered that most of them did not want the university, which they regarded as pushed on them by an Englishman (Wiseman) and used by the Roman-trained Archbishop Cullen as an instrument of policy against them. The Jesuit Provincial in Dublin had already told Newman that there was not in Ireland the class of young men to go to a Catholic university. Newman, still envisaging it as a place of higher education for all English-speaking Catholics, was not at once deterred. As far as the Irish were concerned, he was planning Evening Lectures for the 'mechanics' – some twenty years in advance of his old university in this. But he would need all the official backing he could get, and when he went over again, after Easter, it was to discover that the Brief setting up the university had come from Rome – with nothing in it about the promised bishopric for the Rector.

Archbishop Cullen said nothing to him about it, nor did Wiseman, beyond getting Manning to write a vague letter saying that he 'gathered' it was thought better to wait until the university had a formal existence. This suggested merely postponement, but nothing further happened and no communication was made to Newman. In June, Ullathorne was astonished that nothing had been fixed for Newman's consecration. Years later Newman wondered what would have happened had he refused to be installed as Rector before he was consecrated – 'as another man might have done'. But in fact he never questioned the authorities on the subject; he hated even to seem to be looking for 'honours'. 'It never occupied my thoughts,' he wrote in his memorandum of 1870 on the university. 'The prospect of it faded out of my mind, as the delay was more and more prolonged.' But of course it meant that he was left in a singularly powerless position, subject to the Irish bishops and without even a seat on the committee for the university.

Newman, guessed, at last, that Cullen had something to do with it, but the evidence has only recently come to light in the Archives of

Propaganda, which are opened, like a serial judgment day, a hundred years after the arrival of letters, manifesting the words of the dead to the world. There are Cullen's letters, persuading the Roman officials not to make Newman a bishop, because of the jealousy of Englishmen in Irish affairs and the expense of maintaining an episcopal Rector. In later letters Cullen complained of Newman's own behaviour and methods, which shocked him by the freedom he allowed the students and the laymen he appointed to the staff. It is clear that even Cullen, the only Irish bishop who had supported the idea of a Catholic university (because Roman policy was against 'mixed' education) really expected nothing more than a college, a kind of lay seminary, controlled by priests. But Newman expected the young men to keep horses and went riding with them himself, he encouraged music and debating societies and even, horror of horrors, supplied them with a club room and a billiard table, so that they could enjoy the favourite game of the day without resort to the places of entertainment in the town. 'All this makes it clear that Father Newman does not give attention to details,' wrote Cullen in October 1855. Or perhaps that Father Newman had different ideas of undergraduate discipline.

Then there was the sordid question of finance. Newman spent a lot of time and energy trying to gain the support of the gentry for an institution which at first anyway would benefit them more than others, and as the university was primarily for laymen he thought there should be a committee of laymen to run the finances and that the accounts should be audited. He pressed this idea from the start but never succeeded in getting the bishops to agree to it. There was no audit, and yet Newman was continually criticized for unnecessary expenditure when he drew from the fund as he had been invited to do. It was inconvenient and irksome, and the few influential laymen in Ireland who supported the university were disgusted by it.

But Newman's attitude to laymen was one of the principal causes of Cullen's suspicion; he appointed clever young laymen as professors and lecturers, sometimes men who had been associated with the

Young Irelanders; he was on friendly terms with these dangerous fellows, and they were devoted to him, rallying to his aid in any emergency. And then Newman's educational aims seemed startlingly modern – scientific faculties and a school of medicine (which became the most flourishing of all his foundations) sprang into being. What was more, Newman gave lectures to the faculties assuring them a proper intellectual freedom, just as he allowed the students a proper moral freedom. And who was invoked as the patron of all this liberty? Mary, the *Sedes Sapientiae*, seat or throne of Christ, the Wisdom of God.

Newman's attitude to learning and his mild impenetrability in maintaining it, came out more as time went on, but it was apparent from the beginning. All through May and June 1854, before the bishops had ratified anything, he was busy arranging hostels, appointing deans, tutors and lecturers, writing to possible professors, working out entrance examinations and lecture lists. He took a lease of 6 Harcourt Street and set up his own establishment where he lived whenever he was in Dublin during the next few years, with a bunch of students of different nationalities. He started a University Gazette, to familiarize people with his intentions and as a place for announcements. It came out weekly and he wrote most of the first numbers himself, corrected the proofs and saw to the distribution. For this Gazette he wrote some amusing sketches on the entrance examination, which give a glimpse of his own methods – how encouraging to good intentions, but how penetrative of ignorance covered up by surface glibness! The first number of the Gazette appeared at Whitsun, just before his formal installation as Rector. As usual he had been rushing up and down England just before and remarked to Ambrose, 'I hope I shall not go to sleep tomorrow at High Mass, or at the Archbishop's sermon.' He was apt to drop off while public speaking was going on, but managed to stay alert for this occasion.

Newman was now Rector, and after the vacation opened the first session of the university with a lecture on *Christianity and Letters*. After a hectic month he went back to Birmingham for Christmas, where Bernard Dalgairns was upsetting the house with his idealism and his criticism of others. When he had to leave, Newman made St John Rector in his absence, and he was soon writing, 'I feel with F. Bernard under me what you felt with F. Wilfrid under you.' Dalgairns and Faber both had a genius for getting their own way while proclaiming absolute obedience to superiors. Ambrose, with his collection of fowls at Rednal, his precious plants and his liking for a quiet smoke, was not at all Dalgairns's idea of a perfect saint. To have him as Rector made Bernard more Savonarola-like than ever.

Back in Dublin Newman was planning a university church, to be paid for by the rest of the Achilli fund. He asked John Hungerford Pollen to design it. Pollen was an Oxford man and had been a member of the group at St Saviour's, Leeds, but after a retreat in Rome decided he did not have a vocation to be a Catholic priest. Almost at once he met and fell in love with Maria Laprimaudaye, one of a family of Evangelicals of Huguenot descent, friends of Miss Giberne's, who had all come over with Manning. Maria was only sixteen and Pollen thirty-four, but the marriage was a happy one; the pair came to settle in Dublin in the autumn and were greeted with a note of welcome from Newman: 'May it be an auspicious messenger, crowned with flowers and dressed in its best,' he wrote.

Pollen later looked back with pleasure on those Irish days. 'What a time it was! Reading, thinking, writing, working, walking with him in times of recreation over the pleasant fields, parks and gardens of the Phoenix; listening to talk that was never didactic and never dull.' In his diary Pollen noted: 'To see Fr N. and with him to the Zoological. His wonder at and speculation on the design and end of beasts; their ferocity; their odd ways; birds especially. Back home to tea with us.' Visiting Zoos was to be a favourite expedition with Newman till he was over eighty. Pollen summed up his memories of Newman in Dublin: 'He shed cheerfulness as a sunbeam sheds light, even when many difficulties were pressing.'

Difficulties were certainly pressing, the chief of which was having to live in two places at once. Newman later reckoned that he had crossed St George's Channel fifty-six times in the service of the

University. The weather, this first winter of the Crimean War, was appalling. Ambrose wrote of the miseries of the unemployed in Birmingham; Newman was praying daily for those who died in the war. He thought it unnecessary and hated it. 'We have enveloped ourselves in illusions and shams, as John Bull always does,' he wrote to Mrs Froude. This year she made the decision to become a Catholic and though William, her husband, a marine engineer, was too much of a sceptic to come with her, he allowed his children to do so – thus Hurrell Froude's nieces and nephews became Catholics. In March 1855 Newman wrote a series of letters on the war for the *Catholic Standard*, entitled 'Who's to Blame?' afterwards reprinted in *Discussions and Arguments*. He used his old signature 'Catholicus' and the letters show his interest in political theory and practice and exhibit a realism only not cynical because he emphasizes the relative value of all human activities.

Keeping house had its own small trials, what with Irish cooks and lively students of different origins. Newman added to them by taking on Brother Frederick, one of Faber's young converts from Elton, who had disgraced himself in Birmingham by making proposals of marriage to a girl while still wearing his Oratorian habit. As the lay brothers did not take vows he could leave and marry, but he was eased out of religious life by coming to act as a servant in the university house. 'He is simply relieved and happy,' Newman wrote to Ambrose, 'and sings in the kitchen with astonishing compass and volume.' In 1879, plain Thomas Godwin then for many years, the ex-Brother recalled the Dublin days. 'Little do the outer world know how beautifully the family was managed – I think I can see the Father sitting in his little room receiving first this one and then the other, directing, guiding, calling each by their names as if he was their very father. Then there were the jolly recreations which might be termed musicals or extempore plays or charades, we never lacked amusement of the highest and most innocent order. They would bring me up bodily to sing a favourite Bass song . . .' This took place just below Newman's room. After he left, 'we soon got in a mess,' recorded Thomas Godwin, recalling the petty rules of his successors.

Lively as the house was, the chapel was the centre of it, and the young men came voluntarily to Newman for confession. Writing to Richard Stanton, Newman put first of his blessings: 'You know I have a chapel with the Blessed Sacrament here.' Always, the presence of the Lord under his roof was the source of his peace and strength. He was back in Birmingham for Holy Week where, as usual in these years, he sang the Christus in the Passion story – the shortest part and traditionally sung bass, which is interesting considering that Newman's speaking voice is remembered as pitched fairly high: 'silvery' is the word often used.

Back and forth he went and this summer took his holiday at Rednal, whence he wrote to Mrs Bowden about the first year of the university. 'It is swimming against the stream to move at all – still we are in motion.' Although it was all his doing he did not feel he was quite the man for the job. 'A Rector ought to be a more showy, bustling man than I am, in order to impress the world that we are great people ... I ought to dine out every day, whereas I don't dine out at all. I ought to mix in literary society and talk about new gasses and the price of labour, whereas I can't recollect what once I knew, much less get up a lot of new subjects – I ought to behave condescendingly to others, whereas they are condescending to me – And I ought above all to be twenty years younger and take it up as the work of my life. But since my qualities are not these, all I can do is to attempt to get together a number of clever men and set them to do what is not in my own line.' And certainly he gathered some distinguished and able men, both English and Irish; it was not their fault, or his, that the Catholic university did not develop as he had hoped.

During this summer vacation of 1855 Newman wrote *Callista*, his second and last novel, which was published later the same year. Some thought it was written to rival Wiseman's *Fabiola*, just out, a novel of the early martyrs of Rome, which enjoyed a great success. It may have reminded Newman of his own idea, first sketched in 1848, but the two books could hardly be more different. Most of Wiseman's characters were nobly born and the good ones beautiful –

the villains were hideous. All the Christians were perfect saints and the pagans monsters of depravity. The events took place in imperial Rome, with plenty of archaeological detail from the new excavations. Newman, on the other hand, fixed his story in an obscure Roman provincial town in North Africa, where the local Christian Church was in a state of disintegration. Callista was allowed to be pretty (and intelligent) but she made her living painting pagan images before her conversion. The Romanized pagans were decent sensible men, except for the old woman who had taken up occult practices (horrific in description) and a few men on the make. The visitation of the locusts and the riots in which a Christian cook is killed by the mob are vividly orchestrated and the psychological flight of the corrupted Juba strangely startling.

It is interesting that Newman did not choose the fifth century, which he knew so well, and which Charles Kingsley had just used in *Hypatia* for a glorious fling against celibacy and dogma, but this earlier period, just before Christianity emerged from the underworld of persecution. Not for nothing does the Christian community appear at the end of the book inside a mountain cave, celebrating the mystery of Christ's sacrifice. *Callista* is short and deceptively simple, but it expresses the poetic and intuitive side of Newman's nature, full of psychological insight and touches of irony, but essentially the story of a human soul who finds life in giving her life for Christ, her heart made whole in his love.

11

THE ORATORIES IN OPPOSITION

It was in the autumn of 1855 that the quarrel began between the two houses of the Oratory which was to end in official separation. The occasion of it was a dispute over the Rule, but the cause lay deeper, in the increasing opposition between the two groups, polarized by their different attitudes to the problems then facing the Church. There are always dissensions going on within the Church, which do not always issue in schisms, as at the time of the Reformation. In the last great internal struggle, spilling from the seventeenth into the eighteenth century, the party ultimately defeated were known as Jansenists; in the nineteenth century Jansenism was still a smear-word, much as Modernism has been since the beginning of this century. The bad side of Jansenism was moral severity, the good side conscientiousness; but since some of the leaders of the movement were intellectuals, any intellectual approach to Christianity was liable to be labelled Jansenism and suspected as heretical. Since the French Oratory had been implicated in Jansenist ideas, it became the habit of the London Oratorians to stick the label on Newman's back. He was intellectual, therefore 'French', not Philippine, almost Jansenist. By contrast, they were Italian, devotional rather than intellectual, and ultra-papalist.

When Newman was thinking his way into the Church the Pope had been Gregory XVI, conservative in much the same way as the legitimist régime of Charles X in France; but when Newman reached Rome he found Pius IX reigning, at that time a mild liberal. The Revolution of 1848 soon changed all that. Forced to flee from Rome, which was temporarily converted into a Republic by Garibaldi and Mazzini, Pius was only able to return by means of the

French army, for France was already giving up its own recent revolution and looking towards Louis Napoleon, who became the Emperor Napoleon III in 1852. From that moment Pius IX looked with suspicion on everything liberal, stuck grimly to the Papal States in the face of the national movement towards unity known as the Risorgimento, and became during his long reign the symbol of immobility in political affairs. The weaker he became in world affairs, the more his spiritual authority was exalted, his supporters creating a mystique about his person, as if he were almost an embodiment of the authority of Christ. Ever since the ruptures of the Reformation there had been an over-emphasis in the Church on the virtue of obedience – the Pope now became an almost supernatural father figure whose will must be obeyed as if it were the will of God. Of course, this did not prevent his curial staff from trying to manipulate his will; it merely gave a mystical force to the rubber stamp signature of their bureaucratic decisions. This authoritarian image of the supreme father appealed strongly to Faber and other converts, who had suffered from the uncertainty and indecision of authority in the Church of England. Besides, the Pope was a long way off and it was easy to practise obedience at a distance. Newman, on the other hand, was too near to be ignored. In 1850, when the London House was given its autonomy, Faber suggested that Newman should retain sweeping supervisory powers; these he refused, but agreed that for three years he should be consulted on important decisions. That period was up in 1853, and Faber had been elected once again as Provost; Newman had been taken up with the beginning of the new university since then, and in London they thought he had virtually given up the Oratory in its favour. By 1855 the house at Brompton was in full swing, Faber had become a popular preacher and devotional writer, and they felt themselves much more truly the exponents of the Philippine ideal than the house in Birmingham, that humdrum community, coping with factory workers, the prison, the workhouse and so on.

Oratories have always been small independent groups, but in Italy and other countries they usually grew up as such. It was the fact of

Faber's joining him, with his tail of Wilfridians, which had forced Newman to start two houses at once, and he had always been aware of the difficulties this would entail, in a country so closely united by rail and post as was England in the nineteenth century. What he had not foreseen was that Faber and the London group should come to lose confidence in him, not merely as their Oratorian founder, but even as a Catholic, so that they could feel he was merely a half-converted intellectual, while they were well on their way to sainthood, swimming with the popular tide of ultramontane supernaturalism.

The trouble began when the London Oratory, without telling Newman, wrote to the office of Propaganda in Rome for an interpretation of the Rule on the question of hearing nuns' confessions – the spiritual direction of communities of women. This was something Oratorians were not supposed to undertake, since it took them away from the community centre, but which they were doing to oblige Wiseman. The idea of writing to Rome about it was their own; it would confirm their independence to correspond directly with Rome. The first Newman heard of it was when Bishop Ullathorne said he was glad to hear a rescript from Rome was coming to dispense them from this provision of the Rule; Dalgairns had undertaken similar work for the nuns at Stone, which they had felt some qualms about, but which the bishop encouraged.

Newman was taken aback to discover that, through the action of the London Oratory, his own could be threatened with a binding order from Rome. Ullathorne was embarrassed to find that Newman had not been consulted and did not even know that Propaganda had written for his opinion, as bishop of a diocese in which an Oratory was situated. It was particularly annoying to Newman, because, as the adaptor of the Rule for England, he knew that the Oratories already had the right to interpret it according to circumstances; application to Rome was unnecessary.

Newman's council of the four Deputies were even more annoyed, for they regarded it as a deliberate gesture of independence, not to say rebellion, on the part of the London Oratory. Newman was once more going to and fro across the Irish sea and in Dublin he was laid low with a carbuncle, which shows how the strain of his double life was telling on his health. From there he sent a letter addressed to the whole London community, beginning: 'My dear Father Faber, I write this letter to your Congregation. I transmit it through you and hope you will read it to them.' This was because he knew Faber was liable to act without telling the rest, but it mortally offended Faber, who felt Newman was trying to set him aside and address the community apart from him. He was so hurt and indignant that he could not bring himself to write to Newman at all till the following May, six months later. Newman told Brompton that their request had been 'unintentionally on your part misunderstood by (Propaganda) to come from us as well as from you.' He therefore asked them to draw up a petition to Propaganda to recognize in some way the independence of the two houses and asked that it should be sent first to him, as Founder, for transmission to Rome.

London's answer came from the Deputies, saying that they had not asked for a dispensation from the Rule but an interpretation for themselves alone, and that it would be disrespectful to write again until they heard what had been decided. Newman thought this meant that they were trying to put things right with the Cardinal's aid, but soon afterwards a letter arrived from Wiseman's secretary which showed that nothing was being done. He therefore sent Brompton a more peremptory letter. 'You have (unwittingly) done us an injury. We feel it. We ask you to repair it. You can. Do as you would be done by ... I repeat my request, distinctly, formally, more earnestly. Rather, since justice comes in, I make it a demand.'

The reply to this, written by Stanton as Secretary, made Newman realize how angry his intervention had made them. It was formal but long and gave three resolutions to the effect that they did not think it right to petition Propaganda further, and refused to do so. This letter was a shock to Newman; he felt that even if they thought the petition unnecessary, they might have done it when they realized his anxiety on the subject. He wrote a short note to Stanton in reply, summing up his feelings: 'Tell them, I never loved them so much as now, when they have so exceedingly wounded me.' And he asked them not to answer. It was a mistake to put his feelings on paper, for the London Oratorians soon reduced the whole of his case to hurt feelings.

But there was more to it than feelings, for as Newman had said to his own community: 'Alter the Rule and you alter the vocation.' A religious Rule is the constitution of an order or Congregation, and Newman thought that if one house could get it altered from Rome without the knowledge of another, no one would know where he stood, or what he was pledging himself to keep. As Founder in England, it was Newman's duty to safeguard future houses by preventing this happening, and it was this necessity which sent him off to Rome in the middle of winter.

He spent Christmas at Edgbaston but was in Paris by 28 December and arrived in Turin on New Year's day, 1856. His plan was to visit the Oratories in North Italy and, without mentioning the London Oratory, try to discover the general view on questions connected with the Rule. He had no idea that the London Oratory, having got wind of his departure, had written off to the Superiors of the Italian houses, and to Propaganda, to warn them not only that Newman was coming, but that he was aiming at a *generalate* over the English Oratory – abhorrent word to the democratic sons of St Philip. The ground was thus prepared against him, and the journey was exhausting; snow, rain and the Austrian authorities did not help, bringing on St John's asthma and almost landing Newman in prison because he was down on his passport as 'Doctor' and, as he told Bowles with amusement, afterwards, 'the title of Doctor is often assumed or professed by revolutionary Germans.' In spite of all this the visits were a success, and the London House received some unsolicited testimonials to their itinerant Padre from the Italian Superiors, praising his learning and his courtesy and assuring them that he had said nothing against them and seemed to have no ideas of a *generalate*.

On they went to Rome, and here, under cover of twilight, Newman did something unusual for him – he walked barefoot into the city, a cold miry walk at that time of year. He did not tell anyone this but St John later told Neville; knowing Newman's dislike of exhibitionism, he added that their long cloaks hid their feet. Nevertheless it shows how strongly Newman felt the importance of the cause for which he had come to Rome.

Everywhere they went they saw Stanton's curly handwriting; documents from London, containing they knew not what, lay on every official desk. The critical interview was with Barnabò, the Prefect of Propaganda, soon to be a Cardinal, for English Catholic affairs still passed through this office. He was exactly Newman's own age, a bustling shrewd little man of business, who greeted his distinguished visitor with the words, 'So you've run away from Dublin, Dr Newman?' as if he were a truant schoolboy. But later, when Newman suggested that the London Oratory should have a Brief of its own, to ensure independence, he said it was not necessary. Newman's Brief sufficed for the whole of England and any other Oratories must be founded through him. Thus Newman discovered that his powers were greater than he had realized.

Their audience with the Pope was satisfactory; he was pleased to hear of their work in Birmingham, with a word of praise for what the women were doing, gave them his blessing, and when Newman asked it for the London House, gave that too. They saw friends as well as officials in Rome, settled some university matters, and went off with a Paschal Candle given them by the Pope, by steamer to Marseilles and then on by rail and boat, going straight through London to Birmingham, whence Newman, after only a week to recover – in Rome he had once nearly fainted from sheer exhaustion – hurried back to Dublin.

The London Oratorians had been much alarmed at Newman's dash to Rome; they imagined he had gone to report against them and to gain some special power to overrule them. Excited letters had gone to Wiseman from Faber, when it was discovered that Newman had written to the Cardinal without informing them. Wiseman showed Newman's letters to Faber, but not Faber's to Newman. His view was that Newman's 'noble wounded feelings' ought to be 'soothed' but he did nothing to effect this, nor to restrain the excited emotions of the Brompton community. However, when Newman, on returning from Rome, merely sent the London House the Pope's blessing, they were relieved, and even triumphant, thinking he had made his journey for nothing. As to the original occasion of the trouble, the rescript had arrived in the interval, and with habitual Roman caution merely allowed the hearing of nuns' confessions for a period of three years. Silence fell between the two Oratories, but it was an uneasy silence.

In March Antony Hutchison wrote a long private letter of explanations, which Newman refused to read; in order to restore confidence, any communication must come from the whole body. Then, in May, just after Newman's university church in Dublin was opened, Faber at last broke his long silence and wrote a reproachful personal epistle. 'You have cast me from you, perhaps justly. I do not doubt that you have had much to bear from me ... I feel as if there were on your mind a long series of jealousies, doubts and misconstructions, which it would be hopeless for me to remove ... Now is it quite impossible for you to forgive us, to be a Father to us again, to destroy ye scandal of ye unvisiting Houses? What exactly is it in our conduct which has angered you so greatly – what can we do to repair it – is it such as to justify a break among St Philip's sons? ... I do not want to make any excuses. You have never let us make any explanations. We hardly know what to explain ... True to you I have *unfalteringly* been ...' As usual, Faber had reduced the whole episode to a personal misunderstanding and he interpreted Newman's actions by what he supposed were his feelings.

Newman never expected such misinterpretations; the more he stuck to facts, the more cold and calculating he was thought to be. When he replied, after charitably putting down Faber's long silence to his poor health, he said, 'Great confusion arises from going to and fro, beginning formally, continuing informally, and thus dissipating responsibility as I am sure you will see.' Faber did not see; he dashed off another letter, all about their own feelings in London. As to their refusal to write to Propaganda at Newman's request, Faber asserted that the Cardinal had said they must not think of it. If he did, it was not in his letter to Faber, advocating the soothing treatment of Newman. 'We had no suspicion a refusal would have wounded you so,' wrote Faber now. But when they *had* learned it, they had merely taken steps to put Newman in the wrong with the Italian Oratories and at Rome by accusing him of trying to exercise a *generalate* over them.

Newman's reply was to repeat that he would listen with sympathy to anything that came from the whole Congregation. To Ambrose he remarked that he feared Faber might feel this a comedown – 'or at least *he* feels *he* shall be put aside.' At last on 21 May 1856, came the formal letter – and it was nothing but a lengthy apology for having hurt Newman's feelings. Unsatisfactory as this was, it at least gave Newman the opportunity to explain to the London House why their action in applying to Rome for an interpretation of the Rule was dangerous to the stability of the whole institute. Moreover, this had been done without consulting him, either as founder or as head of the Birmingham House, though others had been consulted. 'I expostulated; and with what effect? ... First, they gave me no notice of what they were doing; then they put aside my expostulation; now they ask my blessing. Do they ask a blessing on their unanimous, their persevering refusal to co-operate with me in any way whatever, in providing against the recurrence of what they know I feel to be a great danger?' He forgave the rudeness of their refusal, but pointed out that so far they had done nothing to 'remove a difficulty, which, as I reminded them, may one day be theirs as well as ours'. This time, he did not fail to accompany his formal letter to the Secretary with a private note to Faber.

But the official reply, when it came, was a complete puzzle to him, for instead of acknowledging the difficulty and suggesting some safeguard, they thanked him for his forgiveness of their rudeness and said that his view of their application had never struck any of them at the time. 'They seem simply to decline to do anything,' Newman said to Stanislas Flanagan, who bluntly called the Londoners humbugs. Newman said, 'I suppose they mean to go their own way, relying on their own caution and my journey to Rome, that there will be no fresh collision. But I fear there will be a multitude of little rubs, do what we will.' To Ambrose, he wondered if Faber, living so much away, *could* govern the others; Faber's frequent collapses meant that he was nearly always at Sydenham or staying at Arundel Castle, or with W. G. Ward, who had inherited an estate on the Isle of Wight. Newman now guessed that the Londoners had found his original letter 'domineering and unjust' but this did not explain their present attitude.

However, as he felt there were signs of softening, he took two steps intended to improve the situation, which unfortunately only made it worse. He invited Faber to preach at his university church in July and sent to Cardinal Wiseman Faber's five proposals of 1850 for securing Newman's direct control over the London House, which he had refused as unconstitutional, and his own suggestion (accepted) that for three years he should act as a kind of court of appeal – as in fact he did, during the Achilli trial, to save Faber from being deposed by his exasperated subjects, though of course he made no mention of this. Instead, he pointed out that the next three years were not up before they were acting in a spirit directly contrary to both their own, and his, arrangements. He sent a copy of this brief missive to London.

In Edgbaston they thought he should have given more explanation with it, but Newman insisted that he only wanted to give facts, and that Wiseman 'would not stand a long statement, but when he saw the Resolutions of F. Faber he would say to him, "How is this? I suppose you *have* observed the spirit of these resolutions, though perhaps not the letter?" and I thought that F. Faber would not have the face to say he had, and so would be bothered.' If Newman had been Wiseman, that was what he would have said, and if he had been Faber, it would have bothered him. But their actual reactions were quite otherwise. Faber sent their recent letters to Wiseman, to show how they had grovelled to Newman for his pardon. Perhaps one day 'the long series of misunderstandings may be unravelled, so that he may see how he has wilfully put away from himself a House which your Eminence knows has been faithful and true to him as its Founder under St Philip.' But he excused himself from preaching in Newman's church.

Faber's view that it was all a misunderstanding, which could have been cleared up had Newman merely called at Brompton and discussed things face to face, has generally been the view of outsiders, at the time and long afterwards. But his going there, to receive more fulsome apologies for wounding his feelings, while the London House continued to go its own way, would simply have appeared to give his public approval to them. And this, in fact, was all Faber wanted. He did not at all want Newman to exercise any authority, or to do what Newman wished him to do. This is plain enough from his next step, which was to send two representatives of the London House to Rome, to petition for a separate Brief, so that they could be completely independent of Newman. Of course he did not know that Newman had made the same request in Rome, and learned it was unnecessary.

Stanton and Hutchison departed in great secrecy on 1 July, and their letters from Italy reveal the true attitude of their community, anxious to get rid of all connection with Newman and full of scoffing remarks about him – they called him 'the Serpent' and talked of his habit of 'shooting round corners'. But they were surprised to find, at the Italian Oratories and in Rome, that no adverse impression had been created against them, and Barnabò, though he laughed at Newman and called him 'Il Babbo' – daddy – startled them by saying that they did not need a Brief, for as long as Newman had set them up, they were not 'bastards'. However, the two young Oratorians persisted and finally secured their separate Brief, with a clause ensuring that no other Oratory should be founded in London. Newman had always wished to have another, in the East End, with Robert Whitty in charge. Although Whitty had by now left the Oratory and later joined the Jesuits, he always remained Newman's friend. Faber was determined to have this clause inserted; he must be the representative Oratorian in London, with no rival.

Their chief ally in Rome was George Talbot, fifth son of the third Baron Talbot of Malahide, a fussy little man whose position as a Papal Chamberlain gave him more influence than was good for him. Talbot pleased the London Oratorians by saying that 'Numman', as he called him, was 'crochetty' – had been crochetty with *him* over the Achilli documents. Talbot abetted them against Newman, as he was later to abet Manning against him. They also called on Miss Giberne, and found her unexpectedly sympathetic and ready to recall that when Newman was young 'he always had a shocking temper!' She was evidently out of hers, because, said Hutchison, Ambrose had picked a quarrel with her on Newman's behalf. If this was true, it was probably an attempt to curb Miss Giberne's unin-hibited devotion, for, grateful as he was for her help with the witnesses, Newman had certainly found the exuberance of what she idiotically called her 'spiritual love' for him, embarrassing. This little awkwardness between them was soon to pass, but at the moment Miss Giberne (who was now fifty-four) attached herself to Stanton and Hutchison, and was for ever coming to their lodgings to play hymns on the piano.

Two letters of Faber's to Hutchison are the only ones of his which deal with the row between the Oratories to survive, besides those to Newman. They reveal how anxious he was to get the exclusive clause in the Brief. Wiseman had been consulted from Propaganda and Faber rushed round to make sure he was on the London side. He was agitated to hear that Newman had been in town – 'I suppose it was to ye Cardinal about ye one house.' In fact, Newman had come to see the dentist. Faber wrote again on 25 August: 'It strikes me that if ye Padre writes a motivated letter against ye one house in London, you will have to make a regular attack upon him.'

In this letter Faber also repeated a lot of gossip brought to them by Dalgairns, who had finally left the Birmingham House to return to London on 15 August, the feast of the Assumption. 'The whole house, Bernard says, is extremely united in condemning us, not regretting ye row and considering themselves a very successful house, and all that they could wish. He describes their feeling against us as something awful.' He said that the Congregation as a whole was told nothing, the Deputies did everything, except that 'ye Padre transmitted from Dublin bitter papers, which Ambrose was ordered to read at General Congregation. One of these papers lashed them to a perfect frenzy. One passage about our house was as follows: "I have to tell you, my dear Fathers, that you are despised: you are voted slow and looked down upon. And what is more, I also am despised." Bernard said it seemed as if his object was simply to inflame their passions.'

If Bernard Dalgairns had said that, it was untrue. Newman had said, 'We have been despised', but he added that in his own experience it was when he had been most despised that he had done most for God. 'What is more, I also am despised', was not what Newman had said, but what Faber thought he felt.

Dalgairns's own account of his leaving Newman was rather different from what Faber's gossip leads one to expect. He had never settled down at Birmingham, for he missed the hothouse fervour of the London community. Restless and dissatisfied, a year ago he had been to France for a retreat under the direction of a noted Jesuit, Père Ravignan, to whom he had poured out his feelings that Newman and his colleagues were not truly spiritual men – notes remain to give his point of view. The Jesuit had tried to make him see that his dissatisfaction arose from his own pride, and he had returned to Birmingham to make a new start. But by the summer of 1856 be had come to the end of his tether, and another holiday in France, this time with Lorain, the priest who had trained him ten years ago, had convinced him that he must leave, and return to the London House.

He was already in touch with Faber; in fact, he seems to have been aware of their correspondence with Rome the year before, in which he had an interest since he was directing Mother Margaret's nuns at Stone. All along, he had felt more sympathy with London than with Birmingham in the dispute and disapproved of the papers Newman sent from Dublin, on the historical origins of the Oratory, because they showed that from the beginning intellectual work had been an integral part of its mission, starting with the famous history of the Church by one of Philip's first disciples, Cesare Barone, later known as Cardinal Baronius. Now, on 14 August, he told Faber how hard it was to 'snap a chain' which had bound him to the Padre for so long, begging him not to speak of it in case it got round to Newman. 'If only I could have submitted my *rationale* to the old gentleman. Yet how can a man remake himself?'

The very next day he got his opportunity, for the whole house was meeting to vote approval of those papers, which Newman had written in March because he realized how few of the present community had been with him at Maryvale, let alone in Rome. They were dry in tone, because Newman disliked gush about their vocation, but Flanagan, for instance, found them intensely interesting. But they were the antithesis of Dalgairns's outlook; he was that most difficult of beings, anti-intellectual intellectual.

Feeling he could not approve, he asked to see Newman alone before they voted, and the meeting was adjourned. Dalgairns told Faber a few days later how he had gone in fear and trembling to Newman's room and announced his 'settled conviction that the idea of the London House was more like the historical Philippine idea than that of Birmingham'. He ended by 'putting the question point blank to (Newman), "Do you consider I have the spirit of the Birmingham House?" He showed a most amusing respect for an intellectual conviction,' Dalgairns went on, 'and asked me once or twice if it really was intellectual, and then he said I had a right to hold it.' Newman sent him away and said he would come presently and let him know what he thought. 'After three hours of anxious suspense, he came. I cannot tell you how kind he was. Do you remember an expression in *Callista* about "eyes as blue as sapphires of the eternal city"? His eyes looked then just like a saint's, and he spoke and acted like one, so disinterestedly, so gently. He said how much he loved me; he then said he felt quite sure he had no resentment against the London House; and lastly he said that since I had asked him the question he could not but answer that I had not the spirit of the Birmingham House ... Then he gave me his hand, which I kissed ... How very small I feel beside him; if I were not such a restless selfish blackguard I could live with him ... The dear old boy behaved so generously I must take care not to wound him.'

In fact, though he was sorry to see Dalgairns go, Newman was relieved that he had taken the decision himself, for he had been wondering 'how he could bear us or we him' (as he put it to Ambrose), since he had so identified himself with the views of the London House. Dalgairns's departure to London on the score that it was more Philippine than Birmingham, left Newman the delicate duty of speaking to his own community on the subject. He was forced to criticize Dalgairns, in discounting his criticism 'of themselves, but he began by praising his virtues and blaming his own deficiencies as Superior in failing to guide him properly. Nevertheless, had Dalgairns been a saint, there was bound to have been a convulsion, 'on the sudden introduction of a new element, definite in its kind and powerful in its influence and free in its action, into a constituted community'. The language recalls the essay on Development and shows Newman's insight into the socio-psychological life of a community of persons.

Newman then perceptively diagnosed the negative side of Dalgairns's zeal. He had severely censured others as unspiritual, while himself failing in everyday duties which he found dull. The devotee of spiritual direction had complained of the routine of hearing parish confessions, and though he had grumbled that the Fathers had not enough to do, he had not taken up Newman's suggestion that he should work up the mission in Smethwick. Above all, whereas the sign of the presence of God was peace, everyone would agree that Dalgairns was restless in all he did. 'This simply to my mind invalidates his testimony about our want of St Philip's spirit altogether.' So they must love Dalgairns still but need not adopt his views; his criticisms, by bringing out their own latent spirit, could do them good. 'We *have* an idea of the Oratorian vocation though we don't bring out a scientific definition of it.'

So Dalgairns went back to London, but not to contentment. He and Faber never could do each other any good. Five years later Faber would write to him, 'I often pine for you as you came from Birmingham. All that suffering gave you a wonderful odour of God's presence and of prayer – which these studies have evaporated.' Criticisms of Dalgairns's books came ill from Faber, who admitted to Hutchison that he was miserable without a book on hand. But as his were 'devotional' he thought they had nothing to do with what he called 'literary hankerings'.

Meanwhile, the Oratories were not reconciled. Newman had agreed willingly to the Brief, much to the surprise of the Londoners, and had not even complained of its exclusive clause. He told his own house that it was better that the two Oratories should go their separate ways, as if they were of different orders, and he strictly forbade them to talk of the quarrel to outsiders. The Deputies jibbed a little at this; they felt Newman had been badly treated and they knew that in London the talk was pretty free – Faber was showing letters about to his friends and justifying himself by creating an impression of Newman's 'sensitiveness'. But Newman insisted on silence, telling Stanislas that 'it is a lesser evil that I should be thought tyrannical than Fr Faber proved to be double-dealing.' That was his considered opinion of Faber's behaviour, and he did not see how to defend himself without attacking Faber, which he refused to do.

But the gossip in London continued and it undermined Newman's personal reputation among influential Catholics. He was sensitive, touchy, resentful. Silence in Birmingham was interpreted as sulk.

12

THE DEFEAT OF THE *RAMBLER*

The trouble between the Oratories contributed to Newman's decision to resign from the university at the end of his three-year term of office, in 1857. He felt that he was getting nowhere in Dublin and that his presence was needed in Birmingham. In the spring of 1856 he warned Archbishop Cullen and in October made known his intention to the Irish bishops. But nobody seems to have taken it seriously till March 1857, when he wrote his official letter of resignation, naming 14 November as the date of his retirement. The reasons given were that his health would not stand the continual travelling and that he must be with his community. He wrote separate letters to all the bishops, differing slightly in wording and tone according to their friendliness to the university.

Now there was general consternation and Cullen himself, who had been so difficult, refusing to answer Newman's letters and writing adverse reports of him to Rome, called round to persuade him to stay. 'The poor Archbishop has just gone,' Newman wrote to Ambrose afterwards. 'I say "poor" because he was evidently so nervous and distressed, as to melt me internally, though I was very stiff, or very much moved, both at once perhaps, during that short interview.' Newman did not change his mind but by June he was reconciled to continuing as non-resident Rector for a further year 'but it will be a very large pill for the Irish clergy to swallow and I doubt the capacity of their throat.' If he was to stay as a mere figurehead, a working Vice-Rector was a necessity. The bishops invited Newman to suggest one, but when he named a layman, shocked silence ensued. By the time he left, in November 1857, no one had been appointed. At the end of his non-resident year, all connection with the university ceased, though not with his Irish friends.

In 1872, when Newman was going through his Irish papers, he found a letter from one of these Irish friends who feared he must think badly of the country. Newman wrote on it: 'It was not Ireland that was unkind to me. The same thing would have happened in England or France. It was the clergy, moved as they are in automaton fashion from the camarilla at Rome.' By that time he had suffered a great deal more from the division between clergy and laity and knew how it was helping to destroy the opportunity to meet positively the intellectual and practical challenges to Christianity in the modern age.

In his opening sermon in Pollen's university church, which he called *Intellect, the Instrument of Religious Training*, Newman had put his aim with clarity and force. 'I wish the intellect to range with the utmost freedom and religion to enjoy an equal freedom; but what I am stipulating for is, that they should be found in one and the same place, and exemplified in the same persons . . . I want the same roof to contain both the intellectual and the moral discipline. Devotion is not a sort of finish given to the sciences; nor is science a sort of feather in the cap . . . an ornament and set-off to devotion. I want the intellectual layman to be religious and the devout ecclesiastic to be intellectual.' Why? Because it was useless to fight the battle of truth with moral weapons only. 'The influence of sanctity is greater in the long run, the influence of intellect is greater at the moment.' The young were especially liable to be carried away by ideas. 'Youths need a masculine religion, if it is to carry captive their restless imaginations and their wild intellects, as well as to touch their susceptible hearts.' Too few people understood him, or even listened. For the university sermons he delivered and later printed in *Sermons on Various Occasions* he had, as he once told Ambrose, an audience largely of 'lawyers and old ladies'.

But although Newman had decided that he could not fulfil his aims in the university of Dublin, he hoped to work towards them in England, where he expected that his talents and those of his community would be used in some project of intellectual influence as well as in pastoral cares. 'It seems to me that a time of great reaction and great trial is before us,' he wrote to Ambrose St John in May 1857. Once more he felt, almost as in 1833, that he might be '*wanted* in England' – that there was a work which only he could do. 'It makes me wish I were to live twenty years in full possession of my mind – for breakers are ahead.' Newman did get his twenty years, but he could not foresee the strange way in which his influence was to be brought to bear through the deepest frustrations and humiliations of his own life.

At first it looked as if positive, useful work were to come his way at once. In August 1857 Wiseman wrote to inform him that he had been entrusted with the supervision of a new translation of the Bible. Taught by his experience with the Irish bishops, Newman asked to see the actual decree of the Synod. Back it came, ratified in Rome. Now he accepted the charge and during October wrote over twenty letters to the heads of Catholic colleges and professors of theology, asking for suggestions and advice. Ward and Manning were on the list, but the majority were not converts. The replies are interesting. Catholics at that date used a version based on the Douay and Rheims translations by the exiles of the sixteenth century, revised and approximated to the Anglican version authorized by King James, by Bishop Challenor in the eighteenth century. Most of the men consulted wanted an entirely new version, and paragraphed, not divided into verses; all were delighted that Newman had undertaken the work.

Newman was lucky in that he had, in Ambrose St John, a man who had studied Hebrew and Syriac under Pusey at Oxford, and knew German; Nicholas Darnell also knew German and was a first-class Latinist; and Edward Caswall had been very successful in translating Latin hymns. Assistant translators from outside were to be invited and Newman went into all the practical details, the kind of type, the method of revision, and the costs. In order to meet the latter he suggested that he should temporarily hold the copyright. Wiseman, as remiss in answering letters as Cullen, answered this within three weeks – in the negative. Silence ensued for nearly three months. In February 1858 Wiseman spoke of final approbation being necessary from the Holy See and advised Newman to show Ullathorne his arrangements for revision. Newman replied that he had already done so and repeated his request about the copyright, saying he would hand it to the bishops as soon as costs were met. Silence once more.

In November 1858 Newman made a private note on what he supposed was the reason for this strange behaviour. He had first heard of the idea from Ullathorne in 1855 and he now guessed that the Synod had originally passed the decree then, 'with the intention of the London Oratory doing it, and my chiefly giving my name and general superintendence', as he had then been in the thick of his university work. But just when the decrees went to Rome, the quarrel between the Oratories began. 'The Cardinal found his plan marred, and therefore waited till the last minute, hoping things would come straight.' But they had not by the time the decrees came back, ratified, from Rome in 1857, and Wiseman, though forced to take some action, no longer wished Newman to be in charge and so played a delaying game. Probably Newman was right, for, when Faber was dying in 1863, he told Newman he knew how badly he had been treated over the Scripture translation. At any rate, though Newman had already spent £100, a lot to him at that time, he was never given the signal to go ahead. In this day of many translations, so often marred by banalities, one regrets those Newmanic cadences, so clear and so musical, which never saw the light.

The year 1858, during which the Bible project gradually receded from sight, was an extremely disappointing and anxious one for the Birmingham community. In January Stanislas Flanagan went down with bronchitis and was so ill that Newman sent him to a specialist, who reported that both his lungs were affected by tuberculosis and that he must spend the rest of the winter abroad. When this news arrived in Birmingham, Henry Bittleston had just been struck down by a severe pleurisy. 'I am like Job with one trouble after another,' Newman wrote to Stanislas, 'Eliphaz and Bildad saying it is because St Philip has given me up.' Under the circumstances Stanislas felt he ought not to go abroad, with the new American novice, Robert Tillotson, who was also delicate. 'I want you and Robert out of the country *as soon as possible*,' said Newman firmly. '*Get off*.' They went.

Bittleston was so ill that his life was despaired of; he had several relapses but eventually recovered. After Easter he was sent out to Stanislas at Pau and Tillotson came back, only to develop a bunion on his foot.

Newman took on the offices left vacant by the invalids, including that of novice master. Apart from some who came and left the only novice who persevered was young Harry Ryder, who had been with Newman in Dublin till his father, in a sudden huff, had removed him and his brother Lisle, to whose lie-a-bed habits Newman turned a blind eye. Although George Ryder sided with the London Oratory, Harry persisted in his vocation to Newman's Oratory, where, as there was already a Fr Henry, he took the name of Ignatius. He was clever, musical and good-looking, and was to become Superior after Newman's death, but temperamentally they did not quite hit it off, and Ignatius was later to play the part of critic on the hearth; that he was able to do so says much for the freedom within the group, since he was thirty-six years younger than Newman.

At this time Newman went back to the work of a parish confessor, which he had had to give up during his university days. He was reluctant, fearing that his anxiety over it would destroy the peace of mind he needed for intellectual work. But once back in the confessional he settled to it, and did not give up till he was eighty and a Cardinal. His advice was much prized by the humble parishioners. 'Old Mrs Brennan has found me out,' he remarked, reminded how few Fathers were left who had heard confessions in Alcester Street when, he feared, he had made mistakes. There he had had factory boys, now it was mostly girls and old people. One little girl remembered all her life how, at her first confession, he had come out to comfort her, hearing her tears of fright.

There were alterations going on in the buildings. By now all the lay brothers had gone and there was a succession of unsatisfactory servants. Things were stolen and someone was spying, picking pieces of unburnt letters out of Newman's fireplace. (So he did burn *some*!) At the beginning of June an accusation was made against one of the Fathers which prompted Newman to deliver a special Chapter Address, asking them to observe two rules: '1. Never to put your arm round a boy's neck or show any other familiarity towards boys. 2. To observe the rule of the Roman Oratory, which I got leave, not wisely, as I now see, to omit from our body of rules. I say "not wisely" because people so weakly take offence at innocent practices.' The rule was, not to allow boys in the Fathers' rooms. Newman had evidently thought such a rule only necessary in the corrupt times of the Italian renaissance. But he had always been careful to guard against gossip about women; they were only allowed in the public rooms. Needless to say, Miss Giberne had succeeded in getting Fr Gordon to show her Newman's room, before the house was officially opened, and was impressed with his little low bed, as she told him years later, when they were both over eighty.

Ambrose St John went abroad for his holiday, on the lookout for lay brothers. To him Newman wrote in June, defending his right to 'croke' occasionally; it seemed to him justified by the utterances of Job, Jeremiah and the Psalmist. Nor did he do it to the whole world. But his present situation did cause him to complain to St Philip, since it was for his sake that Newman had involved himself in the responsibility of a household – 'almost as much as if I had married'. He was thinking over recent events. 'I now, so far, pity poor Fr Dalgairns in his restlessness here, from understanding it better (considering our disorganized state and the malign action of St Philip's own people, my sons, upon us) – though I trust I shall never be so unfaithful to St Philip as he was to me.' Newman's devotion to his patron was very real and simple, as to a revered friend and master, and it was most painful to him that the London House considered he did not understand or follow St Philip. And now St Philip seemed to desert him.

The summer continued on its chaotic way. Neville was lamed falling out of a pony cart; Ambrose, when he got back, went down with crippling lumbago, and Newman was frequently left alone in the house, with all the odd jobs to do, including a baptism, which agitated him, as he was unused to the Catholic rite and discovered afterwards that both the parents were Protestants. Then Miss Farrant died, one of two sisters, friends of Bittleston's, who were just about to start a hospital for the poor. In his review of the year, read to the Congregation, Newman said of this scheme: 'The waves went over it.'

The waves seemed to be going over another scheme too, that of a school for boys. The influx of educated converts meant that Stonyhurst and Downside were overflowing and the schools attached to the seminaries, such as Oscott, were hardly up to the standard required, either in teaching or care of the boys. Newman's lay friends were pressing him to open a school, and though it was not generally an Oratorian work, Newman had allowed for the possibility in revising the Rule, in view of the circumstances in England. But just after he had got out a prospectus and begun writing round, it seemed that the money could not be raised, so that it seemed that the project had come up only 'in order to fail'.

Newman told his community that he found such discouragements puzzling; he did not expect St Philip to save them from snubs, since their saint had made great psychological use of humiliation as a method of spiritual growth, but there was no obvious reason for the failure of good works, started in good faith. In private, he began to note down rumours from London. Some years later Manning and Talbot grumbled to each other that everything got round to Dr Newman in the end. In the small society of literate Catholics it was inevitable that gossip should be reported to its object; Newman's habit of noting it gives today something of the atmosphere in which he lived, now that the ultimate silence has settled on those busy tongues. It was clear enough already that Newman's character had been destroyed; Harry Ryder came back from a holiday in Brompton and asked Ambrose St John 'how it was that he heard there I positively hated Fr Faber'.

Cardinal Wiseman had been finally turned against Newman by an incident when he proposed to dedicate his latest book jointly to

Newman and Faber. Feeling that his name was simply being used to back up the London Oratory, Newman asked if his Birmingham house could be associated with him; in this way he hoped to make plain his independence, and Faber's, without hostility. But Wiseman was annoyed. 'He stood before the fire a long time and then brought out "the insolence of Dr Newman" or "the fellow", I don't know which,' Newman noted. This was reported by Sir John Acton, who had been a little boy at Oscott when Newman was received. Acton was a unique phenomenon, a Catholic aristocrat who was also a first-class scholar, having studied under Ignaz Döllinger, the great German church historian, in Munich. The Actons had many connections in Italy, and Sir John's mother, of the German family of Dalberg, had married Lord Granville as her second husband; through his stepfather Acton was introduced into the circle of the great English Whig families. He was now twenty-five, very clever, very serious, very upright and perhaps a little arrogant towards the rest of this stupid world. But as a witness, no one could be more reliable. It was he who told Newman that Faber had shown his letters to his friend, now Duke of Norfolk, who was so shocked that he said, 'shall we then never have a saint?' And he was now evasive about supporting Newman's school. Acton also heard that Faber was saying that everything Newman had done as a Catholic had failed. Faber was later to deny this and blame it on Ward, but as in so much, these two evidently agreed on Newman.

In this winter of 1858-9 Stanislas Flanagan was visiting Oratories in Sicily and Italy, and through him Newman discovered how the London Oratorians had accused him of aiming at a *generalate*. What lay behind the actions of the London House now became plainer to him. The only defence, however, which he allowed himself, was to send a careful answer to his lay friend, Robert Monteith, who had been a friend of Tennyson's at Cambridge, and a Catholic since 1846, and who had asked the truth of the Dedication affair. Newman said he had taken the step 'not under the influence of personal feeling, but in a matter of grave duty and with a definite object'. He did not explain his object; that would have involved making charges against

Faber. Of course this kind of defence only convinced friends who were already unable to believe that he had acted out of hurt and angry feeling, as Faber made out.

It was while his personal reputation was in this unfortunate state that Newman became involved in the affairs of the *Rambler* magazine, early in 1859. The *Rambler* had been started in 1848 by John Moore Capes, one of the married clergy converts who had to take up a lay career, and he intended it for 'the present condition of the *English* mind, entering into all subjects of literary, philosophical and moral interest'. He had written at once to Newman for advice, and for a time Newman was indeed a frequent adviser, though he was able to do less once he was involved with the new university in Dublin. During the fifties Capes had personal troubles, both domestic and religious, for he was assailed by difficulties of faith which later caused him to drop out of the Church – though he came back some years before his death. In 1858 he sold the *Rambler*, Sir John Acton taking two shares and Frederick Capes (John's brother) and Richard Simpson, acting editor, one each. Before the end, Acton had to subsidize the paper. He wanted the *Rambler* partly as a political platform, for he was shortly to enter Parliament as member for Carlow, in the Whig interest of his stepfather, Lord Granville. But he also wanted it as an intellectual platform from which to address the English Catholics, who, he felt, needed to broaden their minds.

Most of the editorial work was done by Richard Simpson, another married clergyman convert, a clever man with a lively sense of humour, who was writing a biography of Edmund Campion, the Elizabethan Jesuit and martyr, and was to become a respected Shakespearean scholar and perceptive appreciator of Jane Austen. Simpson, like most of the converts, was interested in theology, and would throw out speculations in the Oxford style, expecting argument; unfortunately seminary professors took them as heresies and tried to get the *Rambler* censured. Simpson was nearly twenty years younger than Newman, Acton more than thirty years. They were anxious for his support and advice and held him in respect, even though they might call him 'Noggs' to each other, after Newman Noggs, one of Dickens's characters.

The first clash with authority was caused by Acton's calling St Augustine the father of Jansenism; when this was taken amiss he commissioned an article by his old teacher, Dr Döllinger, showing the historical connection of ideas, which appeared in December 1858. As a consequence Faber seems to have tried to get Wiseman to delate Döllinger to Rome for heresy; Acton, hearing of this from a friend who had seen Faber's letter, told Newman of it when he called at the Oratory on 30 December 1858. 'He was quite miserable when I told him the news,' Acton wrote to Simpson, 'and moaned for a long time, rocking himself backwards and forwards over the fire like an old woman with toothache. He thinks the move provoked both by the hope of breaking down the *Rambler* and by jealousy of Döllinger.' Acton was surprised to find Newman so frank, talking of 'the natural inclination of men in power to tyrannize; ignorance and presumption of would-be theologians.'

Next day Newman wrote Acton a long letter, urging him to keep theology out of the magazine; Döllinger also gave the same advice. The priest-scholar was not in fact censured this time. But, significantly, the rock on which the magazine nearly foundered was not theological, but an article on education in the January number by Scott Nasmyth Stokes, a school inspector. He advocated Catholic co-operation with Government measures and though he had written the article before the publication of the English hierarchy's decision not to do so, the Cardinal was seriously annoyed and proposed to censure the magazine, which would effectively put it out of business. A last-minute suggestion was offered: the paper would be spared if Simpson resigned.

Ullathorne was deputed by the bishops to ask Newman to conduct this delicate operation, which he reluctantly undertook in order to save the magazine. Simpson visited Birmingham and agreed to resign if a suitable editor was found; if not, he would publish the whole transaction. Newman transmitted all this, with excuses for Simpson, who was in a difficult position, with the March number in type, expenses looming and his brother seriously ill with a mental breakdown at the same time. Wiseman was merely annoyed at what he called 'Dr Newman's stipulations' and proposed to go ahead with the censure.

Faced with the imminent destruction of the *Rambler*, Acton and Simpson resigned the whole property to Newman himself. It was rather like asking him to carry a box of explosives through a burning house. He was naturally unwilling to undertake the responsibility, but as with the *British Critic* twenty years earlier, he agreed in the end, rather than lose a periodical which he felt was doing useful work. Wiseman was gloomy about this transaction, sure that with Newman as editor the *Rambler* would finish off his moribund *Dublin Review*. Newman's reply, that there was room both for a religious quarterly and a literary bi-monthly (which he intended to make the *Rambler*), elicited no response. Presently Newman wrote again; assuming silence for consent, he had accepted the editorship, after much prayer and consultation, on 21 March 1859. Silence from Westminster, as usual.

Newman's association with the *Rambler* proved to be brief, but his editorship identified him with it in the minds of those most hostile to it, for the rest of its chequered career. Not wishing to cast any slur on Simpson or Acton, he made no public reference to any change of policy; indeed, he did not wish to change the principles of the magazine, but only its tone, blue-pencilling some of the smart remarks in the March number. He made two innovations which Acton admired and tried to keep going later: a correspondence section and a résumé of current affairs. His editorial *savoir-faire* was still excellent and promised well for the future.

But the bishops and seminary professors were still watching with hostile eyes; many people did not know Newman had become editor. An adverse critique appeared in the *Tablet*, which was known to be controlled by the Cardinal's circle, and Newman was in correspondence with its editor when on 22 May Bishop Ullathorne called at the Oratory. Newman made a memorandum of the interview, in which Ullathorne, saying that the *Tablet* had expressed his own views, added: 'our laity were a peaceable set; the Church was *peace*. They had a deep faith; they did not like to hear that anyone doubted … I said in answer that he saw one side, I another; that the Bishops etc. did not see the state of the laity … He said something like "Who are the laity?" I answered (not those *words*) that the Church would look foolish without them.'

Here was the crux: Newman saw the needs of those who did have doubts and difficulties, who did not live in a closed ecclesiastical world. When Ullathorne observed that things might be said in books which were unsuitable to periodicals, 'I granted; but did he mean to give up Periodical Literature to the enemy? I said, those who did not like it, need not take it in.' But that is a suggestion never appreciated by those who like to control the minds of others! Then Newman rashly said that nothing would please him more than to give up the editorship, but he could only do so by returning the magazine to its owners, Acton and Simpson. To his astonishment Ullathorne jumped at this offer – he could do so after the July number. It had not occured to Newman that the bishops thought Simpson less dangerous than himself! But he had to agree; as he said afterwards, he could not continue to edit a magazine against his own bishop's declared wishes.

'Your retirement is an irreparable blow,' said Simpson, shocked at this new turn in the 'persecution'. Could they have his assistance still? His advice? Could Ward be told? No, Newman hastily replied to this last request: 'I would do it myself, but he is so great a blab. I don't think he *can* keep a secret.' In the event, Ward took on the *Dublin Review* and made it the platform of the strongest papalist views and the organ of Westminster, now dominated by Ultramontanes. Already opinions were polarizing for the battle of the sixties.

In the July number of the *Rambler* appeared Newman's own article *On Consulting the Faithful in Matters of Doctrine*, interesting in itself and of crucial importance in his life because it determined the attitude taken up towards him by the officials at Rome. In the May number he had put in an editorial paragraph on the education issue, apologizing for any annoyance caused to the hierarchy but defending the right of the laity to be consulted on a question which concerned them so nearly and remarking that only recently they had been consulted on a matter of doctrine, as to their belief in Mary's immaculate conception. Dr Gillow, the leading theologian at Ushaw, not knowing that Newman was the author of this paragraph immediately wrote to attack what he regarded as a heretical and subversive idea. In the correspondence which followed Newman pointed out that he had used the word 'consult' in the sense in which we consult a barometer – the bishops had been asked to discover the faith of the people. Afterwards he worked up his defence into an article, bringing out his meaning with examples from the early centuries, when many bishops had taken up Arian ideas but the body of the people had remained faithful to the orthodox beliefs.

At the Synod of Bishops in July this article was held up to reprobation by Bishop Brown of Newport, and Manning, then Provost of the Westminster Chapter, was deputed to speak to Newman on the subject. He was so diplomatic that Newman did not realize the seriousness of the matter. Manning suggested he wrote *theologically* on the subject, but Newman thought it a mere suggestion and did not take it up. Bishop Brown, feeling that nothing was being done, then wrote off to the Secretary of Propaganda, denouncing Newman for writing what was 'totally subversive of the essential authority of the Church in matters of Faith'. Newman had given an 'unsatisfactory answer' to Gillow and the Holy See itself ought to deal with what 'might have been the writing of a Calvinist'. He ended: 'There are in the writings of Faber many objectionable passages – but space fails me'. Newman was the scapegoat for all the converts, as became clear in Brown's letter, to Talbot, and in a second to Propaganda written on 30 October. On 3 December Talbot wrote to Ullathorne of Newman: 'He has lost the confidence of many in consequence and the *Rambler* is beginning to be looked upon as a very dangerous periodical'. It is uncertain whether Ullathorne received this letter before he left for Rome, but anyway he said nothing to Newman about it.

Newman was in bed with one of his worst colds when Ullathorne returned to England in January 1860, but he got up at once when he heard that the bishop wanted to see him on an important matter, and went the two miles to Pugin's Gothic episcopal fortress (pulled down a hundred years later) late at night, to hear that Barnabò had shown Ullathorne Brown's letter and said, 'Le Pape est beaucoup peiné.' Ullathorne advised writing to Wiseman, and this Newman did, drafting a careful epistle in which he requested the passages of the article objected to and offered to explain them. He then waited for Wiseman to take the steps he had promised Ullathorne he would take, to clear Newman at Rome. Unfortunately Wiseman took no steps. Propaganda sent him a list of suspect passages but he did not forward it to Newman. He showed Newman's letter to Talbot and Manning, but not to Barnabò or the Pope – in 1867 Barnabò was to express surprise at this, since Wiseman had been at Propaganda but had said nothing on the subject. Wiseman had a heart attack in Rome and was suffering from diabetes, but his illness did not prevent him from writing to Faber, or from prosecuting his case against his coadjutor Archbishop Errington, a Catholic of the old school who disliked the Romanizing methods of Manning at Westminster and had annoyed the Pope by coolly taking notes during an interview. Wiseman had secretaries; Manning, supposedly Newman's friend, was with him in Rome. Nothing whatever was done by anyone.

Four months later, in May 1860, Manning wrote to Newman to say that on his return Wiseman would bring the matter 'to an acceptable termination'. Nothing more was said to Newman, but a year later Barnabò wrote to Ullathorne asking why Newman had done nothing. From Rome in January 1862 Ullathorne wrote saying he was trying to set things right, presumably by talking, since no records remain. At Propaganda Newman continued to be regarded as a writer of heretical articles who did not trouble to defend himself and who was responsible for all the views printed in the *Rambler*. Unaware of all this Newman was writing to Miss Bowles in 1863, 'I kept silence and the matter was hushed up. I suppose so, for I have heard no more of it, but I suppose it might (*pel bisogno*) be revived in time.' It was.

Meanwhile trouble went on for the *Rambler* and in 1861, after the May number had carried Acton's précis of Döllinger's lectures on the Pope's temporal power, Cardinal Antonelli (the Papal Secretary of State) sent a letter to Wiseman demanding the suppression of the *Rambler*. This did not bring an end to it only because, on Burns's refusing to publish it, Acton transferred it to a non-Catholic publisher. It was the height of the agitation about the Pope, when he had lost all but Rome itself of his States, and it was the point at which enthusiasm for his earthly sovereignty began to merge into a mystique of his supernatural mission. Faber published two sermons, *Devotion to the Pope* and *Devotion to the Church*; in the latter, Acton, with reason, felt that he was 'distinctly pointed at' in a warning against periodicals, and was irritated by Faber's suggestion that opinions were validated only by the holiness of their authors. As to the Pope, Faber found him a kind of eighth sacrament. Jesus was never ill or old, but his Vicar could be, and so focus our sympathies, 'I have an irrepressible feeling,' said the irrepressible Faber, 'that it will be especially well in heaven with those who have especially loved on earth the Pope who defined the Immaculate Conception.' He even identified opposition to the Pope with the sin against the Holy Ghost, which cannot be forgiven.

Manning, who had been saying that the Pope's temporal sovereignty would soon be defined as part of the Catholic faith, was sent to warn Acton of the censure expected from Rome, and Acton told Newman. While Newman thought it might prove impossible to carry on the *Rambler*, he disliked the political pressure, and said Acton should not allow himself to be bullied into giving up the government foreign policy, if he agreed with it – in favour of the Risorgimento. Newman also took the bold step of writing to Manning to say that if the Cardinal was going to use his inaugural address to the new Accademia of the Catholic Religion to promote the papal policy, Newman would resign from membership.

Manning knew just how to neutralize such a brave but naïve gesture. He replied that he did not know what the Cardinal was going to say: would it not be better if Newman, instead of resigning, *did not join* yet? Thus Newman was prevented from making his gesture, so that Acton and his friends began to think him timid, while Manning was confirmed in his suspicions of Newman's disloyalty.

In the spring of 1862 Acton turned the *Rambler* into a quarterly and rechristened it the *Home and Foreign Review*; its high quality was generally recognized and much appreciated by Newman, but the English bishops continued to criticize it in their pastorals. Finally, after studying the Pope's Brief to the congress of Catholic scholars assembled at Munich in December 1863, Acton decided that it discountenanced free inquiry in scientific and historical research, and felt he could not continue his review in direct opposition to the declared policy of the Holy See. He printed his famous article, *Conflicts with Rome*, in April 1864, and made that number the last. From that time the moderates and liberals among English Catholics had no organ of opinion, the field was entirely held by papers and magazines controlled by the Ultramontanes at Westminster. It was a situation which prevented any but the views of the extremists from being canvassed in England, and materially affected the attitude to the First Vatican Council.

13

ORDEAL BY REJECTION

It was towards the end of 1859, after the many failures of the last few years, that Newman, in an effort to understand what was happening to him, began to write down his thoughts in an exercise book with a marbled cover. The entries were made at rare intervals but are all concerned with his own life; they are now published in *Autobiographical Writings*. He began on 15 December with the Latin text of Christ's saying that no man who puts his hand to the plough and looks back is fit for the kingdom of heaven. 'I am writing this on my knees and in God's sight.'

First in his mind was the effect of the process of ageing on his personal relationship with God. 'Old men are in soul as stiff, as lean, as bloodless as their bodies, except so far as grace penetrates and softens them. I more and more wonder at *old* saints ... O Philip gain me some little portion of thy fervour. I live more and more in the past, and in hopes that the past may revive in the future. My God, when shall I learn that I have so parted with the world, that, though I may wish to make friends with it, it will not make friends with me?' He felt that when he was younger he had really 'put the world aside' for the service of Christ, but he now realized that the power to do so had partly derived from the natural enthusiasm of youth. 'When I was young I was bold, because I was ignorant – now I have lost my boldness because I have had [sic] advanced in experience.'

Here he was interrupted by the demands of life, a fearful cold, and Miss Giberne's attempts to enter a convent – at fifty-seven she was a difficult novice and tried several places in England before settling at Autun, in France. On 8 January 1860 Newman picked up his exercise book and tried to recover the lost thread of his reflections, attempting to unravel the puzzle of his failures as a Catholic in comparison with the success, in the sense of his great influence, he had as an Anglican. But again he became absorbed in what had actually happened, and the unkindness he had received from others. 'I have no friend at Rome, I have laboured in England, to be misrepresented, backbitten and scorned. I have laboured in Ireland, with a door ever shut in my face.'

If this had made him shrink into himself, it had also turned him more to God – 'while I have Him who lives in the Church, the separate members of the Church, my Superiors, though they may claim my obedience, have no claim on my admiration, and offer nothing for my inward trust.' For this reason, it was difficult not to feel attracted by the returning sympathy of Anglicans – 'certain persons who have deliberately beat me down and buried me for the last ten years'. And so he feared this was a temptation to look back from the plough, and prayed, this time with a deeper understanding of what it could mean, his '*lifelong* prayer' that he should be 'set aside in this world'. St Philip helped him here, with his famous prayer: to despise myself, to despise no other, to despise the world, to despise being despised. But that made him anxious again, on behalf of his Oratory, a dwindling group of overworked middle-aged men. This time he was interrupted by another cold and the news that the Pope had been pained by his writing heresy in the *Rambler*.

This episode prompted him to write, in a memorandum, 'All through life things happen to me which do not happen to others – I am the scapegoat. It was the Cardinal who got off the Achilli matter, while I suffered, as now Döllinger gets off, not I.' (Had he known it, Faber was getting off too, for lack of space in Bishop Brown's letter to Rome.) Not only his role as scapegoat interested Newman, but the regularity of its occurrence. He saw himself as the mythical Sisyphus, 'rolling my load up the hill for ten years and never cresting it, but falling back. Thus I failed in the schools in 1820; then I slowly mended things and built myself up into somebody with a prospect of something in 1830, and then on 5 May I had to retire from College offices and was nobody again. Then again I set to work and by 1840 had become somebody once more, when on 27 February 1841 No. 90 was attacked, and down I fell again. Then slowly I went on and by 1850 I had as a Catholic so recovered my ground that the Pope made me a DD when on 28 July 1851 I delivered the lecture in the Corn Exchange which delivered me over into the hands of Achilli.' At that time he had wondered if, at the end of the next ten years, he might be 'had up before Rome'. Now this had come to pass.

After this, he thought, there was nothing left but to die in 1870. Yet the curious pattern was repeated; the success of the *Apologia* was to build him up once more, yet the publication of his letter against the infallibilists in 1870 threw him again 'under a cloud' but by the end of the decade he was a Cardinal; in 1890 he died. It was indeed a strange rhythm, like the gathering and breaking of slow waves one after another on the shore.

For Newman, the years round about sixty were the worst of his life, the time when the sense of failure and uselessness weighed so heavily on him as to affect his health, though he knew the symptoms were caused by nervous anxiety. Part of his unease was on account of the Oratory school, which had started successfully on St Athanasius's day, 2 May 1859, but had been more and more taken out of Newman's hands by the headmaster, Fr Nicholas Darnell, now in his early forties and ambitious to rival the public schools. Darnell treated the school as his, never asked Newman's advice and ignored his suggestions. He was even planning to remove it to a better site without consulting the Congregation; his confidants were the lay masters and rich lay friends – his colleagues in the Oratory concerned him less and less. And as time went on there were gathering criticisms outside, that the boys were not taught their religion and that the punishments were too severe. While Darnell was in fact in command, it was Newman who was ultimately responsible – though one of his trials at this time was that people were saying he was no longer fit for such responsibility.

As usual, Newman noted the evidence of this gossip and kept the letters of those who wrote to him in concern about it. Stories were circulating that he was in his dotage, physically and mentally breaking up, and so nervous that he ought not to be allowed to say mass. One of the lay masters, a clergyman convert, Robert Moody, denied saying such things when Newman faced him with it, but friends insisted that Mrs Moody had certainly spoken in London of Newman's mental decay. They were not the only ones to do so, and there was an unpleasant episode of anonymous and scurrilous Valentines sent to Newman and the other Fathers.

Newman certainly came near to nervous breakdown in these years, though he carried on his normal work throughout; mentally he was alert enough, making notes on his old favourite subject of the relation between reason and faith, which were at first intended for a large book – put aside when he realized that he was suspected of unorthodoxy and later to be transformed into *The Grammar of Assent*. Emily Bowles, who had tried her vocation in Mother Cornelia Connelly's new order of the Holy Child Jesus, but had come out to live a life of charitable work in the world, left an account of a visit to Birmingham in 1861. She was welcomed by Newman 'as only he can welcome'. She would never forget 'the brightness that lit up that worn face as he received me at the door, carrying in several packages himself'. But when they were talking in the Guest Room, she noticed a change in him. 'He had not only aged disproportionately to the time but his grand massive face was scored with lines which no lapse of years had written there. They were too evidently lines of intense grief, disappointment, and the patient bearing up against the failure of hope. Whenever he spoke, the expression softened, but when at rest, and his conversation was frequently broken by short fits of absence of mind, there was even a look of terrible weariness akin to lasting depression of mind – It gave me at first the idea of some personal displeasure, but I soon found that this idea could not be entertained.' She discovered that it had something to do with the school, but the details she only found out afterwards from others.

The final crisis over the school came at midwinter 1861–2, and caused another upheaval within the Oratory itself. As a community experience, its details are interesting, but since they are now available in Newman's *Letters and Diaries* the briefest account must suffice here. The occasion of the explosion was Nicholas Darnell's determination that Mrs Wootten, the chief Dame, or matron, must leave at once; if she did not, he would resign, and his threat of resignation was supported by all the lay masters, who would go with him. He presented this ultimatum with such impatience for an immediate decision that Newman had the utmost difficulty in gaining time for all the Fathers to say three masses while they thought and prayed about it. Meanwhile, Darnell was already telling and writing his version of the affair to all his friends. Newman also found that Mrs Wootten's chief fault, besides what Darnell considered excessive coddling of sick or delicate boys, was that she had criticized the headmaster's acting without consulting Newman about the proposed transfer of the school – sites had even been inspected. The quarrel between them was not the trivial affair that Darnell represented it to be.

Newman was determined that the Congregation should decide, but when they voted for his view rather than Darnell's (that the school was the Oratory's and the ultimate responsibility his) Darnell could not bear his defeat and resigned from the Oratory as well as the school. He was extremely upset by the way things had turned out; Pollen, with whom he stayed in London, heard him crying in his room at night. But although he was given six months' leave in which to change his mind, he could not bring himself to climb down. And in the summer Stanislas Flanagan left too; he had postponed his departure because of the school débâcle, since he did not want it to be blamed on that. Newman felt that it was the long succession of failures which he could not stand. He went back to Ireland, but remained a friend and correspondent.

Darnell had left precipitately, followed by most of the staff, whose resignations Newman had accepted. It was January 1862 and somehow the school was opened only a few days late. Ambrose St John became headmaster and they secured as senior master Thomas Arnold, son of Dr Arnold of Rugby, who had written to Newman from Tasmania at the time of his conversion, 1855–6. Newman had made him Professor of Literature in his university, but the pay was very poor and the post in constant danger of being suppressed, so eventually he accepted Newman's offer, and a house near the Oratory for his growing family. Arnold's name, of course, was an asset to the school. Newman himself did some teaching and later he adapted the Latin comedies he himself had played in at Ealing School, and got the boys acting – they long remembered the vigour he put into rehearsals.

Now that he was able to run the school as he wished, Newman's health began to improve. In 1861 the doctor had *ordered* him to take a holiday and drink wine – he was not to imagine it gave him a headache. He went with William Neville to Cambridge, and later to Ventnor, Isle of Wight, writing vivid and amusing letters back to his community. His friends now discovered how poor he was, and part of the expenses of his next year's holiday was defrayed by presents. Newman was extremely worn out, but again his letters from Deal are full of lively descriptions of the place and the people, his lodgings and the dreariness of *East Lynne*, which he had taken from the library only to find, as he told Ambrose, that 'it got more like medicine every page I read on.' He got half through the first volume but then reported 'I positively can't take any more.' The characters were cut out of paper and the author had not the faintest conception of dialogue. Newman was a great reader of novels and fond of Trollope, though complaining that he sometimes could not *end*. Thackeray was also a favourite, though he felt the later books fell off.

Deal proved unsatisfactory in many ways and Newman enjoyed Ramsgate much better. He was joined there by Austin Mills, who was suffering from sciatica; Mills was one of the Cambridge converts who had joined Faber, but, allotted to Newman's Oratory, remained faithful to the end. At Ramsgate Newman took cold plunges in the bath and relished the meals, which were served by an ex-scout from Oxford. He told Ambrose of gossip against the school. 'You see, tongues are at work, frightening people with the suspicion of our being crypto-heretics.' He apologized for letting off steam but Ambrose replied, 'It is rather a rollicking kind of despondency, which says "never say die" all the time as the refrain to the song.' He was right; the tone was different from the bewildered pain of the year before.

But Newman still had not worried out his problem to its conclusion, and in January 1863 he once more took out the marbled exercise book and began to write about the gossip against the school; it was still said that the boys were not being trained in their religion, though now Newman himself was giving them instruction, in St Philip's chapel during the sermon at High Mass – and many of them remembered his very words, his look, all their lives. Newman was aware that the criticisms were really directed at him and that his silence in public – for he had published nothing in recent years – was considered sinister, not submissive. Ambrose was on holiday at Brighton and met one of the ex-masters of the school, who explained Newman's unpopularity very simply: 'Why, he has made no converts, as Manning and Faber have.'

Suddenly that gave Newman the clue and he saw the whole of his course since 1845 with new eyes. This was when he wrote of his blunders in Rome, his snubs from Wiseman. 'And then, when I came home, at once Faber was upon me, to bully me, humbug me, and make use of me.' That was how it looked now. He went on to note that all this opposition and mistrust was not a problem in itself (St Philip too had suffered this sort of thing) but because it had destroyed his influence and his usefulness. People who might have come to him were put off. 'I am passé, in decay; I am untrustworthy; I am strange, odd; I have my own ways and cannot get on with others; something or other is said in disparagement.' God had certainly worked through him in the foundation of the Oratories (he specifically included the London House – 'the instrument of so much good'), of the university and the school. But these were works of his *name* – 'what I am speaking of is what belongs to my own person; – things, which I ought to have been especially suited to do, and have not done, not done any one of them.' The bitter paradox was that the very people who had prevented him doing these things were the ones who complained that he was doing nothing.

Suddenly Newman realized that all his work had made no

impression whatever, chiefly because it had been aimed at the education of Catholics and not at conversions. 'Manning then and others are great, who live in London and by their position and influence convert Lords and Ladies. This is what was expected of me.' His activity in education, suggesting that Catholics were actually in need of improvement, had even annoyed people and encroached on the existing institutions. Then, in writing, '*I* should wish to attempt to meet the great infidel etc. questions of the day, but both Propaganda and the Episcopate, doing nothing themselves, look with extreme jealousy on anyone who attempts it.' Then again, on the Pope's temporal power, 'I, thinking that they would be obliged to rely more on reason, a truer defence, than on the sword, if they had it not, am lukewarm on the point; and this lukewarmness has been exaggerated into a supposed complicity with Garibaldi!' Rumour had it that Newman had contributed £50 to Garibaldi's funds.

So Newman wrote all this down as he saw it and put the book aside again. But in May Miss Bowles wrote from London, anxious to know the truth behind the gossip she heard, and reporting Acton's laments – 'he does so fully *appreciate* what we all lose by your silence.' She had been to Oxford, she had been to Littlemore – Newman's trees had all grown up – she had been to St Mary's and reported 'they are retouching and restoring every bit of it.' To her it was Newman's Via Dolorosa. Touched by her sympathy he wrote a long letter, in which he let her into the secret of his present silence, the suspicions and difficulties behind the scenes. Propaganda was too rough and ready to understand intellectual conflict. 'It likes quick results – scalps from beaten foes by the hundred.' In the old days there had been much freedom of discussion in the schools of different nations and Rome was only the ultimate court of appeal; now, Propaganda came down at once on any private person who said anything doubtful. 'How can I fight with such a chain upon my arm?' Newman said. 'It is like the Persians driven to fight *under the lash*.' But he admitted that he was afraid of hiding his talent in a napkin and when people asked him why he was not doing more, 'then, since I think I could do a great deal if I was let to do it, I become uneasy. And lastly, willing as I am to observe St Philip's dear rule that "we should despise being despised", yet when I find that scorn and contempt become the means of *my Oratory being injured*, as they have been before now, then I get impatient.'

Many years later Miss Bowles wrote of this letter as heartrending. 'It filled me too with awe, as if I had seen the rock stricken and the long restrained imprisoned flood rushing forth.' Yet the tone of this letter is different from the 'inarticulate cries' Newman had written earlier; it is even touched with scorn when he speaks of the low-mindedness of those who thought him soured because he had not, after all, been made a bishop. In essentials Newman had mastered this, the most painful frustration of his life, before he had any hope that things would change.

In this summer of 1863 Faber was dying. He had been dying so many times, had so many quasi-miraculous recoveries, that people hardly believed it, but this time it was true. He had Bright's disease, complicated by dropsy. His friend Antony Hutchison had already become seriously ill and was confined to a wheel-chair; he too had a relapse and was to die within a short time of Faber. In spite of Faber's success as a preacher and writer of devotional books and hymns, he had had many difficulties lately, not only from his ailments but from the state of his Oratory. One of the Fathers had left in a blaze of scandal – leaving the rest sobbing in each other's arms, according to Faber's description. Faber wrote notes to his novices addressed 'My dearest Pet' but was sarcastic about them to Hutchison; he was irritated by Dalgairns, who was again unhappy and restless, and he was now so often away that he had no real control over the house.

Hearing Faber was so ill, Newman asked if he would like to see him, and when Faber eagerly accepted the offer, he called in July, on his way abroad with Ambrose. It was the first time they had met since the quarrel seven years ago. Both of them had aged in appearance; though Faber was only forty-nine he was immensely stout and his hair was white. The doctors only allowed Newman fifteen or twenty minutes in the sickroom. The same day Faber dictated a letter to Herbert Harrison, a favourite novice, pursued, as so often with Faber's young men, by indignant relatives. 'Fr Newman has been this morning and spent full twenty minutes with me – we went into everything – no woman could be tenderer than he was – the whole interview was effusive of more than kindness, of downright love – all is right and righter than right. We held each other's hand the whole while, and talked about our old friendship and next through the breach – he begged me to pray for him when I was before the throne of God – you would have been strangely moved had you seen his face when he came to leave and looked down upon me and said in a voice of the most consummate sweetness "St Philip be with you, Father." I said, smiling, "He will be if you tell him to be, and now Padre give me your blessing," which he did in silence but with great solemnity. Fr Philip says tears were in his eyes when he left the room.'

Newman went straight off from Dover for what proved rather a hectic holiday, Paris, Trèves, the Moselle, the Rhine, and Aix, where he fell downstairs and wrenched his arm. They met William Neville at Spa and Ambrose went back, while Newman stayed an extra week at Ostend, and it was there that he wrote down some notes on his interview with Faber – at this time still alive, for he had once more revived (after a tremendous death-bed farewell of all the community) and was even able to sit out in the garden.

'He was nearly the sole speaker,' Newman wrote, on 11 August, 'for he seemed to wish to disburden his mind ... He said he had loved me best of anyone in the world next to the late Duke of Norfolk.' (Faber's friend had died suddenly, after a very brief time as Duke.) Faber then confessed that he was pained to think how he and his were adding to Newman's trials, mentioning the translation of Scripture, and then going on to speak of the quarrel, insisting that his own house had acted against his advice in the first application to Propaganda. On this, Newman made some *Remarks*. 'My own view about Faber, poor fellow, is not much changed by the above.' He recalled the evidence that Faber *had* spoken against him, and thought that he seemed as if he were 'arguing with himself that he had not been unkind to me; rather than boldly saying he had ever been a hearty friend. How different e.g. would Ambrose have to speak, if he were at the last!' Ambrose would know that whatever else he had done wrong, he had always been loyal and true to Newman. 'Dear Faber has not been so, and feels it.'

Newman felt Faber had thrown some light on 'that mysterious matter, the London House's treatment of me'. Newman now realized what the various moves of the London Oratorians had been and pieced together what had once puzzled him so much that he had said he could no more see into it than into a deal board.

Faber lingered on through August and September, receiving a blessing from the Pope and a kind letter from Cardinal Wiseman, a comfort after a recent estrangement. He brightened up to tell a priest that he would lose his soul if he settled in Oxford – the anti-intellectual supernaturalist to the last. There were more alarms, more revivals, but at last he died peacefully on 26 September, conscious to the last, while mass was being said for him. Newman and Ambrose St John went up for the requiem.

When Newman returned from the continent he had found a letter from Keble who reproached himself for his long silence. He was seventy and spoke of himself 'as if dying'. Newman said, 'I trust you will live long, and every year more and more to the glory of God.' At the end of his affectionate reply he wrote, 'Never have I doubted for one moment your affection for me, never have I been hurt at your silence ... It was not the silence of others.'

One of those others had suddenly turned up in Birmingham on 30 August, when Newman was arranging the books in the library. After twenty years, Frederic Rogers came to see him. He was now fifty-two, married but childless and Under-Secretary for the Colonies. Newman wrote to Ambrose, 'when he first saw me he burst into tears and would not let go my hands – then his first words were "How altered you are."' But soon Rogers was crying out, 'Oh how like *you*!' Rogers himself wrote to his wife of his pleasant day, though he felt Newman was overworked and in a way that was not his line, thrown away by the communion to which he had devoted himself 'and evidently sensible he is so thrown away'. Newman took Rogers round the church, in its usual state of alteration, and as he was leading the way Rogers 'caught a kind of impatient and half-mournful "Ah, tzt" … which seemed to say, "why is he not with me, why can't I often be talking to him in this way?"' They talked about Birmingham, politics (Newman said they had been like two clocks keeping time) and Ward, whom Rogers had recently met and who had given him the picture of Newman as left in the cold which no doubt coloured his view of what he saw. 'A joke at Ward's expense was not unacceptable, and it was a pleasure to get a good hearty laugh out of him in the old fashion.' But Newman laughed more often than Rogers imagined, even during these difficult years, to judge by his letters.

The first of these connections with old friends still Anglicans had occurred when Newman had met William Copeland, once his curate at Littlemore, in a London street, and persuaded him to come and see him in Birmingham – 'Do let us have a long confab.' Copeland had passed the word round that Newman would like to be visited. It was a curious thing that he should just now be picking up these old friendships. For on 30 December 1863 he received by post a copy of *Macmillan's Magazine* in which there was a review of volumes VII and VIII of Anthony Froude's *History of England*, initialled CK. The sender had drawn a heavy cross against the following passage: 'Truth for its own sake, has never been a virtue with the Roman clergy. Father Newman informs us that it need not, and on the whole, ought not to be: that cunning is the weapon which Heaven has given to the saints wherewith to withstand the brute male force of the wicked world which marries and is given in marriage. Whether his notion is doctrinally correct or not, at least it is historically so.'

14

THE GHOST OF OXFORD

As soon as Newman read that he had taught that truth was no virtue he wrote to Messrs Macmillan, drawing their attention to this 'grave and gratuitous slander'. Within a week he received a polite letter from Alexander Macmillan, who had heard him preach in St Mary's long ago, enclosing a note from Charles Kingsley, the writer of the review, who confidently asserted that his words were just and cited Newman's sermon on *Wisdom and Innocence*, published in *Sermons on Subjects of the Day* in 1844. He said he was happy to hear that he had mistaken Newman's meaning.

Newman had not guessed Kingsley's identity. As he told Macmillan, he had thought 'Here is a young scribe, who is making himself a cheap reputation by smart hits at safe objects.' Charles Kingsley, however, was now forty-four, Chaplain to the Queen, Tutor to the Prince of Wales, Professor of Modern History at Cambridge and a novelist at the height of his popularity: *Westward Ho*! was written during the Crimean War and *The Water Babies* had appeared in the last year. The letter of apology which he designed for publication was almost more insulting than the original remark. 'Dr Newman has by letter expressed in the strongest terms, his denial of the meaning which I put upon his words. No man knows the use of words better than Dr Newman; no man, therefore, has a better right to defend what he does, and does not, mean by them. It only remains, therefore, for me to express my hearty regret at having so seriously mistaken him; and my hearty pleasure at finding him on the side of Truth, in this or any other matter.'

Newman objected to this so-called apology and gave what he considered the 'unjust but too probable popular rendering of it', in a parallel column. Thus: 'I have set before Dr Newman, as he challenged me to do, extracts from his writings, and he has affixed to them what he conceives to be their legitimate sense, to the denial of that in which I understood them. He has done this with the skill of a great master of verbal fence, who knows, as well as any man living, how to insinuate a doctrine without committing himself to it. However, while I heartily regret that I have so seriously mistaken the sense which he assures me his words were meant to bear, I cannot but feel a hearty pleasure also, at having brought him, for once in a way, to confess that after all truth is a Christian virtue.'

Evidently Kingsley did not find this gloss amusing and missed the point, for he repeated his reference to the sermon as the basis of his allegations in his amended apology, which appeared in the February number of the magazine, 1864. 'Dr Newman has by letter expressed, in the strongest terms, his denial of the meaning which I have put upon his words. It only remains, therefore, for me to express my hearty regret at having so seriously mistaken him.'

'*Mean* it! I maintain I never *said* it, whether as a Protestant or as a Catholic,' Newman represented himself as retorting, in the imaginary dialogue he composed a few days later. He had consulted his lawyer friend, Badeley, as to whether the apology was sufficient, and Badeley had replied, 'Most decidedly not.' It would not pass in a court of justice or in any society of gentlemen and was a disgrace to the writer. In fact, it was an affair of honour, only one step removed from a duel, and as such the newspapers were soon to take it.

Newman took up the challenge, though he feared it might lead to a controversy, not only because the accusation gave the lie to his whole life, but because Kingsley had used him as a scapegoat for 'the Roman clergy'. As he put it in his pamphlet, would not offence have been taken had he said, 'Dean Milner or the Rev. Charles Simeon informs us that chastity for its own sake need not be, and on the whole ought not to be, a virtue with the Anglican clergy' and when challenged for proof had said, '*Vide* Simeon's Skeleton Sermons *passim*.'

The atmosphere in which Newman took up this challenge can be gauged from some attacks which had been made on him in the summer of 1862, some eighteen months earlier. Mr G. Noel Hoare had been reported in the *Lincolnshire Echo* as demanding, at a public meeting, what had become of 'that "giant" of intellect and sanity, John Henry Newman?' Answer: he was living in Paris and had become utterly sceptical, ridiculing the Romish persuasion altogether. Nonsensical as this was, it was typical of rumours going about, and as it gave his name, Newman wrote a fighting reply, which he sent to the *Globe*, declaring that he was living in Birmingham, detailing his work and asserting his whole-hearted belief in the Catholic faith. He also said that the thought of the Anglican service made him shiver and the Thirty-Nine Articles made him shudder. As he explained to a pained Anglican friend, 'it is one thing to shiver at the Anglican service, quite another to take delight in the devotion of which it was the occasion.' But this distinction between the objective mutilation of the central Catholic rite and the personal devotion of which it was nevertheless an instrument, was not taken in by the journalists, and a great uproar arose. An especially violent attack in the *Saturday Review* was widely reprinted, after the custom of the day, in other periodicals. 'Dr Newman must have relished, with the oiliest smacking of controversial lips, the chance which invited him to construct that griping antithesis,' the Saturday reviewer proclaimed, and spoke of 'controversial bile secreted without natural discharge for thirteen years.'

Some people thought the same at the beginning of the controversy in 1864. Newman sent his little dialogue to Badeley, wondering if he should do something more staid, though whatever he tried seemed 'ditchwater' in comparison. Luckily, Badeley pressed for the original 'champagne', which was published on 12 February, Macmillan appearing as 'Mr XY'. Five hundred copies were printed; two more impressions had to be taken before the month was out. Newman's brevity and humour won him a hearing and the *Reflections* were reprinted in weeklies, monthlies and even in quarterlies. The matter was taken as a kind of boxing match and the laughter showed that Newman, with all the odds against him, had won the first round. When Kingsley's reply came out in March the

Athenaeum observed, 'How briskly we gather round a pair of reverend gentlemen, when the prize for which they contend is which of the two shall be considered the father of lies!'

'*What, then, does Dr Newman mean?*' Kingsley demanded, in high indignation that he should be laughed out of court. On 9 March he wrote to a friend: 'I am answering Newman now and though of course I give up the charge of conscious dishonesty I trust to make him and his admirers sorry they did not leave me alone. I have a score of more than twenty years to pay, and this is an instalment of it.' Since he had never met Newman, and had been up at Cambridge, he had no wrongs to revenge; it was Newman's influence he hated – it had nearly turned Frances Grenfell into an Anglican nun. From this fate Kingsley had rescued her, marrying her in spite of her upper class family and ideals of dedicated virginity. Kingsley, a stammerer who made a cult of virility, was an odd mixture of enthusiasm, belligerently anti-celibate, an admirer of the Teutonic races and despiser of Latins, an ardent believer in science and a defender, if erratic, of the rights of the working man. His pamphlet was deadly serious, a confused tirade against the evils of Romanism, with Newman as the arch-deceiver, at once credulous and subtle, outwitting honest Englishmen with his 'cunning sleight of hand logic', and double significations. 'What proof have I, then,' Kingsley demanded, 'that by "*mean* it! I never *said* it!" Dr Newman does not signify, "I did not say it; but I did mean it."'

Newman called this 'poisoning the wells' because it prepared readers' minds against him, so that whatever he said, he would not be believed. Kingsley's pamphlet arrived on Palm Sunday, 20 March. Newman was the celebrant of the principal services of Holy Week, as usual, after spending the Wednesday in retreat. He did not begin his answer till 10 April, but he had already decided what to do. In the second part of his answer he said, 'When I first read the Pamphlet of Accusation, I almost despaired of meeting effectively such a heap of misrepresentations and such a vehemence of animosity.' But he soon decided that what gave unity to Kingsley's accusations was his belief that he was attacking a *liar* – the representative of a corrupt moral system because he had voluntarily accepted it. Even when he wrote the sermon in question, Newman had been a secret Romanist, corrupting the Church of England from within; his whole course had been that of a deceiver and a hypocrite.

'My perplexity did not last half an hour,' Newman said. 'I recognized what I had to do, though I shrank both from the task and the exposure it would entail. I must, I said, give the true key to my whole life; I must show what I am that it may be seen what I am not, and that the phantom may be extinguished which gibbers instead of me. I wish to be known as a living man, and not as a scarecrow which is dressed up in my clothes. False ideas may be refuted indeed by argument, but by true ideas alone are they expelled.' His plan was to write the history of his own mind.

And so it was born, the book that Newman afterwards called *Apologia Pro Vita Sua* – in defence of his life. It came out like a serial in weekly parts, which Longmans had agreed to publish, emphasizing the importance of immediacy and continuity. Bound in stiff buff paper they came out on Thursdays, the first two, on Kingsley's method and how to deal with it (omitted from the book edition) on 21 and 28 April at 1/– each and the historical parts, which were longer, at 2/– throughout May. Newman worked all out, up to sixteen hours a day, and once for twenty-two hours running, with Rivington's man at the door to take his copy to the printer's. The whole task (with appendices on specific charges) was not completed till 12 June – two months of intense labour and strain – an amazing achievement for a man of sixty-three, who not long before had felt himself breaking down under the stress and frustration of his life.

Newman used old letters and papers and was anxious to check facts with his Anglican friends – it seemed providential that so many had recently got in touch with him again. Rogers and Church helped most, delighted to get mentioned in the text, Rogers only sorry to appear unnamed as the 'intimate friend' who put Froude's Breviary into Newman's hand in 1836. Some friends, as well as old enemies, were apprehensive, but Newman contrived to tell his tale with such skilful charity that he did not offend even those who had thwarted and snubbed him throughout his Oxford career. Provost Hawkins wrote on 6 June to express his great pleasure at 'such very kind feelings towards myself and others of your old friends'. On 28 July Keble said, 'I see no end to the good which the whole Church, we may reasonably hope, may derive from such an example of love and candour under most trying circumstances.' And Keble had been one who had doubted the wisdom of the enterprise.

Everyone was reading the serial of Newman's life. Miss Bowles wrote from Oxford on 6 May, 'men are carrying those brown pamphlets in their hands, reading them as they go along.' Nor were these merely Newman's contemporaries, or the generation of his Oxford disciples, now middle-aged; young men were reading them too – Gerard Manley Hopkins read them and so did Thomas Hardy. It was probably the last part which especially appealed to them. It was first called *General Answer to Mr Kingsley* and afterwards *Position of my mind since 1845*, both boring titles (Newman was not good at titles) for a bold sketch of the mysteries of existence and the case for a divine revelation, with the idea of the Church as the living body which kept and developed it through the ages. It was in this part that Newman touched on the supposed conflict between revelation and science, the relation of reason with faith, and the balance of freedom and authority within the Church. Newman began now, what he later developed to a fine art, the policy of using the necessity to defend the Church against an external attack as an opportunity to state the moderate Catholic view to counteract the vagaries of Ultramontane extremists. Considering Newman's delicate position within the Church at the time, the balance is marvellously kept, but Manning and Ward were sharp enough to see what he was doing, and dislike it.

The *Apologia* could only have been written when it was written, twenty years after the Oxford Movement ended, because it was not until 1864 that Newman had passed through a parallel, though different, period of personal crisis in the Catholic Church. The second was a deeper experience, but more hidden; the truth about it was not known to many till long after his death. But the two experiences illuminated each other, and in writing the history of his religious opinions till 1845, Newman saw them with the eyes of one who had come through a further ordeal of rejection, passive rather than active, and had gained a more profound understanding, not only of his own life, but of the fact of the Church in the human dimension of history.

Of course people continued to disagree with him, but it was now with reason and respect. The *Apologia* was a tremendous success and once more Newman was an influence in the land – indeed his influence was far greater than it had ever been. All kinds of people wrote to him on all kinds of questions, from now till the end of his life; enthusiastic Americans christened their babies Newman; philosophical Indians sent sheets of discussion across the ocean; devotees begged for photographs, the rage of the moment; and an endless stream of ladies and musicians wrote for permission to include *Lead, Kindly Light* in their anthologies. Perhaps this hymn was so loved by the Victorians because it expressed trust in the midst of doubt, a light in darkness.

And everyone began to call at the Oratory, even Jemima' s grown-up sons, forbidden till now to see their wicked uncle, even Monsignor Talbot – but he missed Newman, who was in London, breakfasting with Rogers, visiting the Zoo and the British Institution pictures, and having his photograph taken. Newman reported on Talbot's visit to Ambrose: 'He went on to ask what I *did* – did I read? Austin said he did not know – but he saw me take out books from the Library.' The deadpan answer seems to have been Austin Mills's *forte*; he was not to be pumped by 'bumptious Romans' as Edward Caswall called them. But Talbot was bent on flattery and wrote inviting Newman to preach in Rome to an audience superior to anything he could command in Birmingham. This provoked from Newman, in his curt refusal, the famous retort: 'Birmingham people have souls.'

Birmingham people, and the diocesan priests, showed Newman that he was still regarded by them as the champion of ordinary believers, ordinary Catholics. An address read at the diocesan synod moved him so much that in his reply, as a priest who was present noticed, 'he was gasping for words and yet he never used an awkward or useless one.'

'What is the use of influence except to influence people?' Hurrell Froude had once demanded, and Newman certainly hoped he could use his new celebrity to meet the needs of the day in his own field of action, which was, in a broad sense, education. Since the comparative failure of the university in Ireland, English Catholics had begun to send their sons to the two universities in England – possible now that the anti-Catholic oaths and subscriptions had been lifted. When, in August 1864, a five-acre plot in Oxford was offered to Newman, he saw at once the advantages of such a site, stretching from St Giles back to Walton Street. His idea was to resell parts for schools, convent, perhaps a Catholic College, perhaps an Oratory. The price was over £8000 but Hope Scott urged a subscription and offered £1000 himself. When Newman consulted Ullathorne the bishop said he would put the Oxford mission in his hands – a new church was urgently needed. Newman had not expected, or even wanted, this parochial responsibility, but he was pleased to have the bishop's confidence. A circular was drawn up and copies sent to some friends, but it was not yet put into public circulation.

Rumours soon went round that Newman was to return to Oxford, and Pusey set up a wail of despair, sure that this would renew the controversy against Catholicism, whether Anglo or Roman, which he thought now dormant. In writing to his Anglican friends Newman spoke of his painful feelings at the thought of return, which he would do only if it proved to be God's will. To Catholic friends he talked of his hopes for the new mission. He was not being double-faced or swaying between two moods, but he certainly felt the pull of contrary emotions. 'We want to erect a great centre of Catholicism in Oxford, which may last and grow more important as time goes on,' he told Mr Fullerton in November. That *centre*, a typically Oratorian idea, was not intended controversially. Earlier he had said to Wetherell, Acton's associate on the Review, 'What I *aim* at, is not immediate conversions, but to influence, as far as an old man can, the tone of thought in the place, with a view to a distant time when I shall no longer be there.' He did not mean he thought his own death distant – at this period he was still expecting it very soon – but he foresaw the future when doubt and scepticism would spread from the few to the many.

Newman puzzled his contemporaries by being at once so ancient and so modern. He was at home with the martyrs and Fathers – and with scientists and factory girls. He practised fasting and penance but he read novels and travelled by train. A venerable sage, he talked the slang of the moment. Puseyites were disconcerted by his modernity; Catholics by his antiquity. He saw things historically, and yet in the light of eternity: the cross of Christ was still the measure of the world.

Manning had commented acidly on the *Apologia* that it was 'like hearing a voice from the dead', but as soon as he heard that Newman might be returning to Oxford, he became alarmed at the effect this voice from the past might have on the future, and immediately began to take steps to prevent it, acting through Wiseman and Talbot in Rome. There was a bishops' meeting on 13 December and on 19 December Ullathorne called on Newman to tell him that Wiseman wanted the universities prohibited under censure to Catholics, and had become very excited when Ullathorne opposed him. In the end, the prohibition was reduced to a dissuasive and its publication was postponed till the matter had been referred to Rome.

Ullathorne wanted Newman to wait, but he felt he would rather 'be off the business altogether'. There was no use in going to Oxford if no one had confidence in him, and when he had no confidence in Barnabò at Propaganda. He offered the land to the Oxford Mission but Ullathorne could not raise the money without Newman's name – nor could Newman, if he was not to go to Oxford himself, and there was no point in his going if the university was to be out of bounds to Catholics. In the end he asked Pusey to offer the site to the university, and the university bought it.

There was alarm and despondency among the leading laymen, who felt that the bishops were preventing Catholics from becoming full members of the educated society of the day; they quickly got up a petition to Rome, which went off at the end of January, with the support of three bishops, Ullathorne, Grant and Clifford. Serjeant Bellasis, already in Rome, wrote to Hope Scott, 'Someone or other is undermining Newman at Rome, and they say he is not a safe man and they quote some article of his in the *Rambler* and some passages about the Church of England in the *Apologia* and there is no one here to defend him. My belief is that whoever it is is more bent on keeping Newman away from Oxford than on keeping young men away.' It was Talbot who was undermining Newman at Rome, as his correspondence with Manning shows; there is also some evidence that had the *London* Oratory gone to Oxford, opposition would have been negligible. The lay promoters of the memorial were treated with careless rudeness by Barnabò; the case had already been decided – adversely to them.

On 15 February 1865 Cardinal Wiseman died. He would have enjoyed his own funeral – it was a splendid function. Thousands who, fifteen years earlier, had been ready to lynch him, watched the procession with respect. But the Chapter of Westminster had not forgotten their grievances and when they met to choose three names to be sent to Rome for the new Archbishop, they defied their Provost (Manning) by putting Errington at the head of the list. An upright, hard-working traditionalist, English in outlook and central in theology, Errington was certainly a good man for the job, but he had already been winkled out of his post as coadjutor and was not popular at Rome. Although the name of Henry Edward Manning was not on the Chapter's list, Pius IX chose him to be Archbishop of Westminster. Talbot, who had done much to influence his choice, exulted; so did W. G. Ward, who was now editor of the *Dublin Review* and making it the organ of extreme Ultramontane views in England.

Manning, pale and intense, was consecrated bishop on 8 June at St Mary Moorfields, by Ullathorne, assisted by Grant and Clifford, the three chief moderates in the hierarchy. Newman was present among the secular clergy. He was staying with Rogers and went home on the same train as Church, who got out at Didcot, for

Oxford. This fraternizing with Anglicans sealed his fate with Manning, offended because he had cried off the banquet. Even before Manning's election Newman had remarked in his journal (opened for the first time in two years): 'Faber being taken away, Ward and Manning take his place. Through them, especially Manning acting on the poor Cardinal (who is to be buried tomorrow) the Oxford scheme has been for the present thwarted.' The whole entry is interesting, for its complete change of tone, which Newman himself noted. 'I don't know that this recklessness is a better state of mind than that anxiety,' he characteristically observed. He had ceased to worry, partly because though he was still kept out of work, he felt he was indirectly acting through the *Apologia*, 'and because its success has put me in spirits to look out for some other means of doing good, whether Propaganda cares about them or no.'

Propaganda could not prevent him increasing his influence by his publications. *The Dream of Gerontius* was first published by Fr Henry Coleridge (second son of the judge who had condemned Newman in the Achilli trial) in the *Month*, soon to become the Jesuit literary periodical, in May and June 1865. Newman was surprised by its immense popularity (long before Elgar's music), but he was encouraged by it to collect his verses into one volume, and this too went into many editions, each with variants, for he tinkered endlessly with his lines, even though he regarded his verses as a relaxation, to be composed while shaving, or lurching, slightly seasick, on the ocean.

Another relaxation taken up again after a long interval, was music. Rogers and Church sent Newman three fiddles to choose from, and after cutting his fingers on the strings, and then having 'a good bout at Beethoven's Quartetts' which made him 'cry out with delight', he chose one and often played it, alone at Rednal or among the second fiddles of the school orchestra. He had never had such a good instrument. 'I never wrote more than when I played the fiddle,' he told Church, in thanking him. 'I always sleep better after music. There must be some electric current passing from the strings through the fingers into the brain and down the spinal marrow. Perhaps thought is music.' Newman held his fiddle not under his chin, but in the old-fashioned way against his chest. When he became too old to play, and one of Church's twin daughters married, he gave the violin to Mary, the one who did not marry, and became her father's biographer. I cannot discover what happened to it afterwards.

Soon after this, going while on holiday to see Keble, Newman found Pusey there as well. It was an overwhelming meeting. He hardly recognized Keble at first, but soon saw in him 'the old face and the old manner'. Pusey, however, was enlarged to twice the size, 'as if you looked at him through a prodigious magnifier,' Newman told Ambrose, with a paunch and a condescending manner. Newman felt at this meeting a pain 'not acute but heavy. There were three old men, who had worked together vigorously in their prime. This is what they have come to – poor human nature ...' Pusey, he remarked, was 'full of polemics and hope'.

Pusey's chief polemic came out in the autumn under the title *Eirenicon*, though far from being peacemaking it was largely an attack on Mariolatry and the infallibility of the Pope, as proclaimed by Faber and Ward. Newman had not intended to answer Pusey but two things led him to change his mind. One was Pusey's attempt to drag him in on his own side by quoting from his Anglican works and the other was the knowledge that otherwise Ward in the *Dublin* and Manning in a pamphlet would be his only takers. Having made up his mind Newman went out to Rednal on 28 November and had finished his *Letter to Dr Pusey* by 7 December. It was published on the last day of January 1866; a fortnight later 2000 copies were sold and Newman was correcting it for a second edition. This is an indication of his new fame; so is the fact that his literary earnings, declared for income tax, rose from £95 to £1100 in this year. All the time he was working on it, particularly when correcting the proofs in January, he was suffering from trying and painful symptoms of what turned out to be stone or gravel, though he was able to note on 17 January "½ past 2 a.m. got rid of the *causa mali*.' His doctor told him he was very lucky and put him on to drinking cider.

209

The first part of the *Letter* set out the Catholic doctrine on Mary, drawn from the Fathers; the second was called 'Anglican Misconceptions and Catholic Excesses in devotion to the Blessed Virgin'. Newman made a distinction between doctrine and devotion and showed how often the Church had condemned superstitious practices. With some compliments to Ward ('still in the vigour of his powers') and Faber ('departed amid the tears of hundreds') Newman said firmly that 'they are in no sense spokesmen for English Catholics.' Faber's Anglican brother Frank was pleased at his words about 'Fred' whose poetic nature and need for emotional outlet led him to 'over-colour'. Fred's brother might be pleased, but Fred's friends in London, who regarded him as a saint, were very annoyed. Hardly a number of the *Dublin* appeared without a eulogy of him; poetical fancy and sensitive piety were poor stuff to those who heard Faber compared to St Philip, St Francis de Sales, St Bernard, and even St Augustine – *not* as the father of Jansenism, of course.

In fact, while Anglicans found the *Letter to Dr Pusey* a reasonable defence of Catholic doctrine and practice, it roused the Ultramontanes to furious indignation. Talbot wrote to Manning to stand firm. 'I am afraid that the *Home and Foreign Review* and the old school of Catholics will rally round Newman in opposition to you and Rome.' Talbot thought every Englishman naturally anti-Roman. 'Dr Newman is more English than the English. His spirit must be crushed.'

Manning agreed; he replied that he saw much danger of 'an English Catholicism, of which Newman is the highest type. It is the old Anglican, patristic, literary, Oxford tone transplanted into the Church ... In one word, it is worldly Catholicism, and it will have the worldly on its side, and will deceive many.' All Manning's opposition to Newman was based on this conviction that his interest in education was worldly and his Catholicism half-hearted.

Manning did not make known his opposition openly, but Ward made no secret of his disagreement, a frankness which Newman much preferred. He wrote to Ward on 16 February 1866, 'I do not feel our differences to be such a trouble as you do; for such differences always have been, always will be in the Church; and Christians would have ceased to have spiritual and intellectual life if such differences did not exist. No human power can hinder it; nor, if it attempted it, could do more than make a solitude and call it peace ... Man cannot and God will not. He means such differences to be an exercise of charity. Of course I wish as much as possible to agree with all my friends; but if, in spite of my utmost efforts, they go beyond me, or come short of me, I can't help it, and take it easy.'

Unfortunately, Ward and his friends, sure that they represented 'the Church' would not take it easy. An angry letter appeared in the *Tablet* by E. R. Martin, the Roman correspondent of the *Weekly Register* (a paper owned by Henry Wilberforce). Martin hysterically attacked Newman for causing grief and pain in Rome – his works ought to be on the Index of Prohibited Books – so unlike the sainted Faber and went off into grumbles about Englishness, intellectualism, and how Protestantized the old Catholics were. This roused the old Catholic Bishops Clifford and Ullathorne to write letters in Newman's defence. But the knowledge of this hostility in Rome made Newman decide not to write next on infallibility, as he had intended.

'Recollect, to write theology is like dancing on a tight rope some hundred feet above the ground,' he wrote on 16 April to Miss Bowles, who had pressed him to take up the vital question. 'It is hard to keep from falling and the fall is great. Ladies can't be in a position to try.' He compared his recent effort to introducing the narrow end of a wedge and making a split. 'I feared it would split fiercely and irregularly, and I thought by withdrawing the wedge the split might be left at present more naturally to increase itself ... Better not to do a thing than to do it badly. I must be patient and wait on God. If it is His will I should do more, He will give me time. I am not serving Him by blundering.' Others had not his restraint.

On Palm Sunday, 25 March, the bishop for the second time offered Newman the Oxford Mission. Newman was not keen; he felt that the bishop simply wanted to get his church built, and he foresaw the difficulties ahead. Nevertheless, he did not like to refuse. His lay friends were as enthusiastic as ever and there was another, smaller, piece of property available in Oxford. On 8 June he told the bishop he would take the mission if direct permission was obtained from Propaganda for him to start another Oratory without leaving Birmingham permanently. He was still thinking of those accusations of attempting a *generalate*; yet the real objection now was simply himself – the influence he would exert in Oxford, drawing Catholics not merely to the university but into Englishness, intellectualism and all kinds of iniquity. On 26 June Manning was writing to Talbot urging him to get strong declarations from 'Rome' against 'Protestant' universities. 'I think Propaganda can hardly know the effects of Dr Newman's going to Oxford.' And when Cardinal Reisach was sent to England to inquire into the state of Catholic education, his visit was carefully managed to exclude Newman, though he came to Oscott and met Ullathorne there. Newman did not even know he was in England till the faithful Miss Bowles wrote asking why he did not come to town to meet the eminent visitor. The Cardinal did not meet the man most concerned with the education of Catholics and when he left England Manning was able to report to Talbot, 'He has seen and *understands* all that is going on in England.'

In his reply to Miss Bowles Newman expressed his thoughts on the general situation with great force, anticipating 'with equanimity the prospect of a thorough routing out of things at Rome – not till some great convulsion takes place (which may go on for years and years, and when I can do neither good nor harm) and religion is felt to be in the midst of trials, red tapism will go out of Rome ...' He saw the Church sinking into a sort of Novatianism, an early heresy characterized by narrow exclusiveness. 'Instead of aiming at being a world wide power, we are shrinking into ourselves, narrowing the lines of communion, trembling at freedom of thought, and using the language of dismay and despair at the prospect before us, instead of, with the high spirit of the warrior, going out conquering and to conquer.' He despised the reliance on Napoleon III and his armies. 'But the power of God is abroad upon this earth – and he will settle things in spite of what cliques and parties may decide. I am glad you liked my sermon – the one thing I wished to oppose is the coward despairing spirit of the day.' His sermon on *The Pope and the Revolution* was ill received by the Ultramontanes; some were trying to get it put on the Index.

On Christmas day 1866 Ullathorne sent Newman a copy of a letter from Propaganda, granting permission for an Oratory at Oxford. But he had left out of it an injunction that Newman himself should not be allowed to go there. Ullathorne was trying a political game for which he was not clever enough, playing both sides along in the hope of getting the Oratory into Oxford without a rap from Rome. At this critical moment the first number of the *Westminster Gazette*, owned by the Archbishop and edited by his future biographer, Edmund Sheridan Purcell, came out with an '*on dit*' paragraph, saying that Newman 'had abandoned his plan of going to Oxford, in deference to the opinion of a most eminent prelate'. Feeling that this was 'a shadow of things to come' Newman took it round to Ullathorne who, in spite of knowing the injunction, advised him to wait, and insisted that when he got to Rome he would 'have it out with the lot of them'. Meanwhile, he wrote to the *Gazette* and got a courteous apology from Manning himself, who was coming to Birmingham and hoped to see Newman.

Newman was not keen; he told Ullathorne frankly that he did not trust the Archbishop. 'Certainly I have no wish to see him now – first because I don't like to be practised on; secondly because I cannot in conversation use smooth words which conceal, not express my thoughts, and thirdly because I am not sorry he should know I am dissatisfied with him … However I propose to call on him, that he may not have the advantage of saying that I have not done so.'

To Miss Bowles, who was still pressing for action, Newman gave some explanations. Of Manning he said, 'I think this of him – he wishes me no ill, but he is determined to bend or break all opposition. He has an iron will and resolves to have his own way.' He told her how, on becoming Archbishop, Manning had wished to make him a bishop (thinking, with Propaganda, that Newman was sulking because an honour had been snatched from under his nose): 'I declined – I wish to have my own true liberty ... He wanted to gain me over; now, he will break me if he can.' Manning had not offered him a *place*. 'The only one I am fit for, the only one I would accept, a place at Oxford, he is doing all he can to keep me from.' Miss Bowles had urged him to fight and defend himself; Newman replied that he had done so, privately, on important matters (the *Rambler* article and Ireland) but when he did not feel it was his duty, then 'to fight is, not bravery, but self-will'. His conclusion was that God works for those who do not work for themselves, but only for him. 'Of course an inward brooding over injuries is *not* patience but a recollecting with a view to the future is prudence.' Unfortunately, in London he was credited with just that brooding on injuries which his silence seemed to show.

But, urged by his lay friends, Newman did put out his circular for the church at Oxford at the end of January 1867 and almost at once £5000 was subscribed. Manning wrote off to Talbot in great anxiety on 1 February, 'We are slipping sideways into the whole mischief.' The next move was a rap from Cardinal Barnabò, directed at the school, which Newman thought unfair, and said so in his reply, which he ended '*sed viderit Deus*' – but God will see to it. Bishop Ullathorne thought it would be better not to leave it all to God and urged Newman to go to Rome himself. He decided to send Ambrose St John and Henry Bittleston – the latter had never been to Rome. 'Do not lodge in a religious house,' he told them, 'Ambrose will get sore throat, asthma, lumbago and gout.' Off they went in April. The weather was very cold. The Oratory was to take over the Oxford Mission in May.

Meanwhile Manning was kept informed from Rome not only by Talbot but by Herbert Vaughan, the young disciple he had got put in as head of the seminary at Ware, in order to Romanize it, willy nilly. Vaughan reported that Barnabò said Newman gave him the stomach ache and added that if Newman wanted to found a Catholic College 'one could hardly feel a scruple at removing him from Oxford with a pitchfork.' He evidently felt no scruples at the methods already being used. Then suddenly E. R. Martin weighed in again, as Roman correspondent to the *Weekly Register*, saying that the Pope had prohibited Newman from going to Oxford, and announcing that he was no longer trusted at Rome. 'That fool, Martin,' as Vaughan called him, had gone too far too soon; he created a sensation among the English laymen concerned and Monsell immediately collected 500 signatures for an address to Newman, which appeared, with his reply, in the issue of the next week, 13 April 1867. 'We feel that every blow that touches you inflicts a wound upon the Catholic Church in this country,' said the distinguished laymen.

In the excitement of the moment Ullathorne felt he must let Newman know of the 'secret instruction' that if Newman went to Oxford himself the bishop was *blande suaviterque* (gently and softly) to call him back. The phrase stuck in Newman's throat; he used it ironically in several letters to friends, feeling it implied he was thought to be 'a vicious animal' who might 'kick out or jump at their throat' and that the bishop must have got 'immense credit at Propaganda for years, for his wonderful skill in keeping a wild beast like me in order'. Ullathorne begged Newman not to say publicly that he would not go to Oxford and set off for Westminster, where Manning showed him the *one* letter he had written to Propaganda ... and changed the subject when the Yorkshireman suggested that he might have written to others in Rome.

Not long afterwards Manning was indeed writing to Talbot saying that Ullathorne ('I must suppose unconsciously') had been used by Newman's party. He was wrong, but that was how he imagined Newman acted. Manning wrote his letters in separate sentences, sometimes numbered like verses of the Bible or items in an inventory. This one must have crossed with a long screed from Talbot dated 25 April which, printed by Purcell, has often been quoted. The laity were beginning to show the cloven foot, putting into practice the doctrine taught by Dr Newman in his article in the *Rambler*. 'They wish to govern the Church in England by public opinion ... What is the province of the laity? To hunt, to shoot, to entertain.' They had no right to meddle in ecclesiastical matters. 'Dr Newman is the most dangerous man in England and you will see that he will make use of the laity against your Grace. You must not be afraid of him ...' Manning was annoyed; he was not afraid of Newman. But, he insisted, 'a word or two of mine might divide the Bishops and throw some on his side.' An open conflict between Newman and Manning would be 'as great a victory to the Anglicans as could be'. He saw it all as a campaign among enemies.

In Birmingham letters from Ambrose and Henry were eagerly awaited, but it was soon plain that they were innocents abroad. They went expecting black looks and were met with smiles and compliments, only gradually discovering the charges against Newman. Ambrose was able to refute the tale that Newman had stood upon his rights as Founder in 1855 because he had been with him, but when Barnabò suggested that Newman had shown his jealousy of Manning's elevation by absenting himself from the banquet, poor Ambrose could only say, 'You really don't know the Father at all if you think so.' Then it all came out about the *Rambler* article and that Barnabò thought Newman had refused to answer the charges made. When this news reached Newman he turned up draft of his letter to Wiseman, asking an opportunity to explain himself; he got Ullathorne to write down his part in that affair, and for good measure added his original *supplica* of 1856 for the separate Brief for the London Oratory. When Barnabò was shown these documents he was 'flabbergasted', reported Bittleston. He immediately changed his tune and told Ambrose, 'I know Manning, but Newman I love.' And Talbot played the same tune – he had never said anything against Newman. Even the Pope assured them that he knew Newman was 'tutto ubbediente' – altogether obedient – and sent his blessing.

So that was satisfactory – or was it? The Oxford question was not finally settled when Ambrose got home on 23 May, the weather, as Newman noted in his diary, 'cold and gloomy, leaves and blossoms shrivelled up'. The Fathers were already taking turns of duty at Oxford, but Newman himself did not, could not go. In August he heard that a new rescript was coming from Rome, declaring Oxford university to be a proximate occasion for mortal sin; parents who dared to send their sons there would come under censure. Newman did not wait for this decree to become public; on 18 August he resigned the Oxford Mission, for the second time, into the bishop's hands.

It was a layman, Sir John Simeon, who summed up the situation: 'All that can be done to spoil a great and noble future is in my poor opinion being done.'

15

THE POWER OF THE POPE

The idea of calling a Council, the first since Trent three hundred years earlier, came to Pope Pius IX at the time of the publication of his encyclical *Quanta Cura*, with its attached *Syllabus of Errors*, at the end of the year 1864. It was a mark of Roman confidence in the new Archbishop Manning that he was one of those secretly consulted the following spring. Because of the war between Austria and Prussia the announcement of the Council was deferred until the eighteen-hundredth celebration of the martyrdom of Saints Peter and Paul, held at Rome on 29 June 1867. The date was then fixed for the following year, but the preparations took so long that it was not opened till 1869, on 8 December, feast of Mary's Immaculate Conception.

Although the Council was officially convened to discuss the changes of discipline made necessary by the lapse of three centuries, there were persistent rumours that there would be a definition on the doctrine of the Pope's infallibility. Whether or not this would be so, the Ultramontanes had already begun a campaign in favour of it and their exaggerated claims soon raised tempers to fever pitch. Papal power is not an abstract theological problem and the debate was carried on in popular newspapers with passionate partisanship.

As to the Syllabus, which declared the papal policy against every form of liberalism, Newman heard the first rumours of it from his friend William Monsell, who was in Rome at the beginning of 1864. Monsell, later Lord Emly, was that rare bird, an Irish gentleman converted to Catholicism; a friend of Gladstone's and Member for Limerick from 1847 till 1874, he drew from Newman some of his shrewdest comments on political and ecclesiastical affairs. He wrote in agitation that the Pope was about to make some general prono-uncement adverse to the principles of toleration and political liberty. Indeed, when the Syllabus appeared at the end of that year (in England even the bishops read it first in *The Times*!) it seemed to do just this, and there was a tremendous outcry. Instead of explaining the status of the document, the Catholic press, now almost wholly dominated by Westminster, merely gloried in the Pope's blast against modern errors, and Ward instantly declared that papal encyclicals were part of the infallibly true teaching of the Church – in the *Dublin Review* for April 1865, and later in a letter to the Weekly Register of 29 July.

Newman wanted to write to that paper saying simply: 'I beg leave to say that I do not subscribe to this proposition.' He was dissuaded on the advice of the ex-Oratorian Stanislas Flanagan, now living in Ireland, who said that there must come a reaction against such extreme views. Newman agreed, but he noted that 'if there are no protests, there will be no reaction.' This was the problem, for the infallibilists insisted that their opinions were the only orthodox teaching. In private letters to Pusey towards the end of 1865, Newman put the moderate position clearly and then remarked, 'As to Ward's notions, they are preposterous.' They were; Ward was ebulliently announcing that he would like an infallible papal pronouncement delivered at his breakfast table every morning with *The Times*. Later, he was to find his wilder ideas unacceptable even at Rome, but in England he was regarded as the spokesman of Catholic theologians.

Although Newman himself did not write on the subject, Fr Ignatius (Harry) Ryder composed a critique of Ward's views which he called *Idealism in Theology* – 'Ideal' Ward was still trying to make facts fit theory, disregarding history. It came out just after the news-paper attack on Newman in 1867; indeed the other Fathers wished it held back from publication. But Newman welcomed this contri-bution from the younger generation. 'My monkey is up!' he wrote to Ambrose, full of fight. 'As to clamour and slander, whoever opposes the Three Tailors of Tooley Street must incur a great deal, must suffer – but it is worth the suffering if we effectually oppose them.' The 'Three Tailors' had issued a manifesto which began, 'We, the people of England ...' Manning, Ward and Talbot were Newman's Three Tailors, and he would not recognize their right to speak as if they alone represented the Catholics of England. He himself sent Ryder's pamphlet to Ward with a letter in which he said, 'I rejoice that now my own time is coming to an end, the new generation will not forget the spirit of the old maxim, in which I have ever wished to speak and act myself, "*in necessariis unitas, in dubiis libertas, in omnibus charitas*." (In necessary things unity, in doubtful things liberty, in all things charity.) But he also told Ward, on 9 May, that he was making a church within the Church, like the Novatians of old or the Evangelicals within the Establishment, 'by exalting your opinions into dogmas, and, shocking to say, by declaring to me, as you do, that those Catholics who do not accept them are of a different religion to yours. I protest then again, not against your tenets, but your schismatical spirit.' It was a strong expression of disapproval, though he ended, 'Bear with me. Yours affly. in Christ.'

Ward, who was convinced he was expressing the spirit of Rome and so must be right, paid no heed. He went into action against Ryder, not only with a retaliatory pamphlet but in articles in the *Dublin Review*. Ryder brought out a reply early in 1868 which he ended with a protest 'against the practice of turning the easy chair of a lay reviewer into a Cathedra of religious doctrine'. Ward retorted once more, Ryder wrote a Postscript, Ward answered that. He could always have the last word in the *Dublin*. Nevertheless, the controversy gave publicity to theological opinions other than those of the Ultramontanes, and many priests and lay people wrote gratefully to Ryder and to Newman. They could not believe Ward's exaggerations were true doctrine but were worried that they seemed to have the backing of Rome and of their own hierarchy. At the Council the individual bishops were to discover their own office and power but before it they seemed unable to prevent the Archbishop of Westminster from carrying them along in his train.

Newman's position was the more delicate because those who opposed the Ultramontane line most violently were men who had been professors in his university or had taught in his school, or were associated with the *Rambler*. While the historical objections they raised were valid, their style was often as pugnacious as Ward's, and they sometimes repudiated infallibility in any form, which Newman never did. He maintained that Popes had always acted as if they had the right to the last word on disputed matters, thus sharing in Christ's guarantee to his Church that the Holy Spirit would guide it into all truth. What he objected to was a sweeping application of infallibility to all the pronouncements of any Pope and the way in which the proponents of such views anathematized everyone else as unorthodox. Familiar as he was with the history of the early Councils, Newman had no illusions that unity in the Church meant utter uniformity of ideas.

It was in 1868 that Newman, now sixty-seven, made a visit to Littlemore, going by train direct to the little station, and so missing out Oxford. A legend grew out of this visit, because Newman was seen leaning over the lych-gate, crying. A pathetic story was made out of it, though Newman in fact had gone on to sit in the garden of Mr Crawley, an Anglican friend, where villagers came hurrying to see him – one, as she afterwards told Anne Mozley, felt she could never let go of his hand. The idea of Newman, old, poorly dressed, lonely and despised, weeping over the past, appealed to many, but though he might cry at the sight of that loved place, his mood at this period was generally calm and cheerful, as letters and journal entries show.

For though he was frustrated in his special work in defence of Christianity, he was content in his life within the Church, which continued as active as ever. Besides taking his turn at preaching and hearing confessions, keeping up with his considerable correspondence and many visitors, he was now beginning serious work on the book which became *An Essay in Aid of a Grammar of Assent* – a typically tentative title. In his notes Newman often referred to it as 'Certitude' – and that is its subject, the same that he had dealt with thirty years earlier in the university sermons on Faith and Reason. His mind was in full vigour, and although he had some minor physical troubles, including something wrong with one eye, his health too was improving. He suffered less from the debilitating colds of his middle age. He still walked the seven miles to Rednal quite often, though now Ambrose or William Neville sometimes drove him there in the 'basket' – a little pony trap. When he visited Switzerland with Ambrose in 1866, he went up the mountain paths 'like unto a very active lamplighter,' said his younger but fatter friend, left sweating behind. All the same he found travelling tiresome now and did not go abroad again, though he made circuits of friends in England for many years to come.

On the score of age and health, however, Newman managed to get out of going as a theologian to Rome – for he had been invited to take part in the preliminaries of the Council. After Ambrose's representations in Rome in 1867 Propaganda wrote to Cardinal Cullen in Dublin, and he, though he had treated Newman so ill over the university, now vouched for his orthodoxy. However, Newman felt that it was not in his line to take part in conferences. 'I never have succeeded with boards or committees,' he wrote in a memorandum. 'I always felt out of place and my words unreal . . . I never could make my presence *felt*.' This was perfectly true; right from the times of the Tracts Newman acted best as an individual writer and the inspirer of a group of friends. He was no politician. At managing other men he was no good at all.

Manning, however, was above everything a manager. And although he successfully managed to keep Newman out of Oxford, he did not like to hear it said that there was any difference between them. In 1867, therefore, he initiated a correspondence with Newman, designed to placate him if possible, and if not to put him in the wrong. He conducted the operation through Frederick Oakeley, now a priest of his diocese, but an admirer of Newman from Oxford days, who perhaps hoped he was bringing two great men together. The exchange (printed by Purcell in his biography of Manning) should be read entire, for it is revealing of both men, and amusing in a way certainly not intended by its initiator. Briefly, Manning asked what Newman found 'wanting' in him; Newman replied, frankly but without much hope, as he confessed to Oakeley, that he could not rid his mind of mistrust. Manning immediately retaliated with a numbered inventory designed to show that it was *Newman* who had begun the opposition. Most of his evidence was mistaken; for instance, he believed an attack in the *Rambler* had been inspired by Newman, who had not, in fact, seen it till it was in print. In his reply, Newman proved that Manning's suspicions were groundless. Whereupon Manning retorted that whether or not they were true, they were generally *believed*. Newman pointed out that this was hardly a reason for Manning's opposition *now*. They ended in dead-lock, promising to say masses for each other's intentions.

Two years later, in 1869, it looked like starting again, when Manning was attacked in a pamphlet by Edmund Ffoulkes (a convert who presently returned to the Church of England) who charged him with suppressing Newman's letter of explanation about the deleted *Rambler* article, referring to some pamphlet which he said Newman had dissuaded the author from publishing. (It was in fact an appendix to William Palmer's French translation of *The Pope and the Revolution*.) Manning wrote to Ullathorne: 'The accusation … touches me not only personally but officially and not me only but the Holy See.' Ullathorne went straight to Newman who wrote a denial that he had ever thought or said that Manning had suppressed any letter of his to Wiseman. Manning was not appeased; he wrote to Ullathorne that he had wanted to know 'not whether such a report was believed by him or by you, but whether you had ever heard of it'. To Newman himself he suggested that he might help him track down the offending (unpublished!) pamphlet. Newman then made this reply: 'My dear Archbishop, Thank you for your kind letter. I can only repeat what I said when you last heard from me, I do not know whether I am on my head or my heels when I have active relations with yourself. In spite of my friendly feelings, this is the judgment of my intellect – Yours affectionately in Christ, John H. Newman.'

Manning was deeply offended and noted, 'His last was in terms which made a reply hardly fitting on my part.' Manning then set off to Rome for the Council and Newman went to Rednal to finish *The Grammar of Assent*.

The book appeared on 15 March 1870, the very day that the *Standard* newspaper carried a version of a private letter of Newman's, written on 28 January to Bishop Ullathorne at Rome – 'one of the most passionate and confidential letters I ever wrote in my life,' he told Sir John Simeon afterwards. Newman's letter was a protest at the methods of those who were campaigning to get the definition of papal infallibility on the agenda of the Council, and by the time its pirated text appeared they had succeeded in their aim. Manning was a moving spirit in this campaign, abetted by the Roman Jesuits who ran the *Civiltà Cattolica*, a paper which, like the French *Univers* and the English *Tablet*, had for months been taking a high tone against all opposition. Vaughan, now editor of the *Tablet*, had proclaimed that the declaration on the dogma was inevitable and that afterwards: 'Doubtful books will be condemned; rash speculations from science reduced to harmony with revealed truth ... The decisions of the Council will come home to every Catholic hearth and home, to every College, to every seminary and Religious House. If they did not they would fail in their scope of healing the evils of our age ... It is the increased executive force which the Definition will place in the hands of the Holy See that, in the human point of view, is the real secret of the opposition.' Exactly.

In his letter Newman named these Ultramontane papers, saying that they were spreading fear and dismay among Catholics who 'practically, not to say doctrinally, hold the Holy Father to be infallible'. In spite of this, 'suddenly there is thunder in a clear sky, and we are told to prepare for something, we know not what, to try our faith, we know not how. No impending danger is to be averted, but a great difficulty created. Is this the proper work of an Ecumenical Council? ... When has a definition *de fide* been a luxury of devotion and not a stern painful necessity? Why should an aggressive and insolent faction be allowed to "make the heart of the just sad, whom the Lord hath not made sorrowful?"' He described the confusion of Catholics, 'one day determining to give up all theology as a bad job and recklessly to believe henceforth almost that the Pope is impeccable; at another tempted to believe all the worst that a book like Janus says' – *Janus* was the pseudonym under which Döllinger, Acton and the liberal militants were lambasting the papacy with historical scandals – 'and then again angry with the Holy See for listening to the flattery of a clique of Jesuits, Redemptorists and Converts'.

Newman ended, 'With these thoughts before me, I am continually asking myself whether I ought not to make my feelings public; but all I do is to pray to those great early Doctors of the Church, whose intercession would decide the matter to arrest the greatest calamity. If it is God's will that the Pope's Infallibility is defined, then it is God's will to throw back "the times and the moments" of that triumph which He has destined for His Kingdom; and I shall feel I have but to bow my head to His adorable inscrutable Providence.'

Newman's 'intervention' went off like a bomb – with far greater effect than any article or pamphlet would have done. Because he spoke privately he had actually named the papers and the 'clique' and this naturally extremely annoyed its members, who liked to think they were 'the Church'. This outspoken comment reversed the beginning of reinstatement at Rome which had been the result of Ambrose St John's embassy in 1867; Newman took his ten-yearly plunge downhill again, into the cloud. But at the time he was quite glad to have his views thus publicized. He wrote to the papers to protest, of course, against this use of a private letter and failed to recognize as his own the phrase 'aggressive and insolent faction' – not surprising, since his much altered draft is almost illegible. But he did not disown his views.

Sir John Simeon, who had seen the letter circulating in London, told him the words were in it; peering again at his draft Newman discovered them, and had to write again to the *Standard*, taking the opportunity to explain that by faction he did not mean the majority of bishops said to be in favour of a definition, nor whole religious orders, but a mere 'collection of persons' drawn from all ranks. He was not perturbed by his slip, he told Sir John Simeon; it had simply given him the chance to clarify his meaning. The whole episode was providential. 'Would anything more make my mind on the matter more intelligible to the world? I think not.'

Ullathorne, who swore he had only shown Newman's letter to bishops of the minority, Errington, Clifford and Moriarty, was upset at the advantage taken, though he agreed with Newman's sentiments. The letter appeared in the French press too and grateful letters came to Newman from his friends there. Louis Veuillot, the intransigent editor of the *Univers*, who printed old Latin hymns with 'Pius' substituted for 'Deus', hit back by saying Newman had never thanked him for his aid in the Achilli trial. Cuttings from his own paper were sent to him to prove that he had been thanked. Dalgairns now stepped into the limelight; he used the fact that he had been sent with Ambrose to do the thanking to come out with a long piece of sob-stuff about Newman's noble wounded feelings, dissociating himself and the London Oratory from any complicity with his sadly detestable views. Bishop Moriarty was one of many disgusted with this; Dalgairns's diatribe against liberalism prompted him to observe: 'Restore the principle of intolerance and what will become of the London Oratory?' He was glad Newman had not answered. 'Let no abuse tempt you to break silence.'

Abuse was perhaps not quite the word, for everybody now felt it necessary to speak respectfully of Newman even when they accused him, as Vaughan did in the *Tablet*, of trying to teach the Universal Church and thinking he knew better than six hundred bishops. As usual, friends begged Newman to write at length, but he resisted. It was not the time for theological meditation; the important thing was to stop a dogmatic declaration being rushed through like a political measure in an emergency. 'You are going too fast at Rome,' he wrote to Robert Whitty, who had once tried to be an Oratorian but failed under the dreadful alternative of Faber or Birmingham and was now a Jesuit, but not one of the clique. '... We do not move at railroad pace in theological matters even in the nineteenth century. We must be patient and that for two reasons, first in order to get at the truth, and next in order to carry others with us. The Church moves as a whole; it is not a mere philosophy; it is a communion; it not only discovers but it teaches; it is bound to consult for charity as well as for faith.'

Manning and the infallibilists, however, were determined to rail-road the definition through, and they succeeded, though their triumph was limited by the modifications imposed by the large minority, headed by the French Bishop of Orleans, Dupanloup (who had tried to persuade Newman to come as his theologian), and the German bishop, Ketteler of Mainz. All the same these, still dissenting, absented themselves from the final session on 18 July so as not to offend the Pope, who would be present, and who was known to favour the definition. 'Tradition?' he had once said with a chuckle, 'I am tradition!' That last session took place in a tremendous thunderstorm which simple Protestants regarded as a sign of divine wrath. Among the crowd of reporters was Tom Mozley, as correspondent for *The Times*, a bearded and elderly Tom but still as fond as ever of a tall story or a dramatic scene. '*Placet* shouted his Eminence or his Grace, and a loud clap of thunder followed in response.' The zealots shouted, '*Viva il Papa Infallibile! Viva il trionfo dei Cattolici!*'

The next day war was declared between France and Prussia, and the Council was suspended and the bishops went home exhausted. By September Rome was in the hands of Victor Emmanuel; the papal government came to an end and the Pope became 'the prisoner of the Vatican'.

'The definition of July involved the dethronement of September,' said Newman to Monsell, in December. And to Miss Holmes he wrote in the same month, 'As to Rome, I cannot regret what has happened. There is one thing worse than open infidelity, and that is, secret, and the state of Rome was such as to honeycomb the population of Italy with deep unbelief, under the outward profession of Christianity.'

When he saw the wording of the definition itself, on 23 July, he noted that he was 'pleased to observe there is nothing in it strong or startling'. With his historically and theologically trained mind he saw that the eventual effect might even be to restrict the Pope's power. 'Hitherto he has done what he would, because its limits were not defined – now he must act to rule,' he wrote to one inquirer. But it was not so easy for an ordinary person, whether Catholic or not, to understand the meaning of the decree, especially when Manning came back from Rome triumphant and began to put pressure on people to accept the new dogma (as interpreted by the ultra party) with full internal assent. Many consciences were strained and as the victims often wrote to Newman, he became more and more aware of the immediate effects of the definition.

'I never expected to see such a scandal in the Church,' he wrote in February 1871 to Maskell, an Oxford convert (a married clergyman) who had written a pamphlet to combat Manning's Pastoral and wondered if he ought to publish it – Newman congratulated him on what he had written. 'Such scandals, I know, have been before now, and in Councils – but I thought we had too many vigilant and hostile eyes upon it, to allow even the most reckless, tyrannical and heartless ecclesiastics, so wounding, so piercing religious souls, so co-operating with those who wish the Church's downfall.' Nevertheless he was sure that God would heal the offence, and that 'things will in time gradually settle down and find their level ... The voice of the whole Church will in time make itself heard, and Catholic instincts and ideas will assimilate and harmonize into the credenda of Christendom, the living tradition of the faithful, what at present many would impose upon us, and many are startled at, as a momentous addition to the faith.'

Just because he saw the whole business in perspective, he was continually urged to write on it, but for some time the opportunity did not offer. He told Maskell that if he had written in 1871 he would probably have been reported to Rome and perhaps put on the Index, 'and thus should have made matters worse instead of better.' In that year the troubles of France, the fall of Paris, the Commune, took up public attention; in 1872 it was Germany, with Bismarck's Kulturkampf against the Catholics, in part provoked by the intransigence of the Vatican decree. 'It is time for Fr Newman to speak out,' said Monsell to Hope Scott. But Newman said, 'What good would it do to Germany?' Yet he did write a letter to *The Times*, which had published an article saying that if the Pope were to order another massacre of the Huguenots, Catholic opinion would now be bound to obey as if it were a divine command. Newman said: 'No Pope can make evil good. No Pope has any power over those eternal moral principles which God has imprinted on our hearts and consciences. If any Pope has with his eyes open approved of treachery and cruelty let those defend that Pope who can.' Whether Gregory XIII had a share in the guilt of the massacre of St Bartholomew was a fact to be decided by historians. 'But even if they decide against the Pope, his infallibility is in no respect compromised. Infallibility is not impeccability. Caiaphas prophesied.'

'Just what we would expect from Dr Newman,' commented the *Echo*, but like the rest of the general public thought him an exception among Catholics. In fact, during these years Newman was again forced to defend his good faith – there were persistent rumours that he did not believe the decree, had left or would leave the Church, was unhappy and longed to return to the Anglican fold. In public he had to declare himself formally; privately he often said things like, 'Be sure there is as much chance of my turning Anglican again as of my being the Irish Giant of the King of Clubs.'

In August 1874 Newman opened his private exercise book, unused since the happy entry on *The Grammar of Assent* four years before, and once more wrote, as he had done in the years before the *Apologia*, of his depressing feeling that he was 'doing nothing at all'. He meant, doing nothing 'about the divinity of Christianity etc.' Some Catholics, especially some of the Jesuits, thought him 'too free and sceptical'. But he ended with his usual confidence that God would provide for the need. 'Why need I fash myself about it? What am I? My time is out. I am passé – I may have done something in my day – but I can do nothing now. It is the turn of others. And if things seem done clumsily, my business is, not to criticize, but to have faith in God ...' In October he went back to the subject again, startled to discover how little he had written in the last fifteen years. The two chief reasons for his silence were the suspicions in influential quarters and the difficulty of writing without a 'call'. A few weeks after he made this note the last great call of his life suddenly came.

On Guy Fawkes day, appropriately, Gladstone brought out a fierce *Expostulation* against the Vatican Decrees, maintaining that the Pope could now command Catholics to act contrary to their civil allegiance on pain of eternal damnation. 'Depose Queen Victoria or go to hell' were now predictable alternatives – though Gladstone put his case in the measured terms of his public orations. Although Manning wrote at once to *The Times* to deny it, Gladstone's pamphlet had a huge success and went rapidly into cheap editions, unusual even in those pamphleteering days. Rome was mental slavery and the Pope had made a new religion, repudiating 'the ancient Church'.

An avalanche of letters now descended on Newman. 'All eyes are turned on you,' said one. Jesuits, Dominicans, Bishop Brown (once Newman's delator, who had repented and even tried to get him to be his theologian at the Council), Dr Russell of Maynooth, old Phillipps de Lisle, Monsell (now Lord Emly), and even Lord Acton (created Baron in 1869), joined the chorus. Acton had had a sparring match with Manning, whose ecclesiastical threats only made Acton's aristocratic hackles rise. 'I take it no interpretation holds that is inconsistent with tradition and with former decrees,' he had written to Newman. Although his old master Döllinger was excommunicated, Acton managed to remain in the Church.

Newman needed no urging; his time had come. In defending the Church against Gladstone's attack, he would be able to give an explanation of the definition in a legitimately minimizing sense, clarify the relative position of conscience and papal authority and put the exaggerations of the recent campaign in their place. But it was a delicate task. He made several false starts. 'I am very bold – and cannot be surprised if I make some people very angry,' he told Monsell. 'But if I am to write, I will say my say.'

'Some people' were, of course, Manning, Ward, Vaughan and the rest. (Talbot's mind had given way in 1869, just before the Council, and he spent the remainder of his days in the famous asylum at Passy in France.) Newman gave no names, but they recognized themselves when he said that 'there has been of late years a fierce and intolerant temper abroad which scorns and virtually tramples on the little ones of Christ.' Not wishing to attack Gladstone, who had not attacked him, Newman dedicated his pamphlet to the young Duke of Norfolk, the son of Faber's friend, who had been at the Oratory School. The Duke was shy at the compliment, but as the first peer of the realm, and so the first Catholic layman, he was the obvious dedicatee.

The *Letter to the Duke of Norfolk* was published early in January 1875, but before that Newman was besieged by eager editors who wanted to be the first to serialize it. Of all his writings, except the *Apologia*, this was the most immediately successful. It completely reversed the public attitude. It is quite extraordinary to read the newspapers of the time and see their tone change with a few weeks. When Gladstone's *Expostulation* came out *The Times* said: 'But that the Roman Catholic Church has brought itself into direct and visible antagonism with civil allegiance throughout the world has now become unquestionable to all but that portion of Roman Catholics who are content to believe without reasoning. The popular press, less measured, expressed the same scorn. Yet the reaction to Newman's *Letter* was a real understanding of the Catholic position. Gladstone himself wrote to him. 'You may from the newspaper of this morning perceive that yesterday was a busy day with me, for I had to fold my mantle and to die,' he said, referring to his retirement from the leadership of the Liberal Party. He thanked Newman for the 'genial and gentle manner' of his treatment and told a friend that Newman's wonderful style always had an exciting effect and made him 'wish to shout and do something extravagant'. He did write a reply, *Vaticanism*, in which he allowed Newman to have proved his point about civil allegiance, but insisted still that a new spirit had entered the Church which would change everything to mental tyranny.

But now the newspapers did not follow him. Misunderstandings were cleared up; from the Anglican *Guardian*'s review it is clear that it was news to them that dogmatic decrees needed interpretation from theologians and were not oracular utterances. And since this was just what Ward and his friends had wished them to be, many Catholics also were relieved to find this not the case. Miss Bowles spoke for others when she wrote of the 'burthen' which she had been rebuked for feeling – 'but your dear noble fearless Letter has unloosed and thrown it off for ever.' As usual she passed on London news: Ward was in a terrible state about the *Letter*.

There comes a point in the life of every doctrinaire when reality breaks into his abstract world. Ward now suffered some of the pain his theorizing had inflicted on others when he read of those who trampled on the little ones of Christ; he had to take a double dose of chloral to get to sleep. In an exchange of letters with Newman, Ward revealed that he believed a Catholic thinker or writer should aim 'so to think and write as he judges the Holy See ... would wish him to think and write.' He never could see why this was not the whole duty of a Catholic theologian.

Newman's *Letter* was unpopular in certain circles and the indefatigable Fr Bottalla of the *Civiltà Cattolica* sent several critical articles to the English Catholic press. It was a sign of Newman's success in calming a dangerously hostile situation that the *Tablet* refused to print them. They appeared in the *Catholic Times*, which meant they had less official backing. The *Tablet*'s policy was no doubt guided by Manning, who wrote to Rome on 9 February urging that there should be no condemnation of Newman, since his pamphlet was doing much good. He did not let his distrust of Newman influence him when the good of the Church was at stake. But though his nominee Rector at the English College in Rome, O'Callaghan, told him that the notion of Newman's opposition to the Pope was now completely dispelled, Manning did not pass on this pleasant news to Newman, even when the latter sent his congratulations on Manning's being made a Cardinal, as he was on Easter Eve. To the end, Manning remained suspicious of

Newman's loyalty, but this time he did not prevent him from doing his own work.

Newman was naturally watching for official Catholic reactions. When Cardinal Cullen made an approving reference to him in a Pastoral, he wrote to thank him, and took it as a hint that all was now well. Meanwhile, from less august personages, letters of gratitude poured in. And, their fears of mental tyranny assuaged, converts began to come again.

16

THE UNEXPECTED

It was sad that so many of Newman's most loyal friends, those who had most wished him to 'speak out' had died before he was able to do so. Serjeant Bellasis died in January 1873, after a long illness; his sons were at Newman's school and two were later to join his community. Newman had dedicated to him *The Grammar of Assent* 'in remembrance of a long, equable, sunny friendship'. In proof this was converted into 'funny friendship' and someone who was present when Newman noticed the slip said he had never seen him laugh so much. Bellasis had been delighted at the dedication, saying: 'I wonder what he can have to say about the old Serjeant?' The boys felt Newman was like another father to them, he was so kind.

Newman had written the *Grammar* for the ordinary intelligent reader, and asked Miss Holmes for her comments on the last hundred pages, 'for they were written especially for those who can't go into questions of the inspiration of Scripture, authenticity of books, passages of the Fathers etc., etc. – especially for such ladies as are bullied by infidels and do not know how to answer them.' Agnes Wilberforce, whom Henry called his 'most intellectual child' and who had been involved in just such an argument, demanded the book eagerly, and in spite of Newman's calling it a 'dry, dull, humdrum concern' she enjoyed it all. In this last section Newman draws out from history and from the universal experience of moral obligation, the accumulating probabilities that Christianity is a true revelation of the divine creator; final acceptance is an act of will and duty, but it cannot be accepted till it is seen to be credible. Newman once observed that this was the way both factory girls and philosophers were in fact converted. It was a diagnosis of experience as well as a theory of belief.

Newman's approach to this great question was so original that he had to put up with a great deal of misdirected criticism from theologians and philosophers. In May 1870 he told Miss Holmes: 'It amused me to find that Allies and Dalgairns found my book difficult. I don't say it is not – but I know that, among clever men, they are the least clear-headed that I know – and I have long thought so.' But now he had enough confidence in himself to leave the book to make its own way. He did not answer criticisms; did not even read some, knowing they would be off the mark. Telling Fr Henry Coleridge of the suspicions his *Development* had at first aroused, he remarked wryly, 'Now at the end of twenty years I am told from Rome that I am guilty of the late definition, so orthodox has it (his theory) been found in principle.' And he suggested that those Catholics who thought he ought to be 'answered' should first 'master the great difficulty, the great problem, and then, if they don't like my way of meeting it, find another. Syllogizing won't meet it.' In August 1869, when afraid his book might be stopped, he had given Henry Wilberforce his opinion of these rigid traditionalist critics. 'Our theological philosophers are like old nurses who wrap the unhappy infant in swaddling bands or boards – and put a lot of blankets over him – and shut the windows that not a breath of air may come to his skin – as if he were not healthy enough to bear wind and water in due measure. They move in a groove, and will not tolerate any one who does not move in the same.'

Henry was the second of his old friends to die in 1873, in the spring. During his last illness Newman went to see him at Woodchester; he found him sitting in the garden and looking, as he told Jemima, 'inexpressibly like his father – most strangely so'. Newman went to the funeral and was asked to say a few words, which he found it difficult to do from the pressure of his feelings. The *Weekly Register* reported: 'His grief, his simple unstudied language, and gentle voice were inexpressibly touching.' He said that Henry, in leaving everything to become a Catholic, had become 'a fool for

Christ's sake'. Later that year, when Sam Wilberforce, now Bishop of Winchester, was thrown from his horse and killed while holidaying at a noble house, Newman was struck by the different fates of the two brothers. Robert, the theologian of the family, had finally become a Catholic, but had died in Rome suddenly, of a fever, in 1857; Newman had found it hard to accept that untimely death. Even the eccentric eldest brother, William, had become a Catholic, and many of the younger generation; when Sam's own daughter did so, he is said to have cried, 'Emily has lost me Canterbury!'

On returning from Henry's funeral, Newman found a telegram announcing the death of Hope Scott. His young daughter begged Newman to preach at the requiem: 'He loved you so.' And so on 5 May, at the Jesuit church in Farm Street, he preached the sermon *In the World but not of the World*, afterwards printed at the request of the family, speaking of Hope Scott's upright professional life, his unobtrusive charity and the sorrows of his repeated domestic bereavements. Newman almost broke down as he spoke of his friend's last hours, but managed to reach his conclusion: 'Farewell, but not farewell for ever, dear James Robert Hope Scott ...'

To the Duchess of Norfolk, whose daughter had been Hope Scott's second wife, and died young, Newman wrote: 'As for me, I too am like a tree stripped of its greenness and strength in losing first one and then another of my dearest friends.' The deaths of these faithful laymen who had stood by him in his trials left great blanks in his life. There was an end to the long series of letters, coming and going, the sharing of past memories and present interests. But the greatest loss came not long after the success of the *Letter to the Duke of Norfolk*, when on 24 May 1875, Ambrose St John suddenly died, at the age of sixty.

'Ambrose died of overwork,' Newman noted. As well as the School, he did much in the parish, often six hours in the confessional, and he was Father Minister, in charge of the household. His brother's widow and children were always needing his help. On top of all this he sat up at night translating the book by Fessler, Secretary of the Council, whose minimalist interpretation of the decree had received the approval of the Pope himself. 'Fessler was the last load on the camel's back,' mourned Newman afterwards, blaming himself because it was undertaken in his support.

The doctors thought Ambrose was ill with heat-stroke, but at first it seemed as if he had gone off his head. He was ill and feverish for several days, out at Ravenhurst Farm, which he had recently bought to secure playing fields for the school. Even in his wildest state he would obey Newman; he was not violent, but incoherent and shouting. The danger seemed over by 24 May; the doctors pronounced him recovering and said there should be no permanent mental derangement. But he was still not normal when Newman had to persuade him back to bed that evening; he sat on it, eating bread and butter, with his arm so tightly clasped round Newman's neck that, as he noted later, 'I laughed and said, "He will give me a stiff neck."' When he got free, Ambrose took his hand and gripped it so tight as to hurt him; Newman had to get someone else to loosen it, 'little thinking it was to be his last sign of love'.

Newman then went back the mile and a half to the Oratory. He was wakened at midnight with the news that Ambrose was worse; when he got to Ravenhurst he found him already dead. He had got into bed at about eleven and lain down 'with great deliberation, gravity and self-respect'. William Neville was about to give him some arrowroot when he suddenly sat up and then slowly fell back, dead. 'I said mass for his dear soul an hour after I got to him,' Newman wrote, in the notes he made afterwards.

Newman's first biographer, Wilfrid Ward (son of W. G. Ward), without giving the source of his information, wrote, 'Newman threw himself on the bed by the corpse and spent the night there.' There is nothing in Neville's notes, or his own to suggest it. It was well after midnight when Newman reached Ravenhurst Farm and an hour later he was saying mass. He then took up his usual duties, as his diary shows. But the loss was heavy.

Ambrose died just before St Philip's feast and the church was crowded for the requiem. Denis Sheil, later a Father of the Oratory (he died in 1962, aged 96), a boy at the school, remembered how

Newman, as he was giving the absolutions to the dead, after the mass, broke down and wept; the boy heard a strange noise all over the church and for a moment thought the people were laughing. But they were crying.

Newman admitted to Miss Bowles that he had violent bursts of crying, which weakened him, and he dreaded them. 'I do not expect ever to get over the loss I have had,' he said to Miss Holmes in September. 'It is an open wound, which in old men cannot be healed.' He was seventy-four when he lost this faithful friend, and nothing much more could be expected to happen to him in this world.

Soon there were more losses; Mrs Wootten died in January 1876 and was buried in the plot at Rednal, the other side of the ground from the Fathers. Miss Bowles came to fill the gap at the school and stayed five years. Numbers had dropped and financially the school was an anxiety; it was to pick up again later. Then, in January 1878, Edward Caswall said, 'I think I'll go to bed' – and then 'fainted away and died, so peacefully we could not tell when he went,' Newman recorded. Caswall had suffered from heart trouble for several years and his death was not unexpected, but he was greatly missed.

But now, at long last, young men were coming once more to join the Oratory. The first was Richard Bellasis in 1876; two came the following year and one in 1878, so that Newman could say to Miss Giberne (Sister Maria Pia, at Autun): 'I think Ambrose is helping us, who was so anxious that we had no novices.' And to the Congregation, after Caswall's death, he said that they were now entering the normal state of a religious body: 'its members change but it remains.' This address, one of the few remaining from later years, shows him still meditating on the Oratory, which meant so much more to him than outsiders realized. At last his little community was beginning to renew its youth.

During these years, his own seventies and the century's, Newman was at work on a task that had been begun when his ex-curate William Copeland, still an Anglican, had persuaded him to republish his Oxford sermons: he was editing his own complete works. He had got Copeland to be editor of the Sermons (though in fact they were simply reprinted) because he was afraid of more trouble at Rome if he did it himself; but when this venture proved a success, he went on to bring out one volume after another, dedicating them to friends old and new and annotating them – the notes, besides being useful, are often amusing in their detached comments on 'the author'.

But Newman was not always in his room at Birmingham; he often went visiting, to Derby to see Jemima and Anne Mozley, to Bath to see his cousin Louisa (Fourdrinier) Deane, whose daughter Emmeline's portrait of Newman as a Cardinal hangs in the National Portrait Gallery, and to London often, to stay with the Coleridges (the elder son of the judge who condemned Newman in 1853, who himself became Lord Chief Justice of England) or with Richard Church after he became Dean of St Paul's. Once, standing at the back of Wren's great church, listening to the chanting of the psalms, he was seen off by a verger, and it got into the papers that a poorly dressed old man had been turned out: 'It was Dr Newman!!' Church, abroad at the time, was upset when he heard of it and wrote asking the true story. Newman admitted he had been shown out, after refusing to go and sit in the choir, but insisted that his clothes were 'simply new' as he wore them so little. But to judge by photographs they probably looked antique and crumpled – did Victorians ever press their clothes?

While the Church family were still living at Whatley in Somerset, Newman spent a day with them in 1870, enjoying the summer beauty of Longleat and shocking the twins by not being familiar with *Alice in Wonderland*. The children sent him *The Hunting of the Snark* and Lewis Carroll (Charles Dodgson) was delighted when he was shown Newman's letter of thanks.

Just before Christmas 1877 came the surprising news that Trinity College wanted to make Newman its first Honorary Fellow; after anxiously consulting the Fathers and his bishop Newman gladly accepted. And so it was early in 1878 that Newman returned to Oxford for the first time since 1845, with Neville, another Trinity man. He called on Pusey and saw the new Keble College; he visited his old tutor, ninety now, and blind. Hearing his step on the stairs Mr Short cried out, 'Is that dear Newman?' Before Newman returned to Oxford as a Cardinal, Short was dead. Once more Newman had exercised his uncanny gift of coming to those separated from him for years, just before they died. He had done it with Keble; he had done it with Isaac Williams in 1865, and many others. After this first visit he was invited to the Trinity Gaudy – no orgy now – and would have gone but for the lameness troubling him at the time; he sent Neville instead. But in September that year he wrote in his diary, 'Went to Oxford by myself and back, and went to Littlemore.' In October he told Anne Mozley, 'I went boldly into my Mother's garden and was amazed how beautiful forty years had made it. Perhaps Rednal will equal it forty years hence.' (He managed to get Anne to visit Rednal, once.) It was to Jane Mozley, his niece, that he said, 'I am to be painted for Oriel. It is a wonderful change of feeling – and wonderful that I should have lived to see it – but I could not have been painted *unless* I had lived.' The portrait, by Ouless, hangs in Oriel Hall.

Newman had not only lived through an age since he had left Oxford, under a cloud of scorn, for Rome; he had lived through one of the longest pontificates of modern times, for most of it under a still heavier cloud, suspected of disloyalty and unorthodoxy. Pius IX died on 7 February 1878, and the Pope who was elected and took the name of Leo XIII was altogether different. Thin, shrewd and intellectual, with his bright eyes and wide humorous mouth, Leo wanted to show his new policy by creating Newman his first cardinal. The rumour appeared in print in England in the summer of 1878 but Newman dismissed it as most improbable. The Duke of Norfolk, however, on behalf of the Catholic laity of England, took up the matter with enthusiasm.

Manning, of course, was not enthusiastic and though he did not openly oppose the idea, managed to convey to Rome that Newman would refuse the offer. The misunderstanding arose through

Newman's fear that he would be expected to leave his Oratory and live in Rome, but Ullathorne, who had forwarded the letters to and fro, could not imagine how Manning had turned anxiety into refusal. When *The Times* announced that Newman had refused the honour, Newman was upset, fearing it would be taken as an insult to the Holy Father. However, thanks to the Duke of Norfolk, and to the fact that Manning quickly altered his attitude when he saw how it would be taken, the suspense of six weeks was ended when the official letter at last arrived at the Oratory on 18 March 1879. Newman was to be allowed to remain in his Oratory and yet be a Cardinal. He accepted it with happiness, regarding it as a sign of approval for his work from the earthly head of the Church. 'The cloud is lifted from me for ever,' was his refrain.

Newman went to Rome to receive the Cardinalate, arriving there on 24 April 1879. He was seventy-eight and very frail, going down almost at once with a severe cold, but luckily not till he had seen the Pope. He wrote to Bittleston on 2 May, 'The Holy Father received me most affectionately – keeping my hand in his.' He asked about Newman's community. 'When I said we had lost some, he put his hand on my head and said "Don't cry."' When the other Fathers were called in, Leo asked them, 'Is England pleased?'

England was pleased; English reporters were present for the great occasion on 12 May, with eyes only for Newman among all that eminent throng. The *Guardian* said, 'His words ... pass verbatim along the telegraph wires like the words of the men who sway the world.' Newman's words, on receiving the biretta, might have been spoken by him forty years before at Oxford, for they were a challenge to that 'liberalism in religion' which thinks one creed as good as another since truth can be proved of none. He saw this disease, or flood of scepticism and doubt spreading into the future but had no fear of it; the Church must go forward in confidence and peace, leaving the outcome to God, who over-ruled all. Newman was pale but serene, and managed to speak with clarity. 'Dr Newman's face looked quite like that of a Saint,' said a bystander, and Italian ladies called him 'bellissimo'.

After the ceremonies were over he was ill again and could go about very little in Rome. On the way home he had to forgo a visit to Dr Döllinger, whom he still hoped would return to communion in the Church, and to Maria Giberne in her convent at Autun. It was a great disappointment to her. 'We must submit ourselves to the will of God,' he wrote to her from England. 'What is our religion if we can't?'

However, by the time he reached Folkestone on 27 June, Newman was able to call on several people, including Bloxam at Upper Beeding in Sussex. Into Bloxam's scrapbook went a cutting from the paper to record what happened when Newman alighted from the train at Bramber, 'the courteous Stationmaster ... presented the illustrious visitor with one of the famous Bramber white roses.' Bloxam insisted on giving Newman his print of San Giorgio in Velabro, his titular church in Rome – what could be more suitable than this ancient building dedicated to England's patron? Ever after he showed 'the Cardinal's room' – where he had washed his hands – to suitably reverent visitors. Bloxam always referred to Newman as He with a capital H, but when he later made one of his rare visits to the Oratory and kissed the Cardinal's ring, Newman made him sit in the biggest chair and took a small one himself.

At last he reached Birmingham, and so as not to disappoint the parishioners, changed in the cab into all the splendid garments which had been presented to him by the Catholic Union, the lay organization. It was pouring with rain, of course. He went straight into the church, blessing the congregation as he passed, and after a visit to the Blessed Sacrament in St Philip's chapel, was conducted to the sanctuary, where he sat down, leant his head on his hand and said, 'It is such happiness to come *home*.' Ryder wrote afterwards, 'He was wonderful to look upon as he sat fronting the congregation, his face as the face of an angel – the features that were so familiar to us refined and spiritualized by illness, and the delicate complexion and silver hair touched by the rose tints of his bright unaccustomed dress.' He spoke of the joys of home, of Nazareth, of St Philip's family, of the Holy Father's kindness, thanked them all and gave them his blessing. Young Lewis (Harry) Bellasis wrote to his mother, 'I wish you could have heard the sermon. It made us all cry, more or less.'

The Cardinalate was not an end, but another beginning, for now every kind of organization began to present addresses – the devoted Neville collected over sixty, with Newman's answers, for a book that was published after his own death. On the feast of the Assumption, 15 August, there were no less than five – one read by the Duke of Norfolk and two by Lord Ripon. Newman made simple replies, grateful for their kindness, saying that Cardinals ought to be 'a living memento of the Church's unity' and as such he accepted the honour done to him, while feeling hardly up to the office so surprisingly allotted to him by Providence in his old age. He usually managed to include a reference to the Pope's intended encouragement of learning and intellectual inquiry. But it was all rather tiring. 'I am very sleepy' is a remark which appears frequently in the little notes Newman still found time to write to his friends.

But he assisted at High Mass on Christmas Day and preached the sermon – and at that very moment his sister Jemima died in Derby. Since the death of her husband he had linked up with her again, and had played Beethoven with his niece Jane, but things had never been quite the same since his conversion. Harriett had died long ago, in 1852 and Charles, extraordinary Charles, was to die in 1884. Newman managed to journey to Tenby to see him before the end; he was well looked after and remained a socialist and an atheist till the last. Newman chose the text for his tombstone: 'Despise not O Lord the work of thy hands.'

It was in 1880 that the official reception for the new Cardinal was held in London at the Duke of Norfolk's house. Newman had noticed that in the Consistory he had been named as head of the Oratory *of London* – London was England, abroad, and Birmingham nothing. He could never forget he had been accused of trying to exercise a *generalate* over the London House and was still determined to make it plain that the two communities were quite independent; but he hoped that now, as a Cardinal, he could pay an official visit to Brompton, to show goodwill. Therefore he arranged to make a public call and assist at Vespers – but the reception would be held in the Duke's house.

It had to be put off from April to May because of a fall in February when he cracked two ribs. However, he was in good form by May and carried off the social ordeal in fine style. Fr John Norris, now the headmaster of the School, was his companion and wrote home how he was 'talking away most vigorously' at dinner. Afterwards there was a great crowd to be presented; one of them was the poet and critic Matthew Arnold, son of Dr Arnold of Rugby and brother of the younger Thomas, whose path had so often crossed Newman's – he had left the school and the Church in the sixties, but in 1876 had come back to the Oratory to be received again. As for Matthew, he had already corresponded with Newman, who greeted him warmly. He was amused at the sight of everyone kissing Newman's hand – even a non-Catholic Lord 'mumbling it like a piece of cake'. *Good Words* could not get over the scene either: 'fine ladies going on their knees before him in London salons'. It was a far cry from the days when Judge Coleridge had lectured Newman in public for his moral deterioration since joining the Roman Church.

A far cry, too, from the days of Tract 90, when, a few days later, Newman was entertained by the President and Fellows of Trinity College at Oxford, the guest of honour for the Gaudy. On the Sunday he preached both morning and evening at the new Church of St Aloysius, just where the Woodstock Road leaves St Giles, and where the Jesuits were now in charge of the mission. Fr Henry Coleridge, appropriately, presided on this occasion. Newman spoke in the morning on the Holy Trinity and in the evening on the Lord as the Shepherd of Israel, the office delegated to St Peter – thus gently underlining the doctrine which had forced him out of Oxford thirty-five years ago.

The *Oxford Herald* was indignant with Trinity College for 'allowing him bed and board' thus to preach Romanism, but the College remained unrepentant and celebrated the Trinity Monday

Gaudy with 'a conversazione in the College gardens, which were illuminated by limelight'.

Rogers, now Lord Blachford, called these events 'triumphal processions', remarking that it was an extraordinary historical event 'that a Prince of the Church should go about receiving indiscriminate homage in London and Oxford with the applause of all men'. Warmly, he insisted, 'it is you, by being you, that have done it.' Newman replied that of course it was 'overwhelmingly gratifying – but equally, or still more, surprising, as if it was not I.' And, typically, he wondered if there would not be a reaction.

There was no reaction. Newman was accepted by England as a Cardinal – one might almost say he made the office of Cardinal acceptable to England. Millais painted his portrait for the Duke of Norfolk and addressed him as 'you dear old boy'. Newman asked the fashionable artist some technical questions on behalf of Maria Giberne and ascertained that he too was familiar with ivory black. Louis Barraud, a famous photographer, took his picture, getting the right expression when the old man's face brightened up as Neville began to talk of the Zoo – he was then eighty-four. At home in the Oratory the only thing that distinguished his dress was the red skull cap, or red biretta, he wore. He liked still to be called 'the Father' – appearing in the Decree Book as 'His Eminence the Father'. He celebrated his eightieth birthday by pontificating at High Mass in the vestments presented by the Oratory School Old Boys, afraid that otherwise he would never wear them. Afterwards, Lewis Bellasis told his mother, 'I actually caught him *running* down the backstairs to breakfast.'

The new young Oratorians were devoted to the old man, but both Fr Norris and Fr Ryder went through difficult patches, though both emerged to lead successful and contented lives, and both became Superiors in turn after Newman's death. Newman was never a despot – indeed, the renegade Arthur Hutton, after he had left the Oratory and the Church, called him King Log and said he even overlooked open scandal till forced to act. Perhaps this refers to the sad case of Henry Bittleston, who seems to have mixed up his accounts and left, ostensibly to become a Carthusian. He was really too old for that and went to live with a priest at St Albans; Newman wrote him affectionate notes, anxious that he should keep warm. Bittleston was the only one of the six Fathers to whom Newman paid tribute at the end of the *Apologia* to die outside the house. Arthur Hutton, a convert, had annoyed Newman by a piece of rudeness to Anglicans in a book which he had tried to get through the press without first submitting it to his Superior. He left with a Catholic schoolteacher whom he married and later recovered sufficient faith to take up his Anglican ministry again, cashing in on his Oratorian experiences after Newman's death by writing pieces for the papers criticizing his character. He was the only one of the younger generation to fail Newman. The rest built up a strong community in the years to come.

Newman wished to use his new position to further the causes he had at heart, and he encouraged Lord Braye, an ardent young convert, in his efforts to get Catholics allowed at the universities. In the seventies Manning had founded a Catholic College in Kensington, where the students would take the London University examinations ('godless' rather than Protestant!) but Mgr Capel, the Rector, had to resign after a resounding scandal and the experiment collapsed under a huge debt. But Manning remained adamant on the ban on the older universities; curiously enough it was Herbert Vaughan who raised it, after he had succeeded Manning at Westminster. Owing to Manning's mistaken policy Catholics had lost thirty years of participation in English higher education.

In 1883 there was an attempt by clergy of all denominations to stop the Affirmation Bill going through Parliament, and Newman caused something of a sensation by a letter which was widely reprinted. As he told a friend, 'Christianity has ceased to be the religion of Parliament for many years', so that, as he observed in the letter for the press, 'it as little concerns religion whether Mr Bradlaugh swears by no God with the Government, or swears by an Impersonal, or Material, or Abstract or Ideal something or other, which is all that is secured to us by the Opposition.' The same Newman still, seeing through shams with his prophetic eye!

All this year Newman was preoccupied with the problem of the Inspiration of Scripture, then the most critical question before Christians – '*the* difficulty' as Bishop Clifford put it, urging Newman to answer an article in the *Nineteenth Century*. Knowles, the editor, was amazed at the freedom of interpretation which Newman showed the Church could have, and accepted the article which was printed in February 1885 and caused a good deal of excitement, especially in intransigent Catholic circles. 'If poor Dr Ward were still alive, he would be already in the field against you,' wrote one correspondent. Ward had died in 1882, but up spoke bold Professor Healy of Maynooth, editor of the *Irish Ecclesiastical Record*, asserting that the merest tiro in the schools of Catholic theology would see how startling were Newman's statements. Soon afterwards he was made a bishop and when Newman sent him a specially bound copy of the Canon of the Mass, he was contritely grateful. Newman had put his answer into a *Postscript*, which he had to publish separately, since he found that the *Nineteenth Century* had a year's copyright of his article.

Newman's last venture into controversy was an answer to Professor Fairbairn, Principal of Mansfield College, the new Nonconformist centre at Oxford, who wrote on 'Catholicism and Religious Thought' in the *Contemporary Review* with adverse criticisms of Newman himself. Newman's answer *The Development of Religious Error* appeared in the same review later in 1885 (he asked about the copyright this time!) and was republished, with additions, in pamphlet form the next year. In it he quoted from his sermons of 1832 to show the continuity of his thought on the subject of Reason as the instrument of the World – human society organized without reference to God. 'It has triumphed over time and space; knowledge it has proved to be emphatically power.' Against this could religion hope to be successful? Of course Newman thought it could, but not an emasculated Christianity without dogma – reason must have its place within religion.

Dr Fairbairn continued to believe that Newman distrusted Reason because his own intellect was sceptical. He might have been surprised to know that Cardinal Manning agreed with him – he told friends that Newman's works were riddled with scepticism. However, all was apparently peace between the two Cardinals now, and when they met in the new Oratory church at Brompton, in 1886, at the funeral of the Dowager Duchess of Norfolk, Newman is said to have remarked afterwards, 'What do you think Manning did to me? He kissed me !' When Manning won the 'dockers' tanner' in the dock strike of 1888, Newman wrote to congratulate him. Manning showed his best side in his social work; it was the intellectual situation he did not understand.

Newman was always better understood by laymen, whether Catholic or Anglican. Lord Coleridge, now Lord Chief Justice, wrote to a friend in 1882: 'I cannot analyse it or explain it, but to this hour he interests and awes me like no other man I ever saw. He is as simple and humble and playful as a child, and, yet, I am with a being unlike anyone else. He lifts me up for a time and subdues me – if I said frightens me it would hardly be too strong ...'

Perhaps it was this quality which Mark Pattison felt when he was dying in 1883, an embittered sceptic, and received an affectionate message from Newman. 'When your letter, my dear master,' wrote Pattison, 'was brought to my bedside this morning and I saw your well-known handwriting, my eyes filled so with tears that I could not at first see to read what you had said.' It was January and Newman had a cold, but he got up and travelled to Oxford with Neville, who recorded that his meeting with Pattison was happy and that though he said nothing of it, he seemed satisfied. Pattison died that spring.

William Copeland died in 1885; the last turkey – Newman had once thanked him for his 'kind turkey' which he sent every year – arrived for Christmas 1884 when he was already ill. 'My very dear Copeland, God be your strength and your life, my very dear friend,' Newman wrote. He died peacefully the next summer. The same year Maria Giberne died quite suddenly in her convent at Autun. To Anne Mozley Newman said he could not be sorry for her death – her friends were all gone or going. Her community remembered her as 'très gaie'. All her drawings and memories came back to the Oratory. Right up to her death Newman was corresponding with her and warning her, when she had lost her teeth, 'Unchewed meat is as dangerous to the stomach as brick and stone, or a bunch of keys. You are not an ostrich. I am very *serious*.' He was then writing on the anniversary of 'my dear Mary's death' – the unforgotten sister who had died in 1828 – 'an age ago'.

Nobody was forgotten; when they died their names went into the little anniversary book with its cross-stitched cover, made by Mrs Pusey long ago in her last illness, in which, in beautiful script, she had written the name of the baby christened by Newman, which had died in the first year of life. Every week, nearly every day had its memorials and Littlemore parishioners jostled with Fellows of Oriel, Anglicans with Catholics, nuns, children, duchesses, theologians, doorkeepers – a long human litany. Almost the last loss was Frederic Rogers, who died on 21 November 1889.

It was only in 1886 that Newman himself really began to fail. He had a long period of weakness that autumn but recovered again. He was losing his sight and his writing became very shaky and straggly; Neville had to take over his letters. In October 1888 when he was eighty-seven he fell down in his room and knocked himself unconscious; everyone thought he was dying and he was given the Last Sacraments, but again recovered. On his eighty-eighth birthday he was present in the sanctuary for his favourite Mozart mass, and the school children gave him a bouquet. He now found it hard to hold himself upright and at times his memory wandered. Vaughan, now Bishop of Salford, wrote to Manning, 'I hardly knew him: doubled up like a shrimp and walking with a stick longer than his doubled body.' Newman referred to Cardinal Manning and Provost Manning as to two different persons but, though Vaughan did not notice it, spoke courteously of both.

The occasion was the funeral of Bishop Ullathorne, who had only recently been persuaded to retire to Oscott. In 1887, calling on Newman, he had been astonished and awed when the old Cardinal slid to his knees and asked for his blessing. 'I felt annihilated in his presence,' Ullathorne wrote, 'there is a saint in that man!'

Newman said his last mass on Christmas Day 1889. He knew he was too infirm and blind to say it any longer with safety, though he continued to say a 'dry' mass in the hope that it might become possible to celebrate once more. St Philip said his last mass at Corpus Christi, Newman at Christmas – 'they are cognate feasts,' he had said in 1847, celebrating his first mass in England at Christmas, as his very first had been at Corpus Christi, in Rome.

Some time during this last year he said to Neville: 'I am not capable of doing anything more – I am not wanted – now mind what I say, it is not kind to wish to keep me longer from God.' This had to be said to poor Neville, whose whole life was devoted to looking after Newman in his fond, muddled way. He delighted in every rally, reporting joyfully at the end of term in July 1890 how Newman had 'talked with all comers .... received everybody in the cloisters – gave the prizes and in the evening followed the Play.'

Early in August Newman had a special visitor – Harriett's daughter Grace, whom he had not seen since she was three years old; he held her hand while they talked. Thus once more a separation was ended on the eve of death – this time his own. He caught a chill that day.

Neville was making his bed ready on Saturday 9 August when he was surprised to see Newman come into the room 'unbent, erect to the full height of his best days in the fifties; he was without support of any kind. His whole carriage was, it may be said, soldier like, yet so dignified: and his countenance was most attractive to look at; even great age seemed to have gone from his face, and with it all careworn signs; his very look conveyed the cheerfulness and gratitude of his mind; (and what he said was so kind) his voice was fresh and strong: (it was his own musical presence) his whole effect was that of power combined with complete calm.' The words in brackets were added in pencil; it was one of several attempts made by Neville to express this experience, which he afterwards felt suggested Newman's readiness to die. But at the time he thought him exceptionally well.

In the night, however, Newman called him and said, 'I feel very bad.' Others were fetched, the doctors; Newman was sinking. He revived for a short time on Sunday morning and asked Neville to recite the office with him. But by the time he received Extreme Unction on Monday he was unconscious and so did not receive the Viaticum. There were no last words. Newman went out of this world as quickly and quietly as he went in and out of the rooms in it, surprising people who expected a more formal presence. He ceased to breathe at a quarter to nine in the evening of 11 August 1890. This was the day he had passed over every year, as he once said, 'as if walking over one's own grave'.

In Upper Beeding Bloxam flew the flag of St George at half mast and the church bell was tolled.

The body was placed in an open coffin in the Oratory church and hundreds filed past; thousands lined the roadside all the way to Rednal as the funeral procession went by; all the papers in the country came out with tributes of admiration and pride in the man who had once been so bitterly denounced and derided. Newman was buried, at his own desire, in the same grave as Ambrose St John, so that even in death his name should not stand alone on the stone cross that marks the place where his bones rest. But in the cloister leading to the church of the Oratory there are tablets on the wall to the memory of departed Fathers. Newman, who had composed graceful Latin tributes to those who died before him, wrote a very simple one for himself which yet expresses his whole life: 'Out of shadows and images into the truth.'

Ex umbris et imaginibus in veritatem

Note on Sources

My original biography was based principally on the Archives of the Birmingham Oratory, which as well as about 20,000 of Newman's own letters, contains thousands from his correspondents, his diaries, memoranda, and the memoirs of friends, besides newspaper cuttings, pamphlets, photostats from Roman and other archives, etc.

I also used letters from Faber and Dalgairns and others at the London Oratory, Brompton; the Manning papers at St Mary of the Angels, Bayswater; college correspondence at Oriel College, Oxford; Bloxham's scrapbooks at Magdalen College, Oxford; letters in the possession of Mr Basil Johnson, descendant of 'Observer' Johnson; and family material shown me by Miss Dorothea Mozley, descendant of Jemima Newman.

Naturally I used the Victorian biographies of Newman's friends and enemies but quotations from his own letters are taken from the originals.

A more detailed work on sources was included in the original volumes.

INDEX

Fount Classics

THE COMPLETE POEMS
With Selected Prose
Gerard Manley Hopkins

Gerard Manley Hopkins (1844–1889) was born into a devout Anglican family in Stratford, Essex, and converted to Catholicism in his final year at Oxford. He became a member of the Society of Jesus and was ordained in 1877. After some years as a priest, he became a professor of Classics at University College, Dublin, but died from typhoid four years later at the age of 45.

He displayed remarkable poetic creativity throughout his life, though on becoming a Jesuit found this ability difficult to reconcile with religious devotion. Through the teaching of Duns Scotus he came to recognize the importance of allowing individual talent, and hence his poetic gifts, to be exercised in the service of the Church. Sadly, his poetry was rejected for publication in his lifetime, though in later years it was regarded as innovative and highly influential.

Hopkins is best known for his nature mysticism, exploring the revelation of the divine within the natural world. This complete collection of his surviving verse is complemented by a selection of extracts from his notebooks and sermons, specially chosen to reveal the essence of his mystical vision.

Fount Classics

MY CONFESSION
Leo Tolstoy

Leo Tolstoy's literary stature rests almost entirely on his two masterpieces, *Anna Karenina* and *War and Peace*. Less well known are his books on moral and religious themes for which he was dubbed 'the conscience of the continent' in his day. These books were inspired by his mid-life conversion to the Christian faith.

His approach to Christianity was quite distinct. He disliked the dogma, insisting on the simple, practical truths of Jesus' teaching and emphasizing the importance of the individual conscience in upholding these truths. He saw that spiritual insight was often granted to the simple and uneducated in society, promoting a radical change in his own lifestyle.

Written immediately after his conversion and widely praised by his contemporaries, *My Confession* traces the development of Tolstoy's faith and morality. It is an absorbing account of the influences on his life and literature. In a frank, autobiographical style, he reveals the complex intellectual, moral and spiritual turmoil which brought him to the brink of suicide, and the faith through which he eventually attained, to some degree a peace of mind.

Fount Classics

THE PILGRIM'S PROGRESS
John Bunyan

Written in prison, where Bunyan had been sent for unauthorized preaching, and first published in 1678, this classic story has been described as the most popular work of Christian spirituality written in English, and as the first English novel. It describes the road to the Celestial City, by way of Doubting Castle, the Delectable Mountains, Vanity Fair and other places whose names have entered the very fabric of the language.

Fascinating as literature, entertaining as story, profound as spiritual teaching for the soul's journey, *The Pilgrim's Progress* is 'a masterpiece which generation after generation of ordinary men and women have taken to their hearts'.
Hugh Ross Williamson

THÉRÈSE OF LISIEUX
Michael Hollings

The most influential and most popular saint of modern times, Thérèse Martin died virtually unknown outside her Carmelite convent in 1897, at the age of 24. After her death came the 'storm of glory', the miracles and the acclaim that swept her statue into every church and her spiritual teaching into the mouths of Popes.

Thérèse's 'little way' of prayer was a message for humanity of our time, and the publication of her own writings made it known around the world. This vivid biography brings the reader into the closest contact with the life and world of Thérèse, often in her own words, and serves as an ideal introduction to this 'little' mystic who inspires millions of Christians.

'... quite an exceptional book ... It is a joy to find such an interpreter as Fr Hollings ...'   *Catholic Herald*

'... a gem of brief and yet deep biography – an account which is sensitive and totally dispels any preconceived notion of sentimentality in connection with 'the Little Flower'. Father Hollings comments with great understanding on her writings and special contribution to spirituality ... It is by far the best book I have ever seen on this extraordinary woman.'   *Methodist Recorder*

'... few other books can have conveyed the kernel of St Thérèse's message so succinctly and so relevantly for men and women in today's world.   *The Tablet*

Fount Classics

AUTOBIOGRAPHY OF A SAINT
St Thérèse of Lisieux
Translated by Ronald Knox

St Thérèse of Lisieux, the 'Little Flower' who died in 1897 virtually unknown outside her convent, is now recognized as the most popular and influential saint of our times. She was canonized in 1925, and successive Popes have recommended her as an authoritative spiritual guide for the twentieth century and beyond.

The immense popularity of Thérèse is largely based upon this book. It is her own personal testimony. Written at odd moments in school exercise books and on scraps of paper, it gives a vivid human account of the life of a saint from the inside; intimate, spontaneous, and sparkling throughout with a delightful humour.

This first complete, authorized translation by Ronald Knox was described by the *Sunday Times* as 'wholly lucid, natural and enchanting'. The *Church Times* said it was a 'joy to read'. *Autobiography of a Saint* is not only a pre-eminent classic of Christian spirituality, but in this edition also a classic of the translator's art.

Fount Classics

THE DIARY OF A COUNTRY PRIEST
Georges Bernanos

The diary of 'M. Le Curé' consists in his own words of 'the very simple trivial secrets of a very ordinary kind of life'. He tells of his manifold activities as a parish priest – his relations with his colleagues and his superiors; his handling of the spiritual and moral difficulties of the parishioners.

Written with simplicity and honesty, the result is a classic and sometimes poignant novel, telling of one who is irresistibly called to serve God.

'Georges Bernanos was one of the most remarkable personalities and writers of his generation. His theme was almost invariably the struggle for the soul of man between forces of good and evil: to him the Beatitudes were the greatest reality, and the onslaughts of the devil no mere figment or abstraction … The characters of his most typical novels often seemed not to be on quite the same dimensional plane as ordinary human beings. They were perhaps of the same family as some of the creations of Balzac and Barbey d'Aurevilly, and yet his own. Literature was for him a kind of sacrament.'   *The Times*

Fount Classics

LETTERS TO A NIECE
Baron F. von Hügel

Baron Friedrick von Hügel (1852–1925) was celebrated as a man of great scholarship and religious devotion. He was deeply committed to the Roman Catholic Church, recognizing the importance of organised religion alongside its intellectual and mystical aspects.

Von Hügel played a major role in the so-called modernist movement of his day that encouraged people to have a direct relationship with God. He dissociated himself from it when it was condemned by the papacy. Always enthusiastic about new ideas, he welcomed the tension between scientific development and religious faith as a positive challenge to the believer.

In *Letters to a Niece*, von Hügel offers spiritual guidance in response to the events, sometimes distressing, of his adult niece's life. Informal and extremely personal, the letters provide a fascinating insight into the character of this spiritual giant and are published to commemorate the 70th anniversary of his death.

Fount Classics

SEEKING GOD
The Way of St Benedict
Esther de Waal

The spirit of St Benedict, greatest of saints, transcends the centuries and unites all believers in Christ.

In the new edition of this classic work of spirituality, Esther de Waal shows how the Benedictine Rule, practical and totally relevant for today, can guide us towards a growth into wholeness, a balance in every aspect of our being – body, mind and spirit – through which we can become truly human and truly one with God.

'... an engaging introduction to the Benedictine idea ...'
Church Times

'... an extraordinarily good book ... neither simpliste nor swamped by scholarship, though very alive to it.' *The Tablet*

'... superbly enkindles the spirit of St Benedict ... Anglican and Catholic ecumenists and Benedictines and Cistercians and lay people seeking God should be very grateful to Esther de Waal ...' *Catholic Herald*

Fount Classics

REACHING OUT
The Three Movements of the
Spiritual Life
Henri Nouwen

This classic work of spirituality is a response to the question: 'What does it mean to live a life in the Spirit of Jesus Christ?'

Nouwen finds it to be a lonely business, as Dante also found when he said, 'In the middle of the way of our life I find myself in a dark wood.' However, we can and must reach out to our fellow human beings and to God.

'The plan and concept of this book are excellent. Fr Nouwen is particularly good on the whole business of getting to know ourselves ... he says it well and with considerable insight.'
The Tablet

'It is quiet and impressive, giving an impression of wise maturity. At the same time it is full of insight into contemporary situations, the work of a man who has an intimate knowledge of people.'
Church Times

'There are great riches for us to find here, as Nouwen explores areas of spirtuality rarely touched on in our own evangelical tradition.'
Church of England Newspaper

Fount Classics

LETTERS OF SPIRITUAL COUNSEL AND GUIDANCE
John Keble

John Keble (1792–1866) possessed an outstanding academic mind, gaining a double first-class Oxford degree when he was 19 and displaying from an early age considerable poetic talent. He was ordained in 1815. His first publication, a book of poetry entitled *The Christian Year*, was so extraordinarily popular that he was rapidly assured of nationwide fame and admiration.

Resisting the trappings of success, he rejected senior posts in the church in favour of life as a rural parish priest in Hursley, Hampshire. He remained, however, very much in the public eye. In 1833 he delivered a controversial sermon condemning political interference in ecclesiastical affairs, on the grounds that the authority of the Church is divinely ordained. He later became adviser to the Tractarian movement, which sought to return the Anglican Church to its Catholic roots. He urged the importance of sacramental confession and encouraged the revival of the daily office.

The letters in this book were collected and first published after Keble's death. During his lifetime he offered sensitive and thoughtful advise in response to many requests for spiritual guidance. He reveals himself to be a man of wisdom and humility, with an innate understanding of the pastoral role.

Fount Classics

FINDING GOD IN ALL THINGS
The Way of St Ignatius
Margaret Hebblethwaite

St Ignatius of Loyola, the sixteenth-century founder of the Jesuits, left behind him a living tradition of prayer in his Spiritual Exercises. Over the centuries these have been enormously influential; today there is more interest than ever in Ignatian spirituality, among ordinary people as well as religious professionals, and across all the Christian denominations.

In this book Margaret Hebblethwaite interprets the ideas of Ignatius for the present day. She combines sound practical advice on how to set about praying with an understanding of the deep mystery and beauty of prayer; prayer which can lead us, not to leave the world behind, but to make full use of all our God-given opportunities so that we too can learn to find God in all things.

Margaret Hebblethwaite was born in 1951, studied at Oxford and at the Gregorian University in Rome. She is a founder member and former committee member of the Catholic theological Association of Great Britain. Her books include *Motherhood and God* and *Basic is Beautiful*. She is currently assistant editor of *The Tablet*.

Fount Classics

IGNATIUS LOYOLA
Philip Caraman

St Ignatius, founder of the Jesuits or Society of Jesus, was born in 1491, the year before the discovery of the New World by Columbus. He grew up in a golden age of the Spanish court, himself a courtier, a night, a gambler and a ladies' man.

Philip Caraman is a member of the Society of Jesus and a historian of world renown. His previous books include *The Lost Paradise*, the story of the Jesuit Reductions in Paraguay and the subject of the film *The Mission*, and the international bestseller *John Gerard*.

'A brilliant and beautiful achievement.'   *Elizabeth Longford*

'A vivid and veracious biography which all can enjoy for its human and historical interest.'   *A. L. Rowse*